THE EYES THAT LOOK

The secret story of Bassano's *Hunting Dogs*

Julia Grigg

UNIVERSE

Universe
an imprint of Unicorn Publishing Group LLP, 2018
5 Newburgh Street
London W1F 7RG

www.unicornpublishing.org

A catalogue record for this book is available from
the British Library

ISBN 978-0-911604-61-7

Design by Vivian@Bookscribe

Printed and bound in Spain by GraphyCems

For VG

The eye is more powerful than anything, more swift than anything, more worthy than anything

LEON BATTISTA ALBERTI

• • •

Dogs do speak, but only to those who know how to listen

ORHAN PAMUK

CONTENTS

PROLOGUE

Francesco

25 March 1589, Casa Grande, San Canciano, Venice

The Feast of the Annunciation, blustery weather over St Mark's basin. On a day like this, towards the end of March, the light lengthening, spring looking as though it's decided to begin, I'm reminded of my first time in this city. 1566, I was seventeen, my first time away from home, come to get pigment for the paintings Father and I were making in the studio back up north in Bassano.

At Chioggia I marvelled at the way the land stops where the water begins, dissolves into glinting grains of sand. I'd never seen the sea before, dipped my fingers in, put them salty to my lips.

The lagoon, Venice there across it, rising right out of it. (Could it really be?) Flushed pink and gold by the setting sun's red rays, great domes, spires pointing at the sky, almost merging with the clouds. As we neared, I stared and stared. It's like that print of Father's, the one by Albrecht Dürer I've had to copy so many times. Dürer's city soars up, towers and turrets topped by banners streaming out in the wind, in the foreground little curly waves, a fabulous sea monster swimming away.

What I saw was like something from a fable. I'm sure I murmured my wonder out loud, asking, 'Can this place be true?'

It's real enough, Venice. I was soon to discover that. With hindsight, I'd caution you: the city's surfaces may glitter but they're rough to the touch. The Venetians, they're real too, each of them with a story to tell. Should you be thinking of trading theirs for yours, whatever tale you've carried with you across the water, get yourself to the Rialto. But be ready to bargain hard.

6   My story began with two meetings, one expected, one not. I was to be there only ten short days – enough time though, for everything to change. Giorgio, my new friend, warned about the city too, laughing as he ruffled my hair, 'Francesco, my lad, for an artist, nothing is ever the same once you've seen Venice.' He was right.

7   After my first meeting, here in this mansion where so many years later I have my studio, after being ushered into the presence of Maestro Tiziano Vecellio, for me, everything did change. I was a lad from the hills, a lad who prized yellow stockings, who most likely still had sticks of straw in his hair. An audience with Venice's acclaimed master, the master whose fame has since gone so far afield the whole world's lauding him now as 'Titian' – why wouldn't such an audience transform me?

8   Excruciating, it was, as it happens. Afterwards I never wanted to speak about it. How could I make anyone understand what it's like, shedding a skin? Who shows sympathy to the grass snake struggling to slough off its old one? Who gives a care when it emerges vexed, spitting, half-blind – but newly-branded?

9   Then the same day, a second meeting, this one by chance. Giorgio. Signor Giorgio Vasari. If it weren't for Giorgio would I ever have understood where inspiration comes from, about the courage innovation demands, about what has to be sacrificed if you're to turn a vision into a reality? Would I be the person I am now?

10   I was green. Green. But on that day my future beckoned. I quickly learned to look at life through Giorgio's eyes: either you're up high on Fortune's wheel or you're down. In the struggle that's our existence you're welcome to try and force the Lady's hand. But success? It is she who decides.

11   Once on my quest, it didn't take me long to realise our fates are all intertwined. I was never alone on my journey, even when to other eyes it looked as though no one was by my side. And so, in the pages that follow it is right that mine is not the only voice to tell this story, the story that's defined me as an artist and a man: the story of the dogs and the painting.

ONE
Francesco

CHAPTER ONE

24 March 1566, Venice

What would it be like to drown in paint, to fall right in, have it close over your head, the viscous stuff flooding your lungs, stifling your cries for help? That was the fear making my mouth dry, my legs leaden in last night's dream – well, no, call it a nightmare. Last night, my first in Venice.

I do sometimes dream about painting, or drawing, especially when something I'm working on is difficult – but this? I was standing in a chasm, a river rushing at me, furious, foam-flecked, charging between rocks. It was red, reflecting a sky the same colour louring above. This roaring torrent, dizzying me, splashing its gore up on to my shoes, somehow I knew it was paint. Fine spray was hitting my face, so I could smell it, of course. And its hue, its particular shade of redness: it was Titian's red.

So, even before I met him, Titian and his reds conspired to wreck my sleep. As is the way with nightmares, there was horror but no resolution and this morning, jolted into wakefulness, half of me was still there on the riverbank, teetering, unable to back away, aghast I might fall.

I'm down from the north, come with my uncle to re-supply our studio back there. The highlight of my stay? Visiting Titian. Father, planning it all, said, 'You'll learn from Titian. Soon as you're off the boat, get yourself to the Santa Maria Gloriosa church. Study his altarpiece. Study it well before your Uncle Gianluca takes you to the *Maestro*.'

Out of earshot, I'd muttered, 'Need I bother?' Son of a renowned painter, grandson and great grandson of one, I thought I was sitting pretty as a Bassano of Bassano. I *didn't* think about it, in fact. My fate, my future, no sweat: I've some talent, adequate skills to tackle what's expected of me. An apprentice for now, yes, but with excellent prospects, entitled, heir to the Jacopo Bassano studio.

Yesterday, for the sake of keeping in Father's good books, I went, despite how distracted I was feeling. Because Venice *is* distracting. At first it beguiles you, dazes you with the azure of its dancing water, the rose and gold of its shadows. Then it grabs you by the arm, pulls you in and you're lost in the mysteries of its little alleys, bewildered to find your way barred by water, confused that the little bridges all look the same.

And the noise! Hardly had I left off gawping at the Grand Canal's great palaces before we were on the Rialto, thrust into its uproar, its shoving, sweating stink. Whistles, cackling laughter, shouted commands, words I couldn't catch. But anyhow, words are superfluous for some things I soon found: like the woman who licked her lips, brushed her body against my hip before pressing close, whispering. Stepping back, her smile was wicked.

Steering me past, Uncle was hissing, 'Everything's for sale in Venice, lad. Shop wisely.'

I soon realised how right he was. We must have passed a hundred stalls loaded with goods a thousand times more curious and colourful than the wares of any pedlar who's ever come up to Bassano. As it turned out, Father's advice was sound. At least for a painter. I saw Titian's altarpiece, his *Assumption of the Virgin*. I studied it and I was humbled – because you could lump together all the gaudy goods ever hawked on the Rialto across all time and, truly, that painting makes a much, much braver show.

Immediately I was inside the church I could see it, far away under the east window. Closer to it, my first thought was '*How?*' How do you imagine and then how do you achieve something so stupendous? A work over twenty feet tall. Arresting. In the foreground those stalwart men with their backs turned were throwing out their arms in astonishment. And craning their heads up to heaven, just as I was doing, straining for a last glimpse of the gorgeously robed Madonna.

The painting is an exaltation: on three planes, three workings of the colour red, heightened with the rich glow of gold towards the top. So much red, it captivates your eyes. Captivated, they have no choice but to ascend too, Titian forcing you, body and soul, to yearn for that shimmering glory. I wondered whether he'd had a plan how to achieve that effect. Or is *that* what this thing '*genius*' is, something you're possessed by at the crucial moment brush begins to stroke colour?

Father doesn't hold with genius.

'A modicum of talent is essential for beginning, yes,' he says, 'after that, it's training. Training for the hand, but equally importantly, for the eyes. Your eyes, son, it's what they are *for*. For looking.' How many, many times have I heard it? '*Look, boy, look. And keep on looking. Only that way will you see.*'

I stood there, eyes wide and *looking*. Looking at my first Titian, convinced by it that Father is wrong, my conviction making me dare to dispute his teaching for the first time. In that moment, absolutely certain that a spark animating some *does* exist, I realised it's those fortunate few who will lead the way, will achieve things never done before.

Casa Grande, San Canciano

Today, as a result, I'm all anticipation arriving with Uncle Gianluca at the *Maestro*'s mansion, a big place they call the 'Casa Grande'. It lives up to its name. Lush lawns stretch away. There are fountains and, in one corner, a bird house where doves flutter. Not white, but dyed all colours: pink, blue, peach and pale green – imagine. The mansion has a big hall, a great, mirrored chimneypiece where a fire blazes. You can glimpse bronze statues on plinths, and down corridors there are heavy striped gold brocade curtains on windows of glittering glass. Breathtaking.

What a revelation: a painter living like *this*, with all the rich possessions of a nobleman, with so many servants. With adulation from the public too. Uncle and I are just two among a crowd of people, men but also women, some poor, but many fancily dressed, milling around the steps waiting to pay the *Maestro* tribute.

17 A flunkey's white-gloved hand directs us to the studio. People dash back and forth here. There are many apprentices, those on the move harried-looking – I can sympathise with that. The ones crouched over their sketchbooks frown, peering up at a nude male posed on the dais above them. The place is very busy but very organised: through one doorway there's a whole room just for preparing the pigments; through another, trestle tables where workers stretch canvases on to frames. It's a powerhouse, humming with purpose, so totally different from our studio in Bassano.

18 Back there, it's sober, earnest and so quiet. My younger brothers, supposed to be learning the basic skills, do their best to keep out of Father's way, so nearly always it's just me, alone with him.

19 And nothing pleases Father more than working in his studio, shabby though it is. He'd stay there all hours if he could. It looks terrible, it really does. He allows no one to touch anything, so it's a mess. Lizards scuttle away at our approach, leaving their tracks in the dust coating the shelves where years' and years' worth of sketches and used-up materials are piled, all awry. A pigeon has made its nest behind one of the beams. Of an evening we hear it strut up and down, do our work to its *cluck cluck clucks*. First job for me in the morning is sweeping the benches free of droppings. No, no, there's none of Titian's sparkle and sheen for us in Bassano.

20 Here with the *Maestro*, a witness to all this grandeur, suddenly I see there are other ways to earn a living from paint, ways very different in style from ours, reaping rewards on an entirely different scale. Summoned to cross the studio's shining marble floor to where the Maestro stands at his easel, the idea stirring in my mind brings a smile to my lips. I'm thinking, *I'd like to be like Titian*. I step forward jauntily.

21 The *Maestro* turns: a fierce face, grey, a corrugated forehead. He pushes a lock of hair from his temple with the back of one hand. A red-collared hound rises sleekly from near his feet, stretches, makes a great yawn. Uncle speaks our names. Titian doesn't smile. He pats the dog's head before extending his hand. At me, he barely glances. Instead, he thrusts forward his palette. Shoved right at me, what can I do but take it?

For me to hold, huh, as though I'm one of his servants? He steps with Uncle over to the window, their shoulders and heads inclined.

Excluded, I turn to the *Maestro*'s easel. An *Annunciation*. He's been working a blazing red. There are fat blobs of it on the palette, already I've got some of it on my hands and a streak on the sleeve of my best blue velvet jerkin. Mother will be *furious*.

I look again at the canvas: Titian's been throwing gobbets of the colour on to the Virgin's dress. They gleam there like fresh blood. It's not the red in the composition that slaps me to attention, though. It's the gold and the dazzling whiteness. It's the burning light around Gabriel and the Virgin, light that billows out of a turbid sky broiling with clouds, cupids and a dove on outspread wings. Mary is startled from her prayers by the crack that's split the heavens. Veil lifted but eyes cast demurely down, she looks from under her lids at the great shining archangel whose expression alerts us he brings news of some portent.

I can only gasp at the force of the image, recognising how astonishingly new and different Titian's style is in this painting. Stock-still, staring, I hear his voice.

'Gawping, is he, your nephew? Never seen a painting before?'

The *Maestro* has come close and is jutting his chin up at my face, eyes blazing. I feel his breath hot, and ugh, a fine spray of spittle.

'Well, he wouldn't have, would he?' He grasps at Uncle's arm as he jerks a thumb at his *Annunciation* and says, 'Not one like this, anyway, huh? Not up there in that northern backwater where his father insists on hiding himself.'

Reaching forward and yanking the palette from my grip, his laugh is a harsh croak. He turns again to Uncle, claws again at his sleeve. 'Became quite proficient depicting animals, didn't he, your brother-in-law? Yes, I got one of his little works off a dealer a while ago. Bassano wanting to vaunt his skills, obviously – he'd jumbled every sort of exotic creature on to the canvas.' He waves an arm towards the apprentices, 'Useful for reference, at least. For my *garzoni* to copy, you see, the lions, the camels, etcetera.'

I wince. That's what he's like is he, the *Maestro*: no grace, just a rude old goat, full of spite? '*Quite proficient … little works … **jumbled**'* what kind of comments are these about my father and our studio? Titian can say what he likes, exactly how he likes because he's famous and rich, can he?

I don't know where to look but somehow, I'm aware of Uncle Gianluca's embarrassed expression, the little pursed *o* his lips make as he registers Titian's contempt for my father's achievements.

In the next moment we are dismissed. Taken aback, my uncle avoiding my gaze, I'm still fascinated and cannot break away. Uncle doesn't move either. Inexplicable – but what we find ourselves doing: shuffling to Titian's side as though some kind of force is keeping us there. We watch him, stooped, shoulders hunched, as he brings that damn palette so close up to his face he's almost rubbing his nose in the colours.

Stiffening limbs, weakening sight: you would expect that, wouldn't you, from an old man of nearly eighty? But *no*: Titian, grasping his brush, is at the canvas, arms up, an all-out attack. Forget weak, this old man's strong. Strong. The force of that jabbing brush – then the daubing, then, brush rejected, he pushes at the thick colour with his *fingers* and his *thumb*, spreading it, smearing it. Could I work paint like that? My fingers tremble, wanting to.

It is then that something happens to me, me the bystander who looks on, who seethes but who also admires. Titian, this man who's ignored me and disparaged Father, he's hateful – but the painting he's making, the painting is a revelation. It's … well, it's *gawp-worthy*. I'm helpless against its powerful message, so clearly articulated *despite* the blurred and muddied colours the *Maestro*'s applying with his short, chopped brush strokes, his daubing and smearing. This interpretation of his is so strong and it's so *new*.

I don't know how to describe what's going on in my head. It's as though I've been thrust suddenly awake by a bell clanging in my ears. It's as though something is dying in me, destroyed by this first-hand evidence of the mastery and the vigour it takes to be Titian. Yet at the same time something new has begun to grow. No, it hasn't *begun* to grow, it is there, sprung fully-grown into my mind. With this new thing surging through me, I feel I'm being burst open. Ambition, that's what it is. I'm envious and ambitious and inspired, all together all at once and for the first time.

My heart thumps. I'm unsteady and my mind swirls. Plunged into Titian's nightmare river and helpless, it's as though I'm being swept along in its tumultuous, raging red. Red, red, as red as the blaze of anger the *Maestro* has made me feel. There is a roaring in my ears as the torrent takes me down. I'm going under, under.

My mind is racing: is *that* how you must be if you're to have a Pope, a King, an Emperor running after you, pleading for a portrait? And that 'spark' I had wondered about, that must be what Titian has. Isn't that what I've just seen in action? My God, I am thinking, this is how Titian has been doing things for more than fifty years: changing style, reaching for more, for perfection.

'Come, lad. We're leaving.'

Uncle G nudges me but my feet feel stuck to the floor. Look at this place! My eyes are not big enough to take it in. Around me, Titian's rewards are all too plain to see: the man made rich, *so* rich, fame heaped on him to excess. That thought is back in my head, it has burst in again and it's bigger now and it's urgent: *this* is the place I want to be, in this great house. And the Maestro's career, *that's* the career I want.

I can't say anything to Uncle. What will he reply anyway, if, pathetically, I ask how Titian could mock me as though I'm a dolt, could sneer so about Father? As for the envy that gnaws at me, there's no way I can express it, nor my sense of futility – futility which borders on self-disgust as it hits home how paltry anything I've achieved is, set against the artistry of the man whose working practice we've just witnessed.

CHAPTER TWO

Fortunately, later I find someone I *can* express myself to, the man I had encountered earlier while waiting with Uncle G in Titian's lobby. Giorgio Vasari: bright-faced, smiling, introducing himself as 'author.' A writer, the first I've ever met. He had offered me his hand, pulled mine to his chest, held it there in a strong grip. His cuff was of creamy lace, starkly contrasting with his badly stained hand, the knuckles blue-ish, fingertips totally black. Ink: so ours is not the only occupation to leave its mark.

His meeting with the *Maestro* over, Vasari was making his way out in leisurely fashion, greeting and chatting as he went.

We fell into conversation, prompted by his question, 'And you, young man are…?'

'Francesco, Signore. Jacopo Bassano's son.'

'Bassano, Bassano? Do I know that name? Let me recall what I know of it. Ah yes, something's coming back: did I not hear that da Ponte, as he was once was, is now *Bassano*?'

I'd nodded. Our name change is known in Venice, then, Signor Vasari remarking how our town has followed fashion and linked Father's artistic output to itself, ensuring it gains stature by being associated with his acclaim. 'Yes, Jacopo. I met him here in Venice, oh, twenty-five or more years ago, I suppose it must be,' he said. 'He's busy?'

Very soon I was to understand the importance for an artist of an interrogation by Signor Giorgio Vasari, the writer. The name, well, I recognised it as he said it. As, of course, would anyone who'd claim the slightest knowledge of painting or sculpture. The two Vasari volumes, we have them in Bassano. I could picture them, ancient and very yellowed on Father's shelf: *The Lives Of The Most Excellent Painters, Sculptors and Architects.* Once or twice I'd browsed the pages. Noticing he mentioned many artists of Florence but no Venetians, I had wondered why that was.

1550, Signor Vasari told me the work came out. Just a year after I was born. He quickly explained what he's done since his first success – beginning straightaway, in fact, on a second edition to be published as a third volume, revising and expanding the first two but also including living artists. For years and years he's been travelling all over and meeting with the artists of today to get their life stories, write them up – and rank them.

'Thousands of miles I've covered and taken the details of more than two hundred artists' biographies,' he said. Then, a little pompously to my mind, he added, 'I need to push on now to finish, busy though I am with endeavours of more importance to me, my painting, my architectural plans. I shall just have to dash the work off and get it on to the presses in double quick time. Can't delay longer because people are mad keen to get my views.'

Never mind his pomposity, what he said got me thinking. 'No one before has ever ranked artists in regard to their historical importance, have they?' I asked. He shook his head. I was realising, yes, he had been the first to contrast and compare artists' different ways of working. I was thinking, this is *interesting*; Vasari learned about them, judged them, then found the language to describe their achievements and justify his decisions.

'But this time it's different because now you're compiling living artists? And because this time you've come to Venice?'

Looking at me levelly, he nodded. It was dawning on me how crucial it was for Father to have *his* biography in this second edition of Vasari's, to ensure his rightful place is acknowledged – and, an added bonus, to stifle Titian's mean criticism.

And crucial for me as well. I must also be there in the book if I'm to have any chance of success in the future. Why *not* me too?

So, when I come away angry yet also agog from meeting the *Maestro*, I'm pleased to find Signor Vasari still there, gratified he invites me to go with him.

'You want to talk? Well, come then, I'm in need of a break after quizzing the *Maestro* most of the morning.'

Yes! I want to hear more from this writer, what he means exactly when he says he wants to help 'advance' artists through his new book. So I leave Uncle G to his business at Casa Grande and follow where Giorgio leads. A gondola taking us along the Grand Canal, then we cross Dorsoduro to the Zattere on foot, where we walk head-on into chill spray blown on a bitter wind. Then Giorgio pulls me out of the grey weather to sit in the warm half-dark of a tavern by the bridge across to Campo San Barnaba. Right away he tells me, yes, I'm to address him by his first name.

Giorgio seems to like my company and with him, saying what I want to say flows easily. Perhaps I open up to him more than I should. I have to admit that all the time we're talking it is in the back of my mind that maybe he can also help me live the way I want to live.

Giorgio goes on, all generosity about the *Maestro* and what he will be writing about him.

'Ah, Titian, yes,' he says. 'Love him, that's what we must do. Study him, imitate him and above all, praise him.'

Love him, that ogre? *Show* him, more likely.

Perhaps my expression says something or perhaps Giorgio can read my thoughts because next thing he's jerking his face close to mine and instructing, 'Francesco, never forget that envy's a driving force, one you should welcome.'

Among the many things Giorgio speaks of that afternoon, uplifting things such as 'grace' and 'unity' and 'harmony', he declares, more than once, that his goal is the 'betterment of the noble arts'.

I grasp on to that. Am I wrong or is he hinting there's a way that, through his writing, he'll better *me*, help me get to be where I've just decided I want to go? If he is, he's cryptic. Standing up, he makes an elaborate mime of someone holding a book in his hand. Eyes rolling, languidly he flips invisible pages over. The serving girl laughs at his oddity as she passes by, laden with her clinking tray.

Then those eyes harden and flash as he darts me another question. 'Ambitious, are you, Francesco? Best think ahead, then, think how to promote yourself.' He taps a finger on his imaginary page. 'Thought about what will get you noticed? You'll need more than that winsome smile you wear so nicely, the one you beam at me so often.' Now that finger of his is tapping my elbow, 'Ever considered what this is for? You need to use it. Don't ever think you can rely on someone else to push you to the front of the queue to get what you want.'

What I want? I want him to be *clear*. Does he mean he'll include something favourable about Father and me in the new edition of his *Lives*?

Before I can ask my question, he gets his own in, 'What's impressed you most about Venice?' That's Giorgio's thing: questions, so many of them. Often he'll go off completely at a tangent. And laugh. Several times I suspect he's teasing me. Or taunting.

How to reply? If I'm honest, my most lasting memory will most likely be the willowy Venetian women, their pale faces, silver-gold hair, their disturbing, swaying walk on their high, high heels. But I don't want Giorgio to think me vulgar, so I decide to say, 'One sight I'll never, ever forget is those coloured stars they call "fireworks".'

I ask if he knows who invented them. He shrugs, mutters something about 'the Orient'.

One night out walking, I tell him, I was startled by a screeching sound and a loud whistle. Then there were streaks of light against the sky, as they went shooting, these fireworks. Then *bang bang bang*, the streaks burst out into red, green, blue, white. *Flap flap flap*, all the pigeons flew up, squawking their distress. Above, the coloured shapes, stars, spangles, snowflakes drifted silently down. The beauty of it. I opened my palms to catch one but somehow they'd vanished. There was a heavy harsh smell in the air. People threw up their arms and their caps, cheered.

Giorgio laughs his ready laugh when I tell him, 'I was stopped dead in my tracks. My jaw must have sagged open like a true bumpkin's.'

CHAPTER THREE

4 April, on board on the Brenta canal

All bumpkins one day have to return to the soil in which they were rooted. For me, today is that day. The wrench I felt leaving Venice was awful. In such a short a time I've come to care about that place so much.

Early this morning Uncle and I left from the Rialto to cross to Chioggia. I made sure to sit where I could look back all the time we were on the open water. Serene on her lagoon, half-swathed in a veil of grey-green mist, as though too shy to salute her admirers, that was how the lovely city appeared for my last view.

La Serenissima. Not serene for me, my visit. After meeting *Maestro* Titian and Signor Vasari, I woke every morning my head boiling with ideas. I ran everywhere in the city, trying to take it in, quickly sketching scenes I didn't want to forget. Any spare moment I got from helping Uncle G, I hung around the places where the painters congregate. I passed over a coin for *un ombra di vino* and sat in a corner listening, wanting to learn as much as I could about the work such fellows do. There's lots of it, it seems.

'Enough for me too,' I ask, 'when I manage to get back here?'

'Never fear, young sprout, we'll find something to occupy those idle hands of yours,' one of them told me. They discuss quite openly who has been commissioned to paint what, as well as the contract details, the price a patron's paying. They josh and sometimes cuff each other in a jokey way when they part – but I bet that's masking jealousy. Giorgio refers to it as 'competition', the contest between them to close the most prestigious deals. Clearly, it's hot and keen.

The sun's beginning to dip, by now Venice way back behind us. Our barge has travelled north all day on the new canal cut through the marshes. Wanting not to be here, not to be heading *this* way, it's like having a bad belly ache. Ugh, going back, back to Bassano. Back to my hometown, back to the studio, back to being at Father's beck and call.

It'll take us a week to get there. Seven achingly slow days: the canal, the long drag through the plain, then the many winding turns of the river until finally we begin to climb into the line of dumpy little hills marking the start of the Dolomites. Edging forward, we go only as fast as the team of oxen can haul us. Their every thudding tread on the towpath dins into my head how much I'm regretting I have to go. And my anguish is added to every time I hear the crack of the bargee's whip lashing at the poor beasts' backs.

My uncle glances my way, concerned I'm moping, I suppose.

'Where's your smile today, lad?'

How can I explain? I try for a grin. 'Uncle, if I must go home, I wish it would go faster.'

He shrugs at that, leaves me to my thoughts.

Anyway, it's not as though I have a choice. Only at home can I get started on what I want to happen. Bassano *is* a backwater. The old goat Titian was absolutely right about that. No offence Father, but my future *has* to be in Venice. How though, am I to get that over to you?

According to Giorgio, if you're after fame, you'll have to wrestle it out of your fate. In that Dorsoduro tavern he said, 'Lady Fortune's got you, Francesco Bassano, on her wheel and is turning you no differently than the rest of us. You want special favour? You'll need to be strong because that, she grants only to the brave.'

Well, since being in Venice, special favour, and fame to match Titian's, those are the things I do most definitely want. And Father must be made to see that since I'm almost eighteen, *I* should be the one making decisions about my future. I'll have to steel myself to ask him, 'When am I to have a life I can call my own?' It's possible he has never even considered the question, just assumes I'll follow family tradition, be under him until he dies, working on his backgrounds and *staying* in the background.

Before leaving for Venice I'd taken Cennino Cennini's handbook off the studio shelf to check what he says about an apprentice's training. Cennini writes that thirteen years are required to perfect every skill, to develop 'real ability'. Don't ever leave off getting practice, he says too, 'neither on holidays nor workdays'. Ouch, so I'm to be grateful for the odd day off Father does allow.

It's not yet thirteen years, my training. I was seven when I started in the workshop, the small jobs: fetching, carrying, bottle-washing, boiling up sizes. Now I'm seventeen. I should *at least* have journeyman status. I'd produce my best painting and present it to the officers at the Guild as my masterpiece. While waiting on their verdict I would pluck a sprig of white heather for luck and pray to St Luke, patron saint of artists, to take me under his protection and advance my cause.

Once my accomplishments had been recognised then I could do it: go to Venice, join the artists' crowd, advance myself, eventually become a 'Master', take commissions in a studio of my own. But there's fat chance any such plan will get Father's agreement. I can just hear him, see that wagging finger, 'Francesco, you're too young for such ideas.' But Father has to realise I must get going. If not, these ambitions of mine will come to nothing. No Father, no more time-wasting for me in backwater Bassano, no more dogsbody slaving in your shadow.

So I'll do this, I'll *challenge* him: 'Father, let's take Titian as a measure of whether I'm too young. How old was the *Maestro* when he painted his great *Assumption*, the one you sent me to see? *Twenty.*' Yes, Father, I'm telling you, Titian was just twenty.

══◦══

'*Oy – o, oi, oi,*' the bargee shouts from the stern. From either end of our craft a polesman leaps on to the towpath. The oxen halt, the men heave the ropes to moor the barge. Each night we stop like this and make a fire to cook our meal. My job is to forage for kindling.

Uncle calls, 'Bring some green branches. Let's get up a bit of smoke and rid ourselves us of these annoying insects.'

Coming back laden with a couple of logs and a load of sticks, I find the polesmen with a good catch in their nets. While one of them scrapes clean a battered frying pan, the other spills a mess of pinky-grey guts back into the canal. Fried fish, my mouth waters. We'll be filling our bellies well tonight.

═══◇═══

'Turning in now, lad?'

It's getting late but will I sleep if I go to my bunk?

'No, Uncle G, I'll stay on out here awhile.' I bid him goodnight and move closer to the fire, wrap my cloak round me, lie back. We shared a flagon of ale with our supper but with all these thoughts my head is swirling as though I've taken grappa, gulped it down too fast.

All the thinking has come to something, at least. I've decided from now on I'll be calling myself 'artist'. Giorgio was right when he told me I should realise it's not my grandfather's day anymore, when someone with my skills would have been just a 'painter'.

I'll use the term 'artist', anyway, although Giorgio doesn't. His word is 'artificer', which he claims combines something of the artist, something of the artisan. Complicated, to my mind. But however you phrase it, Giorgio's opinion is that to succeed today you have to insist your work is recognised as refined, as achieving a higher level than craft, different from being a goldsmith or a carpenter.

He's right. Take Grandfather, my namesake, old Francesco, he was always busy with something – but for most of what he did, I'm sure he received little acclaim. He could be called to work on just about anything involving putting paint on to a surface, and had no choice but to do it. Father says he remembers as a boy watching him busy as often with a signboard for a hostelry or an embroidery design for the

Castle's ladies as with an altarpiece or a fresco. That's *not* the career I want.

Another of Giorgio's questions was about patronage, 'Francesco, tell me, how d'you define yourself – in relation to the patron, that is?'

I floundered: *define* myself? Giorgio, knowing exactly what he was driving at, had his thoughts off pat. He said the relationship is no longer like it used to be. Back then, *before*, the artist was tame, just a paid performer, because the patron's ideas about the composition were all that counted. '*Now* it's different. The patron comes to the artist and the artist agrees to *lend* his style.'

'You mean the artist doesn't have to do everything he's asked to? But if he refuses, how's he to live?'

'Yes, right, he listens and has to accommodate as best he can the patron's wishes, of course, because that's his livelihood. But individuals are beginning to understand they're entitled to act in a new way, to demand a part in deciding *what* the work's to be.' Giorgio was smiling again as he said this and then he asked me, 'So Francesco, do you see how much better this is, better, I mean, than being just a mechanical medium through which a painting or sculpture's achieved?'

Yes, I did see, I got it. It's only 'some few' individuals though, Giorgio said, who realise they must be in charge of how their ideas are interpreted. Now I understand, that like Titian, these are the innovators, unafraid. The ones that rise way above the rest.

'Some few' only. Am *I* to be among them, surging ahead of stick-in-the-mud imitators, celebrated for a style I constantly adapt and improve?

Titian, Titian, oh no, not that name in my mind again. I can't think of the *Maestro*, our encounter, without remembering my fear as that red river raged in my dream, without feeling that anger rise like bile at the back of my throat again. I can *never* let my father know how obnoxious Titian was to me, how insulting about him.

Despite that, I got something out of that audience. Got angry enough to want to get even with him, that's what. I'll *make* Titian realise I'm not a talentless nobody. And if that anger works like a shot of courage in my veins for when I confront Father about my independence, that's all to the good.

I've stayed out here longer than I meant to. The sky's drained of daylight and all I can see is stars studding a sheet of deep grey-blue from horizon to horizon. Clear, cloudless and no moon, just those million brilliant stars. I kick the last shards of log into the fire's embers before launching off the bank and on to the deck. Stumbling down into the hold's darkness, I feel around for a quilt to wrap myself in. Yes, it's cold enough for frost, I'd say, if the temperature drops any further.

11 April, on the Brenta

Today, awake early, bedroll folded, I'm positioned for the best view as the barge rounds that bend ahead. Once beyond Cartigliano, we'll soon *at last* reach Bassano. All through yesterday the tip of Monte Grappa was visible on the horizon. Almost May and yet the summit is still white. The sky glowers purple-brown in the east but a shaft of sunshine breaks through and briefly tinges the peak a delicious pink, as though the snow cap glows from inside.

My father is forever painting our mountain. Whenever he talks about his apprentice years in Venice he says it didn't suit him there. It was too painful for him to be away from home. He missed our high country's pure air and having sight of Monte Grappa, the grandeur of its profile, silver-gleaming in the mornings, rose-red at sunset.

From back down there in the stern Uncle waves, 'Almost home, Francesco, only a few hours more now.'

The pastures have come on fast in the time we've been away. The spring wheat is rising and flattening green-gold, gold-green, rippling in the gusts sweeping over it, moving the way the muscles do under the coat of a spaniel when it's hunting down a hare.

Ah yes, *there* it is, just coming into view a way upriver, Bassano, my hometown: the old wooden bridge spanning the Brenta, the tall yellow and brown houses stacked down the slope, the castle jutting up proudly to the east. And looming over it all, barricading us in from the ice-capped ranges to the north, the dark bulk of our great mountain.

All very handsome but all very dull. Nothing will have changed there, that I can guarantee. I suppose there's no reason it should have, just because for the first time in my life I've been away for three weeks. Anyway, I won't be staying long. Yes, I'm going to move on, I have to. My plans, Father, somehow you've to be persuaded to hear them. *What* is the trick that will get you to let me go my own way?

CHAPTER FOUR

11 April, at the house by the bridge, Bassano

'Only the best reds and blues, remember,' Father had said before we left. 'Vermilion red especially, and the purest lapis lazuli. And this time I'm after a lot.' As always, he was concerned about getting value for money. His fist clenched over the coins he'd just counted out in his palm, he shook it by my ear so I heard their jingling while he warned me against Venice's cutthroat merchants. 'Hard, those men, hard, Francesco. Their arms will need a proper twisting before you'll squeeze a reasonable price out of them.'

I have to grin, remembering my tall father, who almost never jokes, contorting himself to mimic a merchant bent double and squirming, his elbow yanked behind him, mouth opening and closing silently as though screaming.

Only thanks to Mother secreting me a small purse did I have anything at all to spend in Venice. And as for the blue scarab ring on my middle finger, *that* I'd better swivel round into my palm. If Father spots it, it'll surely qualify as an extravagance. Were I to tell him the truth, that no money changed hands – no, I tossed a lucky dice, won it playing cards – well, that would not excuse me in his eyes.

We *did* bargain hard with those merchants, nailed them, and got Father's vermilion and all the rest. We've delivered it; we've stacked it in place. Home and in the hall, I'm dumping my knapsack by the stairs when Father's voice reaches me just as I'm about to push open the salon door. I hear my name. And the angry tone.

I freeze, my hand dropping from the latch so its *clack* won't give me away. I step forward tentatively, avoiding the uneven floorboard with the piercing squeak. Balanced on one foot, my ear is pressed to the door.

'Where is he? Where is he, Elisabetta? I was expecting them back on today's barge. They should be here by now.' Is this Father being really angry or is he just enjoying raising his voice, having a good grumble at Mother, she always so mild with him?

Now I hear her, worried-sounding, 'Perhaps Francesco's been taken ill. Please the Lord they haven't had to stay on in Venice, that damp place. Especially with the spring weather so cold.'

'Well, I'm not surprised it's gone awry. You know my opinion of Venice. When did anything good ever come from that place? We agreed Francesco is of an age now to get a sight of the city, but it was a bad idea, sending him with Gianluca. If they linger down there it'll hold me up.' Yes, he is annoyed. That is the groaning way he sighs when he's frustrated.

'Husband, I know you think Venice air carries bad humours. Dear oh dear, Francesco's weak chest, his cough … what if he's caught a chill?'

'Well, I couldn't delay any longer. For my new work I need vermilion. Country scenes it's to be, Elisabetta. Landscapes – but unusual, with plenty of country folk in the foreground. Colourful and embellished, heavy with detail. And I want to get started.' Another sigh.

I wish I weren't hearing this: Father talking of new paintings. I've known him like this many times before. There will be a brief period of hectic activity while his enthusiasm is hot. I'll suffer terribly in the studio, badgered every minute as he commands, 'Do this, go there. No, not there. There, yes. But no, no, not there, try it here,' until he's satisfied the materials are in order, the composition's correct and all is set so we can resume our normal schedule of sketching out designs and applying paint to canvas.

Is Mother listening? 'I must check Francesco's not forgetting to take my syrup at night. Two spoonfuls,' she's saying. 'How he complains of its taste.'

Ugh, Mother's right, I do. It is disgusting. Acrid. I want to gag each time I try to take it down. These cures, I've been on one or other of them since that first time I coughed as a child of six.

Father's answer is not all that sympathetic. 'My dear, the boy's always coughed. And hasn't the apothecary always warned that whatever we try, your syrup or my herbal concoction, they *may* soothe but will never stop him hacking? Besides, the boy doesn't let it bother him too much, does he?'

'Ah no, he never does. Our Francesco was born with that sunny smile on his face, I do believe.'

'I'll be wiping that smile *off* his face fast if it turns out he's dilly-dallied down in Venice.'

Well, I'm not smiling now – too busy pressing my fist to my mouth to stifle one of my oh-so-famous coughs, damn them all. At the same time I'm straining to hear if anything more is being said. But the only noise is something muffled coming from Father. Whatever he's saying, it's no longer in that angry tone.

Mother's reply is clear as she sings out, 'Yes husband, I'll sort out what you want, so you can start very soon. Tomorrow or the next day.'

He's gone. I breathe in deeply once more, clear my throat, push the door, jump down the steps. Mother is on the settle, her hands busy as usual, needle in one, piece of linen in the other.

'Mother, are you well?' As I sit beside her she shifts slightly, her face showing no surprise at my sudden appearance. But when I smile at her I see that soft and satisfied expression taking it over, the one I often notice when I'm with her, the one I sometimes thinks she keeps only for me. My nose twitches: lavender. Wherever she is, my mother, there'll be that fragrance, that tang. She hangs the great blue-purple bunches from the rafters to dry every autumn, and she's always stitching at those little sachets she tucks in amongst our linen.

One strand of her dark hair is straying from her topknot, hair in which these days there is a gleam or two of silver. Her brown linen skirt is strained at the seams where she's patting at her belly. And she's sitting strangely, her back leaning at an angle.

So, there's to be another infant in the crib, bawling, spoiling our sleep. I've told Mother that with four girls already in our family, another boy would be best. Another brat for me to show the ropes. I've done it for two siblings already, first Giovanni and then Leandro. If it *is* a boy, we'll be four Bassano brothers. I like the sound of that.

'Your father's after you,' Mother says.

Only just back and already it's started. I say nothing but try to put on a surprised face. Maybe Mother is speaking knowingly, though. Is there just the hint of a smile dimpling her cheeks? Did she hear me come in the front door and can she tell from my face I eavesdropped? I've never managed to keep much from her.

She's looking at my chest, not my face, though. She pushes back from me. 'You've outgrown this, son, the stitching's straining. And look at this here.' She slips warm fingers against my wrist, showing me my frayed cuff. 'This doublet is worn out. And on your tunic I see you've three buttons missing. Come to me on Saturday for measuring. After the Easter feasting is over I'll get the tailor.'

'Let me choose the colour?'

'You and your colours. Something to set off those new yellow stockings of yours? You always do like to look bright.'

'Mother, ask the tailor to bring fabrics for you to choose from too, something that will sit well against this.' I've remembered the slip of fine stuff I've brought for her, straight from the bodkin of a Venetian lagoon lace-maker. I pull the tiny package from my jerkin. She takes off the wrapping, holds my gift up. It's light like a feather, creamy in colour with a chain of daisies woven in the border. Enough for a collar or perhaps a pair of cuffs.

'Burano work?' she says and gives me her special smile. 'You're a dear boy.'

I want to boast, tell her how I bargained with the poor woman, beat down her price. I bite the words back somehow, look at Mother and instead say, 'You should wear rose and apricot, figured muslin, not this heavy stuff, these dark shades.'

She laughs. 'After the baby, after the baby, son.' She pats at her belly again, making a circling movement on it with her palm. Suddenly there's loud noise from next door: banging, clashing of metal on metal, the sound of a heavy vessel fallen to the floor, hitting the flagstones with a resounding clang, clattering.

Someone on the rampage; an intruder in the kitchen? I'm half-launched up from the settle with my hands clenched into fists when I see that Mother's bent over, rocking. *Her* hand's pressed to her mouth, failing to muffle her laughter.

'Francesco, sit down.' She looks up, her cheeks all red. 'It's your father in there. With his new idea, the one that's been – how should I say it … fermenting? – while you've been away.'

Father in there, in the kitchen, fermenting like our apple cider? This is too good. Mother sees my grin of disbelief. Another bang, this time the door, the outside one, closing. She takes my hand, clasps it between hers. 'Son, your father has decided he'll paint ordinary things. Just now he explained there's to be rich detail in his new paintings, especially in red.'

Earlier, she tells me, Father had asked what work she does in the spring season.

'Mystified how to answer him, I was,' she says. 'Because son, as you well know, in the spring my work is about the house and garden and the smallholding, just like it is at any other time. But your father wanted to know what is *particular* to the months of April and May. Well, son, I told him. "Husband", I said, "spring's the time when the poultry begin to lay again and our sheep are lambing and the goats give their richest milk. We make cheese, lots of cheese."'

Then she'd said to him that should anyone trouble to go with a net to the Brenta, April is a month when the river shallows would give up a good catch of young eels, which she'd sugar and fry with onions. She'd explained to Father that eels help eke out the salt fish of our Lenten fasting. Then after Easter, should the hunters do well and come in from the hills with a spring hare or two, she'd jug them in that dry red wine from Vicenza and stew them with juniper berries to a tenderness just the way he likes it.

As she finishes Mother looks just a little triumphant and I ask her how my father took it. She tells me he'd chewed for a bit on all she'd listed, then said he'd want to see her utensils, select a few and keep them a while to use in the studio.

'*Utensils*, eh Mother? Ordinary things, indeed. This is a departure, a bizarre one.

What did you say to him?'

What else could she do, she replies, but promise to gather together her best copper basins and dishes, a bucket or two from the dairy, a spoon, a sieve?

'He's puzzled me with this, son,' she tells me. 'He has been so busy up to now with drawings for portraits and preparing the big altarpieces. The payments have been coming in in timely fashion. I hope this new-fangled thing won't put an end to that.'

I'm sharing her wonderment. 'Yes. This *is* new.'

'He's aflame with it, Francesco, whatever it turns out to be. Tomorrow it'll be clear to you, I'm sure, when he sets it all out.'

Aflame? I know how it is to be scorched by the heat of Father's demanding new directions. I put a hand to my own face. It's on fire. My chest always reacts when I get emotional and sure enough, it's constricting. I splutter a cough: a bad bout's coming, I can tell. To hell with it, I have to stand up, bend over. Mother is up too, beside me, tutting and reaching to pat my shoulder.

Back there in Venice with Giorgio my audacious idea for twisting Lady Fortune's arm, wresting a different future from her, didn't seem so difficult to achieve. Back *here*, it's suddenly feeling impossible. Does that mean I've already given in? Finally, the racking stops and I can straighten up. But I need air. And some space.

'I'm going to walk awhile, Mother.'

'Wrap a shawl round that throat of yours, then and don't stay out too long, will you?' I'm almost at the door when she calls out, 'And Francesco, if you want to keep peace with your Father don't even think about getting into one of your drinking sessions with your chum Stefano.'

CHAPTER FIVE

3 May

I'm making vermilion. For chalks. A big stock. It's always the bravado of that brilliant orange-red Father wants for his most important works. Me and red, I can't get away from the colour. Ambition, this new feeling I have, that's red. It's as red as fire, the fire I feel in me, burning me.

It will take all day and more, grinding the vermilion down to get a powder fine enough to free the brilliant colour which the black blocks of mineral conceal. Soon the heel of my palm will be completely stained and red deeply engrained around each finger nail. Like a butcher's boy.

In Cennini's manual for apprentices it's perseverance he emphasises for handling vermilion – that's if it's quality results you're after. He says, 'If you were to grind it every day, even for twenty years, it would keep getting better and more perfect.'

Perfection, that stern-faced taskmaster, and Father, he of the wagging finger, both are in my head. They goad me as I smash the blocks into manageable nuggets before starting on the merciless grinding. The pile of pigment grows slowly – I wouldn't want to count how many beads of my sweat sully its blood-like hue.

To impress my brothers, Giovanni and little Leandro, I try to make it look light work. It's not, it's hard. But at the same time it requires delicacy, a matter of judgement – which is why I can't delegate to the boys.

The two of them will have to step up soon and take some of this load of studio work from me, though. Father will most certainly need their help if my plans for independence ever come to anything. Not that I've spoken a word to him after being home from Venice three weeks already. Ambition's fire may be burning me but by all the saints, it's as though I've gagged myself. And why would I do that? Simple answer: if I don't ask him, I can't hear the word '*No*', can I? I'd give anything to avoid Father forbidding me.

Giorgio was very firm with me when we were in the tavern in Venice.

'Hunger for fame, lad, that's what makes artists struggle against the odds. And against each other. But you lad, you're telling me *your* struggle is with your father.' He pushed his point home. 'You've been thinking in due course your father's mantle will float down from the sky and fall softly around your shoulders. That Jacopo's acclaim will walk to your door, knock and enter in, eh? But now? *Now* you want fame for yourself. And soon. Isn't that it?'

He said it with a smile, that superior smile that's there infuriatingly on his lips all the time. But the irritation I felt wasn't enough to make me break away. Something was telling me I should heed this man and might actually stand to gain.

Since that conversation I've thought a lot about what 'struggle' means to me. Perhaps I'm just not ravenous enough. Hah, is that it? Any hunger I have is assuaged by Mother's stew, her fish soup with leeks, her buttered macaroni. Such a good appetite for her suppers – but working one up to confront my father? – that's another matter.

I check on Giovanni and Leandro. Their two dark heads are bent over the table as they cut the squares of parchment needed for rolling up the chalks. Leandro's knocked the cone of pigment with his knife and sprayed his face in fine fashion. I want to laugh but keep my expression stern. The boy's eyelashes are red and furred. He blinks at me, nose a-twitch like a little harvest mouse.

'Clear up here and then clear off, the both of you,' I tell them.

Describing my family to him, Giorgio caught on immediately that we Bassano boys, being the fourth generation making art in Bassano, are part of what you can rightly call a 'dynasty'.

Oh yes, Giorgio, on that day we met I was glad you invited me to ride in the gondola. When we left from Casa Grande's jetty we were alone, the gondolier insisting the craft be balanced by the signori sitting facing each other. I was grateful for the chance to study you, your bright face under that mop of curls, how you perched like a cocky bird on the edge of the blue velvet seat. You're not young but you don't act old either.

Once I saw quicksilver. I wasn't more than ten. I remember that Bassano market day in high summer, a hawker touting the substance as a marvel not to be missed.

He calls out to Mother, 'Signora, let your boys see this. There's no harm,' as he throws the three of us a cheeky grin. We jostle into the circle around him. Mother stands close behind us, reaching down to pull little Leandro up, sling him on her hip. The man uncorks a flask, pours out a gleaming, grey-black substance on to a slate. It forms a mysteriously perfect ball and then rolls effortlessly around as he tips the slate this way and that, slowly, then faster, faster.

It *is* a marvel, neither truly solid nor truly liquid. The hawker pokes at the ball with a stick, showing us how its metallic perfection shivers and breaks when touched. But then we see the particles immediately re-form, unperturbed, simply becoming many smaller spheres, all still as round as ever, and continuing to roll.

Well, in the gondola, looking across at Giorgio Vasari: those shining eyes in that smooth, gleaming face, something about him made me think of quicksilver.

Drinking with Giorgio in that San Barnaba tavern was where, for me, it all started – even if I didn't know it then. By the time I had drained my third glass of good Rhenish I'd agreed to the task he'd in mind for me. He dangled a bait; I gobbled it down, hook and all.

'You'll have to wait awhile to gauge the benefits,' were the words he tantalised me with, 'but for now, you can go to work to furnish me what I need. Believe me, you can but gain.'

His last question to me was, 'You'll move on what I need? And do it soon, mind, because I won't wait long.'

I didn't answer. He must have known his hook was caught in my flesh though, because after a momentary pause, he did so for me. 'You'll move on it and I'll hear from you. Good lad. Write to me, I'll be at my house in Florence.'

He strode off, waving his cap at me before clapping it on his head. I was to do the legwork, he was to get what he wanted. Yet I'd been the one clutching his hand in thanks, grinning and grateful as we parted.

During the monotonous days of the barge journey I went over and over the bargain we'd struck – if bargain it was. How many times did I reconstruct our conversation to try and understand exactly what Giorgio expects from me if he's to do his part and include Father – and me, too – in this second edition of his book?

My task? He had made it sound simple. 'Just go and find me a story, lad.'

A story, that's what, something relating to one or more of my father's paintings. Or to a drawing. Giorgio said he liked drawings. 'I'm making a collection of them, in fact, something quite unique,' were his actual words.

Father draws a lot, as it happens, not just preparatory designs, nor just in charcoal. He experiments with coloured chalks on coloured grounds, his favourite combination red chalk on blue paper.

But I had to ask Giorgio again – so I'd be sure I'd heard right. 'A *story* about a drawing or a painting?'

'Yes, that's it. Something you'll provide me, Francesco. So I won't need to get up to Bassano, meet your father, do yet another interview, make notes, all that time-consuming palaver I've had more than enough of, believe you me. I'm very close to finishing the manuscript and now, above all, I'm looking to keep my narrative lively. I need to "lift" it with as many amusing anecdotes as possible,' he said. 'So, once you're back home, you're to be thinking of what your father has done that might intrigue my readers, entertain them, even surprise them.'

Amuse, intrigue, entertain? Not words I'd associate with Father, nor his work. Would Giorgio explain more? No.

'You'll know when you find it,' was all he would say, that smile of his still alight, of course. From that day on, wondering how to even begin looking for such a thing has become the reason I lie awake, toss from side to side, punch the pillow. Night after night.

11 May

Only today, a full four weeks later, up here in the attic's stifling heat, do I get a glimmer of an idea about how to satisfy Giorgio. In our household Father wants nothing thrown away. All our worn out and broken things are thrust up here, haphazardly piled, poised to trip the foot or bang the head. I push past a battered chest and some lumpy cotton sacks to get a place to stand upright. Mother's lavender bunches hang low from the rafters here, the fronds tickling my nose.

Up here to source props for our new paintings, I'm seeking a large double-handled wooden bucket. Mother said its crack couldn't be mended. Father wants it for his painting *Spring*. The cracked lip can be ignored. Or a dairymaid's hand can be posed to cover it.

Yes, my father's finally come clean about his new idea. We're to work on four seasonal paintings, a 'cycle', he calls it.

'Since we're starting in this month of May, we'll celebrate everything about spring in the countryside with the first one, a pastoral scene showing folk at their daily work. After *Spring* will follow *Summer*, *Autumn* and then *Winter*, as you might expect,' he says, a half-smile on his face for once. 'We'll have our own people portrayed just as they are. Naturally, I mean, no fancy dress. They'll be wearing their own clothes. We'll show them using their tools and implements. We'll show their animals.' He waves out an arm, 'We'll have Monte Grappa in the background of each one.' Of course.

A scene with so much happening in it all at once will need careful planning. Father's plan was to include a lot of folk: men, women and children. I was for limiting the complications, but not he. I've come to agree he's right: if we're to do these scenes, let's go all out, bring in models to pose, and paint the pictures so they truly represent country life. At least it'll be a change from staid portraiture.

The bucket must have been thrust somewhere under the dust sheets draping anonymous sticks of furniture because I can't see it. From idle curiosity I heave open another battered old chest. It's filled with fabrics. Hoping I might find a pillow to replace the lumpy one on my bed, I reach a hand in and grope around. I feel two hard shapes I can't identify. The light is not good and so I lean down, reach further in and lift the things out, one by one. Underneath, there's a folder and I take that too.

I close the chest, put the two shapes down on its lid. They're models, models in clay. Two dogs, one lying down, the other standing with one paw raised. Even in the dim light, it's my impression they're finely worked. These are not children's toys. I don't open the folder, which has a dark green cover and is tied with a red-checked ribbon, but put it under my arm, take a model in each hand and back down the steps.

═◊═

Later, opening the folder, my mind begins to race. Sketches spill out, pages of them. Some are done with delicate pen strokes in sepia ink, touched with white highlights, not like anything Father does. But most are unmistakably his style of heavily accented charcoal with some coloured chalk. I note that the marks and broad, slashing strokes have often been rubbed so they blur together.

They are sketches such as I've never seen. Such subject matter I *have* seen: dogs in different poses. Father makes no secret of his love for animals. All animals, but with special affection for dogs. He honours that feeling by often placing dogs prominently in paintings, even in religious scenes. Like in *The Parable of the Good Samaritan*, with which I assisted Father a good few years ago. The Samaritan binds the gashes on the unfortunate traveller's head and legs, tipping fine oil from his flacon, while to the right of the scene two hounds busily lick up spilled drops of blood.

No, it's not the subject, it's the *composition* that sets apart these sketches. What's unusual, no, *unique*, is that the sketches depict the dogs – neither of which, incidentally, looks showy or even well-groomed – as filling the entire expanse of the paper. If you were to frame them, the image you'd see would be the hounds and nothing else. I find it astonishing. Positioning them centrally like this is unheard of, going against everything I have ever been taught about the conventions of portraiture.

I'm puzzled and at first think perhaps there must be other sheets of paper which are missing. Sheets which, if added, would show the dogs as being part of a larger composition. That would make sense. There would be the dogs' master portrayed, for example, probably formally posed and finely dressed. Or perhaps his infant son, equally richly attired. Or the dogs would be there as adjuncts to a Bible scene, the way Father added them into *The Good Samaritan*.

Then I notice something else: a series of small vignettes in the corner of one page, working drawings, just thumbnails really, each one different. But each one depicting only the two dogs and, in each case, taking up the entire area of the charcoal-line frame in which they're enclosed in. What strikes me is that they're *exactly* like the preparatory drawings one would do for a client who's wishing to commission a portrait.

Father has used the simplest of formats: one hound in profile, the other with head three-quarters turned. There's no detail in the background, just the sky, coloured with a brave blue chalk. The result is natural and yet poetic.

Once, I asked Father a question about portraiture. He pulled out a little volume and thumbed it until he found a quote from a treatise by Leon Battista Alberti from more than a hundred years ago. '*The painter represents the dead to the living … so that they are recognised by spectators with pleasure and deep admiration for the artist.*'

Is that what Father aimed at here: portrait-making in the classical mode, but of *dogs*? Because it's quite clear he wanted the painting to be more than a mere likeness. Much more. He's gone deeper. In these sketches he's conveying the two hounds' individual characters. Just as a gifted portraitist should.

Very excited by this, I have to jump up and pace about. There are so many questions to which I want answers. Who was it that commissioned Father for something as radically different as this? *Was* a painting ever, in fact, made from these sketches of his? If so, where is it now? And as for the dogs, why were ones in such less-than-superlative physical condition chosen to be honoured in this way?

And then, what about Father – if he did undertake such a very unusual portrait, did he ever again do anything else like it? So innovative, such a departure from the norm – it's extraordinary and well, it's also *brave*.

I can get Uncle Gianluca to help me with the facts. There's very likely a record of the commission in the workshop accounts he's kept all these years. But if *this* is the story that'll satisfy Giorgio, then what I need is juicy flesh to hang on the skeleton of those facts.

God help me, I see an ordeal ahead. Tackling Father, I'll be put to pains first to explain how it happened, me meeting Giorgio, learning about his new book. Then what will it take to convince Father of the importance of getting a good mention in that book? Without that, there's zero chance of me getting the information I want. A simple task you say, Giorgio? Oh no. It's complicated, complicated.

CHAPTER SIX

30 May, on Monte Grappa

I'm taking a walk on the mountain. I decided to leave my worktable. I still had stuff to do but I'm letting it go to hell. I follow the usual track out of town, at first broad and sandy but as I strike higher through the chestnut woods, the going gets steeper, the path deeply rutted. Above the tree line it's craggy terrain: massive boulders jut from the coarse scrub and the landscape is all greenish-grey; in the distance a line of crevasses plunging into a deep valley.

'Breathe, son. Nowhere on earth has finer air than Monte Grappa,' Father had called out to me one time walking up here together, an icy blast almost whipping the words from his mouth. Always swept with wind, you need to raise your collar when it comes barrelling across. If there's sun, you'll be narrowing your eyes against the glare of the beams bouncing from the snowfield at the summit.

I'm on a narrow sheep track when my eye is caught by something in the sky, a pale flicker, some sort of hawk wheeling into sight. Soaring over me, it's making a wide arc, feathery-tipped wings moving strongly up and down. Straining my eyes, I spot the bars on its long tail, the three broad dark stripes, and the pale underwings. From lower down the mountain another comes, gaining height as it leaves the woods' edge. Their *cree cree* call reaches me faintly as together they ride the air before moving away in dipping, dancing flight.

'Honey buzzards, a mating pair, by the looks of them,' I say out loud, swinging myself up on to an outcrop for a better view. The swifts will be here in a day or two then, I'm thinking, darting and shrieking, dozens and dozens of them, swooping around the Castle keep. Birds – they're blessed to have wings, able to propel themselves wherever they will, drawn down south when the weather's inhospitable in the mountains. Would I could fly off south. South to Venice.

Not to be for me, though. Despite how badly I need to tell Father what I want, I've given up. God, how it grates. But I can't do it. Each time I'm readying to talk about getting my independence I start gasping for breath, get sweaty and fear I'll be sick in front of him.

It would be better, I thought, if I could put what I want to say in a letter. So I tried writing, lighting a candle, using my evenings to crouch over a paper, quill in hand. How many times did I inscribe a page with 'Dear Father …'? But that was no good either. Abandoned, ripped into pieces, those pathetic drafts litter the floor by my desk.

Tonight though, tonight's going to be different. Tonight I'll be getting at least some part of what I want. Because yesterday I did this, at least: went to Father and spoke about the clay models and the sketches of the dogs.

Finally, nearly three weeks after finding the things, I asked if he'd a few minutes, would he give me a hearing? At first he was puzzled, didn't seem to recognise what I was describing and busied himself scratching at his head with the end of his paintbrush.

'Show me what you've found, son,' he said eventually. I put the models in his hands. I think I caught his face softening a little as he took them. 'Cara,' he said, placing the model of the recumbent dog on the table and stroking one fingertip down its red clay spine. 'And ah, there you are, Bruno.' He took the other one from me, the standing dog, and grasped it by its middle to hold up to his face and meet the gaze of its deep-set clay eyes.

I explained as briefly as I could about Giorgio, how we had met and what I now seek as material for his book. Father did seem to listen. All the while he hadn't taken his hand off the model he'd called Cara. When I finished, he nodded. He pulled the pile of sketches towards him and leafed over one or two. His face had that narrow-eyed look it wears when he's at his most critical.

I was twitching with nerves as he pored over the largest drawing, the one that so perfectly captures the poses of the two clay models. His frown cleared as he seemed to make up his mind. 'Francesco, I'm too busy today but tomorrow we shall sit together and I'll tell you about the painting for which these things were the preparatory work.'

I must have started.

'That pleases you, I see,' he said and in his usual decisive manner added, 'Your mother will be with us because she was there at the time this work was done. See the date in the corner of this page? 1548. You, lad, were not born – but if I recall rightly, you were already on your way to joining us.' He actually smiled at me as he said tonight he would warn Mother to be ready.

I risked his annoyance by asking one question then and there. Well, it was more of a statement. 'Father, these models, I've never seen you make anything like this.'

'No, these are Paolo's,' he said before he turned away.

What will Father have to tell me? Something about Paolo, whoever Paolo is, or was, for sure. About Cara and Bruno, dogs whose names he remembers all these years later. And about the drawings of them, certainly. And more importantly, about the painting for which they were prepared.

Father noticed I had started. It was when I heard him say the drawings were done for a painting – confirming there *is* a painting. I'm going to learn, I hope, why he, and this Paolo who worked in pen and ink, made the studies of the hounds, who commissioned him for the portrait subsequently painted, and where that portrait is now. Taken up with these thoughts and muttering away to myself as I climb, it is only on reaching the highest rock's flat top and sliding down to rest my back against a boulder, that I notice the sky. It is a terrifying sight.

It is as though a wall of black cloud a mile high and who knows how many miles wide is coming towards me. Roiling and surging, coming fast straight at me. Suddenly the lightning starts, the black wall cracking open in three or four places at the same time. It sears down in great jagged shafts, which retract, only to sear again. It is so vivid I feel I should be able to hear it sizzling. Smaller blazing lines of light shoot out unevenly, many-fingered, either side of the ends of the shafts, turning the black wall into a flickering tracery of brightest silver. An enormous thunderclap roars in my ears and makes them sing.

Leaping up to scramble down the rocks, my left foot twists and I stub my toe. I tumble headlong. I try to break my fall, snatching at boulders but, instead, my hands scrape against them. My palms stinging, I land on my side. The air's gone flat and sultry and from this viewpoint, the sky above me seems tinged a strange mauve colour. I'd lie here for a moment or two if I could, but the look of the weather so alarms me I struggle up and start to run as best I can along the path.

My feet slip and my ankles knock against rocks and twisted stumps. I am pouring sweat. The rain begins before I reach the tree cover. In a sweep of high wind, it comes horizontally to hit my shoulders. I feel my ears lashed as my hair's blown forward and I can barely see. Despite how my foot hurts, I don't stop running.

I'd rather not relive what it takes out of me to get back down to Bassano, how agonising the long stumbling descent is, all the while my eyes blinking tears of pain from the twinges shooting up my leg. The wind does not let up for a single instant, gusting in and backing off out, still breathily hot somehow. That sweaty warmth doesn't last though, and the cold has got to me by the time I'm within sight of the covered bridge and my favourite of the town's taverns, *The Three Quails*, hugging the end of the bridge, ancient, shabby, always welcoming. I'm planning to get home and get dry clothes on, bathe and bind my foot, but could it be the rain's just easing a little? Then that lamp above the tavern door, it's twinkling so invitingly. I change my mind.

The river is in spate. Shouldering the door and pushing into the steamy warmth, I can hear the old bridge coming under strain, creaking and groaning alarmingly, its wooden supports taking a terrible battering from the current. Through the window you can look down at the water and as I sink thankfully on to a stool, the river below is running very fast and high, churning and broiling in furious flow under the bridge. I look around for Stefano but he's not in his usual corner nor propping up the bar. It seems tonight's teeming rain has doused my friend's thirst for ale.

Upstream the torrents must have started hours ago. This rainfall, combined with the river already being swollen with snowmelt, makes for a dangerous and unpredictable time for Bassano. We're no strangers to floods here, usually they occur in spring and they're mostly on a manageable scale. But there have been some memorable ones when the Brenta's come roaring uncontrolledly down into the valley through the narrow pass. Mother talks of the huge flood that happened in the year before I was born. It was summer that time too, the river rampaging and destroying the bridge. In its flow it brought with it an entire shepherd's hut, wrenched-out trees, root balls and all, dead calves and lambs, all manner of debris. Water covered the entire valley, cutting off the town for weeks.

This storm has come more suddenly than usual. The Brenta rising like this, we're in for a disaster. Over-brimming the banks, filthy brown water will be swirling everywhere. Anyone with a house on the lower slopes will be retreating to the upper storeys and anyone who has tempted Providence by putting a hen coop on the water meadows is sure to lose their birds. There will be stinking mud dumped a foot deep on the pastures.

Another squall of rain rushes down the river and lashes against the tavern wall. It's as though there's a malevolent giant out there, playing with pebble stones, casually casting volleys in our direction. I peer out at the growing crowd of people massing on the bridge, crushing in to shelter under its canopy. I wonder how long it will protect them from the weather as I hear a clatter and crash, look up into the lowering sky and catch sight of a clutch of tiles being swept off the middle section of its roof. They're twirled in the air as though they're a handful of playing cards and then they're let drop straight down to crash into the water.

The door slams open, six or seven men head in, regulars. Laughing and shouting, they stream with water as they pull off drenched tunics and shake their heads side to side like dogs fresh out of the mill pond. The drops flying, they swipe hands across their faces and laugh some more. There's a sudden, sickening, cracking and crunching sound, jolting me up in my seat, the entire room seeming to sway. The men raise a mocking half-cheer, throw their arms around each other's shoulders, lurch about as they slap backs, clink glasses.

A man leans towards me, 'How long have we been saying the old bridge has gone beyond the point it can take these storms? The town councillors know it's a danger. It goes and we on this side in Angarano will be cut off – a fine pickle, eh?' He spreads his hands and shrugs as there's another thump and crash, the room juddering again. Those hearty idiots raise another cheer.

I've seldom downed hot wine faster than I do that beaker. I want to be across the bridge while it's still intact and take off as smartly as my injured foot will allow. My excuse to myself for scurrying away is that Mother has said she's not feeling well.

CHAPTER SEVEN

In the hall the two older of my four little sisters sit cross-legged, absorbed in a game. Tilting her head, Isabella is throwing one piece up, then another, catching them between her palms. 'Tick tack, tick tack, my jack wins over your jack.'

I bend and gingerly pull a squelching boot off my injured foot. I peel my stocking and wince at the look of the big toe and skin around it, as black as if dipped in soot. I ask the girls whether Mother is feeling better.

'Mother's in bed. Father's up there with her. Supper'll be on the table any minute.' I tug on one of Mariana's braids as I make to limp up the stairs. 'Only broth and yesterday's beans,' she calls after me. 'But Mother sent a message you can eat an egg if you're hungry.'

I've got up to the top floor, yanked my sodden doublet over my head and I'm towelling my hair when I hear the first *boom*. I register the strangeness of the sound at the same time as I feel the shock as a blast of wind pounds the house. Still pummelling down from due north, now funnelled through Bassano's narrow streets, it has gained strength. The room shakes. I put a hand flat on the wall to steady myself and feel its very fabric vibrating under my palm.

It goes quiet, well, not *quiet* because from the street down below there's clattering and banging, shouts and a noise of something cracking, as though a big branch is being torn from a tree. But quieter than when a second blast of wind comes, after another roaring build-up and then the same *boom* louder this time, if that's possible. As it passes over I hear how the house creaks, grumbling and groaning the way an old man complains of his aching joints.

We don't have much to say over supper. The little girls are kicking each other under the table but I'm not going to be the one to speak sharply. Not on a night like this when the dark has come down so suddenly and that wild wind barrelling along the street is making our neighbour's shutters go *bang bang bang* against the wall.

It's strange enough to be eating without Mother presiding, dipping her ladle in the steaming tureen, Father handing out hunks of bread. It dawns on me there is to be no discussion after the meal. Tonight I'm not going to learn a thing about the models, the folder of dog sketches and the painting. It's like being dug in the guts with a sharp stick to realise that.

'Where do storms come from?' Mariana asks. As usual, she's more inquisitive than her brothers.

Giovanni, putting on a solemn face, chimes in, 'Is God punishing us?'

Leandro is silent, his eyes fixed on my face. *Look, boy, look.* He doesn't need to be instructed, that one: a portraitist, born not made, if I'm not wrong.

I try explaining the earth has to breathe just like we do, and sometimes the breaths coming from the high mountains are strong and cold, hitting us very hard here, down in the valley. 'Have no fear of a deluge like Noah's; this won't to be like what we read in the book of Genesis,' I say encouragingly. But I have it half in my mind to josh them that if the waters *do* cover the town we could save ourselves by climbing to the Castle. We could raid the dovecote there for a pair of birds to set free from its heights once the flood starts to recede.

I don't get the words out though, because there's a cry from upstairs. Mother? Not a cry really, more a honking shout, short, urgent, loud, awful. I'm shocked by the sudden image I get. It's of passing by the hog pen the day the slaughtering for the Christmas meats began, the blood, hot, red, steaming as it gushed out under the fence and soiled the snow.

A nervous gurgle from one of the boys.

'The baby. Come too early,' says Mariana, old enough to know that much of women's work.

We sit silent on our stools, the dish of beans giving off savoury steam but no one reaching to dip a spoon in it.

Father looms in the doorway, 'Francesco, over to Angarano quick for the midwife. Your mother needs help.'

I stand, put weight on my foot, gasp and try a step forward but can only hobble. I lurch and bump him, almost fall against him. A spluttering cough forces its way up from my chest. I'm bent over hacking, using my napkin to cover my mouth when he speaks again, 'Lame. And sickly. What a time you do choose to be useless, son.'

I straighten up. Does he know how harsh he sounds? Mother would have reproached him for his unkindness. I want to spit out words that'll fend off further criticism but I pause, seeing his white face and the patches, purple-blue and swollen, under his eyes. He's saying, 'Giovanni, it'll have to be you. You know where Mother Silvestri lives? Second door, left side of the lane after the chapel. Take your cloak, it's tipping down out there.'

Giovanni's going to Angarano, crossing over the bridge, the bridge that could fall? Should I tell them how high the water's got? I wince and it's not my painful foot nor Father's scorn that is causing me to do so.

Father's still issuing my brother with instructions, 'Call in at your uncle's as you go by. Tell Aunt Maria your mother needs her. She should come right away.' The door has already slammed behind Giovanni as Father shouts, 'Put on a hat.'

To me he says, 'Hot water. Snap to it. Boiling, if you can. Bring a bucket up quickly. Get them to stoke up the stove, we'll need more. Then send the maids up.'

Mariana is by Father's elbow, her hand clutching at his cuff. His hand pats abstractedly at her head. 'You know where the linens are stored. Bring plenty of towels. And Leandro, you're to carry up logs for the bedroom. We'll be keeping in the fire. Do *not* go in there. Leave them on the landing.'

Little Isabella's eyelids are closing while Father's ordering us about. Only seven after all, she goes off to bed on the top floor where the two youngest girls are already asleep. We three others do what we've been told. Me, shown up as the weakling, consigned to the kitchen, fussing over the stove alongside the maids, filling pails one by one, slopping them up as best I can to put outside Mother's door. Damn this foot. And damn the mountain for inflicting it on me.

My aunt arrives and goes up with the two maids. They are barely grown and they look at me timidly when I say they are to attend Mother. Perhaps back at the farm they've never helped at a birth while a storm like this rages, the wind battering the house as though they're sworn enemies in a fight to the death.

===∞===

It seems a long worrying age before Giovanni makes it back. Soaked through but grinning, his eyes are gleaming with the adventure of carrying the midwife's heavy birthing chair on his back, tied on with a string around his shoulders. Despite the brave grin he has a hollow-eyed, exhausted look about him.

Mother Silvestri drops her wet cloak, and puffing under the weight of her covered basket, takes the stairs. As the door up there opens we hear Father's voice and a dreadful long groan from Mother.

Giovanni says, the thrill of the outing still in his voice, 'We got to the bridge and it was frightful. The roof was cracking and the floor was heaving up and down ... heaving like – well, like a snake. Yes, it was like a snake wriggling. You could hear the water slapping up over the edge.' He's gabbling, 'No one's about. We could barely see our way. Mother Silvestri, she was scared. She wouldn't step on to it at first, and so I had to push her. All the way across the bridge I pushed her. Pushed her, you know....' I glare a warning at him. 'Pushed from behind her.' The girls giggle and he shoots me a triumphant look.

The four of us spend the rest of the night on the landing. I'd pulled my coverlet from my bed and was half-sitting, half-lying on the floor, near to the door to Mother's room. Mariana and Leandro, night-shirted, had peered from the landing above and seeing me there, fetched their bedding and crept down. Giovanni eventually came in as well, having struggled up the stairs to deliver Mother Silvestri's chair, then eaten what was left of his supper gone cold.

The night is dire. Cowering, fearful, we are as helpless as day-old chicks in a hatchery abandoned by mother hen. Mariana has her head on my chest. One of her braids has come undone and her hair, unravelled, has that childish sour-sweet smell. She's stuck a finger in each ear. But that won't do anything to block out Mother's distress. Each time she cries out her voice is higher-pitched and more agonised. The noises she makes, ugly and strange, are sometimes long drawn-out, sometimes panting and urgent. In between there's another voice, steady: Mother Silvestri. She seems to be saying the same thing, over and over and over again.

The wind does not stop its thudding. We brace ourselves against each of its assaults. They come irregularly and last different lengths of time. Some are harder, some softer. But each time the old house is hit we feel the floor under us shake. It grows colder. From upstairs, one of the girls lets out a whimpering cry.

At first we on the landing had been sprawled out on the floorboards but now we move closer together. Is it an arm, is it a leg? Whichever limbs are against mine, they're keeping me warm, however cramped I am.

I feel crazed as I stare into the dancing dots that make up the dark. I watch their dance and think, how would you paint this darkness? Father once said, 'However black the night, it can be captured in paint.' A *nocturne*, he calls such a work, insisting a light source is always there, a reflection glimmering on water perhaps, or a fading star. '*Look, and keep on looking, boy.* Find it, and through it, illuminate your painting.' Tonight though, I'm defeated. If there is a light source in this blackness, it's refusing to reveal its comfort to me.

CHAPTER EIGHT

31 May

Father's boots thumping on the stairs wake me. Grey light is seeping in, morning. My voice is groggy, 'It's all over?'

'Up, up, son ....' he's leaning over me, reaching a rough arm to shake my shoulder. I smell the grappa bottle has been keeping him company during the night's darkest reaches, along with Uncle Gianluca, the two of them glugging its contents down together by the salon fire.

I am so stiff I groan as I get up. My foot throbs. Giovanni's head is still under the coverlet but the two girls stretch and yawn. No noise of wind or rain hits us now. It is strangely still, the only sound from Mother's room is a little whimper.

The door open, I look in, trying to balance on my good foot while the others are shoving from behind me to get a view. Mother lies against the pillows and we get a little smile from her. Only a small one though, as she pushes a strand of hair from her forehead. By the window Mother Silvestri is squeezing rinsed-out cloths, the water in her basin red. Humming a little tune, she folds and piles the squares in her basket.

The ungainly birthing chair has somehow got overturned, its stubby legs jutting out. I glance and see the smears of red around the yawning opening in its seat. I look away. I don't want to think of how it was put to use helping Mother in the dreadful hours just passed. I shudder. Mother Silvestri, she of the broad back and meaty arms, she'd have been straining to make the baby's entry into the world as easy as possible. Pain impossible for me to imagine. Women's burden, women's wisdom. I shudder again.

There was a struggle and a climax. And I was asleep. Now I feel like Peter in the garden of Gethsemane, faithless, failing to keep the vigil, sleeping when I should have stayed awake. But at the very moment I'm feeling wretched and full of self-blame, the scene in front of me is making me see Mother in a new way. As the Madonna of Bassano. I want to paint her.

If I had my brushes and palette, I would do it right here and now, just as she is, one arm against the blue coverlet, the other cradling the infant to her chest. Its little, napkin-wrapped face is crumpled, a puckered *o* of a mouth pressed against Mother's white neck, tiny pink filigree fingers wiggling where they emerge from the blanket.

'Can I go get my sketchbook and capture this?' I want to ask.

'Greet your new brother,' I hear Mother say. She's smiling at us but her eyes seem wide and strained and her voice comes out high, a bit breathy.

'We have survived this night.' Father has been kneeling in prayer but stands up to say this to us. We're still squashed all together in the doorway. He does not smile. He's far more distraught-looking than Mother, his hair rumpled and sticking up wildly. He brushes a hand through it but it's no improvement.

Voice croaky, he says, 'Our eighth child, our fourth son. The new addition to our family has come early. He is small but we pray he'll flourish and grow to be a fine lusty babe. We have a lot to praise and thank the Lord for.'

Mariana puts her hands together. She bends her head, eyes closed, over them. Isabella, who has pushed in to join us, quickly copies her. My eyes are open and I keep them on my father's face. The brightening morning light reveals him haggard and worn. But I find my main feeling is not to be sorry for what Father has gone through. What I feel is anticipation and relief that things will surely soon be calm again, so that I can learn what I so badly want to know.

———◇———

The air is muzzily warm and heavy with moisture, in the lane the branches of the trees bowed under the weight of sodden greenery. The boys and I, pushed out of the house, scuff at the fallen twigs and broken blossoms. Eerily quiet on the piazza, only three market stalls. No fish, no fruit, the only vegetables tired-looking cabbages and muddy bunches of carrots. We call in at the baker's to find he let his furnace die in the night. Hard biscuits it's to be for our breakfast, then.

Down towards the bridge where the paving is slimed with river mud, Leandro's itching to slide the last steep incline. He will whoop out as he reaches the bottom, fall on his face, stain his breeches with mud and then laugh. I grab his arm. I am in charge and today there'll be no japes.

The bridge is wrecked, most of the roof on the northern side blown away and a great spar wrenched half off from one of the supports that brace it in mid-river. People are crossing in both directions, looking down and stepping cautiously around the yawning gaps in the buckled floorboards. The river, still very high, churns furiously. Personally, I wouldn't want to be risking that dirty grey torrent just inches beneath my feet.

1 June

No supervision for me in the studio today, my father too taken up making arrangements with the priest. There'll be a Mass of thanksgiving in San Francesco, followed soon by the baptism. Mother is still keeping to her bed and he spends most of his time with her. He has barely sat with us at mealtimes. Such meals as they are, that is, just messes the maids make, nothing like Mother's cooking. My siblings have long faces. I suppose we should be complaining less and praying more.

For distraction, I call the boys and we walk out and up to a farm overlooking the town. The farmer is expecting us and together we enter the barn. A horse snorts and a groom looks up, gives us a wave with the hand holding the brush. On the straw in the far corner a litter of puppies suckles at a tan-coloured bitch. They tumble over their mother and roll on their chubby backs. The boys go down on their knees, laugh and point.

'Pick out the most lively-looking pair,' I tell them.

The pups are just old enough to be weaned so the little bitch goes into the inside pocket of my doublet. Her fur is a bit damp, smells sweet. Squirming, she mews in protest but quietens once I start walking. Giovanni has made a sling out of a cloth and carries the other one across his chest. Returning single file across the drenched fields on the muddy sheep tracks, the boys call out from behind me, suggesting names. We settle on 'Fiammetta' for the bitch, in recognition of her rich red coat. We can't agree on the dark male's name.

2 June

The time has come for the baby's baptism but Mother is still too weak to go to the church.

'Get on some clean clothes and stockings and make sure your shoes are shined,' I tell my siblings. They're strangely quiet, not even the thought of the sugared almonds to be shared out later lifts the subdued mood. I adjust the angle of my cap, blue velvet, a plume of orange feathers, the favourite of my Venice purchases. Then I stand at the front door, hairbrush in hand, swiping at the boys' heads as they go out.

Father leads our short procession across the piazza. San Francesco's vast vault is cold but a pale golden light streams through the stained glass on to the flagstones by the font and glows in a jewelled mosaic, emerald, ruby and sapphire. Frankincense drifts from the censer in front of the altar.

San Francesco. Our church is named for St Francis of Assisi, who came three hundred years ago to Bassano on his spiritual pilgrimage. The story told is that, as he walked, a flock of songbirds accompanied him, wheeling and dipping around his shoulders. On reaching the town gate the saint accepted an offer of sanctuary and all the town's dogs ran yelping to greet him, leaping joyously, licking his hands. For weeks he lodged in a humble chapel in Angarano. Every morning, while he knelt in prayer under the pines on the Brenta's bank, those same dogs would arrive. At first sitting quietly on their haunches, they would begin soon to crawl on their bellies, edging as near to him as possible. I picture them: intelligent eyes gleaming, ears twitching back and forth to the inflections of the saintly voice.

Dogs, dogs, ah, dogs. My mind is not on interceding with our Maker for my little brother's welfare. It's back on dogs. I cross myself.

The doors bang open and the two godparents hurry across the nave. Standing close together around the font, we are a small, hushed group. The priest leads us in prayer. The baby makes a little nickering noise, a tiny bubble pops on his lips.

With a firm voice but eyes that look moist, Father speaks. 'Gerolamo, my son, we are naming you today. May you grow strong in the love of the Lord our Saviour and his Son.' The baby's head is dipped in the holy water and we hear the splash, followed quickly by Gerolamo's woeful wail. We cluster round to gaze at his wet face, his blinking eyes. Father, taking back the tiny bundle from the priest, cradles it. My new brother seems feather-light, a precarious scrap of humanity.

3 June

Waiting. It's three whole days now since the storm and *still* Father has said nothing. I'm gnawingly anxious for him to relieve my curiosity. Now I'm worrying too about how pressed for time Giorgio is, since in Venice he had said he was nearly finished with the writing. I'll have something for him, I'm pretty sure about that. I've delayed, I know it – but I *will* get it soon. Giorgio, Giorgio, be patient, please.

Alone in the studio, I'm beginning to plan the composition for the *Summer* pastoral painting, *Spring* being pretty much completed. I've had plenty of time to think about these pastorals. If they are to act as true testaments to the way the Bassanese live, they must capture the changing seasons' moods as well as showing practical realities.

So, in *Spring* the feeling is crisp and fresh; people are hopeful, thanks to the return of the sun and the cheer of witnessing new growth, the animals doing well, a fine cockerel, chicks, a baby lamb. Drawing on Mother's advice, we've pictured the hunters home from the hills, the red-collared hounds having caught a hare. In the foreground goat's milk is being turned into cheese.

I want Father to agree with my idea for *Summer*: that we should deepen and warm the palette to convey heat and abundance. On the studio floor I've set a cloth and laid out copper dishes on it to demarcate where, on the painting's right, we'll have a group of four folk feasting *al fresco*. Ideally, we'll show the repast taking place in the shade of an apple tree heavily laden with small red fruit. I've consulted the source book to copy how a monkey looks, since I want us to put one on the left. I'm including a melon and gourds. And a plate of cherries offered by a young boy, another touch of red. These are all indicative of August's fine fruit crop. In the middle ground, I propose the rich yellow of wheat sheaves, part of an energetic harvest scene that will draw the eye to the painting's centre.

When finally he does arrive Father doesn't even glance at my designs, nor at the things laid out. Something snaps in me and I feel my face flush hot as I decide I'll chance my luck, stand up and get my request in quickly. I do it. I get to my feet and boldly ask him if today he'll give me the information I'm seeking.

He doesn't need reminding what I'm after. Straightaway I get his one word reply, 'No.'

That short sharp word barked at me. 'No.' I'm winded, speechless. Then its bite follows. The effect's like I imagine a snake's bite to be: so small, that darting forked tongue piercing the skin. You'll be out in the hills on a sunlit day, taking the air, taking in the view, and it'll be so sudden and so neat the assault, so sharp and quick the pain. At first you might wonder, is this really happening? But then, oh, the long dragging agony of it, the realisation the poison is seeping, taking hold. How you might grip at your belly to ease the cramp, might thump at your useless limbs as numbness creeps over you.

Father, hunched on a stool, leans forward. 'You'll want to know my reasons. Sit, son and listen.' Resentment is seething in me as he tells me he has reached his decision after long thought and prayer. Voice solemn, he says, 'Gerolamo is God's gift to us. He was almost lost during that dread night. Your Mother's suffered greatly. This boy will be my lastborn.' His tone becomes plaintive, 'He's weak, though. The frailty of the child is our Holy Father's warning to me. And a test.'

He's made a vow, he explains. The Lord sparing my brother, Father has promised that in the future he will only ever devote himself to paintings portraying true religion. These sacred subjects drawn from the holy Testaments will represent acts of worship and praise for the Lord God, his Son and the Virgin Mother. Moreover, he's sworn that from this day on he will give more of what he earns to the needy poor. And then to conclude, he says he has placed his feet on a path of humility and is determined to turn his back on praise, advancement and every other worldly reward he may be offered.

He has closed his eyes. 'Can you understand my reasoning, son? The Lord is showing me it is not for me to seek to put myself above others. I've realised commendation, whether from Giorgio Vasari or anyone else, is simply of no account to me.'

It's all so painful to my ears I can say nothing. I just sit there gagged, looking across at him, arms folded on chest, that worn face with its blind eyes turned to me. Then suddenly, startlingly, I see those eyes are open and hard and he's meeting my gaze and using his firm tone again, 'Well I hope so, Francesco, because we will not be pursuing this opportunity your new acquaintance has offered. I said *not*. No. And that's my final word.'

4 June

Still dark but dawn must be close because the birds have started their throaty chirps and syrupy trills. One particular insistent silvery note vibrates again and again. It must be a wren. Answering notes come from another in the bushes down the slope. Their song drilling into my head, the two of them wouldn't let me sleep on, even if I had a mind to. But I don't – because today I'm leaving, just my saddlebag to buckle before I head for the stables.

I'm to go with Uncle again to Venice. I'm to go *back*. What luck for me since I can't *stand* to be here, starting another day in the studio with Father as though nothing's happened. I can't truly enjoy my release, though, because the reason for it is worrying: Father is sending us off because the baby is not doing well. Gerolamo is feeding but not thriving. Special roots and herbs must be procured so Father can make a herbal concoction for Mother. He has consulted his books and is convinced that *must* help with her milk. Since she won't hear of a wet nurse, Mother will have to be dosed every three hours. Meanwhile, until we've sourced the medicine's ingredients, we must all pray for her to rally and Gerolamo to survive.

After supper last night Uncle came upstairs to give me the news about the journey. I had rushed up there and bolted the door, missed the meal. After my talk with Father I had not wanted anyone to see my misery. And I couldn't have swallowed food. Uncle knocked and called out, 'You'll want to hear this, lad.' I opened the door a crack. 'It's a swift visit only we'll be making,' he explained, telling me Father's orders are that we're to rush straight back with the things he's listed. He is sure his rarefied ingredients can be found in Venice and we're to buy them, however high the price. This time, to make all speed possible, we'll be riding the road. It should be no more than a two-day journey each way – so we'll be back within a week.

I look in on Mother to say goodbye. Father is praying again.Mother sleeps quietly while he, on his knees by the bedside, rocks back and forth, eyes closed, mouthing words I can't hear. He gets up, grunting. I will myself not to look at him as he pushes past me to leave the room.

Gerolamo whimpers from his basket. Mother's eyes open. She pats the bed. I sit and take the hand on the coverlet, feeling it cool in mine.

'I heard what happened yesterday.' Her voice is faint. She makes that little grimace that turns her mouth down at the edges.

I'm pulling at a loose thread from Mother's coverlet as I say, 'He turned me down. After agreeing he'd give me the information I need for Signor Vasari, I waited and waited. And now he's turned me down.' How pitiful I am, my voice coming out as a nasty little whine.

Mother gives me time to compose myself by turning to fuss at her pillows. I cough. I'm trying to clear my throat as she says, voice still very quiet, 'I read your letter to your Father and so I know what else you're wanting from him, son.' I'm staring at her, the blush warming that pale tired face, 'Yes,' she goes on, 'you left a letter on your desk. I think you tried writing to him many times, didn't you? There was one you forgot to tear up. I read it. I'm sorry. But it means I know. And last night your Father told me he's refused you that request as well.'

He refused me that as well, oh yes. 'No.' This time he'd fairly bellowed the word at me. 'You *cannot* be spared. How can you ask such a thing at a time like this? *How* do you think the studio would run if you drop your responsibilities and gad off to Venice? Have you no loyalty *at all* to this family?'

Did I manage to get a word out in reply? I don't remember. I stood there appalled, overcome by regret at having abandoned all caution and pressed him to grant me my independence. I'd had the crazy notion he might concede me something since he knew he'd disappointed me about Giorgio. Bad idea, fool. Father's mind doesn't work like that. All *he* could see was that my asking for something so major was ill-judged and ill-timed. And so he didn't hesitate an instant before shouting his rebuke. Then he pushed open the door.

I thought he'd done with me but he turned, 'This Vasari business: you're thinking there could be some benefit to you in it, are you? A way to advance yourself?' My mouth must have gaped his answer. He laughed harshly and said, 'Right, aren't I? Yes? Well, put a stop to that thought right away, son, brace up and face facts. *Nothing* you've yet done deserves acclaim.'

Father had never been one to strike us but with this, he might as well as have taken the strap to my legs. I had to show him my back and while I was turned away I heard him leave, going down the steps, the noise as the wind slammed the door behind him competing with his final irate squawk. Mother is watching my face. I am *not* going to howl out my rage and disappointment in front of her – but it's hard not to. I pretend to cough so I can first bring my hand to my mouth and then haul out my kerchief and blow my nose.

'I can't do anything about that decision of his, Francesco,' Mother says, 'but I can help you with this.' She slides her hand carefully under the pillows and brings out a slip of paper, passes it to me. Her rounded letters, capitals, two words, a name: ANTONIO ZANTANI.

Gerolamo's crying now. I lean into the basket, pull the blanket round him. He's dribbling and his snotty mess ends up on the palm of my hand. I put it behind me to wipe surreptitiously on my breeches before I pass him to Mother. She has to raise her voice over his bleating. 'That is the name of the Magnifico who commissioned your father to paint the dogs' portrait. Perhaps in Venice…?' The remainder of what she might have said is drowned by a higher-pitched yell from my brother. Mother places the hungry little chap to her breast. I wait to hear more but as soon as there's a moment of silence she says, 'You must go now. Godspeed, son.'

I glance down at the name on the paper and from my face it must be obvious I have questions and they are burning me. I bend to kiss her cheek. I'm drawing back when she says, very deliberately, 'I do not agree with preventing you from pursuing this quest. If it is your heart's desire, go follow it.' I still want to ask my questions but she's put a finger to her lips. Then, in the moment it takes me to shift from one foot to the other, she *does* decide to give me more and says very rapidly, 'The boy who came here with Signor Zantani, Tomaso. His name was Tomaso. He was the age you are now.'

Boy, Mother? She doesn't notice my look.

'Find Tomaso and you'll have your story.' She's pulled Gerolamo close now and is bent over him. With her free hand she waves me off – so she doesn't see the bemused expression that stays on my face as I make for the door.

———✦———

Despite the very early hour and the day's drear weather, I find Mariana waiting in the stable yard and see she's lined up her three sisters to say goodbye. The four of them stand solemnly, all in white pinafores, their faces shiny, their hair tied with blue-violet ribbon, a colour which Mariana must have chosen for them. 'You make me think of alpine forget-me-nots, standing there in a row like that,' I want to say. Forget-me-nots, the first flowers that push up to the sun when the snow in the high passes begins melting. I say nothing. But no need to worry, girls, you I won't be forgetting. Nor your sweet flower faces.

The boys are there too, holding a puppy each. I issue my instructions, 'Don't overfuss them. They're not toys. Give them fresh water every day. They'll need to sleep most of the time.' Fiammetta is draped over Giovanni's arm, her little screwed-closed eyes proving my point.

Leandro holds the black male up in one hand, tickling at its fat round belly with the other.

'Cesare,' he calls as he points at the puppy. Then he takes one of its front paws in his hand and waggles it, so it looks as though the little thing's waving me goodbye.

'Cesare,' I think, 'he whom all the world feared.' Why saddle a dog, which may well not be fierce at all, with such a forbidding name? A name remembered in our history, ancient and recent, as an emperor's, a ruthless Borgia villain's. Boys, boys, what a choice. After all, isn't the presence of one overbearing tyrant in our household enough for you? This thought makes me come out with a snorting laugh. The laughter's top note is resignation. But I feel the monster rage that lurks deeper down – and how it's breathing fire, gnashing its teeth.

I have already grasped my horse's reins when Father walks over, arms out, held wide as though to enfold me. I feel myself shudder, try to step aside, stumble awkwardly on my bound-up foot, wince at how it hurts. He comes up so close his beard brushes my cheek, his voice painfully loud in my ear, 'Son, when you are back we'll be doing some things differently.' I step back, holding my breath, hands clenched on the reins, tense against my horse's neck. Father is pulling at his beard, half-smiling, trying to catch my eye. I hold my head stiffly, making sure he can't. Differently, eh? What makes him think anything he might suggest will make things between us different? Or better?

As though readying to declaim something, his arms are out wide again. 'From now on, son, I have decided we shall jointly sign my works.' I don't speak. 'Yes, you can make yourself a fine flourish of a signature. How do you feel about that, Francesco? Your name to be there with mine on every canvas?' His eyes seem to be gleaming with moisture. It can't be that he's moved, can it? But yes, I see it's his turn to grope for a kerchief and pass it over his face.

Am I going to choke? I keep my head down, my own eyes watering, but mine with disbelief. *This* is his idea of recognising I'm a talent in my own right? This is an offer he thinks will satisfy me? Afterwards, looking back, I realise *that* was the moment I understood what, for me, being hungry for fame means. Well, well Giorgio, maybe I'm not ravenous enough to match the urge you say all true artists must have. But *Father*, in Christ's name, I am not a *dog*, cringing at your feet beneath the table, satisfied with sniffing after any scrap, you, my master, might let fall.

I hoist myself into the saddle and am glad of the advantage of height when I do manage to speak. 'That's just a sop, Father.' There, I say it. His eyes bulge as he stares up at me. Then, caution go hang, I make it worse, 'You know it. And you think I have to accept because I have no alternative.' My anger is making my face burn. Father is still glaring at me but hasn't found the words to reply. I've made him too furious to speak. Good.

Fortunately, across on the other side of the yard Uncle's mount is side-stepping skittishly and over the noise of hooves scraping on the cobbles he shouts, 'Let's get off. That cloud is going to break. We don't need a drenching before we've even started.'

Uncle is right, the sky's darkened alarmingly. Dark and steamy, the weather nicely matches my mood as we wheel round and leave the yard. I do not glance behind nor do I raise my arm to wave goodbye. In the piazza we meet the other riders and clatter out through the gate to the south. The brewing storm makes it feel almost like night.

To me, dark or light make no difference. My eyes are turned inwards. I'm seeing a scene, a scene from the Bible. How appropriate. Because Bible scenes are what we're to be forever working on together in the future, Father, you and I, isn't that what you told me yesterday?

But *I* say no to that. No. My turn to say the neat, nasty word. It will *not* be always together that we work. Because I've decided something, Father. You shall have a religious subject, yes, but it will be one painted by me alone. You want to know what it's to be, my offering? You shall have a *Return of the Prodigal Son*.

You won't be able to miss my point: barefoot and in rags, that's how he will be, the young man I'm going to paint for you. I'll show exactly how the errant son is when he returns to his father, what it looks like when, through pride and wilfulness, he's made himself destitute. My not-so-subtly hidden message will be plain to see: that *that* father at least allowed his son to go off and try things, even if his experiment in independence brought him to nothing.

Ahead on the track the trees are thinning, a long green slope in view. Over the open country a disc of white-ish sun has begun to brighten the sky. My horse is fresh and picks up speed. Before I abandon myself to the glory of a good gallop I push my hand into my doublet pocket, check Mother's scrap of paper is still there.

With only four days in Venice, will it be long enough to find this Magnifico, this Signor Antonio Zantani? How best to do it? I'll have to puzzle that out, perhaps Uncle Gianluca will have ideas. My first challenge though, will be to get him on my side. Tonight I'll let him in on my plan to go ahead regardless of Father. He may well frown. And then he may ask me in his down-to-earth way, 'Aren't you likely chasing a wild goose that's already flapped off down the lake?'

Maybe so. But I'm decided: I'm taking action. On my own behalf. Whatever the consequences, I'll not be stopped now. Damn it, I *will* find out whatever it is that lies behind this portrait of the two dogs. And I will let Giorgio have the information.

TWO

Zantani

6 June, Ca' Zantani, Venice

A draught on my neck? Helena must have had the windows opened while I've been sunk sweating in this sickbed, dragged down in one of those dozes you can't really call sleep. They are open, I know, because I hear the gondoliers. Gondoliers' cries are the true music of Venice. And for their accompaniment, our lagoon seagulls' raucous noise.

I admire the skill of the gondoliers, steering their craft from the Grand Canal into the narrow angled entrance of our *rio*, especially when the wind gusts in the channel. Once round into stiller water, some of them spit out a little chirrup of triumph, before pushing forward to glide fast under our palazzo's windows. Sometimes they call out again before manoeuvring their gondola under the bridge ahead.

She is keen on fresh air in the house, Helena. The weather's warming though, soon will be stifling. Oof, awful, how the canal slime stinks at the tide's turn, would the stench weren't so noxious. When summer's heat leaps on us being indoors will be insufferable. For me, though, whatever the weather, when is there an escape from suffering? Never – except when I'm granted happy dreams.

A dream of spring in the countryside at Maser, ah yes. How did I once describe to Tomaso what spring is like there?

I remember saying something like, 'Fragrance of green growth, tremulous feeling of life and light returning, everything about to brim and bud, the earth born anew.' If not precisely that, then some other such fancy phrasing. It was a citified way of speaking I liked to use with him, just to see the lad's eyes widen, hearing me play with our language's richness. I blush now, excusing myself it was the country air unleashing such foolery in me. Quite probably we'd have been skirting the curve of a field that was still brown and bare, a washed sky with swallows dipping and reeling above our heads. I relished Tomaso's company on those long journeys we made on foot. How many miles of the Veneto's country roads must we have covered together?

Sometimes he would stride out and I, dawdling behind, would look ahead and his blonde hair would be like a shining beacon lighting my way. Usually though, we would be side by side, plenty to talk about: me quizzing him, questions, questions about my new passion, drawing him out on all he knows of hunting with dogs for sport, their bloodlines, training and welfare.

Helena and country air on the other hand, they have never seemed to get along. Always refusing to come with me to *terra firma*, even though I told her she'd love our hunting parties, would shine in the amusing company at the Barbaro's mansion, where the brothers play such amiable hosts. Unconvinced, she never did see that splendid sight: Cara and Bruno running free with the estate's pack of hounds. Nor was she ever witness to my dogs' prowess with the game birds, their delicate, patient pointing and flushing, their skill retrieving the quarry. Their timing and their teamwork.

My dogs. On this warm day it warms me more to remember them racing towards me, paws pounding furiously, ears all frilled and flapping. And then I'm reaching forward to their eager, damp faces, feeling their soft mouths, taking the pheasant or partridge they've brought back to me. Ah, Helena, you missed something, never to have hunted with Cara and Bruno in their glory days. Yes, in my view, you missed the best.

Lying here, I have a headful of memories and too much time to pick them over. Once people praised my knowledge of the arts, granted me renown as a connoisseur. 'Antonio Zantani, the good eye' they would refer to me, my taste admired and aped by Venice's elite. It's true I was an expert on things, my eye never failing in its judgement.

Things, all those things I picked out for my clients as special and beautiful: gemstones, tapestries, bronzes, engraved glass. I was once accused, by none other than Helena, of course, of professing more liking for things than for people. Ah, that was cutting, pronounced with that edge in her voice, the one alerting you something sharp is coming, to startle you, make you wince as when the juice of a lemon squirts in your eye.

Nowadays my reply would be, 'Things, they're just things, aren't they? Monetary value, what does that have to do with anything?' From a lifetime's worth of *things*, with the exception of just the one painting, the special portrait I had Bassano make of my dogs, I can truly say that none of it has meaning for me now. With the time that's left to me, I prefer to give precedence to *days*. Yes, to let my mind range over days from the past, ones I spent in pure pleasure.

With days, it's different when you know they're numbered. Time and again I return to ones out with the dogs at Maser. It was so good to be there, spring's shy green cloaking the woods. Or in autumn, smoky with crackling bonfires, the hillsides burnished with tawny light when we would be turning for home, the huntsmen's cries echoing from the forest depths, shouting out the names of dogs which had strayed from the pack.

'Fiore, *Fiore*! Where are you, Fiore? Scout, Scout, here boy, here.'

Back then, I wasn't in my first youth by any means – but how those days made me feel young.

On this day, I feel old.

'Antonio?' It's Helena, whisking in, asking me, as every day, how I am. I tell her the pain in my sides gnaws less, the cramps in my fingers are easier. It's not the truth. Explaining I hurt everywhere would demean me too much, and as for my eyes, the soreness, I'd rather not discuss it. About my lethargy I also remain silent – what's the point of telling her I see no merit in ever again raising myself out of bed?

Helena used to say, in an appropriately wifely way, that she'd like me to rally, said I would build stamina getting out and about. 'Take a stroll up to Dorsoduro, go and see how your Hospital buildings are advancing, check the designs against the foundations going in for Sansovino's church,' she would suggest. She says things like that less often now – but anyway, if she tried to persuade me, I would reply I'm not up to it. In truth, when I lever myself from the bed my feet are swollen, I'm pathetically weak and my legs shake. In the last days I haven't even brought myself to walk the length of our *piano nobile*.

I am dull, I know, with enthusiasm for nothing. It makes me poor company, Helena's advised me of that more than once. And been proved correct, of course, since recently few of the old friends seek me out. Do I blame them, call them disloyal? I'd shun a sickbed too if I possibly could. I find I hardly care that I'm alone.

Although I *would* like it if my wife were willing to read to me. 'There's always solace in poetry,' is how I would instruct her back in the early days of our marriage. She had the lilting voice of a young girl. I'd coach her in her phrasing of the stanzas. Back then we were barely apart, sharing our reading, discussing everything.

Helena Barozza, she came to me as a girl of sixteen. Sixteen, but her mind lively and with a zest for learning. Such beauty she had, inspiring Pietro Aretino to write those exquisite sentiments about the grace of her eyes, the highness of her brow. Ah Pietro, the poet you are loved my Helena too. Yes, Pietro had seen Helena's portrait, the one I, proud bridegroom, commissioned from Vasari. Following soon after, there was that sonnet by Capilupi in her praise. Once set to music, didn't everyone have *that* on their lips? Its honeyed final stanza, my favourite, I have by heart: '… sweet ardour from her flame makes me melt and burn.'

Nowadays, Helena and I don't discuss anything much. It is Maddalena who sits with me. I'm glad that when her father was widowed and she sent to live with us, I offered to take on her education. Just in some of the finer things, to get a taste for the arts. It has been good to have a niece in the house, to see her becoming refined as her knowledge has increased. We understand each other. Since she became orphaned, I believe what I have arranged for when I'm gone will ensure her future is secure, tranquil and as she wishes it to be.

What's this now? Our house so quiet these days, so very few coming to call on us, it is a shock to hear a clanging bell, someone arrived at our water gate below my window. Whoever is there will need patience since they'll be bobbing awhile on the tide until Luigi comes to ease the door open and raise the grille. There is silence except for the *slap*, *slap* of the *rio*'s ripples. Then I hear the grille go up, screeching with disuse. Luigi must be instructed to get hog's fat to grease its workings. Low voices next, words I can't catch. All goes quiet again until I hear the lightest tap on my door.

'It's Maddalena. May I disturb you, Uncle?'

Maddalena, just seventeen. I see the Barozza family resemblance in her, daughter of Helena's older brother. I need to sit up and dear girl, she helps pull a pillow behind my head. I must be stale but she keeps her smile bright as she leans over and orders my coverlet. Always so modest. Pretty too, her aunt's blonde tresses in abundance, lovely grey eyes.

'I thought you might be sleeping. But Aunt is out and there's a young man asking to see you.'

'If it's a bill to be paid, he'll have to come back for his money. It's your aunt who has the books these days.'

But the person waiting below asks for me. Maddalena explains he is not from Venice. 'The young man's come from the north, I believe,' she says, a particular emphasis on 'young'.

Somehow that piques my curiosity in a way nothing has for weeks. The visitor has apologised for the unannounced nature of his call and speaks of urgency.

'He has told me a little of what his mission is. Only you can help him, Uncle.'

On a sunny afternoon this room is a bowl of light. Maddalena brings my visitor in and leaves, closing the door as I'm trying to pull myself upright. To discern who crosses to the bedside, I have to wince against the glare. My sore eyes impede my vision and my being thoroughly startled by the visitor being shown in may be attributed to that, I suppose. The curls, they are what confuse me, the light behind them not letting me see that this young man's shock of hair is nut-brown, not blonde. His height and slim build, silhouetted against the long window, also contribute to my mistake.

'Tomaso… ?' The name is out of my mouth before I can stop it. Tomaso, walked from my dream. But whoa, am I befuddled? I took no wine when I breakfasted. No, fool, your mind is going – this cannot be Tomaso. You forget so easily that what, getting on for twenty years, has passed? By all rights, Tomaso is a full-grown man by now, a busy farmer most likely, out there on the Veneto flatlands, harvesting his wheat soon and contemplating the crop to come from his vines.

Struggling with the coverlet, wanting to bring out my hand to welcome my visitor, I try to recover my composure. I must look like a just-hooked fish, feebly flapping on the slab, gasping for air.

My visitor pauses and drops on one knee. Sweat springs to my brow and I brush the back of my hand across it before I greet him. He *is* young. He is close enough for me to catch the salt-sweet scent of Venice on him and now I can see there's a gleam in his dark eyes.

'Signore, I am so sorry....'

What, the boy has come here to pity me? Not wanting this, I struggle again, pushing against the mattress on feeble elbows to raise myself straighter against the pillows. Still talking, he does not quite look at me, looks down rather, at the cap he holds scrunched against his bended knee. His accent, his rolled *rrr's* are clearly the soft burr of the north country. A jumble of words, the boy nervous: Bassano, I hear the name Bassano.

I can still assert myself. I lift a hand and it stops his flow. 'Please get up. Take that stool there and sit here.'

He moves the stool where I'm pointing. If I shift carefully on to my right side and lie like so, the pain might abate a little and at least I can see his face clearly.

'I am not quite myself today but please don't concern yourself,' I say. Then I question what brings him to Venice. And more particularly, to my sickbed?

I watch how he coughs, gulps a deep breath and then looks at the hands he's placed now on his knees, fingers splayed. Finely modelled fingers for a country lad and on one a scarab ring of very bright blue. And, I think, if my weak eyes don't deceive, stains of some green colour on the knuckles, a goldish yellow rimming the nails. A painter? A painter and come from Bassano?

That name, I can't help but be taken back there, back to Bassano. The image is clear: the studio with its jumble of canvases, its smell of turpentine, and its windows flung open on a mountain view, that great grey river rushing white-crested under a fine wooden bridge just below. I collect myself, try to peer forward into the boy's face and yes, I'm sure I'm seeing a resemblance to the artist I was with, there in Bassano.

If my visitor is put off by my close examination he doesn't show it. 'May I explain?' he asks, starts to do so even before I've nodded. He believes I commissioned a portrait from his father. He has seen preparatory drawings and clay models. Models? I wasn't aware of those. He thinks it's many years ago these things were made.

'Before you were born, then?' My question slips out. I don't mean to belittle him.

He appears to take no offence. 'Signore, my name day comes in January, the twenty-sixth day. Next year I reach eighteen years.'

A little touch of pride. Oh, the young. So ill-considered of them to wish away the days, to want to add on the years, not appreciating how precious it is, the time they have *now* to be carefree. To me this boy, oh pardon me, young sir, this seventeen-soon-to-be-eighteen *man*, doesn't appear carefree, though. He seems uneasy and he's coughed into that kerchief three times already. His eyes are certainly unusually bright.

My recollection is proved right. He tells me yes, he is the eldest son of Jacopo Bassano, artist, of Bassano in the northern Veneto, and is named Francesco. Jacopo is well, and well occupied on altarpieces and portraits, he reports. A relief then, the boy's not come begging for money just because I once favoured his father with a portrait commission, however significant that was at the time. And I'm glad to hear of Bassano flourishing, to see he has a son to take after him. Four sons, indeed. Francesco tells me of a new infant brother, born a mere few days ago – so Jacopo is indeed blessed compared to a man like me, with none to live on after him.

The lad leans towards me. 'The portrait I am meaning, Signore, is one of *dogs*, hunting dogs.'

Ah, now he has hit on it. I can tell by his expectant stance that this is the nub of why he's here. He knows of the painting, my *Two Hunting Dogs*, his father's rendering of my Cara and Bruno in their beauty. How carefully he pronounced the word 'dogs'. His face is open, eyes bright under dark brows. Young and guileless, it would appear, this enquirer. Yet aware the painting is special – and curious about it.

'I have brought this, Signor. I made a copy of one of the sketches I found.'

I take his book, open at a page with a charcoal sketch of a supine dog, centre, a standing one to the right. An approximation of my portrait, certainly, rough as though hastily done – but quite accurate for all that, recognisable as Bassano's composition for my painting. My painting, which would once have been mere marks like these on a page. My painting – ah, I thought it forgotten by everyone but me.

I feel a pang of regret for all that was lost. Saying, 'Still so much beauty….' I can't help heaving a sigh.

'Signor…?'

I can't explain. The lad would be shocked if I revealed what dark things are being brought back into my mind. However, I find myself saying, 'When they are desperate, people do very cruel and ugly things. In their ignorance and greed, they wreak much harm with their cruelty. You could be brought to despair by it.' I expect Francesco thinks I'm talking in riddles. I must try for a lighter note. 'But look,' I tap my finger on his sketch, my finger that trembles even with this mildest exertion, 'beauty will prevail and beauty will uplift us. Beauty cannot be sullied.'

He continues to eye me, face all bright anticipation. Already convinced there's something very special about the portrait, I imagine the prospect of soon getting the information he wants is warming him. I feel pleasure too, realising my enthusiasm about the work is shared. It's as though someone's put a flint to light my wick and my flame is flaring up. Perhaps it's so because much of my time these day I spend resigning myself to accepting that my end is nigh, whereas now, curiously, I feel quite differently, as though something new is beginning.

My eyes swivel to the wall on my left. Curtains of a particularly fine figured velvet in a shade of deep lilac I've always loved drape its centre part. He is astute, the lad, watching where my gaze goes. He stares fixedly at the curtains and then our eyes meet. I am conscious of how mine are red, sore and unwholesome in contrast to his, wide-open, youthful, dark brown.

'It's *here*, Signore?'

What can he want with the portrait? How has he learned of it? Obviously not from Jacopo. I can understand the lad's father being unwilling to speak of something so associated with disaster. Bad luck can be very long-lived, hold sway over a family, spoil a life – or lives. So what can all this be about? I lean up and manage to point a finger as I tell him, 'If you are to see the painting – *if* I say, – first I must know why you have come to seek it out.'

He explains about a meeting he had here in Venice two months ago with Giorgio Vasari. Vasari, hah! So the fellow's been back in the Republic – but didn't trouble to call on us at Ca' Zantani, did he? Sweet Jesu, in the days of my prime, quite apart from the commission I gave him for Helena's portrait, how much other work did I put Vasari's way? I suppose that from the gossips he will have learned of my indisposition and has shied away from visiting an invalid's bed. What did I say about ties of loyalty unravelling when sickness rears its head?

Francesco is describing the challenge he's been thrown down. Vasari, it seems, has asked my young visitor to provide him with information about the work of his father, Jacopo. Something to be used in a forthcoming book.

'It is an *anecdote* he has requested from me, Signore,' Francesco is saying. 'Anecdote' is another word spoken carefully. 'It's for the second edition of Signor Vasari's *Artists' Lives*. He has been compiling his biographies, living artists this time too, and is almost finished. He seeks stories to enliven his last remaining sections and has told me to find him one.' Then, twisting and twisting his poor crushed cap, he adds, 'I don't have long because he will soon be ready to publish.'

First Vasari issues this lad with a challenge, then he sets the clock ticking. Well, well, is that how things are being done in the world of book publishing nowadays? And, ah, we can look forward to another volume of *The Most Excellent Artists, Sculptors and Architects*, can we? It does not surprise me. Although it has taken enough time. It must be a good fifteen years ago or more that Vasari ravished the whole world with that first book.

It was impossible to ignore. Firstly, we Venetians wanted to see what the Florentine had written about painting. Those of us who'd met him had heard him say we in Venice excel in colour but fail in design. But this book was written in general terms, an introduction to his theories. The hours we spent debating those theories, on topics such as from where quality and style, harmony and unity in art derive!

But if this young lad speaks the truth, it seems these days Vasari's energy has given out and he needs tales and *anecdotes* from others to give his writing spice and savour. Painter, designer, architect, book writer *and* recently founder of an art academy in Florence, as I'm told – for Vasari something is perhaps finally having to give. Choosing my words carefully. I say, 'Vasari is a man who will always make best use of anything that comes to his hand.'

Francesco hesitates, perhaps detecting the scorn in my tone. Slowly he says, 'I have put my trust in Signor Vasari. Did I make a mistake?' Looking at me directly again, he smiles for the first time. It is a questioning smile but a winning one. He holds it, his lip giving just the hint of a little grimace to one side. The lad is not polished but he has charm – and may well know it. Seated so near, I wish he weren't seeing me like this, ill and dishevelled. My hair, by the heavens, when did I last take a comb to scratch at my thinning locks?

'I believed Signor Vasari when he said being mentioned in his book would be sure to further my father's reputation.' His fingers are splayed out on his knees again, denting the cord of his rust-red breeches into little pools where he applies pressure. Yellow hose. With those rugged boots of his, he wears bright lemon yellow stockings. Not the usual attire for a country lad, I'd say and I'm ready to wager that a Rialto stallholder has recently been enriched.

He leans forward, confiding now. *Me*, at least, young Francesco has decided to trust. 'I want Signor Vasari to write of the Bassanos.'

Interesting, the emphasis he puts on the plural. He adds, 'I've a reputation to consider too. I work as my father's assistant now. But I can match his achievements.'

This time there is more than just a *tinge* of pride. My first reaction is to be cynical and I think to smile and lift an eyebrow but then I notice how his jaw is set. He gulps, perhaps recognising how it sounds, his presumption. He has to cough and out comes the kerchief again. But then he looks me in the face, speaks more boldly, 'No, in fact, Signore, there is more to it than that. I want to outdo my father.' He gulps again. 'I have my own style and mean to go far beyond where Father has reached.' He rushes the next words, 'I can't stay up there in Bassano with him. I want success. My future must be in Venice.' He looks startled, as though these notions are unfamiliar to express. His mouth though, that obviously enjoys re-framing this bold thought and he says very deliberately, 'Venice is where I want to be.'

Suddenly I am exhausted by this conversation, by Francesco's youth, his uncertainty, his need for reassurance, his raw ambition. That goad, ambition, I know it too well. Like my very heartblood, it pumped through my life. Because of it, I could never rest. Ambition's twin is fear, fear of failure. Failure, which is like some rotting infection – you dread the feel of it eating at your skin. I have lived with that too. Enough! I groan out loud, wearying of these thoughts. I close my eyes.

'Signore, are you quite well?'

The lad's voice stirs me. I will not frighten him with the true answer. I sense how I am failing. My mouth is dry and I fear a dizzy spell coming on. 'The dogs, you want to see the dogs,' I say, trying to rally. 'Go there, pull that cord,' I croak, pointing to the curtained wall, straining to turn myself that way.

The sun has moved round while we have talked and, lilac velvet drawn back, a shaft falls full on to the canvas, highlighting the dogs against that ethereal sky, making Bassano's very brushstrokes seem to gleam. My heartbeat quickens, as it does every time. Cara, positioned full centre, is glowing with this light on her. Her white coat reminds me of a jug of rich cream.

Francesco drops the cord and stands back, silent. I amuse myself by looking at the back of his head of curls, trying to see the work through his eyes, wondering how it must feel, the painting being revealed for the first time. He showed me his rendering of his father's sketches, so the composition, at least, cannot come as a total surprise.

The first time the canvas was held up for me to view was very different. Although all so long gone in the past, I shudder remembering. How can I not? After the ordeal and all the horror I had been through, then came the shock of that sight, on that day when indeed everything was turning out so very differently from what I'd expected. Nowadays though, it's only dull pain that I feel, the rage and roar and effort of those emotions hard to recall. So I let them go entirely, lie back on my pillows and allow myself the luxury of questioning once again wherein rests the painting's power. As I do, each time I see the portrait afresh. Because for me it has a marvellous power, a power which belies its subjects, dear as they are to me.

The two dogs, creamy Cara splotched with ginger, and dark-eyed Bruno with his gaunt frame and docked tail, are not proud. Their stance is meek, their attitude humble and patient. They are not sleek and they seem subdued as they wait, roughly tied to the ugly tree stump with its sprout of leaves. But there's such dignity. Their comportment is so dignified.

As I think this, I am back with Tomaso in the kennel yard after my first day's hunting with Cara and Bruno in the Maser copses. I see Tomaso's frank open face and I hear again him telling me in his quiet voice, he also with his northern burr, of course, 'Signore, my dogs have their dignity.'

'*My* dogs, Tomaso,' my thought that was not spoken then. My dogs as yes, very soon after that, they were to become. 'Ah yes, my only dogs,' in my mind I add now. Maybe this time I do say the words out loud since, pausing, I feel their shape on my lips. If so, Francesco doesn't hear or chooses not to notice. He is silent, not even coughing now. I have watched enough idiots pretending they know how to read a painting, primping their fingers, moving in, moving back, tilting their heads like tarts, it's refreshing for me to note that this young man is admirably still, completely absorbed. He has been well taught: how to look and keep on looking.

Without turning he says, 'The dogs, they're nothing…' and then he stops.

At this I jerk up, jarring my shoulder. *Nothing*? I am bridling at his impudence but he is continuing, '… no, nothing like other dogs my father has painted. These dogs dominate the composition – yet to me, somehow they seem haunted. They rest, immobile but they are not resting. As for the way Father placed them starkly against all that blue sky, it is as though he pictures them at the very edge of the world. A desolate place, nothing else there but the big tree stump and those sprigs of flowering stuff on the dark earth.'

'What else do you see, Francesco?'

'I am feeling more than seeing, Signore.'

Good answer, lad. I wait and let him feel a little more, standing there, his cap still twisting, twisting in his paint-daubed hands.

'These dogs, do you know them, Signore?' he bursts out at last. The words tumble. 'Because they look out at us in a knowing way. The standing one ... .'

'Bruno.'

'Bruno, Signore, he in particular, in the way he regards us. His eyes, those eyes that look – there is knowledge in those eyes. The other one, lying down, a bitch I think ....?'

'Correct. Her name is Cara.'

'Sitting pretty and keeping her own counsel, but still a part, I'm sure, of what the picture is telling us.'

He does observe well for one so young. Now he points at the canvas, that sunbeam of a smile there again and says, 'Just as I suspected from the sketches, Father has shown them as no prize specimens, these dogs, and moreover, he has them tied to the stump by that rough rope around their necks.' He bangs his fists together, 'There *is* a story here.'

It is my turn to stay silent. He comes back round to the stool and now he is leaning towards me again, hands clasped to his chest, cajoling. 'What is these dogs' story? Signore, will you tell it to me?'

I can almost hear what he adds in his mind: 'I must know this story.' A story. Oh yes, the dogs, for sure they have a story. As do I, even if in the volume of my life I am soon to reach the last page left to turn. It's our story, Bruno and Cara, isn't it? The story of our shared fortunes, misfortunes rather, the rough road I travelled together with you. Along with Tomaso, of course. The story of how the disasters that happened along that road changed all of us.

The pain is back and biting deep, throbbing on the left side now. How much more of this am I to suffer? The lad hears the sobbing sigh I can't suppress and looks up. Even as I grit myself against the pain, the brightness in those eyes makes me want to enlighten him. You are beginning to believe you have found that anecdote you crave, aren't you, lad? – if your luck holds, that is.

I have so much I could tell him, strange as it will be to speak of it, having for so long relived it only in my thoughts. All these years of silence. But who's to tell me I can't change my mind now and confide in this young Francesco? An *anecdote*, he wants. I shall give him that and more. Yes, and between us, we shall have Vasari's appetite well satisfied.

I have to rest my head back, turn my face to the pillow to hide the sudden nausea I feel. Revisiting these memories will drain me further, I fear. But then it's all recorded, is it not? Yes, yes – how could I have forgotten? In my manuscript. Yes, as the worst of my injuries were healing I made sure it was written down. The first days, my impressions, the events, the dreadful calamity. Not all of it – but an account of what I felt able to tell. I remember how I lay in the dark for countless hours, reliving it, the scribe taking down my words. Bitterly painful, so much of it – but I took some courage from the thought it might help me swallow down my disappointment at the disastrous turn my life had taken. Now we need to find the manuscript. Yes, Francesco shall read it and with that, he'll understand enough of what happened.

The lad is waiting on an answer. I direct him with a wave to the carved chest beneath the window in the far corner, tell him to search for a large scroll. It has a canvas cover and is sealed with red wax, the date of 1548 and my initials stamped on it. My sight too poor to see across the room, I discern from the sound of creaking hinges that he is opening the lid.

On the other side of the room, the door bangs open. Helena enters in a flurry, grasping her veil in her hand, throwing her wrap and gloves to the floor.

'Luigi was instructed not to allow visitors,' she says, leaning over me and touching my forehead with the back of her hand. The feel of it is icy. Her perfume, the scent of violets in the spring, envelopes me. She trails the tips of her fingers down to rest them on my cheek but she is not smiling. I sense no tenderness.

'Antonio,' she admonishes me, 'Desist from this. You are too frail for such effort. You've allowed it to exhaust you.'

What, it has come to this, I am to be chastened as though a child caught filching a sweet pie from the larder? She brushes aside my attempt at explanation. 'Cursory' is the word I would use about her response when I try to introduce Francesco to her. I know her too well not to see she recognises the name Bassano.

She can't hide her displeasure and she frowns as she calls across the room, 'Young man, please let my husband rest now.'

Before being ushered out he comes to grasp my hand, asks, 'May I come back?'

Of course I smile and nod my assent. 'Tomorrow, Francesco, come tomorrow,' I croak from a dry throat. I hope he hears. I hope he'll come. From how he is looking, I sense his chagrin. He manages a smile but his eyes quickly go over me to fix on the painting and as he turns to leave, they are still on it. The last I see of him is their over-bright gleam.

Helena sweeps out after him. Before the door swings shut I hear her voice barking something, and I think Maddalena answers from somewhere down the corridor. Once Francesco is seen out, my niece will most likely get a scolding. I hope Helena is not too severe because Maddalena is not at fault. Why in heaven's name should she take blame for the small pleasure I got from the lad's visit?

———

When she comes in later to sit for a few minutes I tell Maddalena that. I tell her too who Francesco is, and more about what it is he wants from me, about what Giorgio Vasari has asked from him.

'He has left the name of the place where he lodges,' she says. 'If you've a message for him, it can be sent.'

I reply I am hoping he will come tomorrow. And that Helena permits him entry.

═◊═

Now alone again, the room is filling with the dusk that seems to come early this evening. Perhaps it has clouded over although I hear no rain. The shutters clatter, the sign of a rising wind, a summer storm that will whip down the Grand Canal, stirring the water until it's coloured like the skin of a green olive, one that has been pickled awhile in some good strong brine.

It falls dark. Too soon, surely? Time passes like that these days, sometimes fast, sometimes slowly. Is it darker than usual this night? No one thinks to come and light me a candle. Although I can no longer see it, I feel the painting's serene presence in the room. And I feel you, Cara and Bruno, here with me. Time is dissolving somehow. Yes, it is as though I move through a swirling, swaying mist. It grows even darker. Yet ahead a brightness is beginning, beckoning me.

I recognise I am in a place I've been before. A place I have loved. Yes, it is in Maser's woods, that slope above a lilting stream, where mossy rocks are overhung with willows and white-trunked birches. Up above me a path leads to where Cara and Bruno are running free in the forest fringe, their backs dappled, first pale yellow with wintry sunshine then dark in the shadow. Leaping and baying, they are joyous, while behind them scuffed orange-brown leaves swirl and flutter in a gust of wind.

Crake, crake, pheasants' musical bark. A brace rises from a thicket, flapping wings of turquoise-purple, iridescent.

I want to follow the dogs, stride out and up after them. They race ahead, tongues lolling, looking back where I come. If only I can walk away from the darkness, let it drop away behind me, if only I can catch the dogs up, then I know all will be well. I have breasted the rise and now come close to where the two of them are flopped down, stretched out, their flanks heaving.

Nearly there. I smell greenery after rain, the lime-y tang of leaves, wet grass and wild thyme trodden underfoot. Where before every step was sharp, grating pain, now there is relief. Now there is only pleasure. Pleasure and glowing warmth. Suffused with it, I am light of heart as I move steadily forward.

'Bruno, Cara, good dogs, wait there, I'm coming.' At *last* I can speak the words I've held back so long. I can plead with them in the way I must, 'Forgive me, forgive me....'

They hear me and turn their heads, ears pricked, regarding me steadily. The film has gone from my eyes. I can see them clearly. Bright-eyed and open-mouthed, they grin. Suddenly I need make no effort, my legs feel strong and my feet sure. Only a few more steps then we'll be together and I'll be able to touch them, stroke them, the tops of their heads, the silky places under their chins. My arm is stretched out in anticipation and I breathe easily, my mind at peace. We will be together, never again to be parted. They are there.

THREE
Gianluca

CHAPTER ONE

6 June, on the Rialto

Ask me, I would say it's an impossible thing he wants, my brother-in-law: this root. But he doesn't ask, just instructs and I, his go-to man, it is I who has to strain to deliver.

'The man-root, they call it,' he said, abashed, I bet, because for once he couldn't impress me with a fancy Latin name. 'It is rare – you'll have to search around. Look, it's like this,' and he wielded a stub of charcoal, drew a stick man, wind-milling.

'A root with arms and legs, a neck, Jacopo?' I was incredulous.

'Arms wide and legs akimbo.'

'*Akimbo?*' I'd have liked to laugh.

'You look *askance*,' he retorted. It wasn't a good time to have teased him and I was a fool to do it, underestimating how stricken he was by his child's sickness. He controlled himself but I knew the danger signs, the ear tips going pink and that mottling high on the cheeks. I folded the stick man sketch, tucked it in a pocket.

He grasped my arm. 'Gianluca, just find it, will you.' Commanding, not requesting, and verging on a threat, 'Get it soon and get back here or the worst will happen, we'll lose Gerolamo.'

So, Venice again, in my least favourite season, high summer when I can't breathe, a sack cinched too tight round the waist. In my least favourite part of the city too, approaching the quays where the galleons offload. A cacophony: rattling anchor chains, cargo thumping *thwack*! to the paving, seagulls' ear-splitting screech, bellowed commands, groans from the line of porters struggling towards me.

'Gangway, *gangway*....'

Whether or not there is room to get by, they come straight on, bent under lumbering rope-strapped bales, bulging hessian sacks. Hunched over, you can only pity them, men used like mules, sweat streaming in the heat. Heat that has got Venice gasping, rendered its citizens more irritable than ever, and all scarlet-faced, as though they're smothering under a feather bolster.

Despite flattening myself against the wall, I still get a knock from the corner of a load. I reach the docks, a few minutes' walk only from my usual hunting grounds, the goldsmiths' shops. The strident chaos is bewildering after the respectful atmosphere of those places, the hushed attention while I finger fine quality things, select just a few, only the best, as brother-in-law-boss-man Jacopo instructs. Then to the bargaining: fierce but always *sotto voce*, battling with locked eyes, clenched teeth.

But today, needs must I endure this, the noise, the assault of smells: hot tar, spilled wine, spices, sickly-sweet and strange, cloying the throat, fogging the mind. After two days' searching, I am down to my last hope. Blank stares have answered all my 'You have man-root?' queries. Just one clue offered by one merchant, 'Try *La Speranza*, she's moored in the *bacino*. Tomorrow the customs officer will let her dock. She's in from Constantinople, Silk Road traders on board. If anyone has the stuff you want, it'll be those fellows.'

No choice but to wait here then, catch the Master, persuade him to have a crate wrenched open, exchange a handful of roots with me for the few coins I've left in my purse. I pray I succeed. That pitiful babe, Jacopo's fourth son, his last child, he confided in me. And not doing well. While we were readying to leave Bassano its wailing made you want to stop your ears.

Jacopo is convinced the roots will enrich Elisabetta's milk. He will take the mortar, pulverise those weird-looking limbs with blows from his pestle and add the pulp to his mountain herb brew. Not that he'll let me see. Whatever he gets up to with the ingredients, he keeps deeply secret in that stillroom of his.

Once when he emerged, flushed-face, handling a noxious steaming pan, I provoked him with, 'You never thought to be an alchemist?' I admit a foul-tasting concoction of Jacopo's manufacture, so hot it burned my mouth, did make short work of a head cold plaguing me – so why should I carp? Would that his remedy helps. And fast. Like all of us, I want this new nephew to grow up and bring more talent into our family business.

At least here in this corner there is shade, slimed and stinking as it is: a fine Venetian stew of fish heads, rotting seaweed and sour urine. The real essence of Venice, I'd say – much different from Francesco's rosy vision crossing the lagoon with me that first time. That day, me, as per usual, racking my brain how to make my too-short time encompass all I'd to get done, I had given no thought to how the city would strike him. Ecstatic, yes, that describes how he was. Out there on the water as we bobbed on the swell, he was saying over and over, 'Glorious, it's so glorious,' arms held up wide to the skyline.

And then, reaching the Rialto, the people: his head nearly twisted off his neck at the colours of their complexions, their clothes. The women: some cloaked head to toe in black, even their faces covered, all but their flashing eyes, others flamboyant in flowing pantaloons made from silk in brilliant hues, garments that billow out and slink back to cling around their frames, as though they've walked free from the Sultan's harem.

'Heady, eh?' I asked him. I remember his nose wrinkling as two beauties slunk past us in a cloud of scent so spicy it can't have come from any flower I could put a name to.

He got about a bit in the few days we stayed that time, raring to see everything. When we weren't negotiating for our pigment with the goldsmiths he was off, coming back late to the lodgings, telling me of great torches seen on the steps of the Grand Canal palaces, bowls of flaring orange flame casting reflections on the water, making multi-hued ribbons waver there, and glimmering on rainbow silks and satins as people stepped from the gondolas.

'The jewels they're wearing, Uncle,' he said, 'all colours, round their necks, decking their hair, dangling from their ears.'

Astounded by the wealth, Francesco also observed the number of sick and poor Venice hosts. How could he not, when you all but stub your toe on beggars everywhere you turn? He told me of the cripple who crawled on oozing stumps through foul mud to get a coin thrown down by a noble in a green velvet cloak.

'A *gold* coin, Uncle. The Magnifico wore a great sword, with a hilt gleaming silver.' I asked how the noble's lady comported herself and Francesco giggled as he answered, 'The lady? Her dress was scarlet and cut *so* low, and the pearls bouncing on her chest were the size of hen's eggs.'

===◦===

I'm wasting too much time here. My tip-off about this ship was sound, I trust. Because if you can't find what you want in Venice, the world's marketplace, then where else is there? And of course, here every type of chicanery and shady deal is to be found. The commerce can be brutalising. If either buyer or seller is too tender-skinned, they'll not survive. Even if you are not dealing, the city will toughen you.

Take Francesco, how he changed during those few short days of his first visit here. The day before yesterday, it was like being woken by a sudden peal of bells, seeing the change that has taken him over in what can't be more than a few weeks. Before we rode away from Bassano I saw the sharp exchange he had with his father and caught the hard look on his face, something I'd never observed before.

That meeting back in March with the writer at Titian's studio, I would say that is when the problem started. Which is mighty contrary because the *Maestro* receiving us was what Jacopo intended as the highlight of Francesco's first time in Venice.

Waiting there at the studio, that was when he fell into conversation with the man, who had been up and down chatting with all and sundry, unable, it seemed, to sit quietly on the steps or lean his back against the wall like the rest of us.

'*Giorgio Vasari, author*,' I overheard. Medium height, fair of skin and dark of beard, that is all I took in, busy planning my tasks, our annual purchase of colours and me under strict instructions to buy large quantities for the new style of painting Jacopo was intending to start on. I did notice Francesco and this man engrossed, then both laughing, the man throwing back his head, slapping Francesco on the shoulder.

We were bidden to our audience soon after, during which I was granted a few courteous words. To Francesco, Titian made some sort of jibe which I didn't quite catch. It was probably nothing, although the lad seemed discomfited. Titian turned again to the easel, his back to us, and I hovered there a moment, just for the privilege of witnessing the *Maestro* work. I would gladly have stayed longer and so I think, would Francesco, because he was very intent, standing there – but I pulled him away, embarrassed to linger.

'Something to tell your grandchildren, my lad.'

The boy was looking dazed, not quite with me. I nudged him, spoke louder, 'Everyone agrees Venice has never been prouder of one of its painters. And the acclaim he gets! Loves Venice though, Titian does. He's stayed here, you know, rather than live at the Spanish court, even though he's been invited there time and again by the King.'

Still no answer from Francesco. Then catching my arm, he said he wanted to ride back to the city with the man I had seen him meet.

'I want to talk more with the Signor. I'm learning useful things. Vasari's a writer, a painter too. And he knows Father,' he said, these words slung back over his shoulder as he waved a hand and scuttled off across the lawn, the Vasari man already halfway to the jetty.

I had framing business to discuss with Titian's people so I stayed on there alone. Thinking back on those moments I remember I wasn't at all sure about Francesco chasing off like that. Should I have stopped him? Well, had their conversation that apparently lasted the best part of the afternoon never taken place, a lot would have been different. That's a fact.

At the outset of this journey of ours down country, the strife between Francesco and his father hung like a cloud, thick and black around the lad's head, the way gnats swarm when there's something putrid. I was glad that on the evening of the second day he sought me out by the tavern fireside. To confide in me. Frankly, when I learned from him what is brewing, my feeling of foreboding those months back seemed well justified. I heard Francesco out on this madcap business: seeking the patron for Jacopo's hunting dogs' portrait, pursuing his writer friend to pass on whatever he learns, hoping that will mean his father gets mentioned in this new artists' directory soon to be published.

'You've already had a disagreement with your Father,' I said. 'You must know the risk you take, going further against his wishes.' Can it be worth it? was my private thought, rebelling and upsetting Jacopo for the sake of this 'anecdote' thing, all simply to please the likes of that Vasari fellow. Besides, how can anyone think it matters a jot, something that happened so long ago?

Francesco made that little grimace with the side of his mouth, the way he's been doing since a child. 'Oh, Uncle G....' and a sigh.

Oh, nephew, you stubborn young mule you, balking against your harness. Obstinacy, deplorable but a family trait. 'I'm answerable to your father, you know.'

'Yes, Uncle.' Another sigh, a hopeful, questioning look thrown my way.

Riding on the next day, it bothered me, not knowing what to do for the best. I am designated Francesco's chaperone – but is it right to hold him back from what he's set on? After all, the boy is practically grown. While I debated with myself I was also thinking, odds are this quest of the lad's will be a fruitless thing anyway.

So, should I follow my sister's lead? Elisabetta has shown *herself* ready to risk going against her husband. Admittedly, she has always indulged Francesco beyond good sense. Now she has really set a hare running by ignoring Jacopo's express instructions. I've seen that slip of paper of hers which revealed the identity of the patron and I sense trouble is likely to come of it, my brother-in-law quite possibly regretting he let my sister learn her letters.

Late yesterday, arrived at the hostelry, I gave in. I told Francesco he was in charge of his own destiny and I would not interfere. That decision taken, I immediately felt better. 'Let's eat now,' I said. However, during the meal I couldn't get out of my mind how, from whatever few hints I've heard dropped over the years about this dogs' portrait, it has always seemed a thing bringing good fortune to no one. Rather the opposite, in fact. But so it goes – and it is almost certainly not worth the breath it would take for me to express that view to Francesco.

CHAPTER TWO

At Taverna Veneziana

You eat well in Venice, dishes with ingredients we never see up in Bassano: sea urchins, whelks, mussels. Best if you're partial to fish though, since tonight we shall doubtless sup again on sea creatures. First to reach the tavern, I drum my fingers awhile before I am asked, 'Your young friend late for the meal? Found himself prettier company, has he?' A wink, a knowing nod.

Francesco falling prey to a seductress? Well, I might have worried, attractive innocent that he is. Never seen a woman naked, I wouldn't wonder. In a torment, he was, I warrant, on the way to Titian's studio, all because he'd heard word of the *Maestro's* nude models. Flushed quite pink while impelled to ask me, 'Is it true Titian has women strip naked and then puts them to lie around all day, displaying *everything*?' I, just a little warm in my loins at the thought too, pretended it was no great matter, answering that the *Maestro* uses the poses for paintings he calls 'mythical poesies'. When Francesco came back at me with, 'Uncle, *that's* poetry I could get *really* interested in reading,' well, I just had to snort my laughter. And he joined in. (When we got there Titian was at work on one of his Virgins. So, no impropriety, not a nipple in sight, not even a bared shoulder.)

Yes, my nephew is grown to manhood now, seventeen, tall and straight, likely soon out-topping his father. He has those curls that crown all the Bassano men. (Although none before with his shade of nut brown. That colour, like the case of an acorn in autumn and just about as shiny, that is all his own.) And the dark eyes, dark lashes, dark brows and the sunniness of his smile are all straight from his mother, sweet sister Elisabetta.

But as to Francesco and vice: no women yet. I have seen him dealing cards and tossing a dice across the square, he thinking himself hidden from view. It'll be as well Jacopo learns nothing of that. Although Francesco has no money to have taken off him, anyway. No, the lad is obsessed with one thing only, to find this Zantani, and get some 'story' or other out of him for Signor Vasari. To my ears that assuredly sounds bizarre.

'Uncle G, good evening,' I hear.

'Francesco, you're here – and ah, good, here is our food. Yes, tonight your first oyster.'

He is nonplussed watching the girl shuck the shell off to reveal the thing, limp and pearlised. His eyes bulge. 'Raw, Uncle?'

I tease, 'That is all there is for supper, I'm told – so I shall see your share of that platterful slipping down your gullet nicely, won't I? One after the other.'

I tell him my success: I've got the root. I spare him the details of the tedium of my wait, hold back on how I exerted my powers of persuasion. About his day, he doesn't tell me. I get the sense something has flustered him but don't probe. Rather, he seems eager I should talk. Often requesting me to recall family history, tonight his question is, 'Uncle, did you not ever want to be the creative one?'

'*Creative*', I think, a fancy kind of word. The girl has brought creamed salt cod, Lenten fare Venice-style. Having to eat fast so Francesco doesn't get more than his share, I take bread, swipe it into the dish and chew while I think. Old Francesco, grandfather to this whipper-snapper here, would never have used '*creative*' about himself. Son of a painter, Old Francesco's work was to *be* a painter. That was his job: he painted stage scenery, shields, banners, you name it, tavern signs his speciality. Bigger things too, like altarpieces – not forgetting his frescos, some in the most prominent places of our town.

Of his children, Jacopo was the one showing aptitude for painting. When that revealed itself as real talent, Old Francesco must have seen a way ahead for his family. Following it, educating and promoting Jacopo, they would be lifted out of poverty. It became a relentless refrain, the old man's bark, '*Study, practise, practise, practise.*'

Repeated, repeated, repeated. That regime in place, I don't remember Jacopo ever again being free to play in the way we used to. No more messing about with a bat and ball with me and the rest of us boys. And of course, eventually a day came when he was told, 'Jacopo, you're to leave Bassano. In Venice you'll be apprenticed to Bonifazio of Verona.'

Gobbling down the good cod, I find Francesco's question easy to answer, 'One with a furious urge to prove himself with paintbrush and palette is enough. Yes, quite enough, if I understand "*creative*" to mean known patterns must be disrupted in order that something new is thrust into the world.'

I was fortunate, brought into the family business soon after Jacopo came home from Venice and married my sister. Fortunate too, to *like* the established patterns, the repetitive work: the accounts, the contracts, my visits to Venice to procure materials and make timely deliveries of commissions to Jacopo's customers. (And that I can have pride too in the skill of my hands: my frames, crafted to show the works off in the best way possible.)

I remind Francesco, 'Don't think there's no challenge to it, by the way. Because how do you reckon a painter's work could ever be produced if there weren't a book keeper behind it, tracking the progress, chasing the pay?'

'We are not in Titian's league though, are we?' Francesco says suddenly.

'Well no, lad,' I counter. 'But our studio does alright, its reputation always bettering in the years since "Bassano" was assigned as your family name.'

Substituting one name for another, sometimes I still don't believe it could happen just like that, pretty well overnight. Jacopo told me how it was: the Council calling a meeting one day, summoning him, announcing what an honour it was to be granted the same name as the town.

'But do you want this?' I remember asking.

Jacopo's answer was a question of his own, 'Who are we to disagree?'

For what it's worth, I still feel a tinge of regret about it, my personal view remaining that for our family, whose house, studio and workshop are positioned right next to the town's pride, its wooden bridge, 'da Ponte' served us well. A perfectly practical name, and moreover, a memorable one.

Visitors coming to our country town nowadays certainly have knowledge of the Bassano legacy, some wanting to study the frescos painted thirty years ago by Old Francesco, as for example his St Christopher, depicted in profile just below the town clock. I've noticed they then often cross the piazza, go through the arch, almost certainly seeking out the Del Corno house, its façade adorned by Jacopo's three-storey fresco.

Then they stand on the cobblestones, agape, immediately transfixed by the central motif, that huge, curvaceous female. Her splendid nakedness, voluptuous breasts, shapely thighs, those are curves worth goggling at. Only after that can they take their eyes to that monkey, those asses, the pig and the lion, the lute and other musical instruments, those sheep, all the intricacies Jacopo wove into his convoluted, lyrical-fantastical border. What kind of an imagination can he have, the man who dreams up that sort of thing? I've thought more than once how different my brother-in-law's must be from the everyday ones the rest of us have.

Francesco pauses to take a gulp from his beaker when I ask how he thinks a fourth Bassano generation will make its mark? I push him, 'You yourself, Francesco, as the first son, how do you rate the talent you've inherited?' He doesn't answer. Do I catch a stricken look on his face? I wonder why. Perhaps he is just embarrassed.

The lad does well at sketching and copying, I've heard from Jacopo, and has ideas of his own he offers up. 'Promising', that is all Jacopo will say, never over-generous with praise. He does drive his children. With mine, I tend to be more lenient – not enough to spoil them, mind.

'Use your eyes, your *eyes*, and look, *look*,' I've heard him say so many times when correcting Francesco and the younger boys. Quite harshly, sometimes. I suppose he feels entitled to be so, since that was the way he was treated. You also have to remember he never spares himself. 'Nothing satisfies me.' Those were his exact words. He even showed me them, written in his own hand on a drawing, next to where he had signed his name.

Anyhow, I'd say you can't fault Francesco on his observational skills, and in Venice during our first visit I enjoyed him sharing some of his discoveries with me.

'Accompany me to San Marco, I'll show you the camels I've found in one of the grand arches over the Basilica's doors,' he said once. Sculpted, he said, along with entwined birds and a man carrying a sheep and bunches of grapes, a sheaf of corn and a strange goggle-eyed sea creature, and oh, some other exotic beasts he couldn't quite distinguish.

We go and he is right. They are high up, his camels, but you can make out the details of their great drooping eyelids, their long curled eyelashes.

'Don't they have a sneery expression as they look down on us?'

'Full of disdain, I agree, even though they are the ones carrying *our* burdens.'

'Uncle, who carved them?'

I don't know, any more than when we enter San Marco, I can enlighten Francesco about the great sweeps of golden mosaic still going up inside the Basilica. I've heard tell mosaicists have worked on them for hundreds of years yet the interior is still not completed. We push into the nave against the exiting throng. Mass over, a procession makes its way down the aisle. Francesco clasps me by the shoulder and bracing ourselves together, we stand on tiptoe.

Over the crowd we glimpse a knot of priests walking together: one, head bowed, carrying a great Bible, another, a soaring gold cross.

'There's the Doge.' Pale in his white and silver robe, moving in his own space, as though oblivious to the way people press around him. Francesco is craning his head up at the gold-glimmering, jewel-toned mosaics in the dome: our great Redeemer, his panoply of saints, his apostles parading around below. Next, fascinated by the panels of marble, the great sheets cladding the columns and side walls, he counts off the colours, 'Violet, blue, grey, beige-brown, rose and brick-red, striated green, dappled black and white.' He whispers close to my ear, 'Look, aren't they patterned just like the beach at Chioggia? You remember, before we crossed the lagoon, the way the tide pushed the sand into those ridges, made them glitter and seem to move?'

Two priests approach us, young acolytes with slender pale hands, pale faces, dreaming eyes. We are ushered towards the door and then we're out on to the Piazzetta, startled at first by the light. Francesco's head darts this way and that, those eyes of his so bright. To our right, the pink-washed building of the Loggetta, pretty with its arching windows and details picked out in gold tracery. Straight ahead the Molo and the grey expanse of the *bacino*, its surface whipped to a froth by the chill wind. That same wind swirls round us, whirling up the petals of some white blossom, making them dance giddily about, whisking them across our faces. Blinded, staggering, we can only laugh.

CHAPTER THREE

7 June, Otello Cannareggio

My bed is strewn with packets for Jacopo along with a stone jar of candied quince to please Elisabetta's sweet tooth. The man-root I'm enfolding in a soft cloth, dampened. 'Keep this moist at all costs,' were my instructions. I finger the wispy tendril protruding from the end of one its limbs, clogged still with red-brown mud from who knows what far-flung place.

'Want to see?' I ask Francesco, hearing him come in. This morning he went off again, no word where headed. No answer now, either. Today we have everything to finish up here, then tomorrow an early start, the two days' ride home ahead. For me, early to bed tonight, offering up a prayer that I'll sleep, sweltering and thundery as the nights are.

'All this to be fitted in the saddlebags somehow: it'll be a squeeze,' I say. 'And you, will you be ready before it is light tomorrow? Your things are scattered everywhere.'

Still he doesn't answer and turning, a glance tells me all is not well. I sit down. 'What…?' my words lost as Santa Fosca's bell tolls the hour. These restless nights its sonorous tones have counted out the small hours for me, *clang clang clang* from the belfry directly across the courtyard. Shutters thrown open now, we feel the bell's reverberations carried on the hot breeze right into the room. I wipe my dripping brow, wait until it's quiet again.

Francesco, slumped on the mattress, hauls himself up. He's half-choked and I catch no words, just a groan. 'Spit it out, lad.' I want to be kind but can't spend the whole of this busy day on his troubles. And troubled he is. No brightness about the eyes today. Instead, it's the twists and turns of a sorry story that I hear, coming out in spurts: a rush of words, a pause, the whole thing patently distressing. And I, anxious to get on, am somewhat tried in my patience, to be quite frank.

I learn he succeeded in his quest, tracked the fellow Zantani down, went to his palazzo in San Toma where, shown in, he was surprised to be ushered upstairs. The Magnifico taken to his bed, in a bad way by the sound of it, sickly a very long while, and now very reduced.

I had imagined Zantani differently. Never met the fellow of course, but assumed he would be fit because, after all, those years back he travelled from Venice to Bassano to commission that painting from Jacopo. Not many Venetian patricians would be up for a journey all that way north just for the sake of a painting. But of course, that was years ago, seventeen, Francesco reminds me. Time has passed since then – and time wrecks us all.

Eventually, Francesco gets to the crux of what happened. Invited by Zantani to explain what he'd come for, he managed to win the Magnifico over and was shown the painting. Turns out it was a prized possession, was there in the room with them all the time – extraordinary! Francesco's voice warms, telling me it is *wonderful*. Now he's on his feet, pacing our dormitory, waving his arms about, trying to indicate the scale of the canvas and how the dogs are depicted.

'*Eloquent*, Uncle,' he says. 'That's the word, isn't it, when something speaks to you? It really speaks, that painting. I'm looking in at the dogs, the dogs are looking out – their eyes looking, *seeing* me, you know – and they are saying to me they have a story to tell.' He's slumped back on the bed and there is that groan again. 'I really want to know that story.'

And then? Then it seems Zantani offered to reveal the background, the whys and hows of the portrait getting painted, all the things Francesco wants to know, the ones his father refused to divulge.

'Zantani announced he'd had the story written down in a scroll of manuscript, stored away in a chest. It's there in the room.' Francesco seems breathless as he says this. What a satisfactory outcome then, I'm thinking – but he is choking again, trying to get out his next words. 'I had it in my hands, Uncle. The manuscript was in my hands. But...'

And then he tells me he was escorted out before he had even opened the scroll's cover, was told he had tired the poor sick man and must leave straight away. Zantani's niece was kind, smiled prettily, Francesco says, but the Magnifico's wife, Signora Helena who had blustered in to interrupt their talk, had a sharp tone to her voice and seemed to be annoyed by the very sight of him.

Perhaps the lad is overwrought. Must be. Because the Signora couldn't really have taken against him just like that, could she?

'So that's where you've been this morning? You went back? And you've read it and now all's alright?'

'No, no, it's terrible.' The heels of his hands are to his eyes, his words coming out muffled, 'I went back Uncle, but I wasn't let in. Three times I knocked. No one came. The blinds were all drawn on the lower windows and upstairs they'd closed the shutters. Then I saw the piece of black stuff they had draped above the street door.' Taking his hands away, he looks at me, eyes wide and reddened.

'*Eeeeoww*....' A desperate noise comes from him, and his face has the expression of a child whose favourite plaything has just been snatched from his grasp. It should be comical – but it's not.

Oh dear.

The hostelry courtyard is hushed except for the cooing doves, pecking for seed in the cracks between the flagstones. *Coo, coo, coo, coo,* soft but insistent. A little breeze gusts into the room and I get a whiff of orange blossom. On this quiet hot Friday, Death walks among us in Venice. You'll hear no footfall as he strides across this *campo* and down that *calle*. Now and then though, he will stop and stoop through one door or another, swing the scythe from his shoulder, reap a life. We sit there, the lad and I, silent on our beds a few moments and then, sombre-faced, we cross ourselves.

So that's it then: Francesco's run up a blind alley, banged his nose. Too bad he is frustrated – but what's to be done? This brings to an end his crazed search. A relief. We can finish up and get off to Bassano in good time. Puzzling how to distract him on this day that's left to us, I decide to take him with me to the Palazzo Erizzo. Best just get on with the work in hand, that's the only remedy I can think of.

And as it happens, Francesco has said more than once that the houses fronting the Grand Canal make him wonder what it would be like to live there, to own the steps down from your private gate to where the water laps. Once he mimed how he'd leap from his gondola to prance up those steps, pretending to teeter on fine high-heeled boots, cloak billowing behind him. How convenient then it is that this morning I'm bidden to one of the Grand Canal's very grandest establishments, a frame there needing some touch-up work, a last task to be fitted in before we leave.

═══◎═══

'Give me a hand with this, lad.' Clambering into the gondola, I pass Francesco my bag, bulky with varnishes and brushes. I never know quite what I'll find on a job. Venice's damp, salty air is no help to the delicate finishes clients like on their frames.

The Palazzo's *portego* has many tall columns down each side. A set of high glazed doors at the far end lead into a garden where there are two pine trees, a patch of very bright blue sky above them. There is a hubbub around the steps at the water gate but we elbow our way through and on reaching the painting, we're alone.

The Last Supper, handsome, dominating the space, declares its patron's piety to the visitors who come and go here. One of Jacopo's large, wide works: greens, soft pinks and gingers its main colours. The components? They are as you'd expect: the apostles break bread with the Lord Jesus, some seated, some standing around the table. As usual, young John is almost asleep, aslouch and heavy-lidded. One of the Saviour's pale hands touches the boy's curls, the other emerging from a dark sleeve's cuff to draw the eye delicately to the lamb they have feasted on. Composed with a sombre background, the light falls from the right and illuminates the apostles' very different expressions. I'm struck again by how tellingly my brother-in-law portrays bewilderment, concern, caution, guilt, denial.

Two footmen appear in jackets of Erizzo livery of royal blue, epaulettes heavily fringed in silver, come to lift the painting off its hooks. They bow but do not greet us. Suddenly I'm inclined to show off my knowledge to these supercilious fellows and say, 'See Francesco, how the steep slant of the table allows its contents to be clearly seen: the bread, wine, the platter with the sheep's head, an orange?'

The lad is ready with an answer the match of mine in pretentiousness. 'Yes, Uncle, you are correct – and does that not also emphasise the apostles' gesticulations?' He must want the footmen, who are tutting and sighing in a tedious manner, to hear of the family connection because he adds rather louder than he need, 'You see Uncle, how my father has used the stance of their bodies as well as their hands to indicate the turmoil in their minds after what the Saviour has just announced.'

The painting placed against the wall, Francesco and I start removing the dust and grime from the frame. Each taking one end, we attack the task with gauze cloths. Only when that's done can I assess the state of the gold leaf. As I whisk I am estimating how many years' worth of dirt we're up against. My, my – all at once it strikes me this *Last Supper* of Jacopo's was completed in the same year as his portrait of the hunting dogs.

'1548,' I say it out loud before I think to stop myself. Francesco looks up, curious, and so I am obliged to explain. 'This painting was in Jacopo's studio when I came back home from Mantua,' I say. 'I believe the money Magnifico Erizzo sent in payment may have been the very first entry I made into Jacopo's books after I started doing your father's accounts.'

'And there's a dog in this painting too,' says Francesco.

'He does like to feature them, doesn't he? That gingerish spaniel, in particular, I mean the sweet little floppy-eared one there. You know that as a bride my sister came to your father with two little dogs? One under each arm, she stood at the door and solemnly told him they were part of her marriage portion. I remember Elisabetta named them Spot and Silky. I'd see her by the fire, stroking their backs and pulling at their ears. Jacopo filled many sketchbook pages with their likenesses.'

I bend to pick a clean gauze. 'Animals, dogs especially, I'd say they're your father's softest spot. Did you ever ask him why he painted so many?' We have made the air around thick with dust and Francesco is preoccupied with sneezing. I say, 'He explained it to me once, saying something like, "You put a dog into a composition, you affirm life. It's like lighting a lamp in a darkening room: hold the flame to the wick and in the next instant you're imbued with warmth and good feeling."'

Working down the painting's left side, Francesco is silent for a while until he stops to wheeze and hack again, bringing out his kerchief to mask that ugly cough of his. Dabbing at his eyes, he says, 'Uncle, the dog in this painting here, you called it "sweet". But those two hunting dogs of Zantani's – they are very different. You should see them: powerful presences, nothing sweet about *them*.'

I choose to say nothing, hoping he won't dwell further on his recent disappointment. We break for a few minutes and we push through the doors into the garden. The sky's earlier bright blue has been replaced with a strange brassy hue, the light thick, almost brown. It has become even hotter. Francesco plumps down on the grass and begins picking at the daisies, plucking them out by the stalk, only to pull off their heads, discard them. Lying down, he throws his arm over his eyes. I close mine too.

'Uncle,' I hear him say, 'You know those dog sketches I found in the attic? Some of them were in pen and ink and signed by Paolo Caliari. And Father told me the clay models were made by Paolo. This Paolo, was he long with Father?'

Relieved that at least this veers away from the main subject that's been upsetting the lad, I reply that Paolo must have spent quite a few months in Bassano with Jacopo, probably the whole summer of the year 1548. He had come from Verona to study with your father, I say, but they became firm friends, by all accounts. He was 'Caliari' then but I explain that not long after, his town claimed him, like Bassano did for our family. So Paolo became known as 'Veronese', and since then has made himself a greatly famous name.

'Veronese, he's *that* Paolo?' asks Francesco. He sits up. 'Here in Venice Veronese is doing work on the Doge's Palace's ceilings and other commissions for high dignitaries, is he not?'

'Yes and no, lad. He's forged a good career, yes. No, because I hear he is not in Venice. Recently left for Verona, to be married back there in his home town.'

Flat out again, Francesco has his eyes closed and after a few moments I hear the faintest snore. This heat is punishing. I decide to let him rest while I get on. Soon enough he wakes, comes into the *portego* and takes up his gauze again. But I say, 'Knock-off time for you for now, Francesco. Go and enjoy the city. Make the most of your last day. Have you watched any of those new Commedia del'Arte plays? You'll catch one in San Marco, for sure.'

While I'm mixing up my varnish I imagine the lad joining a crowd around a booth in the Piazza. These *buffino* shows the troupe from Padua has brought here are all the rage nowadays. Mocking humour, wicked comedy – not sure it's my sort of thing – but the young want to try everything, so why shouldn't Francesco get a taste of their ribaldry?

I finish the application and I'm through. Downing my tools, my brushes cleaned, I pack up and leave, more than enough accomplished to have earned myself a decent dinner. I've a taste for sardines. I'll take a dish of them, in that red sauce that's sweet and bitter at the same time. Washed down with a few jars of the fresh green wine they drink here, that should do me. Defying this heat, I'll get myself a good night's sleep one way or the other.

FOUR

Maddalena

8 June, near Campo San Toma

It must look very odd the way this cloak is bunched up around the bundle I'm carrying. I would never have imagined it so awkward to conceal a scroll about my person. Uncle Antonio once told me poachers wear jerkins with secret pockets large enough to hide a rabbit. I could badly do with a jerkin like that.

Now, however, is *not* the time to care about what I look like – and that's a relief. For such ages I've been thinking I must get free from my aunt's instructions on my appearance.

'*Sit still and look pretty*', that's Aunt Helena's constant refrain. 'You'll never make a good match Maddalena, if you won't respect the niceties of behaviour for a young woman of your background.' She'd like to din it into me every hour of the day that marriage, marriage is my destiny. Oh, Aunt Helena, what a surprise you'll get when you learn what I have in mind for my future. Destiny? Little do you know, dear Aunt, how I've been conspiring with Uncle Antonio to escape from the future you've planned for me.

Thanks to him and his foresight, that escape is all set in place. I'll soon be on my way as now dear Uncle, you've at last been freed from your earthly pain. You were so clever with your idea, agreeing you'd leave me only the smallest legacy, insufficient to attract an appropriate suitor. Lacking a generous dowry, I stand no chance of a match. Not in Venice, where in marriage matters, as in everything else, money alone is what speaks. So, that's it – soon, when my penury is known, for me there will be no other future than a convent.

'Infinitely preferable for you to a marriage about which you're not consulted, wed perhaps to someone who doesn't suit you, don't you think, my dear?' Uncle said when we hit upon the plan. 'Convent life can be convivial for a woman who likes books and good conversation.' I know. I've asked around and heard encouraging things about certain institutions: San Zaccaria, Santa Catarina. I'm not daunted by the prospect, no, in fact, the thought of having congenial company in a tranquil place where I can continue my studies makes me feel positively enthusiastic.

So, with Uncle now about to take up his eternal rest, my life at Ca' Zantani will soon be over. I shall miss it – but without you, dear Uncle, you who gave me another way of looking at things, it could never be the same. God rest your soul, and may the saints shower you with blessings for how you have striven to protect my interests.

And by the way Uncle, you must believe me, it's not for lack of respect for your passing that I've ventured out here on my own. Although I am wondering whether this was a wise choice for a meeting place. Perhaps I've been foolish. I've not even seen the night watchman. Snoring in a doorway, I suppose. But how should I know what to do for the best, me, who's never been out alone in Venice, *ever*? It feels strange to be unchaperoned, unobserved, meeting at midnight. But I'm not afraid, no, because Francesco *will* come. He must have got my message at his lodging. But where is he? That bell striking the hour, what time is it telling me? By now it *must* be after midnight.

Whoever does come must have the lightest of feet because I hear no footsteps nor get any sense someone approaches. Next I know there's the shock of a bump from behind. What is this – an assault? I'm trying to brace my feet but feel them slipping. The hood of my cloak is being pushed roughly forward over my face so I'm in the dark. And now I'm gagged as it's pulled back over my mouth – awful, the feel and the taste of the fusty wool. My arms pinioned at my sides, I'm strongly held, I can't free myself however I twist and jerk.

I want to shout '*Help me, help me, I'm being attacked*', but the hood is tight across my face and anyway, my voice has dried in my throat. Kneed from behind, I'm knocked off balance. I stagger. I'm falling. My attacker has lost his balance too. Together we topple, and like a sack of wet straw, we thud to the ground.

Hitting the paving stones, I hear a yell from my attacker. May he be good and hurt. My own fall has been cushioned somewhat by his body but kicking out and trying to thrust him away, I roll on to my side and am jarred on my hip. My knuckles scrape on the gritty surface. I lie gasping for breath, feeling how cold and wet the ground beneath me is. All of a sudden, I'm let go so I can claw at the cloak to pull it away from my mouth and open it to scream. Nothing but a squawk comes out, though. I try to sit up. My skirt, rucked up above my knees, shows my stockinged legs all awry, staring whitely out against the black path.

My attacker, where is he? I hear him behind me and when I feel a hand on the flat of my back I *can* suddenly make a sound. It comes out as a snarling protest which my fear rapidly turns to an ugly shriek. I flinch and cringe away at the prospect of another blow. I am braced, holding my breath. But nothing happens.

'Signorina, Signorina, forgive me. I am so sorry.'

The voice is coming from in front of me now. I push at the hair that has fallen into my eyes and see someone's half-kneeling there. His hand is out as though offering me help. What is this, though? I know this voice. It's Francesco's, isn't it? *No*, it cannot be that it's *Francesco* who ran at me, grabbed me, knocked me down, rolled me in the dirt. No, not he, who I've invited to meet me so I can help him.

But now that he has pulled me up and we are both standing, I can see it *is* him. I'm so confused. This is very embarrassing. What can have happened that he behaves this way? I busy myself, trying to brush down my skirt, to feel in my pocket for a handkerchief to bind my bleeding knuckles, and to put back up the strands of hair fallen from my headpiece. Francesco is hopping from foot to foot, thinking he's helping, I suppose, brushing at my cloak to get the grit off. He chases after the scroll which fell to the ground during the scuffle and has rolled away into a puddle.

'It was this, *this*,' he is crying out as he straightens up, wiping it against his breeches.

What's he saying?

'This, sticking out from under your cloak. Dangerously. I saw the bulge and thought you were concealing a *weapon*. I thought you must be someone meaning me harm. That message I got, the one that wasn't signed – it was from *you*?' He gives a great sighing groan, 'It must sound stupid but I thought it was sent by a Venetian villain laying a trap to rob me. I decided to show the brigand I'm not a weakling who can be waylaid like that.'

I've got my breath back. A ridiculous mistake. I decide the least embarrassing thing is to ignore how ignominiously we were entangled just two minutes ago. I shall simply stick to the point of our being here. My words are abrupt, 'I called you here because I want you to have Uncle's manuscript before my aunt burns it. Uncle died sometime last night. He will be buried tomorrow. Oh, no – I mean today, since the midnight bell has sounded.'

'My sincere condolences, Signorina. I am so sorry about this.'

'Thank you.' He sounds so kind, my tears, so many of them cried this day, start to brim again. There is an ache in my throat as I wipe at my face with my bound hand. I tell him, 'Uncle Antonio was not well, as you saw, Francesco. He had been very frail for a long time. But his death was very sudden. We – well, certainly I – was not prepared for it. And I am bereft.' Now it is bitterness which I feel rising in my throat and hear in my voice as I tell him more of the day's sorrows, 'My aunt, however, seems not to mourn, indeed, has found new energy and has sprung into action.'

He is looking gravely at me. I blow my nose and decide I want to confide further in him. 'Francesco, today has been terrible, this day that should have been one of prayer and reflection. Aunt Helena has been running around the house in a fury, ridding it of Uncle's things, throwing them on to a fire in the courtyard where they're burning in a great smoking heap. And this before the grave has even been dug at San Michele, let alone before we've been there to bid Uncle farewell. *Why* is she doing this? When I asked, she said the things have bad associations.'

'Bad associations, whatever is she talking about?'

'She would not explain. But I realised it was vital I got to the chest to find the manuscript before she did. So I slipped into Uncle's room.'

The half-light in the chamber, the incense hanging heavy in the air as I tiptoed past the shape shrouded there on the bed, the shape that was once my dear Uncle:

I can't speak of these things to Francesco. He waits while I wipe again at my eyes. 'I grabbed a cloth from the chest and wrapped the scroll in it. I have smuggled it from the house. I am a *thief*. But I don't care. I'm here, you've come, and we have it. At least this is safe from her.'

Francesco, clutching at the wrapping which is starting to come undone, stops at that and turns to me, 'And, the painting – what will happen to the painting?'

'*Will* happen? It's already happened.'

'She hasn't burned it? No, *don't* say that.'

'No, not burned. But given away.'

'*Given away?*'

'To the priest who came to deliver the last rites. Father Matteo, Uncle Antonio's confessor. He has been attending us at Ca' Zantani for years.'

'What can a *priest* want with a painting of dogs?'

'I know it seems all wrong. But according to Aunt Helena, the Father admires the work a great deal. In fact, I'm remembering now that I heard him speaking of it to her once, while they walked together in the garden.'

'So, the Father's a dog lover?'

'It's not that. He said he sees the two dogs as virtuous, representing piety and fidelity, chastity and submission, that the painting can be used to teach such moral virtues. His plan is to hang it in the dining hall at the seminary.'

'Moral virtues, to be learned from a *painting*?'

'He means things like the gaunt state the dogs are in, I think. I recall the Father saying the hounds are like that because they are self-denying. Just as Christ was for mankind. He finds other symbolic meanings in the painting too. I just can't remember any more right now.'

'You, Signorina, do you believe that's what the painting is about?'

'*Not* Signorina. Francesco, I beg you, please call me Maddalena, won't you? The painting's meaning? You've seen the work. And yesterday, you saw the way my uncle looks ... oh, I mean, *looked* ... at it. He felt passionately about those two dogs. That was obvious, wasn't it?'

Francesco's expression tells me he agrees with me, so I add, 'That painting is a portrait of real, live dogs. No symbol nonsense. I'm sure you heard the way Uncle said their names.'

'Yes, I did. Bruno and Cara: their names. Even my father remembers those two dogs' names. But your Uncle's manuscript must explain all this.'

'Yes – but it's so dark here, how are we ever to decipher it? Ah, I know, come – we'll go up here.' I take Francesco's arm. I have remembered the lamp around the corner in the *campo*, the one at the Virgin's shrine on the side of the church. I tell him, 'My aunt gives the priest oil to keep it alight all night. She has been doing that ever since my Uncle became so ill.'

We do not see a single soul. That bell sounds again, a single *clang*: the half hour or one o'clock in the morning? I've lost track of time. Francesco is dealing with the scroll, unwrapping the cloth, letting it drop. To pull the scroll from its canvas covering he has to push in his fingers and tug at the parchment. He fiddles a bit, until with a final jerk it comes away. Lurching back, the scroll in his hands, he lets the cover fall to the ground. He has the manuscript by its edges. But what is this? Something is wrong. Tiny scraps of paper, all different sizes, are detaching themselves from it and scattering all around us. Some fragments are falling straight to the paving, others float away, whirling and swirling in the air above our heads. It's like the white wood ash that blows up in a bonfire's smoke when the last log breaks into embers.

'Oh *no*,' we say, our words chiming together. Francesco says another word under his breath. A curse. Who could blame him for that? Not I. He uses both hands to unroll the thing and we see there's a large hole going right through the manuscript's four or five sheets. Unevenly shaped, the hole is neither a circle nor an oval. It has serrated edges, just as though it's been nibbled. A tangled mass of grey fluff and some things looking like strips of cotton slide down the sheets to fall through this hole and join the mess at our feet. And what's this, falling after: *droppings*?

In other circumstances I'd giggle. Mice. It *has* been nibbled, no doubt about it.

A mouse mother chose the scroll's safe, domed interior to bring her family into the world. She came in from the winter's cold and through the dark weeks she chewed away at Uncle's words to create her neatly spherical nest. Then, undisturbed in her confinement, she doubtless produced a fine brood and they snuggled cosily together in there as she weaned them.

I do not share these thoughts with Francesco, who has sunk to his knees and is pushing the remnants of the sheets as flat as he can, setting them side-by-side on the paving. The light is very weak down there but enough to show all the stains and smears on the very small surface of parchment remaining around the gaping hole. But despite the mess and the area's limited size, after some moments have passed it seems he has identified something. Leaning right over, head supported on one elbow, he is pointing at words in the undamaged top and bottom corners.

'Look at this,' he cries, 'a name your uncle mentions many times. "Paolo". Here and here and here, the man is mentioned. Sometimes he writes this Paolo with the family name "Caliari", other times as "Veronese".'

'Oh, so Francesco, do you think Uncle's Paolo is *the* Paolo Veronese, who has painted so much here in Venice?'

'Yes, must be. That Paolo was with my father for a while. He came to study, they spent a summer together. And Maddalena, I'm just realising that the year Paolo was in Bassano was that *same year*, the year when the painting was done. I got that from my uncle just this afternoon. After that Veronese, so young, came to Venice and quickly got fame.' Then he adds, 'The sort of fame I want.'

He says it so fiercely I have to ask him, 'Fame, Francesco – is that what's most important to you?'

Not looking at me, still poring over the sheets, he is quite gruff, 'It's the avenue to other things, isn't it? To being free, for one. If I had fame and riches, I wouldn't have to answer to anyone. I wouldn't have to suffer being insulted by anyone either.'

Oh, ambitious then, and some sort of grievance – no wonder he's so tense. 'Ah. But for now, what's to be done now about the story you seek?'

He looks up. 'Now? Now I need to hear what Veronese can tell me. Your uncle's story we shall never know, thanks to the mice. But don't you see? The manuscript still has its message. Your uncle's manuscript is directing me to Veronese. We know he spent time with my father while the painting was being made – so he *must* know the story.'

He bends again to the pages, 'Oh, look!' I try to see what his finger jabs at. '*Here*, here's Veronese's name again and next to it, the name "Tomaso". Here again too. Tomaso. The last thing Mother said to me before I left was to find Tomaso. Find Tomaso if I want to find the truth.'

I'm thinking that it will be easy to track Veronese down at one of the several places in Venice which he is adorning with his luminously-hued frescos and paintings. For years he's worked on the coffered ceilings in the San Sebastiano church, noble figures and architectural details presented from a dramatically steep perspective. I hear he did something very pretty for the doors of the organ loft too. And I'm sure Aunt Helena told me at present he's making a painting for the silk weavers' chapel at Santa Maria dei Crociferi.

Francesco is saying, 'Verona, I have to go there. How do I get to Verona?'

'To *Verona*? He's not here?'

'No, Paolo's gone to Verona. Marrying his sweetheart. He'll have to be tracked down there.'

'Can you do that, go there?

'I *want* to – but I can't. We leave for Bassano tomorrow. No, I mean today. We're to take the horses soon after dawn.'

Suddenly he's looking at me fixedly, as though I have answers. 'But I could, couldn't I? Maddalena, think of this: I could take the one road rather than the other. Why not? If I explain to Uncle Gianluca, he may not be happy – but he has no choice but to ride on for home because my father urgently needs him back with the herbs for the baby.'

I'm thinking fast. 'Better if you have a head start, surely? Get across the water on your own before dawn and get going, hire a horse and join up with others riding that way. If you're there at Chioggia ready to leave at first light there'd be no chance of your uncle stopping you.'

'Just slip away? Poor Uncle G, he'll be vexed. And he'll certainly not like having to face my father with the news that I just took off.'

He's wavering, I can see it. I say, 'Francesco, if you're going, you must go now. It's like this: once day dawns Uncle's boatman will be preparing the barque for the funeral. But if you're up for going now, I can wake him. Alberto will *not* like me ordering him to cross you to the mainland. Especially with the day he has ahead of him tomorrow. But I suspect if enough coins cross his palm, he'll agree to do it.'

'You have money for that? Oh, my Lord, I have none,' Francesco says. He makes that gesture the Commedia del'Arte clowns do, pulling his pocket right out of his breeches to show there's nothing there.

I say, 'I have money secreted away, thanks to Uncle's generosity. I have enough for that and to pay for your change of horses along the road to Verona. It's a three day ride, I believe.'

He clasps my hand. 'I must get my things from the Osteria. My uncle's bound to be sleeping. He snores like an old sow most of the night. I'll creep in and leave a note, do my best to explain where I'm going. And why.'

'Go and do that. Then meet me in one hour on the steps just down there on *rio* San Toma.' I point at a place almost opposite Ca' Zantani's water gate. 'See? Just there, where you came and called on us two days ago.'

Two days only? It feels as though I've known all my life about Francesco, about Giorgio Vasari's challenge to him, and about this crazy quest for the story of the dogs in Uncle's painting.

At the steps he is in silhouette against a lantern's faint glimmer, saddlebags over one shoulder, a cloak over the other. I've seated myself in the gondola – because yes, I am going out on the water with him. Something else which, just a few hours before, I'd never have dreamed of doing – but why stop this night of amazements now?

Francesco says nothing about me being there, steps in, stows his things. We sit together, our backs to Alberto, whose grunts and puffs are to let us know how put upon he is. There's not a single other craft on the Grand Canal as we make our way towards the San Marco basin. Any heat remaining from the sultry day is long gone, the sky above us clear, a dusky grey-blue light still lingering. Or perhaps dawn's beginning? It being near to midsummer's eve, the nights are almost at their shortest. Recently I've sometimes found it difficult to fall asleep at all. But no, it's not day yet – a pale moon, round and very full is sitting low down out where the lagoon and the sea meet. We turn our backs on it and head steadily towards the long dark line which is *terra firma*. Are there any lights on the mainland? From here, I see none.

We reach the open water before we speak. The piers which mark the navigable channel loom up eerily, snagged around the base with trailing seaweed, towering over us as Alberto steers past them, one after another. The breeze freshens out here, strongly salty in my nostrils. The gondola rocks a little. I'm acutely aware of everything, so awake it's as though I'll never need to sleep again. I find this half-light night beautiful, euphoric even, a counterpoint to the pain of Uncle's death which I'm clutching inside me, the sorrow that's like a dagger thrust in my ribs.

It seems completely natural for me to reach for a fold of Uncle's great cloak and lift it over Francesco's shoulders. It falls heavily around him and he pulls at the hood, bringing it round the backs of our necks. Like a tent, it shields us from Alberto's hearing, makes it seem natural too that our heads should be so close together. Just for a moment I let myself wonder how it would be if my head were to slip down, come to rest on Francesco's shoulder. I don't know why, but I trust him. I like the smell of him – should I admit to such a thing? My aunt, for one, would *not* think it proper. But if I *were* to rest there I could breathe quietly, let my sore eyes close just for a moment.

I could gather my strength for the sights of the sorrow-filled day that's about to dawn: the grimness of the raw earth around that yawning trench, the long faces of the incessantly intoning black-clad priests, the sounds of psalm-singing and consolatory words that are bound to make me weep once again. And then after all that, there will be the bleak mourning period, the wearing of drab clothes and our jet jewellery. I'll be fending off Aunt Helena as long as possible – she'll want me out of the palazzo as soon as the provisions of Uncle's will are made known. The thought of her fiercely cold anger makes me want to shrink away. But before I take up my new life I would like to have at least a little time to grieve for dear Uncle in the place where I spent so many happy hours with him.

Uncle and his painting: it's because of it that all this is happening. I tell Francesco, 'The portrait your father made: I believe it captured Uncle's feelings for Cara and Bruno. He cared, of course, about dogs in general. He told me once what an old friend had told *him*. Ibrahim was the man's name, a learned Jew from the Ghetto. Uncle was interested in all the scriptures, not just our Christian ones. "There are many parallels to be drawn between what is preached in the different religions," he would say. He and Ibrahim would exchange texts to compare, then meet to converse. They…'.

I am interrupted with, 'Does this have anything to do with the painting?'

I dig my elbow in his ribs and command him, '*Listen*, Francesco and you will learn. Now, my Uncle Antonio was often called a "good eye". Did you know that?'

'No.'

'It's a way of describing a connoisseur of fine things. Uncle learned from Ibrahim however, that in the Torah there is another meaning for "*good eye*". To the Jews, having a good eye means someone is generous. With their money, with their things.'

'Like the parable of the Good Samaritan?' At least I've got him listening to me and he has a point. It is a little like that.

'Yes, yes, similar: the Samaritan who saw the wretched traveller's plight, stopped to help him.'

'I've painted that scene.'

'Yes? I would like to see something you've painted, Francesco. One day perhaps

I will. Anyway, Ibrahim explained to Uncle about the alms the good-eyed, generous person would give the needy: they would amount to one-fortieth part of whatever he owns. These alms, given freely, ensure the person is blessed as righteous. On the other hand, someone mean and uncharitable would give only a sixtieth part of his wealth.'

I have to pause for breath. Is he following me? His eyes meet mine. Good, he's with me.

'I'm talking long,' I apologise, 'but hear this out, Francesco, because it's important. Uncle told me how he had reacted, saying to Ibrahim, "Are we humans not poor creatures? A fortieth part, that's generous, that's *selfless*? The animals do far, far better than us, my friend. Take man's relationship with dogs. What do we provide? Food and shelter. And they, how do they repay us? Why, they give us their everything. Way above a niggardly fortieth. *Everything* dogs have to give, they give us – loyalty and devotion thrown in on top. Am I not right?"'

A silence follows, broken by Francesco coughing. It is quite a bout and even in the dark I can see how his eyes water. He has to heave in a breath before he can say, 'Holding nothing back, that's dogs for you, eh? The Jew might well have not cared for dogs but I'm sure he'll have taken your uncle's point and gnawed on it. Like one would on a good juicy bone.'

Francesco thinks it is clever to mock – and at a time like this? As reproof I say, 'My Uncle was moved when he told me this.' I choke on the words a little, suddenly moved myself remembering the day he confided the story, even then he so frail and white, his hands so thin and too cold. My eyes sting and my nose is pricking and my only handkerchief is the blood-stained one screwed up and pushed into the cloak pocket. I start to fumble for it.

'No, no, use this,' says Francesco, pressing a folded linen square into my hand. I feel his hand warm on mine and the linen smooth, with a faint scent of lavender.

'Maddalena, he was moved because those dogs did something for him. He had them painted in recognition of whatever that was. Somehow, that's connected with his illness too. I'm sure that's how it is.'

Well, yes, it sounds plausible to me.

'Any idea what it could have been?' he asks, adding more quietly, almost as though speaking to himself, 'Because whatever they did, whatever caused him to have the painting made, that will be my story for Giorgio, won't it?'

'No. Aunt Helena's face always went dark and closed if I pressed her about how Uncle became ill. After whatever it was happened, it seems he just faded and faded over the years, never getting better enough to take up his old life.'

Tears are close again. Francesco must know because he pats my hand. I tell him, 'He was a dear and I got very close to him, you know? He was teaching me to appreciate fine things: his medal collection, the new music, unusual polyphonies he had composed by Adriaan Willaert for performance in San Marco. Even as he got more and more frail, he still arranged for musicians to come to Ca' Zantani. Growing up, I was introduced to so many marvels. But about how he got those injuries, no, he would never speak to me about that.' I have to sniff and wipe my nose. 'Anyway,' I add, 'whatever it was, it was long ago, in the year before I was born.'

'How old are you?' Francesco asks abruptly.

'Seventeen.'

'Me too. Born in 1549, the year my father painted the portrait. Well no, actually, he did that the year before: 1548.'

'I didn't know that. It's strange, you know, I mean how the provenance of the portrait, which was without doubt Uncle Antonio's absolute favourite of all his possessions, was something else he would never talk about.'

'Did you ever ask him straight out? With me, he seemed ready to talk about it.'

'He would just clam up. As for Aunt Helena, a frown bit into her forehead every time she set eyes on it.'

'Well, thanks to you, we have the manuscript and so we have the truth. And, Fortune smiling on me on this journey I'm to make, I'll soon have something for Vasari – even perhaps something he won't be expecting.'

Ah, the journey he is to make: will the coins I placed in the purse be enough? They must cover his keep for how many days? And for the horses, and the fee for joining up with a group so he'll be safe riding those rough roads. I reach into the cloak pocket to pull out the purse, one of Uncle's embroidered ones, green with red cross-stitched roses and silky tasselled ties. Every gift he gave was beautifully presented. It clinks as I drop it into Francesco's palm.

'Take these as well,' I say and in a moment my earrings are off. 'Just in case.' I take back the purse, pull it open, slip the pair inside. They were a name day gift from Uncle, delicate and dangly. I hear the tiny *clink clink* they make as they fall on to the coins.

'Then you must take this,' Francesco says. I don't know what I expect from him. He startles me by pulling at the middle finger of his left hand then pressing into my palm what he has taken off it. It feels good, the warm touch of his fingers on mine again. I hold up what he's given me to the moonglow. A ring in a scarab shape.

'This must have been costly,' I tell him, but Francesco is offhand, replying he won it at cards, from some wretch on a losing streak. Not a good sport, the man, complaining each time his hand was bettered.

'It's from Egypt. Gambling it away, along with the rest of the wares from his travels in distant lands, the fellow took a moment to tell me it came from the bazaar in Cairo.'

An exotic Egyptian beetle, crawled out of the hot sand to cross the ocean and find me here. The stone is dark with a distinct gleam, is it black? No blue, I think. I feel how polished it is as I try it on the middle finger of my right hand, the hand that is not scraped.

'Too big. I shall put it on a ribbon.'

He doesn't ask me to wear it around my neck. Nor do I offer to do so. I change the subject and tell him the thing that has been agitating me since I fully grasped what this quest of his is.

'Francesco, you know that *by rights* the story of the painting and of the dogs that you seek, by *rights*, the story also belongs to me?'

'Yes, I know.'

'Well then, I must ask you, will you come back and tell it to me?'

He does not hesitate, 'I will. I mean to repay you.'

'With the fortieth part?' There is silence. He realises I'm teasing him, doesn't he? Perhaps not. He has to clear his throat and his voice, when it comes out, is rather deep.

'Not with the fortieth part, Maddalena. Nor with the thirtieth. Nor with the twentieth, no. It will be with my whole heart.'

I haven't a reply to that. Did he hear my little gasp? I am nonplussed. I should find graceful words to match his. What should I say? Before that though, there's one more thing I *must* tell him. But oh, I'm jolted. With a sudden grating lurch, the gondola reaches the shore.

Francesco, pushing the cloak aside, is getting up. He stands, arms out to balance himself. Then he's gone, launched over the side to land with a thud and splash on shingle in shallow water, with just time enough to lean back in and grab his cloak and bag before Alberto, oar out manoeuvring the gondola in an arc, pushes off, ready to speed us back. I have to twist round to call out, 'Francesco!' Already across the strand, he is clambering on to the footpath.

Does he pause? No. I strain to make my voice louder and it rings out in the stillness, 'Francesco, know this. If Giorgio Vasari won't write the story, *I* will write it.' All I hear is the swish and hiss of the tide, the *crunch crunch* of his steps growing fainter, that cough one more time, and from far off, fainter still, the hoot of an owl. Louder again I call, 'Francesco, I will write the story of the dogs.' We are moving away fast and he has all but faded into the grey-blue but then, just discernible, even as he walks on I see he has one arm raised above his head. The palm is flat, the fingers splayed. Francesco salutes me.

FIVE
Veronese

CHAPTER ONE

11 June, Verona, Casa Badile

'Our young visitor has been asking how I met his father, Jacopo. And that's just one of the things he wants to know,' I call out to Elena. I'm slumped on our marriage bed. I have eased off my boots one at a time and lain back, pulled a pillow under my head and rolled on my side so my face benefits from the stripe of evening sun falling gold across the bedcover. My bride is bathing in the alcove to the sound of falling water.

'Can't hear, husband. Wait to tell me more.' There is splashing and then her laugh, husky.

Eyes closed, behind my lids all is rosy. *Bride, husband.* New vocabulary, to match my new ways. *Wife,* I've got myself a wife and the responsibilities that come with that. Not that I find them onerous as yet, the two of us simply enjoying being *newly-weds.* But there won't be many more days like this. I know it already. Days when I can quit early, long before the light has left the studio, hang up my spattered overshirt, scrub the paint from my hands and face and come here to linger with Elena, spend evenings watching the daylight gradually dimming over Verona's rooftops, the gibbous moon that wanes by a thumbnail paring each time.

No, such ease won't be mine much longer, not with the orders piling up in Venice, the clients fretting for their commissions. Not to mention the two altarpieces in the Badile studio here, which must be finished before we leave. So, for the short while that is left, let me have these hours cocooning with my wife in this chamber, feeling like a fat bee come home safe to its hive.

Marriage, well, I left it as late as I reasonably could – but let contentment come to me, nevertheless. Contentment and a couple of sons, not too much to ask, surely?

My hair is greying. If I don't tip Lady Fortune's cornucopia into my lap *now*, soon it could be too late. Contentment, happiness and beauty: the things they say I capture best in my paintings. Oh, and abundance, of course. Let me taste all of them now, no, let me *live* them.

'*They* say?' the same *they* who also deign to say I succeed better at painting prettiness, light dancing off jewels, shadows in the fold of a lustrous fabric, than I do at conveying deep emotion. I say ignore such critics. Who heeds them, anyway? Besides, I have no desire to paint what I see when I look into a man's soul. And long ago I resolved to ignore all but good praise, to be warmed by words from those I respect, like dear Bassano.

Besides, should I have a moment of self-doubt, I need only finger the gold chain Titian himself awarded me, the one I wear all the time now, accustomed to its weight on my neck and the warmth of its links against my throat. It is fifteen years since the *Maestro* honoured me with it, I, only twenty-three, selected over all the others tasked with painting the ceiling panels of the Doge's Palace and his Library. Freezing fog had hit Venice the day of the ceremony, Titian robing himself against the cold like a king, a great brown bear of a fur cape round his shoulders. I knelt and he lifted the chain over my head and I alone, my head so close to his chest, could see that inside his doublet he wears one of similar design. Had from the hands of Emperor Charles V of Spain, learned later.

That chain, I've drawn it in pen and ink many times, capturing its satisfyingly rounded links and the grey-brown shadows that nestle in its curves. My bride has found a use for it in these last few days too. While we've wrestled and tumbled on the bed Elena has taken to reaching for it, catching it around her wrist and tugging on it to bring my head, my lips to hers.

'Elena, my darling.' She throws herself down beside me, exuding the smell of fine soap, some summer memory of jasmine, rose and lavender. She shakes her hair loose from the linen towel and stretches out on her back. My lovely wife, not a girl, a ripe woman, yes, plucked at just the right time from the tree, a luscious perfect apricot. I put my finger to her cheek, trace her lips, stroke her skin.

She shifts a little, her head heavy on my chest. I can see her eyes are closing, heavy-lidded. I push the damp towel away and my hand slips into her robe to the familiar place where it cups her breast. She murmurs, her lids flutter. Enough of day-to-day affairs, I must attend to the priorities of this moment. Elena murmurs again as I turn my full length to embrace her. I nuzzle my face into her neck, pull her hips closer against mine. I clasp her right hand with my left, stretching our joined arms above us on the pillow. Our lips touch; she tastes of cherries.

Her robe, silky against my fingers, slides open across her thighs. Her thighs feel like silk too, silk and cream as I push them apart and she opens herself to me. I shift my weight over her, my hands grasping her shoulders, my face in her still-damp hair. How easily our bodies fall together, fit together, move together. Bathed in a lilac twilight, I am warm. I'm away, my heartbeat quickening, conscious only of our rhythm and how the arc of my world is blurred, transformed into a glow of deepest amber.

Afterwards she sighs and murmurs, 'Paolino'.

It gives me a start to hear her use that name in her love talk. Only very few get away with calling me that, a name that thrusts me right back to my youth. Childhood and youth: Elena and I were together then too, of course, she a mere suckling babe when I, at fourteen, starting out in work, was apprenticed to her father. The day I knocked at old Badile's door stone dust cloaked me, grey-griming my skin and hair. From *my* father's work. Father was a sculptor but also a mason, a skilled one, but not above spending his days bending his back at a building site. Many of the blocks making Verona into the fine city we have today will have passed through his hands. He tried but eventually gave up hope of training me to handle stone. Realising I'd some aptitude for drawing, he made me apprentice to Badile the painter.

Elena's eyes are open. She shifts to rest her head again on my chest. 'You were saying about our visitor – he goes by the name of Francesco, doesn't he? Tell me more.'

It is as well he found me yesterday morning at the studio when he did, I say. 'He can't have eaten or drunk on the ride from Chioggia. All three days of it. I had to wonder what the state of his nag was when he gave it over to the stable: in a poor way if as wild-eyed and staggering as he.'

'Ridden from Venice to see you, no word sent ahead – what *can* be his hurry?'

'He was all-out, I couldn't press him. In fact, he'd barely the strength to introduce himself to me as Jacopo Bassano's son. He is well-schooled in politeness, you'll see, but he wasn't up to explaining his purpose. He fell into the bed I showed him to. In the intervening hours I'm told he's been fit for nothing but to sleep, wake, drink great draughts of water and down bowlfuls of your stew. And then sleep again. Now he has rested I can see the Bassano family likeness, the height and that head of curls. He's young, not twenty yet, I'd say, and he's rallied of course. This afternoon he appeared in the studio and got started on his questions. His visit here, you see, is all to do with one particular painting by Jacopo.'

'Really?'

'A portrait Jacopo made of two hunting dogs.'

'Goodness, of *dogs*, an unusual one, then, surely?'

I explain Francesco wants to know more of the work, one his father was making when I was there in Bassano, that summer I spent there. 'That was well, nearly twenty years ago, wasn't it? Just before I went first to Venice.'

'*That* summer. You downed your tools one evening, said nothing to Father and went off no one quite knew where. I was too young to see it at the time but the soreness of it, your abrupt departure, that stayed with Father, according to my mother.'

'Ah well, I needed space and fresh influences. At nineteen years old, a hasty youth, not such an unusual thing.' After all, I'm thinking, everyone needs somewhere to go to do their growing up – even if they travel only inside their head.

'Anyway,' Elena says, 'later, when the news from Venice came, word of your successes, I mean, I heard Father admitting he'd not been surprised you had gone because really, there was nothing more he could teach you.'

'How old were you Elena, when I left?'

'Only a toddler, five or so.' She giggles. 'Fond enough of you already though, darling, in my childish way.'

Well then, here is a chance for my new wife to learn what happened while I was out of her sight. 'I went first to Bassano, spent some months there with Jacopo, dear man.' I explain that arriving, I met him in his garden, the showcase he had created for his animal models. Clever things, crafted from painted card and placed all around, very life-like, superbly finished, put there expressly to fool the unsuspecting. Fooling *me*, anyway.

They were Jacopo's idea of a joke: like the hawk on a low branch that startled me with its sharp beak and blazing eyes and the huge rat I feared I had stepped on with my sandalled foot. I still get the shivers, remembering the shock. Recovering and realising the pretext, the artist in me had to admire the techniques: the stippling of the hawk's feathers, the silky gleam of the rat's fur: how'd he achieved them? And their gleaming, golden eyes: so realistic. Now I come to reflect on it, seeing these things was my first experience of Bassano's special affinity with animals.

'I never hear you speak of Jacopo Bassano but with fondness. I think you admire him a lot, and not just for his work.'

'Yes I do, Elena, he was generous to me with his ideas and, as for his principles, I came to admire them. But what prompted me to seek him out was his fame for portraying animals with such aptitude.'

'You went to learn from him?'

'The young think they can master everything – so yes, why not? And Elena, I tell you, the very day I arrived I was struck by a fresco of Jacopo's telling the story of Marcus Curtius. The Roman gladiator is magnificent as he spurs his white horse on to plunge into the gaping void which has opened beneath their feet. The fresco is high over the arch of one of Bassano's gates, the Porta Dieda, and looking up, I saw how I could tell the story from a different perspective, from down there below, as though I were in the hole.'

'And did you paint it?' Elena asks me, rolling on to her stomach, reaching her hand towards my chain. I bat it away but she smacks at my wrist, reaches again. She has spirit, my wife, I am beginning to discover.

'If you promise to release me I'll answer you … thank you, that's better. Yes, soon after, I did, painting the edges of the abyss rimmed by the disbelieving faces of onlookers gaping down. And listen, my dear, I came up with a neat touch: to make the canvas round, like the hole that opened in the earth. You see how much I learned from Bassano, right from my very first day with him? The first thing he asked me was "Did you see the unicorn, Paolo? Not everyone does." A trick question, which I didn't answer because everyone knows that a unicorn, once beyond the forest edge, is invisible. Jacopo appeared not to notice my silence and added "Fanciful displays like these models please my mind – and besides that, making them tries my dexterity."'

'But you too make models.'

'Well, yes. In fact, one of the questions Francesco asked me just now was about my modelling during my time in Bassano. Jacopo had stored in his attic some I made of the subjects of the portrait, the two dogs Francesco is wanting to learn about. He is so enthusiastic about them it made me blush. I told him, "Modelling of figures and animals was my first adventure with materials."'

Elena stirs and half turns to me. 'Why, yes, your mother says that too. She is proud of all you brothers but she's always said you were the one to show your talents the earliest.'

'Ah, she was always fond, dear woman.'

'And a fond story about you I heard her tell often was when you were barely able to crawl and she came across you sitting in some muddy sand outside the house. Smeared with the mud, you were, and had also grabbed up some of it up to pinch at with your fingers and thumbs.'

And just as though it's clay, Elena reaches up to my nose and pinches it between two soft fingers. 'I can just see it,' she teases, 'chickens pecking, a strutting cockerel bigger than you, I expect, and you busy playing with the dirt to copy their likenesses. Very realistic ones, apparently, your mother astonished then and marvelling still to this day about the talent you showed as an infant.'

I remember no more of that conversation because I am blessed with dreamless sleep for a sweet short while before Elena wakes me at the hour for supper. Thank the heavens, Elena doesn't favour the light sweetmeats we newly-weds are supposed to nibble on, morsels eaten with fingers daintily primped. A fine supper of roast pork is on the table. I was salivating while I dressed as the smell of frying onions wafted from the kitchen. Elena has had whole apples baked with the joint too, cinnamon-dusted, a sweetness that bursts in my mouth. Supper, served the same time each evening on a table with a clean cloth. For a disorganised bachelor this is something new in life.

Pit pat, pit pat on the flagstones tells me Bianca comes to my side. She licks at the fingers of the hand I put down to pat her fine white head. Sitting tall, she lays her muzzle on my knee. Since my first Bella, that greyhound bitch of Bassano's, the one which took to me in the months I stayed with him, I have always had a noble-looking, long-legged dog in the house. I've lost count of the times I've put them in my paintings.

'There are the new season's yellow plums, and will a slice of *Asiago d'allevo* cheese suit my husband?' Elena asks, leaving the table after I've wiped the last drop of gravy from my plate. I raise my glass, saluting myself before I drain it. Well, why not? It was timely, my decision to wed and our union neatly achieved. And why should it not be a happy one: a happy union?

Either I'm become mawkish with the wine or that's a phrase, isn't it, that would be fine as a painting's title? I play with the thought that yes, I might use my golden chain allegorically, in a wedding scene. Cupid can be there, holding it in a chubby hand as the thing that will bind the lovers in an eternal bond. A dog, symbol of fidelity, must be there too, of course.

Got right, yes, this marriage business has much to recommend it, I'd say. A full belly and a pliant warm body in the bed every night, a recipe for self-satisfaction for a man in mid-life, if ever there was one. Yes, this woman of mine will bring me rest. 'A rest for your roving eye' my drinking companions would say. What's more though, is that she will manage the books of the business.

Returned with the platter, Elena must mistake my contented sigh for one of fatigue because she says, 'I fear this Francesco's questions tire you, worrying at you when you want no distractions from your work.'

Plum juice dribbling down my chin, I reach for a napkin. An idea is forming in my mind 'Dearest, you could relieve me of him for a few hours tomorrow perhaps. You understand I owe Francesco the courtesy of helping him with his mission, in due return for his father's kindness to me those years ago. But yes, I have the two altarpieces to finish. (I've had to insist the lads come into work, Sunday though it is.) But Francesco, he should see our famed ruins while here in Verona, don't you think?' I ask. Elena nods. 'The Roman arena and the Borsari gate? Walk under the plane trees on the Adige's riverbank and put his head for a few minutes at least into San Zenobio to make the acquaintance of our town's smiling patron saint. A saint with a smile almost as broad as Francesco's, by the way.'

Elena smiles her own pretty smile at that.

I ask her, 'That fine newly-married matron, the Signora Elena, could accompany him, along with her maid, could she not, help our young visitor to know something of Verona?'

'It's Sunday, so *yes*, we could walk out with the young man after Mass.' She seems to like the idea and says, 'And as for our lunch, why don't I have food packed and carried to the Giusti Gardens? In this heat, might it please you to take refreshment *al fresco*? Would you join us there in the almond orchard on the hilltop when you're ready? There will be a breeze up there, as well as the view that Francesco may like to see.'

Uh-oh, I reach again for the napkin, hoping to sufficiently stifle the belch that is the proof of how well I have dined. Elena turns her face discreetly to the side. We both know it is too soon for this tender marriage music we are making to be interrupted by the burping that my bachelorhood has accustomed me too. (And oh, dear Lord, save her in the future, will you, from my snores – not to mention the *basso profundo* of my farts?)

CHAPTER TWO

12 June, the Badile studio, Verona

Sometimes in the studio I walk as far as I can away from whatever it is I am working on, taking myself to the room's furthest extremity, turning abruptly to look back. I do it to trick myself into thinking I see the painting for the first time. Today, my brush put aside, I go to the back wall, spin on my heel and allow the impact of *The Martyrdom of St George* to hit me. Today, for once, I think, 'Yes, that's it, that's right.'

'*Garzoni*,' I call the apprentices around me but do not squander my praise, 'Tonio, Agostino and the rest of you, this is satisfactory work of yours on the backgrounds.' I point here and there where a colour contrast can be strengthened, a texture improved. 'The mane of the horse on the left, stipple it to have more depth. Tomorrow you'll attend to these details please.' Then I let them go and decide to call it a morning myself.

═◇═

I've a good appetite after climbing to the Giusti hill's summit. I hear laughter even as I enter the orchard. Elena has arranged for the lunch cloth to be been laid in the shade and they are all seated around it, the meal already under way.

'You'll be parched,' Elena says, standing to hand me a beaker. The maid steps up, splashes in some cool pink wine. As pink as the almond blossoms are in March when this orchard would stop you in your tracks, a blizzard of whirling petals. As pink as the grid of rooftops, belfries and domes spread out down there below us. Verona from here looks like a map crafted from precious metals, the glinting river snaking its S through the city, grand palazzi on its banks, the glittering straight-as-a-die Roman roads, and out over the plain, sun-shimmer blurring where city and countryside merge.

'Have you admired this vista, Francesco? Come, let us drink a toast to our fine city, why don't we?' I call. They cheer and clink their beakers in appreciation.

'Sit, join us and eat,' says Elena, indicating the platter she holds. She won't sit until I am served.

'Bresaola,' says Francesco, reaching his arm out over the cloth, taking a slice of dark red moist meat, dangling it limp above his lips.

'Pork meat too,' says Elena, looking pleased with herself. Looking pretty too, with her Sunday lace collar unbuttoned over her lemon dress. 'Cotechino salami, your favourite – with mostarda fruit pickles in piquant syrup.'

'Cheeeese,' calls out Francesco, this time his knife spearing a yellow wedge.

'And cake: *pandoro*, with apricots on the side,' adds the maid, cheekily, licking crumbs from her finger.

═∞═

Later Elena supervises the re-packing of the baskets while I, sprawled on the rug, head on a cushion, contemplate basking awhile in the warm sunshine. Am I growing to like this leisure too much? Well, it's Sunday, why not spare myself for an hour or so more from the studio's demands? There is our guest to entertain too. Our unexpected guest, well recovered from his fatigue, who continues to spill his boyish charm on us. Francesco, his smile as persistent as his questions.

As yet I don't fully understand why he needs to hear something from me that surely, his father could tell him? At odds with Jacopo over something, is he – is that it? What can the urgency be to trace this piece of family history? There must be some real urgency because Francesco, you can't relax, can you? I could doze off if it weren't for your restlessness. You fidget, twist and turn as though ants bite at your bottom. Soon you will come out with another question.

Sure enough, you cough that trying cough of yours before saying abruptly, 'How did it come about, the commission to Father for the portrait of the dogs?'

Ah, the commission, that is what you're after now. I remember that day in Bassano well, as it happens. So I shall tell you. Despite my drowsiness, I can't justify refusing you that, since after all it is something I can do while lying here with my eyes closed. 'In effect, Francesco, it was a day in the studio like any other: your father nearing the end of work on a large canvas, me with several different projects on the go. Signor Zantani had been around in the town for a day or two, the lad Tomaso with him. He had already met with your father to confirm what his letter said about commissioning a painting. A Magnifico come personally all the way from Venice to do such a thing, not at all a usual occurrence. Of course, you're aware of that.'

'Yes, indeed.'

'Well, we found out this Zantani was not averse to wanting things done differently from others. That morning, right from the moment he entered, I sensed he had an announcement to make and thought, yes, it's that delicate time. Our fish, swum upstream from the Venice lagoon, is finally surfacing in our Bassano pond. Sleek and fat, in prime condition to take the hook. Reel him in, gently, gently now. He will be beached before he knows it.

'Zantani positioned himself plumb in front of the easel with your father's *Last Supper* on it, the one commissioned for Palazzo Erizzo. Pointing at the huge canvas, he called out very deliberately, "*Maestro* Bassano, this dog here, the spaniel, is similar to the one I wish to be in my portrait." He referred to the dog curled close to the Saviour's feet, small, floppy ears, white coat splotched with brown.'

'Yes, yes, that dog,' Francesco breaks in.

The boy can be brusque: I've noted that. I ignore him. 'Your father duly replied, "Yes indeed, Magnifico, of course. Any hound you favour can be incorporated in the composition."

'In response, I remember Zantani snatching the cap off his head and twirling it, taking two steps toward the window, two steps back and then standing stock-still to blurt out, "I intend the dogs to be the composition." At this, we must have been quite silent because there was time for that fine velvet cap, plumed with viridian green feathers if I recall rightly, to get another twirl or two. Then he said, "The dogs in question – there are two dogs, yes, a couple of hunters – they are not to be just a part of the work. In fact, just the opposite. Because *Maestro*, it is my wish you portray the dogs as the portrait's sole subjects.'"

"The painting is to be only dogs?" Your father's voice was gruff.

"Precisely. Just as you put it, *Maestro*. '*Only dogs*'. The two dogs I shall bring you are to be painted exactly as they are."

'There was still no answer from Jacopo. In the pause I watched Zantani's expectant face, then saw the tic of annoyance that twitched his mouth before (feeling, I suppose, he had no other option) he pressed your father, "And so, *Maestro*, you'll take note now of the details of the commission?"'

'And did he take them, Father, just like that? Nothing said? Did he not have a view on the odd thing the patron was asking for?' I can hear Francesco's puzzlement. 'I can't believe that.'

'What your father proposed was a walk.'

Then the boy's laughter peals out, the first time I hear it, and he says, 'You're not serious – a fat commission on offer and my father suggests the patron takes a walk?'

I laugh too at how ridiculous it sounds. I tell him, 'Why yes, Francesco. What he said went something like this, "*Magnifico*, I propose this. With your permission, I'll finish up here. The morning light, you understand …?" I admired how he could remain apparently quite unperturbed by the extraordinary proposition Zantani had just made him. Your father waved a hand to the north, through the open veranda doors to where the sun was climbing Monte Grappa's eastern side, and then across at the painting. "You see I'm touching up highlights on the pewter flagon. And there is one section here …." his hand went down to the painting's left, indicating a seated man's green robe, "… I'm grappling to get my colouration exact. If you'll allow me, I suggest an excursion later, in the early evening. Perhaps I may show you one or two places outside the town which I believe may charm you?"'

I hear the swish of skirts, get a faint trace of jasmine in my nostrils. I pause and open my eyes to see Elena joining us. I sit up to say, 'Ah darling, come and hear the rest of what I am telling Francesco about my days in Bassano. I'm describing a walk I took one day.'

Elena, next to me on the rug now, pulls a cushion behind her to support her back as she rests her head on my shoulder. Stroking back a strand of hair come loose from its net, I say, 'Elena, one of these days I must take you there. We shall go when the white asparagus is in season and partake of a dish together. Bassano produces the Veneto's finest, especially delicious with a tarragon sauce.

'I walked a lot around Bassano. That year the early spring had been unusually warm and dry so most mornings I was out with my sketchbook. While we walked with Zantani that day I remember describing how earlier, down near the bridge, I'd found three little girls playing a game of stones. I drew them and also a big rough-haired dog that ran up to join the children. How fondly those little girls greeted and hugged their companion. (*That* sketch I've made good use of. Oh, it must be ten years ago now I put the girls in the foreground of my *Supper at Emmaus*. Only two girls in fact, one with her arms around the dog's neck, her little fingers smoothing its fur, the other one wiping at its shoulder with a cloth.)'

Francesco coughs before yawning noisily, not the most subtle of hints. I must be fair to the lad. In this situation, obliged to honour his never-ending curiosity, I had better stop teasing his impatience. I put on a bright voice to say, 'But ah yes, let me get back to our walk. Tomaso joined us so we were four crossing to Angarano on the Brenta's far shore. Bella came along too, loping beside us, her head held high. That dog had barely left my side since the day I arrived. Your father led us down the track to San Donato's chapel where the holy St Francis sojourned. We stepped in for a brief inspection of the old frescos. Then we walked on sandy tracks through the vineyards to where three tall pines marked a grandly gated entrance, behind it a modest yellow stone farmhouse and an assortment of dilapidated barns.

"The lord of the manor has taken himself a bride recently," Jacopo told us, "and word is out that Andrea Palladio is the architect hired to make the place new-fangled and imposing."

'I remember Zantani saying, "Palladio, eh? His reputation is growing, I see – I shall be following his progress."

'After that I don't think we spoke much more because, of course, each of us had Zantani's revelation to chew on. How odd it was, I thought, to be walking the lanes, casually slashing at the hedgerows with a hazel switch, with that burningly unspoken question, "*Why?*" hanging in the air around us. Was it out of surprise, respect, or caution that Jacopo had not asked Zantani straight out: "Why paint the hounds this way?" To me, the Magnifico's idea seemed all topsy-turvy, why would you want dogs forging the central focus of a painting when conventionally, they are never more than secondary elements? As for excluding any human representation, what possible sense did that make?

'Eventually I realised your father had swung us round in a circle to bring us back to the Brenta. And to a riverside tavern, where I for one was happy to rest my legs, wet my lips with that pale green local wine your Bassenese produce. Evening was closing in. And so you see Francesco, it was under the light of swaying lanterns that the commission's details finally came to be discussed. I recall the scene quite precisely: the sky violet, a pale moon, almost full, sailing up it, a cooling breeze from the north reminding us summer had not yet arrived.

'Zantani took his time before he raised his objective again and I believe the second bottle was more than half gone before he cleared his throat and spoke, "This portrait you're to do for me, Maestro. This is what I want … ." He had our full attention then, you can be sure, as he described how he wished the two dogs to be positioned within the frame. Close up. A blue sky, he said, but otherwise no detail specified about the background. He was emphatic though, that the dogs' collars, made to his own design, were to be shown to best advantage. He gesticulated, eloquent with his hands as he spoke about them, collars of silver with a fine filigree finish and gems of red and blue, studding them.'

'Collars?' Francesco asks. 'In the painting the dogs have no collars.'

'No. All in due course you'll learn the reason for that, Francesco,' I say. 'You told me that in Venice you got to see the Magnifico's palazzo, so you've an idea of how fine his taste was – and of the wealth he had to lavish on it. His connoisseurship was famed...'

'Oh yes,' he breaks in, 'at Ca' Zantani even the corridors were hung with tapestries and there were objects displayed in niches, vessels of coloured glass.' He is animated now. 'In fact, when they gave me water to drink I feared I'd crush the beaker. It was so delicate, gilded on the base and made from completely transparent blown glass, imagine that – but with whorls and spirals of white and blue streaking it. I was made dizzy just lifting it to my mouth.'

'And paintings?' I prompt him.

'I expect you can believe I was only interested in the one,' he says and smiles at me. Once again, I'm awarded that beautiful, winning smile of his, charming words to match it following, 'I trust you'll forgive me pressing you, Paolo, but there is still more I want to learn about how *The Two Hunting Dogs* came into being.'

So, I talk on about that time, remembering how strangely tense an occasion it was, the four of us drinking and still no explanation being demanded of the patron about his fanciful notion for the portrait. And none forthcoming. Discussion continued, I tell Francesco. 'Your father, on my left, sat very upright and maintained his inscrutable expression. The country wine appeared to be easing Zantani though and he waved a hand airily as he announced, "*Maestro* Bassano, there'll be no gold leaf in this portrait – but my fee is to cover the cost of ultramarine pigment. I want my sky to be of the finest blue, so there is to be no skimping on quality." Asked about the dogs' pose, he said he would leave it to your father's discretion. "You've worked with enough animals to know how best to depict them." About the dimensions of the work he was also vague, "Well, just make it a good size."

'Your father asked what palette he should employ, besides the use of blue. Zantani was not precise there either. He praised Titian. "He can't be matched for colour, in my view. Keep that in mind."'

Having abandoned any idea of keeping my eyes closed, I have pulled myself up to half-sitting, Elena's head transferred to my lap. I am sure I catch a darkening in Francesco's expression at my mention of Titian's name. Had the lad not spoken of an audience with the *Maestro* at Casa Grande? So what can be bothering him? He should be reckoning himself a lucky young pup to get that close to the best of Venice's best, I think.

My mouth is dry with all this talking and I want to rest my voice, so I finish the tale with, 'We needed to open another bottle before a deal was clinched – but eventually it *was* made, a sum for the fee proposed and accepted, agreement reached for the contract to be sent on later. Your father, he was still inscrutable, but Zantani seemed pleased with the outcome. Certainly, he was generous enough with the coins he threw on the table to cover the cost of all we'd drunk.'

===◦===

We make our way down through the banks of flowering bushes and leave the gardens by the southern gate, Francesco excusing himself to run to another meeting. He has been offered a tour of the town by one or two of the *garzoni*, he says, and darts away across the street.

'No doubt he'll see a very different selection of Verona sights than with you this morning,' I say to Elena as we link arms to walk towards home. 'How was it anyway, your tour?'

She explains, 'He is a keen observer, I noted that, but of all we saw today I'd say what impressed him most was San Zenobio's rose window.'

'Our famed Wheel of Fortune window. Well, he is not alone in being fascinated with the message of that window. We all know we're poor helpless things, our lives determined by Fate – but I'll bet Francesco has never seen a Lady Fortune working at her wheel like that one there.'

'What does it say on it, Paolo, that inscription too high up to read?'

'It is the Lady's warning to us, "Lo, I, Fortune alone govern mortals. I raise up, I depose, I give good and evil to all". They say the sculpted figures represent the four phases of our mortal life: at the top there is the lucky one lording it, there are the ones who clamber up towards him in hope, and then the ones who tumble down in fear of becoming like the prostrate wretch who has been thrust miserably to the bottom. It *is* an oddity.'

'Oddity? It's *he* that's an oddity, that's what I think.'

'Elena, Francesco has upset you?'

'No-o,' she laughs and I am relieved. 'But I find him strange. He may smile a great deal but underneath, I wonder if he's melancholic. After studying the Lady Fortune window he went around head down, repeating a word to himself – but as though through gritted teeth. Latin it was, that much I could catch, so I asked him what it meant. "I shall reign", he told me.'

'*Regnabo*: the motto of the figure who climbs upwards, grasping for more.'

'What can he mean by it?'

'Odd, as you say. He must have had some setback, the lad, and I am guessing what you saw *was* him gritting his teeth. Perhaps he'll tell me what's perturbing him if I ask. Lord knows though, that sounds like yet more time I must find to be with him.'

Elena has not finished. 'And then there're the earrings.'

'Earrings? Sweetheart, whatever is this now?'

'Yes, a pair of earrings. He had them out on the table when I went to fetch him, made no effort to conceal them. He held one up to the light, emeralds and peridots, I would say from the colour. I saw how he *stroked* one as I explained about our walk.'

'You asked him whose they are, what business he has with them?'

'I asked him nothing, husband. I wondered about them a lot, mind, while we walked. But it is not my business to question this boy about his strangeness. That I leave to you.' She laughs, but a hint of a frown tells me my wife's perturbed.

I part from her at our door, explaining I must make confession since I missed Mass this morning. The vespers' bell tolls as I cut through some back alleys. I am thinking that I didn't tell Francesco how the day in Bassano ended. He'll have to know it. I shall need to describe clasping hands at the hostelry door with Zantani and the boy Tomaso, who were to leave early the next morning to travel on to Maser. How Jacopo said, 'Godspeed and a safe return to Bassano. We'll be keeping a welcome for you – and your dogs.'

I shall also tell Francesco how, once out of earshot, I was at last able to demand of his father, '*Maestro*, **why** … ?' Dear old Jacopo, he was calm still, too calm for me because I was feeling unsettled by what had gone on that day.

'Ah yes, Paolo,' he replied. 'You may well ask why the Magnifico wants it the way he wants it. The man has a passion, doesn't he?' He laughed, good-humoured as ever. 'Yes he has, hot like a fever, eh, and who's to guess the ague's source?' This time it was a shout of laughter he let out as he clapped me on the shoulder. 'But don't go thinking we shall ever find out. We're mere artists. We'll never get to know the mystery of what a man's heart needs, nor why he chooses what he chooses to celebrate as beautiful.'

I didn't understand how he could he be so … well, so detached, when this highly unusual request had just landed in our midst. His final words were that he would take his supper with Elisabetta and would sleep on what we'd heard today.

'We may talk more,' he said, fumbling in his pocket for his door key. 'For now, think on this, Paolo: the patron has had his say. The instructions for the work, yes, they are his. But have no doubt about it, when it comes to the work, the *interpretation* – well, the decisions about that will always and forever be mine.'

We did talk more, of course. I could not have stayed silent about the conundrum –
because that was what I saw it as. Would a respected painter like Jacopo really take
a commission that broke all the rules as we know them? And if he would, well, *why*?
What I *did* know was that his reputation from then on would be bound up with
having departed so radically from the norm. He would risk all that – for what? I
certainly hadn't thought the fee agreed was great enough to tempt him to such a folly.

Not long later Jacopo took pity on me, sat me down, set me straight. There were
serious lessons for me in that conversation and, far away as I am from that time now,
I have never forgotten it. I realised I was being made privy to the outcome of an
argument he'd been having with himself. He'd pondered, decided, and now I was
to learn. First though, the questions. On the table between us there was a pile of
brushes. Cleaning them one by one, rubbing at them with a walnut oil-soaked rag
before dunking them in a jug of the same substance, I kept my head down while he
began the interrogation with, 'What is a portrait, Paolo?'

'A representation of an individual, made to celebrate, or perhaps to commemorate.'

'Good. Made by…?'

'Made by another individual, the painter.'

'So you'd see the work as a collaboration, painter and sitter?'

'I would.'

'You would accept that ideas can change, that what individuals deem worthy of
celebration can change too?'

'Yes, I believe a person's taste evolves, especially as we broaden our knowledge.
And then there is fashion: we all fall under its influence.'

'This Bella, are you fond of her?' Startled by this diversion, I saw he was pointing
where the white dog was prone on her side, head and half her length beneath my
stool. I could only nod agreement, wondering where this could be leading.

'Might you care for the dog enough you would seek to preserve her likeness, perhaps particularly so in the case that she'd pleased you with her prowess?' He answered for himself, 'I think you might, Paolo – and I would propose that representation of her would say much about *you*. Yes, about how you want to be seen, how you yourself would like to look back out at the world from within a painting.'

Jacopo engrossed himself in pasting short lengths of pig's bristle on to a strand of raffia up as I tried to absorb this. 'You mean Zantani has somehow *subsumed* himself in these dogs you've agreed to paint? Is that even the word to use for what you're describing? He has invested, as it were, his own individuality in them? In *dogs*, though – Jacopo, can you be serious?'

'Oh, I'm *serious*. You may think differently but for me, all animals – but perhaps especially dogs in recognition of their loyal companionship – deserve better than the status we grant them. If you read what is written about the Great Chain of Being you might be convinced it is right that humans are placed higher than the animals.' He used the newly-mended brush to indicate his bookcase. 'Paolo, you make your own mind up about that, the volume is on the shelf. Read it. Understand though, that I do not agree with its doctrine.' He stood then, shook his head and pushed a hand back through his hair, as though readying himself to declaim something important. 'Such writings of the so-called wise men say animals have no souls. This is proved, they say, because animals are brutes. They do not speak and thus they cannot reason. I do not hold with that.'

'But....'

'There are no buts, Paolo.' He wanted to be finished with it, his points made, me convinced, I could see that. He said, 'Personally, I will not concede animals any inferior status. Answer me this, Paolo: what gives us the right to believe the beasts were put on earth by the good Lord simply to serve the pleasure and convenience of we humans?'

I stayed silent. He continued, 'Nor do I agree animals lack grace. At least, not dogs. For me, dogs have more physical beauty *and* more moral virtue than many humans I am obliged to deal with.' That big face of his broke into a smile then. 'So, you can see it's very gratifying Zantani has come to me for his portrait. Paolo, believe me, I am fully in sympathy with his pride in owning those dogs, as well as with his affection for them.'

'So, conventions go hang! You are going ahead.' Dropping my rag, I got up, extended my hand, took his to shake. 'I can only admire you.'

'And emulate me.'

'I, emulate you? I ….'

'You are doing it already. Look at this.' He reached across to take the sketchbook by my elbow. 'You've many studies of dogs. These for example.' He flicked to the book's centre, 'This shaggy-headed, dark brown dog: it is the creature depicted in the painting you are at work on now, the one of Our Lord with a kneeling woman, or am I wrong?'

I grinned in agreement: my *Conversion of Mary Magdalene*, which I was soon to complete. Which, gratifyingly, Jacopo went on to praise, saying, 'The dog, his form and how he holds his big head, I find they draw attention quite insistently to the left of the work, nudging the eye to glance up to that narrow strip of heavenly blue you have put at the top there. The dog has a significant role in the work as a whole, a counterpoint to all that colour and action centre stage.' He snapped the book shut. 'Paolo. I find it excellent. You've made the dog a chief witness even though the poor cur stands in the shadow.'

I took the book back, thumbed through it. He was right. Unknowingly, I *had* been emulating him. Numerous dogs, yes, featured in my pages. Such as the pen and ink sketches of Bella made just the week before. In one, a few strokes were all I had needed to capture her deep chest and strong, long legs, her alert eyes focused on something unseen. In another, only her head appeared, peeking from the right of a page where a young woman was also pictured, Bella inclining forward, intent, as though bidden to the young woman's side.

Madonna Elisabetta, Jacopo's newly-wed wife, had modelled for that one. I recall we had met as she came in from the garden, basket laden with vegetables. Elisabetta, in a green skirt, had leaned back against the arched doorway. Bella had come and snuffled at her pocket and after accepting a carrot, had sat licking her lips with a long pink tongue. With a few more strokes I'd captured Elisabetta reaching down to finger the dog's narrow collar.

I am late but if I walk any faster I'll be running. As I near the chapel I am asking myself, how much of this reminiscence does Francesco have to hear? All of it, I'm realising, since it can all be considered relevant to the painting he wants to learn about. Before reaching the entrance I slow my steps so that my breathing is quieting as I step inside and slip in to a pew. This is my favourite place for vespers, the chapel small, lit only by a line of candle lanterns hanging in front of a side altar, their flames reflecting on the silvered cross and the votive offerings clustered on the wall behind the crucifix.

The first psalm has already begun, Psalm 112. '*Praise ye the Lord. Blessed is the man that feareth the Lord, that delighteth greatly in his commandments.*' The priest's voice resonates, the verses reminding us of the rewards to be gained from living a blameless life. '*The generation of the upright shall be blessed. Wealth and riches shall be in his house: and his righteousness endureth forever.*' It is a relief to sink to my knees and allow the familiar rhythms to soothe me, to leave off, at least for a while, the thoughts that nag. The ones about perfecting my designs, the ones about mixing the purest colours, keeping the commissions to schedule. And above all just now, about these reflections on my past life.

CHAPTER THREE

13 June, the Badile studio

For someone who's been drinking most of the night in Verona's shadier stews, Francesco does not look too bad in the lemony early morning light that streams into the studio. Although, greeting him, I learn immediately from his garlic-reeking breath that one of his outing's pleasures had been sampling our town's famous horsemeat sausage. Anyway, he is awake enough to pay me attention while I summarise my recollections of last evening while going chapel-wards.

'Dogs you have drawn?' he asks when I get to that part of my account. 'May I look at them in your sketchbook?' I had already searched in the store chest for one of my books from those days in Bassano. He pores over the pages, looks up and enquires whether I'll show him my technique with pen and sepia ink.

'*It is a rare scribe who allows another to see how he holds the knife with which he sharpens his quill*,' I reply. Francesco looks blank. I poke his ribs, 'An old Arab proverb.'

Without smiling Francesco says, 'If I could assist you with something I would be sure to learn from you.' He must be missing handling his materials, it surely being a good few days now since he has mixed paint or applied a brush. Because what are we, we painters, without a pen or brush in our hand? Like a plant deprived of nourishment, we fade and want to die. I can't answer him immediately, out of breath as we heave together to shift a stack of backing boards, unaided, since the *garzoni* are late from their beds this morning. As usual.

Francesco is puffing too but manages to say, 'What I really want to ask you about is Tomaso.'

I wipe at a trail of cobweb clinging to my forehead. 'Tomaso.'

Francesco has one of his coughing fits before he can announce, 'Tomaso is the key to it. All I have learned up to now about Father's painting of the dogs is *what* it is. I am no wiser *why* Zantani wanted it.' He gulps, 'Mother told me I would need to find Tomaso. Do you know where he is?'

'Tomaso? Why Tomaso is at Maser, the Villa Barbaro. He works for the two Barbaro brothers, Signor Daniele and Signor MarcAntonio. He has been in charge of the Villa's construction for some years now.' How many years since I last saw Tomaso? Five. Next month it will be five almost exactly since I was in Maser working on the frescos final stages. Can I ever forget how we sweltered there those weeks in June? Almost too hot for the *intonaco* to be happy, really – although I think most people, looking at my wall and ceiling work now, seem to agree it went alright in the end. We got away with it.

'I am right, aren't I, that Tomaso has the information I want?'

This lad will never let up, will he? But yes, he is right. And I am getting an idea: to go to Maser, take Francesco there. Well, why not? It might be just the thing to suit everybody. I shall pass Francesco's interminable questioning on to someone fresh. Tomaso, after all, is the one with the knowledge of the dogs. Truly, it's his to tell, the story of what happened to Zantani in the forest.

At the same time, I can check the state of my frescos and finish up those missing details I never got round to. And Tomaso? Tomaso, I'll bet, will be glad to welcome us, bringing him news from the city, breaking the monotony of his too-tranquil pastoral life. My new bride will not like me taking off to Maser, of course. But it is a day's ride only, so it would be unreasonable of her to fret over-much. I'll be away no more than a week – she'll taste even sweeter on my return.

I tell Francesco what I have in mind: to leave at first light tomorrow and reach Villa Barbaro before dark. 'You like this plan? It will delay you a few days more getting back home. Write and let your mother know, will you?' I say to him. 'We shall send a rider ahead to Maser to alert them to our arrival. He can go on afterwards up to Bassano, deliver your letter into her hand.' I urge, 'The rider will be off within the hour. Go and write it now, there's a lad.'

I well remember Elisabetta, his mother, sweet lady. Yes indeed, sweet, dark-haired and glowing, and when I first met her, a new bride, just like my Elena. Elisabetta's firstborn, this lively Francesco fellow, was still in her belly. Now she has a brood of eight, the latest boy born only a couple of weeks ago, from what Francesco has said. No, while he is in my care I'll not have Elisabetta worrying about this eldest son of hers, not if it can be helped.

I lean into the depths of the chest and pull out more of my old sketchbooks. I find the one I think I'm after, its marbled paper cover spattered with reddish-brown paint marks. Flicking through the pages, I locate what I am looking for: ten or so drawings over four pages, different poses but all depicting the same big grey-muzzled dog.

'Bruno, there you are.'

One of the *garzoni*, the surly one, Piero, assists me packing the materials I will need into the saddlebags. As he is sorting brushes I push the sketchbook well down into one of the pouches. Francesco is suggesting he would like to help me? And then so he shall. At Maser I can make good use of him. Yes, I shall get Francesco working – and on something he's not expecting to do. At the same time I shall discover whether he has inherited anything of his father's talents.

SIX
Elisabetta

14 June, the house by the bridge, Bassano

Dear Son,

I thank you for your letter received yesterday. It was fortunate Gianluca was the one who saw the messenger come across the bridge and ask for our house. Your uncle took the letter and brought it to me. Thank the stars for that! Things are such here I do not believe your father would have given a good welcome to any missive from you.

I, by contrast, was much relieved to have knowledge of your whereabouts. This morning I have left the baby in the maids' care and have come with my writing materials to the arbour, where I can answer you undisturbed, and also undetected. I find it a very unfamiliar thing to be doing, concealing such an activity from my husband. But I think it is for the best as things stand. I must inform you there has been much distress in the household since your Uncle returned from Venice without you.

The better news to tell you is that baby Gerolamo's health is much improved. He has begun feeding well in the last two days and sleeps more tranquilly. I believe now he actually grows a little every day.

Your brothers are being very attentive and yesterday Giovanni, coming by the nursery at bath time, offered to help me. He hummed a little tune while he plunged his arms in the water. Soon the baby was thoroughly soaped all over, while Giovanni had got himself looking comical with suds on nose and cheeks and splashed all down his shirt. It did me good to laugh, and to hear laughter in the house again.

Your father has been speaking little, neither to me nor anyone else, since Gianluca's return. He is silent at the meals he comes to, while many times he stays through supper in the studio, the door locked. Your uncle took the brunt of his rage when you did not return. I was not there – but in my fearful imagination I see your father's face going black and hear his voice roaring like a prize bull.

Thanks to Gianluca glossing over my part in the business, I have been shielded from Jacopo's displeasure. I hope he'll never come to know you had information from me to help you search out the Magnifico Zantani. He trusts me and I pray I may learn in future to be more deserving of that. I write this sincerely, son, because I believe that if I'd known then the terrible effect it would have on him, your defying him and journeying on to follow this pursuit of yours, I would never have given you that paper.

As for you, Francesco, you are of age soon, my son, and old enough to know that responsibility for your decisions and actions rests only with you. Prepare yourself well for a confrontation with your father on your return home. At this moment I cannot say how that will turn out for you.

Now I must write of things that, from my side, I believe you should know. I do so because it is bothering me that when you met Signor Zantani your impression of his wife, Signora Helena, seems not to have been a favourable one.

Since it forms part of what your father declined to tell you, you cannot know of the Signora's visit to Bassano when you were not yet born, coming to seek help from Jacopo. She explained she wanted your father's advice on obtaining two dogs to take back to her husband in Venice. He was a very ill man, which I do not need to say to you, since you saw that for yourself when at his sickbed.

Your letter having informed me his earthly troubles are at last over, my prayers are for his rest in heaven. May he be at ease in the arms of the Lord, out of pain and receiving his blessed reward for all the years of his long suffering.

Now son, with my words you have learned that it was all of seventeen years ago that the unfortunate Magnifico's suffering began, as a result of what he endured in the forest. The Signora, speaking frankly to me once, said she felt sometimes the pain was in her husband's mind as much as, perhaps even more than, in his broken body.

Zantani suffered greatly my son, but I came to realise that Helena (as the Signora bade me call her after we had talked some little while) was also struck a crippling blow by what took place. I want you to think on that, such a fine lady, gracious (as she was to me at all times) brought so low by cruel fate. Think on that if you please, son, respect my view on this matter and try your hardest to have a kinder attitude to the Signora Helena in future.

I remember it well, the day she came to Bassano: the carriage arriving from Venice, its driver in a fine livery, the sleek horses, the plumed bridles of her outriders. That day was so stiflingly hot we had left off all work and gone to seek the cool of the riverside. Even your father rested in the shade, for a while his crayons and sketchbook idle at his side.

We had gone along the bank to that place where spray plumes up as the river diverts into the mill stream. The bank widens into a meadow, you'll recall, with some fine old trees. On our way we passed a place where the water ripples mid-stream over some flat and rounded stones. I learned something about that place that day.

Your father laughed and pointing to it, told me, 'Look, that's where as boys we used to come in the summer.' Son, for a moment I tell you, he sounded just like a boy himself. 'Yes, us boys would slip out through a back window when the nights got too hot. We'd lie out there under the moon, our backs all wet.' He looked sideways at me, a bit coy, when he added, 'I suppose, as boys do, our talk would be of wenches. Whether or not a dip in the Brenta cooled our hot blood, who am I to say?'

Not finding us at home, the Signora had left her coach at our house by the bridge. Directed to where our group was sitting, she came all the way down that stony path in those delicate city shoes of hers, her maid following. I thought she looked like a queen, head held high and wearing a dress of a yellow that seemed to me as bright as the sun. It must have been nearly noon and the shadows were sharp as she came through the trees, throwing a black lattice on to her, her hair gleaming and her face as pale as the pearls around her white neck.

The impression I gained of her: sure-footed and golden, that never left me. Even when soon after, I learned of her sadness, when I heard through the door to her room (it was too loud to ignore) her sobbing and wailing and protesting as she made her prayers.

Perhaps we should have been better practised at reading the signs of weather in our valley but we didn't connect the unbearable heat that day with a warning of a storm. Our very recent storm, the one on the night I was confined for Gerolamo's birth, I am told that storm also came as a shock to everyone. Out of a clear sky. I also learned that you were on the mountain Francesco, during that storm's approach. I would have you know, my son, since I heard of that I have offered up many thankful prayers for your safe descent.

We had no thought of storm anyway, relaxed under the trees that noonday. For lunch I had prepared a cold chicken pie with chestnuts and thyme, your father praising me for its succulence. Some story-telling diverting us, I recited a fable from Aesop's collection I'd learned by heart. You remember it, the one with the moral concerning working for one's rewards? It tells of the sleepy little dog whose master, pretending to be angry, shakes a stick and says, *'Wretched little sluggard! I hammer all day on the anvil. You, you doze on the mat. As I eat after my toil, you wake up and wag your tail for food. Don't you know labour is the source of every blessing? Only those who work are entitled to eat.'*

By the way, I should like you to know when first able to come downstairs last week I was delighted to find you had secured puppies for the boys. I've told you how I like the spirited temperament of little dogs. Your Father knew, I think, how I missed having a terrier or two about the house. They are a boisterous pair, Cesare and Fiammetta. They gambol on the grass in front of me now. The two of them beginning to eat meat and bones, they get bigger every day.

To finish with my account of Signora Helena: after that day she stayed in our house by the bridge for nigh on four weeks. Because of the great storm, of course, which started almost at the moment she joined us under the trees. We had introduced ourselves, she complimenting the natural beauty of Bassano, pointing gracefully to the curve of the valley and the mountain behind us. In that rather grand way your father sometimes speaks he welcomed her with, 'Ah, thank you Madam. Our mountain, yes, it's against its magnificence I measure myself. If ever I'm to reach Heaven it will be by climbing to Monte Grappa's summit.'

We all got a shock then, looking towards that summit, seeing the sky. It had gone the most odd shade of purple, rich dark purple like the vestment the priest puts on for Easter Mass. Never in my life before, nor all the years since gone, did I see a sky that colour. Nor one that came down like that, so swiftly, a great cloud billowing through the valley and putting out the light of the sun.

The rain came. They were warm at first, the big drops, spotting the Signora's dress, making her look as though we'd thrown a shower of gold coins at her. Then it became heavy, straight down on our heads. It was strange that there was no wind, just the torrents of water and the roar of thunder back away from somewhere behind Monte Grappa.

We abandoned everything and ran for cover. The Signora's maid was trying to catch up the train of the yellow dress as we started up the path, which the downpour was already making riskily slippery. What happened to the Signora's city shoes I can't say, but as she ran splashing ahead of me her feet were bare. We had no umbrellas with us, of course. Just my little summer parasol, so pretty with its painted flowers – but made of nothing but flimsy paper. Your father was trying to protect the Signora with it but, sadly, it fell to pieces. I saw him let it drop from his hand into the mud.

By that time we were shrieking as we ran, yes son, our drenched clothes flapping against us, all but blinded by our flying hair. It was dreadful – but funny too. The dogs yelped as they jostled along wild-eyed beside us, red tongues lolling from their mouths. That deluge, I felt urged by it to laugh wildly and cry out against its force. Not words, just sounds. Where they came from I couldn't tell you but we were all acting in the same demented way by the time we reached the town wall and the first little shelter there, provided by some overhanging roofs.

If she laughed then, Signora Helena, it was the only time I heard it. As you know from many accounts, it proved a great disaster that unending storm that flooded our valley, broke the bridges with the great boulders it brought crashing down, laid waste to the pastures, covering everything with stinking mud that stayed there for months after. No one could get in or out of the town for a very long while.

Completely cut off, we all became low as the rain went on through those weeks, the sky never lifting, foodstuffs in short supply and everything you touched sodden, starved of sunlight and going green-black with mould. I had the animals brought up to the house but that time was high season for their grazing, and we had no feed for them. It was sad to see how they wasted, even while our own stomachs rumbled.

But Helena, she was more than low. She would barely come out of the room we made up for her, making it her prison almost. She was weeping in there. At prayer time she wailed out loud as well as wept. The words she said I couldn't be sure of, except her poor sick husband's name, '*Antonio, Antonio*' often, and other times on a rising note she cried something about 'having a baby, a baby....' Whatever the cause, it was hard to hear, that sorrow she was feeling. Perhaps I should have done more.

I sometimes think I should have offered her opportunities to confide in me, if she so chose. I was a little in awe of the Signora, of course. I was very occupied with managing the household in the difficult circumstances too, and perhaps I'm also permitted to plead my own demanding circumstances: an expectant mother for the first time.

Francesco, dear son, I have to stop now. It seems I must not delay further to conclude this since the messenger who waits on me finishing before he can set off grows impatient. Your Uncle stabled the horse and gave the man a bed last night. He's kicked his heels so far today but the maid tells me he is champing to leave, pressed now if he's to reach Verona by nightfall. Besides, Gerolamo's feed time is approaching and I must speak to the kitchen maid about your father's lunch.

Your letter's made plain to me your determination to uncover the story of the dogs and the painting and I respect your right to have that information – although by saying so I am incautiously going again against your father's wishes.

From my side, I believe there is more to be added to what you have learned from me today and gleaned while visiting Venice and now Maser. Although perhaps already with this letter I have confided more than I should, I *will* complete the story. But I cannot write more now. With no more time, the other events I was witness to must wait to be recounted on your return. That will be soon, I trust.

The messenger will bring this to you at the manor in Maser, where I believe you must have already arrived by now. I hope you are conducting yourself politely at such a fine establishment and remembering the manners we taught you. For my part, I am happy to know you are a good deal closer to your home now. I look forward to embracing you the day you reach us here. May you have the Lord's blessing and a safe passage on all the roads you travel.

Please pass the most cordial greeting from your Father and I to Tomaso and Marina.

This comes with affection from your brothers and your little sisters and fondest wishes from your loving Mother.

Postscript: Son, have you enough supply of your medicine? I fear your cough may worsen if you leave off the dosage. So, I pray you for my sake, be conscientious and take two spoonfuls nightly.

SEVEN

Tomaso

CHAPTER ONE

14 June, Villa Barbaro, Maser

It smells a bit musty in this store cupboard: a good sweeping-out and then a fresh breeze blowing through it should sort it. That window at the back is jammed shut by the look of it. Force it open, grease the hinges, get the latch repaired: something else for the list. One *more* thing that will have to wait until our Master's visit is over. Prioritise, prioritise: have we enough beeswax candles for the dining table to last through his stay? If not, urgent message to the wax-chandler required. Lord knows what we'll do if he can't re-supply us before the Magnifico's arrival. Signor MarcAntonio will not take to dining to the odour of ox fat.

Ah, another box just here. With these, I think we may have just enough. 'Thirty-three, thirty-four, thirty-five…'

'Thirty-three, thirty-four, thirty-five….' mimicking me as she likes to, always when I'm concentrating hardest, Marina is there in the doorway, carrying a tray piled with plucked fowl 'What do you count, Tomaso? Candles,' she says as I hold one up. 'Oh, we'll need some of the good ones for tonight too, unless Paolo and his companion are to eat at the table in the kitchen.'

'Tonight? Paolo? Veronese, you mean, and with a guest?'

'Has word not reached you? Oh dear – they didn't tell you a messenger came from Verona? Paolo will be here this evening. With another painter.' I must show a frown because she says, 'Don't fret, we've food enough. Look at these birds, guinea fowl, cook will stew them to serve with a dish of spiced lentils. What do you say? Enough for them? Ripe greengages for dessert?'

Paolo could have picked a better moment. He has always proved the best of company and we got to like him a lot those summers he worked here on the frescos. But I know he'll be brim-ful of Verona news, while Marina will want to hear about his wedding, he having at last taken a bride. But me, I'll be stretched to find much time for chitchat in the next few days, given Signor MarcAntonio's arrival. This bailiff job, it's no easy ride. Marina and I, even after all this time here at Maser, we're still breaking our backs to put on the best show for the Master each time he visits.

Marina sees me frowning again and pulls at my sleeve to make me look at her, tells me Paolo's message says we're not to be put out, he and his companion will be attending to the frescos much of the time. She adds Paolo's hoping I'll make time to talk with the young man. About what? – I can but wonder. And Paolo's to work on the frescos again? They'll need the scaffolding fetched out of the barn then, and I'll have to send to the village to find that boy who got to be so good at the plaster preparation. More items for my list; the one that never gets shorter.

═══◊═══

Their horses clatter into the yard as suppertime approaches. I take Paolo and his friend in through the kitchen, passing by cook bent over the oven, the fat sizzling as she bastes her roast parsnips. The guinea fowl are stewing, producing that very best of welcomes, the aroma of cooking meat. We are not standing on ceremony with these two and will eat our dinner together at the small table in here, a good idea of Marina's.

Paolo makes introductions and I learn the young man is Jacopo Bassano's son.

'Your usual room is all ready, Paolo. One for you, young man – it's Francesco, is it? – made up right next door. Will you go up before you come and eat?'

'Yes – and my idea is to bring Francesco back down through the Hall of Olympus and the north salon. There's still plenty of light for him to get a good look at the frescos. He needs to know what he's in for before we get to work tomorrow.'

'We're to work on a fresco? *Together?*' the lad's asking as they take the stairs.

He doesn't know what he's to do here? Did I hear wrongly that it's a painter Paolo was bringing with him? Marina comes in, changed into a clean dress for the evening. 'Very beguiling, wife,' I say as she twirls, the skirt of dark sprigged fabric swinging out. She's put a net over her dark hair, tiny pearls dotting it, a match for the string she wears round her neck. I question her about what I heard.

'Oh, he's a painter alright,' she says, 'didn't you see the colour still on his hands?' She tugs my sleeve, 'Let's go upstairs and find them in the Hall of Olympus. I'd like to hear what he's saying, this Francesco. It's not so often we get a completely fresh pair of eyes on all the marvellous scenes that Paolo made.'

We find them at the far end of the long room. It's very quiet, the glazed doors open on the terrace, the only sound the whirr of crickets and the light chirruping of evening birdsong. Paolo leans against the door into the Room of the Little Dog, watching Francesco who's in the position almost every visitor to Villa Barbaro first adopts. In the centre of the room, his head craning back, he's turning slowly around, oblivious to everything but the blue vault of the painted heavens peopled by splendid gods above him.

Marina smiles at me then, stands and watches him too, until she sees he's brought his head back to our level. Then she darts across to him and says, 'Well, how do you find it all?' It's as though Francesco's searching for what he wants to say. Marina allows him no time to answer before she asks, 'Have you worked out who everyone is? Let's start over here and I'll show you.'

Paolo and I move out on to the terrace and perch ourselves on the sun-warmed balustrade. His face looks ruddy, bathed in a ruby sunset glow. He's greyed and his middle is going a bit soft, I notice. But who am I to comment? A family man, settled, and thirty-five years of age when my next name day's reached. I explain the work we've done at the Villa since he was last here: the avenue of trees planted down there, the terraces dug against the hill behind, the damming of the stream to make the pond for the Nymphaeum.

'A Nymphaeum now is it? My, my, haven't we got grand?' Paolo says.

This teasing of his I know from old. I wag a finger at him. 'When our Master

MarcAntonio gets together with his architect, Andrea Palladio, and they start designing together with sculptor Alessandro Vittoria, how can things *not* get grander and grander, eh? It's a simple formula the way I see it: the Master's wealth is put to work creating a thing of beauty that vaunts his status. And that of his brother, of course. Between them, they conceive what is, after all, the finest possible setting for your contribution, Paolo. Frescos that delight everyone who sets eyes on them – and will ever do so.' He looks away, always modest. 'But you're right – so many changes. And now we're nearly finished, there's barely a trace of how the old manor was. You'll want to see for yourself, I know, especially the sculptures.'

'No, I'd no idea of any of that,' Francesco is saying to Marina as they come out to us through the doors. To Paolo he says, 'I hadn't realised the extent of the work here. And you never mentioned the dogs, all the dogs you've put in.'

'I showed him the little pup on the balustrade watching the parrot, and where you've put him again seated by the columns. And then the way you've shown Cara on the balcony across the other side, her ears flapping as she leaps, chasing that monkey,' Marina says. 'You were much more interested in her, the dog you recognised, weren't you, Francesco? I mean more interested than in any clever way Paolo's got the exact likeness of our Mistress Giustiniana and the nanny, leaning over looking down at us.'

'There are all sorts of things you'll see on these walls that I haven't told you about,' Paolo answers calmly. 'Like my brush, the one I forgot when I finished here. Then I believe if you look in that little room to the right when we go in, you'll find my old painting shoes, the ones I left behind.' Francesco laughs disbelievingly. 'Yes, you will. I was tired by the end of it all last time. They clean went out of my mind – but not to worry, they appear to have been immortalised too.' He fixes Francesco with a look, 'Yes, *so* tired that when I left that time there was still an area needing work on it.'

Francesco has caught on with Paolo's tease and seems to be genuinely pleased as he asks, '*Ah*, I see. And it wouldn't be *that* area we'll work at tomorrow, by any chance?'

'Look, gentlemen,' I have to interrupt, 'a start tomorrow could be premature.

Your scaffolding's not in order since we had almost no warning about this.' I hate it when things have to be done overly hastily.

'No need, no need for scaffolding,' Paolo surprises me by saying. 'Come, step inside all of you and I'll show you where we'll be working.'

We go in. 'Just there,' he points to the left of the door to the east room where a stretch of plaster from waist level to floor is only lightly washed with colour. 'Start your fellow off chipping away at the old *intonaco*, as soon he can get going, will you, Tomaso? Ideally before dawn. We need that top plaster off to get the coarse layer below revealed.'

After those months three summers running when Paolo was here, I know the process well. And this time it should go excellently for them, since the weather's perfect. Not humid, no sign of rain but not too hot and dry either. Tomorrow they'll work on planning the design while a new fine-grained *intonaco* layer is applied on top of the old rough brown one. While waiting for the ideal moment to start, the two of them will grind their pigments, choose their palette and mix all their colours so they are good and ready. That ideal moment will come when the fresh smooth plaster is at the just-still-moist stage.

'Aren't you amazed?' Marina's pressing Francesco for his reactions again as Paolo and I start taking the stairs down. I don't know about our guests, but I've a good thirst for some ale at the end of this hot day.

'Have you seen how he's painted our life, Francesco?' I hear her asking. 'The gods up in that splendid heaven, we dutifully admire them in their opulence – but down at this level,' she indicates the wall panels, 'it's our world we see: our river and woodlands and the pretty skies of the Veneto and so many familiar places.'

'Like windows.'

'Windows on to our world, yes, Francesco – isn't it a wonder? Paolo's shown us our dawns, our dusks and all our hours of work and play in between.'

They make short work of the guinea fowl and it's a good thing Marina has an extra loaf on hand to slice up. No one says much during the meal but when the plates are removed and our chairs pushed back, I notice Francesco wears an expectant look and I see Paolo catching it. Leaning forward, his elbows on his knees, he says to me, 'Ah yes, Tomaso, Francesco's keen to hear from you about the dogs which his father painted.'

'You mean Cara and Bruno? Those dogs, how I loved them.' I hear my voice go thick and I have to pause a moment.

Marina, seeing my expression, quickly says, 'I loved them too, when we had them. I mean when they came here after what happened.'

'You had them? After *what* happened?' Francesco butts in.

This lad is *anxious*: what *is* all this about? Hoping it'll calm him, I say, 'Let me start at the beginning.' The beginning, right here at Maser. 'You've had puppies?' I ask Francesco and he nods, his face breaking slowly into a smile. That's better. 'So, you know how it is.'

Another nod. He tells me about a pair of terriers he recently brought home for his young brothers. I question him about them and we have an easy exchange, back and forth with the sort of fond remarks about dogs of which I've a ready store, as does anyone who cares about the creatures. Composed now, I start talking, taking pleasure in recounting my first memories of Cara back when I was a seven year old, just arrived at Maser to live here with my grandparents. My bad fortune was to have been orphaned when my parents died of the pox, falling sick and going within a week of each other.

The good turn of the wheel brought me here where Grandpa and Nonna had always worked for the old Master, the father of MarcAntonio, our Master now, and his brother, Daniele. Fortune favoured me again when Grandpa let me choose a puppy from a neighbouring farm's litter. 'That was Cara. Carota, ginger nut, was the name Grandpa suggested because of her red splotches – but to me she was always Cara because I held her very dear.'

I tell Francesco how she took to me immediately. The smallest in the litter, Grandfather saying of her as she wobbled about, 'Surely, that's the runt?' and the farmer pointing out how nicely formed she was and saying, 'Besides, they often tell you the last-born will be the best fighter. This little bitch could turn out to have more courage than the lot of them, bigger though they may be.' We watched him gently opening one of her tiny eyes with his finger. He told us they were pale, and that was another sign she would be a brave one, or so he'd heard.

Marina, back from the cellar where she's been to fetch more wine, holds the jug close to her chest as she stands by the door to the courtyard. 'The moon is full tonight,' she says with a meaningful look at me.

'Ah yes, we thought we might sit by the water. Shall we go up?'

═◦═

'Unearthly,' I hear Paolo say on an intake of breath as we step into the Nymphaeum.

The semicircle of columns set back against the tall dark trees behind them *is* a startling sight. The Master is so proudly pleased with his designs but I am not yet used to the unsettling effect of these palely gleaming, voluptuous nudes looking down from high on their pedestals. It is *eerie*, the way the moonlight makes their features so lifelike. Prodding them out of their silence, I'd like to ask them, 'Who are you, you women from the classical past? You who observe our daily life, listen to what we say, what do you make of it? Do tell.'

On such a warm night we happily sit for an hour or more out there, sipping at our wine and breathing in the scent of some white blossom that tumbles over the wall nearby. Time enough for Francesco to also hear Bruno's story.

'You got him as a puppy?'

'We never knew where Bruno came from,' I tell him and describe the day he appeared, a brown dog, quietly padding up to me as I was feeding Cara. 'The Master's hounds were housed in another yard around the corner and I assumed the dog had come from there. He was rangy and thin, a little ungainly, clearly not too long out of puppyhood. He lay down, I remember, lowered his head to his paws and seemed to be observing us from deep brown eyes, his expression unfathomably sad. Later in the day I made a rope collar and led him round to the kennels but the lads told me he didn't belong there.

'The dog stood close to my knee, muzzle still lowered. His tail was held low down, but he continued to wag it back and forth, although very slowly. Taking a better look, I saw this was a dog that didn't belong anywhere. His eye was wary as well as mournful, his flanks on the thin side. No brush had touched that coat in a long time.' I conclude my story with a question, 'Well, need you ask what happened next?'

They're all laughing of course, as I finish the tale. 'The Master's hounds were being closed up for the night, leaping and clambering over each other as they were whistled into the kennels. It was growing dark. I looked into the dog's sad eyes and said, "Come on then, you'd better have a meal and bed down tonight with us before we decide what to do next."

'Next morning I found Cara and the brown dog both flat out on their sides, muzzles close, her paws touching his belly. They didn't lift their heads but I knew there were four watchful eyes following my every move. He was a brown dog, so we called him Bruno – what else? And those big sad eyes of his, I'd say that forever after, he never really took them off me.'

Marina yawns and shortly after slips away from the table. The silence between the three of us is companionable. Francesco breaks it. 'The two dogs,' he says carefully, 'I got the impression they had special qualities. You must have been very skilled in your training.'

'Signor Zantani gave you that idea, did he? He always appreciated how I'd taught them obedience. I could never work out where their aptitude for training came from – all I knew was they learned *fast*, took on so many new skills, showed such zest for it.'

'Special hunting skills?'

'Yes. The Master and his brother had just started bird hunting with crossbows here at Maser and Cara and Bruno proved to be fine birders. But I could teach them *anything*, Francesco, tricks, and obedience to all my commands. They were a phenomenon.'

'I'd like to know more of that, the hunting and everything.'

'You would? Let me request the Master tells you about that once he's here. He's expected the day after tomorrow.' I'm thinking my Master MarcAntonio will take any chance he can get to reminisce about those days back then. I must have heard it a hundred or more times, him saying to me, 'You know Tomaso, they were my "glory days" and I'll always cherish them as that.'

Paolo has taken himself for a walk around the pool's perimeter and stands close to one of the nudes, looking up and reaching both hands to smooth over the surface. I'm yawning now. Tomorrow, I'm thinking, so much to get done tomorrow. The rest of this story-telling can wait until then, until Francesco asks for the rest of it, for Zantani's part, that is. Tonight he's had the best part. It may be something he'll regret, discovering what happened next.

CHAPTER TWO

15 June

The sky this evening is a bowl of tranquil blue over the plain, only the faintest streaks of wispy cloud moving across it. The rosebushes on the lawn sloping away below me are giving their best pink and white display, traces of their musky perfume wafting this way. Over the road the gates into the pasture are open and my eye is led through them and down the avenue between the saplings we planted either side. Only a distant spire punctuates the pale horizon.

Sitting together here on the terrace steps, I wish the mood between Francesco and I were as calm as this scene. But he is agitated, I can tell. He and Paolo have taken a break from the painting. A long day, the plasterer sent home mid-morning. By noon they would have completed transferring the design on to the plastered area. I've been barred from seeing the work until they're through – but I can imagine how it was as they waited for the plaster to be ready, resistant to the pressure of a finger.

Then Francesco will have taken the paper cartoon and offered it up against the fresh plaster. The outline of their design will have been perforated with many tiny pin pricks. Paolo will have tapped and tapped again, moving along these lines with his pounce pad, a cheesecloth bag he's had filled with charcoal dust. *Tap tap tap,* a fine dusting of black powder going through the fabric and the pin-pricked cartoon, soon the design will have been neatly transferred to the waiting plaster.

Waiting, but not for much longer, though, having been drying more with every passing minute. So they must have soon started in to get the colour on, first covering where the new area joins with the old. Then with a small, coarse, almost-dry brush they'll have pounded with some force to apply paint over broad areas, the colours mixed with a small pinch of lime to give them body. Building up the colour will have come next, both of them having to work fast now, hundreds of fine clean brush strokes used to put on dozens of coats of clear colour.

By early evening they'll have reached a point when the thirsty plaster is cooperating beautifully, drinking up every stroke. '*Yes, yes, that's it, come on, come on,*' I've overheard Paolo urging his fresco as though it's a woman, one he's encouraging to pleasure him, to do it just how he likes. For this stage, which will last an hour or so, they'll have been using their fine watercolour brushes to feed a thin watery consistency of paint, quarts of it, into the plaster. They will have had a bucket of lime water for thinning as necessary but Francesco, who's had to strip off his shirt in the hottest part of the day, will tell me later he was dripping so much he could have thinned it with his own sweat.

'Don't torment the colour,' that's a refrain Paolo often repeats. 'Let's be kind, let's keep it sweet,' he'll say. At this point he'll have been thinning the mixture with sugar and milk to keep it the right consistency. Just now he's taking a walk to the village but he'll be back to the fresco soon, 'furthering his relationship with it' as I like to think of it. There will be a few hours more painting until the plaster tells him 'Enough!' It will accept no more. Like it or not, they'll have to stop. The plasterer will be called back in to help them chip away any areas of plaster they haven't put paint on. Then it's their turn to sleep, while he has to set to, mixing and spreading *intonaco* through the hours of darkness, readying the wall for their next bout.

Francesco should be fatigued by the long day but he has energy enough to enlighten me about what's troubling him. As soon as he whetted his lips with the first sip of his evening ale he says, 'The letter that came for me….'

'Oh dear,' I interrupt, 'the delay. I am so sorry you got it so late. The messenger who brought it from Bassano was in haste to get back to Verona before dark, so he left it at the gatehouse on the road. Some confusion down there meant we didn't receive it here until halfway through this morning. I hope you weren't overly inconvenienced?'

He shakes his head but his expression is dark.

'It wasn't bad news?'

'No, no. All's well with my family, thank you. And oh, my parents send you and Marina greetings.'

'I'm glad of that.' That agitation is still there though, there's a *'but'* coming, I just know it.

'But … I'm sorry, this story of the dogs: I don't have much time to get it all straight – and there's still so much that isn't clear to me.'

'You're in a hurry, I gather?'

'Oh yes, I am,' he tells me. 'Excuse me for not explaining properly. There's someone – someone important, wanting the information. I don't know how long he'll wait.' He pauses, 'I feel….' Another pause, then it comes out in a rush, 'I feel I'm not being told things.'

I say nothing and he has time to take a great gulping breath before he bursts out again, this time with, 'My mother's letter has me all confused. What *did* happen in the forest?'

Ah, here we have got to it, the difficult part. I don't reply immediately, trying to decide how best to tackle this. Francesco sits and twitches by my side, shifts his weight from one buttock to the other, slaps at his boots. He pushes a hand again and again through his hair while putting more questions. 'Marina was with you in Bassano? I didn't know that until today. And my mother wrote that the Signora came from Venice to ask my father's help in finding dogs to take back there for her husband. I don't understand. What dogs were these? Where were Cara and Bruno? Dead? Was *that* what happened in the forest?'

He gnaws at a paint-smeared knuckle and after a moment adds, 'But then Marina said you had the two dogs here at Maser, *after* … so that can't be.' He sighs, 'Mother's advice was that when I found you I'd have my story. I thought coming here I'd be reaching the end of it – but it's much more complicated than that, isn't it?'

His story? *My* story. In truth, *Zantani's* story, the poor man. Dealt with so badly, his luck truly deserting him. And I blame myself. I should have warned him. I *could* have warned him. Always those three thoughts come into my mind when I reflect on that time. I wish I had advised him – even if he'd chosen to ignore what I, just a youth from the estate, had to say.

How much of this do I have to tell Francesco? If I must recount it, let me keep the thing as short as I can. Ignoring all the questions, I go right back to the time before it all went wrong. Starting straight in, I take a deep breath, 'This is how it was. We were in the carriage, Signor Zantani and I, that is. We had left here and were heading back to Bassano with the dogs, to deliver them to your father for their portrait to be painted, you understand?' Francesco nods. 'They travel in their own contraption, did you know? A sort of kennel on wheels towed behind the carriage.'

They hadn't liked being pushed into the thing, Bruno was growling even as I took his collar. Once the slatted door was slammed shut the barking started, eventually turning into a plaintive yowling from Cara. They say dogs catch your mood. My mood? I was in despair of course, at the thought Cara and Bruno would no longer belong with me. No longer be at Maser. Even though I had left for Venice, sent against my will to work there on that apprenticeship.

But I was obliged to hide any emotion from Zantani, who of course, was all gratified and beaming at being the dogs' new owner. *That*, the despair and misery I was feeling, was why, when we were taking refreshment at the tavern I didn't stay Zantani's hand when he reached into his bag to pull out the fancy silver collars he'd had made for the dogs. Raw with resentment, I thought to myself, if he is so incautious to go flaunting his wealth in a place like this, showing all and sundry how he'll adorn his new dogs with expensive fripperies, well, let him do it. Let him take the consequences.

Francesco's looking at me, waiting – at least he's calmer now he thinks he's getting something from me. I continue, 'That road we took up into the hills has always been known as dangerous, all that deep forest fringing it both sides – but in the carriage and with the dogs, we thought no one would bother us. Wrong.'

'You were attacked?' He gnaws still at that knuckle.

'It was more villainous than that. We knew later it was at that benighted tavern where we'd had the horses watered that they saw us, the robbers. We stood out: Zantani's elegant clothing, his fine leather travelling bag and the way we huddled close over it to inspect the silver dogs' collars, he unwrapping them from their red velvet and inadvisedly pulled them out, holding them up high, the light sparkling off the red and blue gems. Are you surprised we attracted the wrong sort of attention? No wonder those men thought we'd be easy picking. They were right – and it was a bad do for us.'

'Were you hurt badly?'

'Zantani yes, I fear. But not there. We had left the tavern behind and got a little way on the road by the forest before the carriage veered off the road, crashed. A wheel gone. The bastards had loosened the bolts, which held for just a mile or so before working free and falling off.'

'They had planned it all.'

'Francesco, yes – they must have done it before, perhaps many times. With so many isolated spots in these hills around here where no sheriffs patrol, such villains know they can do what they will. I should have been more vigilant but no, sitting ducks we were, dozing in the fine carriage, heads lolling back against the padding. That was before the juddering and shaking started, the carriage lurching terrifyingly as it keeled over, Zantani and I thrown against each other. There was a ghastly grinding sound as it slid on. At last it stopped. I was all crouched over, Zantani splayed out flat on his back. The horses were panicking, we could hear them whinnying and snorting, their harness jangling, the crashing of their hooves as they reared in their traces. Our coachman, Gianni, must have been thrown off his box, all we heard of him was one long groan.

'We got ourselves out somehow and, wanting to look as though I knew what I was doing, I told Zantani I'd handle it, even though I hadn't an idea yet what had caused the problem. "The coachman will help me," I snapped. Of course, a while later it was

Gianni who eventually spotted the bolts were missing and quietly brought out the spare ones he kept wrapped in an oiled rag.

'The first thing I thought to do was to locate the box with the dogs. It was in the ditch, miraculously intact. They were alive! and unhurt it would seem, from the thumping on the box sides and the yelping they were doing as I was letting them out. By that time Zantani was pulling himself up from where he'd been sitting on the grass, his head on his knees. He called, "Cara, Bruno." The two of them, always obliging, leapt up towards him with one concerted, joyful bound, their flanks touching, paws spread as they landed on the verge beside him. Fussing them, he said, "We'll walk in these woods," hefted the strap of his leather bag across his chest and went off.

'If I tell you I looked up then and there was a lone black bird sitting on the dead tree, there in plain sight on a long thin branch forking right out over the path, I bet you would say I had made it up to spice my story. You, Francesco, perhaps don't hold with such omens of bad luck. But I do – and I'll always, always regret I didn't race after Zantani, try to warn him.'

Francesco is fixed on me and I continue, 'The weather broke then, heavy rain falling all at once. It must have been as Zantani sheltered, deafened by the downpour, that they ambushed him. A gang of them, four, it turned out.'

'He was robbed and they beat him?'

'And then left him as good as dead, yes. Why so brutal, I'll never understand. I waited a bit, thinking he would come back as the rain eased – but he didn't and it had started to get dark. We set out to search, the coachman and I, calling as we went deeper into the forest. It was *black* in there. I lost my bearings, could hear Gianni's voice getting fainter, hailed him, told him to keep within earshot. In the end, the place where I found Zantani was quite close to the road.

'It was a terrible thing, Francesco, I tell you, to find him dumped like that, just a sodden heap thrown on the fallen leaves, roped up like a slaughtered beast. I'd have missed him entirely if it weren't for the faintest gleam from the silver fastenings of his cloak. I fell to my knees and was trying to lift his limbs, feeling my hands along them to see where he was hurt. The rain was drenching me as I knelt there and oh, the horror of the cold, thin rain mixing with the warm, sticky blood where it was seeping through his breeches.

'We fashioned a makeshift stretcher for the Magnifico from branches and a hank of rough twine Gianni found, dropped, we supposed, by the gang as they made off. *Somehow* between us we managed to get him back to the tavern, almost dragging him, it felt like, down that never-ending road.'

'And the dogs…?'

'Gone.'

'*Gone?* But what did Zantani say?'

'*Say?* I wasn't sure he was alive, let alone able to speak. Clearly, I haven't got over to you what bad shape he was in. I tell you, he was so broken, he couldn't move and they'd beaten him about the head as well, smashed his face so it was all bloody. I wasn't expecting to hear anything from him but somehow he knew I was there. All he could get out before he lost consciousness was, "I gave them, I *gave* them…." He was trying to tell me something but I'm sorry, they were words that had no meaning to me.'

Paolo comes along the terrace. He gives Francesco's shoulder a friendly shove. 'Ready to finish off?'

I leave them to it but as I go I say, 'I'll have something for you later, Francesco.' Something, yes, I've thought of something. I go up to our room and there I locate the notes I've remembered, a good few pages tied up scroll-like with hemp string, tattered edges to the paper. They are in the chest where Marina has stored her bridal headdress. Her pink-ribboned bouquet, too, which she'd carefully dried. Once a bunch of lovely roses, but now shrivelled and brown, although putting the thing to my face, the lingering scent brings back that happy day. Ten years of marriage and three children separate me from the moment we stood before the priest.

For me, Fortune smiled down in the end. But it was far from evident at the time. The horror of the attack in the forest, and then me falling so dangerously ill in

Bassano during the time the town was flooded: if these bad things hadn't happened, would Marina and I ever have celebrated our nuptials? *Buts* and *ifs* –ah, is it a good idea to dwell on them?

Back then, Jacopo did not think so, which was his reason for obliging me to make these notes, to write of the events, to record everything. 'Stop berating yourself, boy,' he said as I sat in his studio, at last recovering from the fever but out of bed for short periods only. 'What's done is done and you played the hand you were dealt with as best you could. Leave off with the conjecture and the messy emotion and concentrate on the facts.'

I must have looked blank. I was still blaming myself and what I was feeling was worse than blankness: I was devoid of spirit, hopeless. I was fortunate Jacopo's potions had succeeded in repairing my sick body – but nothing could lift my mood. Jacopo, though, would not allow me to continue like that, asking, 'You write, don't you?' I told him the Master insisted all we Maser estate boys learned how, as well as to read, and that I'd also got some Greek and Latin learning. 'You shall make a report for me then.' Determined, he brought paper from his table and handed me a board to lean on, a pot of ink, a quill. 'I want you to write what happened in the forest. Take it steady and keep events in order. Tell all. Tell me the facts, remember, the facts first, your feelings after, if you must.'

Others might think going back over all the evil and wretchedness would harm me – but Jacopo seemed convinced recreating the horrible things I had witnessed would bring about some healing. Looking back, he was probably right. Over how many, many days did I sit in that chair in the corner while Jacopo drew and painted and paced the studio, muttering at his palette and swiping at his great mop of hair? He was painting a portrait of the dogs but must have completed several other works while I laboured away at my manuscript, with its splotches of spilled ink and scorings out and all the rest.

I had never before – nor have I ever since – spent such time like that, crouched like a scribe, my bent back aching and my fingertips blackened by the end of every day. Gradually though, I felt strength coming back to my limbs and my heart a little lighter. Peaceful but painful times, not ones I'd want to repeat. Neither would I now enjoy re-reading my description of those days half a lifetime ago. So let my notes serve their purpose for Francesco. I can't believe there will be much more he'll need to know after he is through with them.

When later Francesco opens his door in answer to my tap, there is a sketchbook on his table. 'Paolo's sketchbook. I've been looking at these in the last light,' he says, pointing to a page where Bruno – it is unmistakably he – is shown in three or four different poses.

'There, that is the detail we've added to the fresco,' Francesco says. 'It's supposed to be your surprise, yours and Marina's, the design we've painted in the Hall. But we shall finish tomorrow – so why shouldn't you see what we've done now?'

In the sketch Bruno lifts his left paw, yes, the old fellow is holding up the paw they broke, those bastards in the forest. I wince, remembering his whole frame covered with cuts and slashes, the congealed blood. He's shown as thin too, just the way he was from the after-effects of the poison.

'And this one here is my sketch, copied from the ones I found in the attic, the ones Father made,' Francesco says, breaking my train of thought as he places another book on the table, a page open at a very similar drawing. Before I can comment he continues, 'We're pretty much done with our work on the dog – but we've more to do tomorrow because I persuaded Paolo that we should paint the ruins of the Roman Arena at Verona as the backdrop to Bruno. It'll be a grand vista – but it will be Bruno who draws all eyes. You'll see.' He darts me a quick look before reverting, as ever, to what he wants to know, asking, 'In the forest, was it you who found the dogs?'

My reply, as it happens, to anyone questioning me about that has always been, 'It was the dogs who found me.' But rather than say that to Francesco, I hand over the sheaf I'm holding. 'In here you'll find your answer.' I stretch across, flip over the first couple of pages. 'This part you already know, so start from here. You will need this candle and flint.' He is pulling the notes into the flickering circle of light as I close the door.

CHAPTER THREE

Page the third

THE DAY AFTER

I am reunited with Cara and Bruno

After a dreadful night I left the tavern before the light was up. None of us had slept. Once we'd got Zantani to a room we had water heated to bathe his wounds. Then we dosed him heavily with grappa to calm his pains – as much as strong drink could. He moaned as he thrashed on the cot and, as for Gianni and me bedded down by the fire, the hours went hellishly slowly. We had agreed Gianni would get Zantani on to the coach due to come through by seven in the morning, and nurse him as best possible while getting him to Venice, home, a doctor.

I could only think of searching for the dogs. I searched and searched, dread in my mind that I'd find their corpses. Nevertheless, through those dawn hours I called their names, whistled, called and whistled. When I heard a yelp and a bark and the sound of them coming through the undergrowth I wanted to cry with relief.

Cara came out of the brush first. All seemed well at first, she putting her paws up on to on my knees, as she always does to lick my hands. I bent down to caress her – but then I got a proper look and I saw the dreadful state of her! Her muzzle was a mass of congealed blood, crusting her eyes and all round her jaws, as though she'd been drinking deep of the stuff. Her coat was so matted with mud it was hard in the feeble light to tell that she's a white dog. She had a knotted rope round her neck, a piece with many other knots in it trailing on the ground. I was running my hands over her back, feeling the dried blood, sticky gobbets of it on my palms. Blood was *everywhere*. A slash the length of her right ear – how could anyone take a knife to a dog? – oozed great fat drops of it.

And Bruno, where was he? Had they killed him, my Bruno? But then he came, all lopsided, head hanging low, limping badly. It was his left paw. He collapsed at my feet and lay on his side and didn't move. My God, I thought my heart would burst. He groaned, hurt badly but at least still alive.

All I wanted to do was to get the dogs away from there, to leave that dark, dripping place and feel sunlight on my face again. To walk in the forest had once been a pleasure for me – but not there, a place that seemed dead somehow, where nothing grew abundantly and no leaf fell.

There was nothing for it but to carry Bruno over my shoulders. Before I heaved him up I loosened the rope he also had around his neck, his perilously tight against his windpipe. With one hand I held together his two back legs and one front around my neck, leaving the injured leg hanging. How he groaned then. His muzzle was close to my face, mouth lolling open, warm saliva dripping down my neck.

'Cara, come,' I said but she wouldn't. She braced her legs and stood there, looking at me. I tried calling her again but this time she ran a few yards down the track which led further into the forest. She would not obey, even when I took a few steps after her and spoke sharply, no matter how many times I repeated, 'No, Cara, this way, this way.'

Page the fourth

I discover a dreadful scene

I should have held her intelligence in higher esteem – because when I gave in and followed where she wanted to lead me it soon became quite clear what she was trying to tell me. In less than five minutes of stumbling through the undergrowth, breasting dripping branches, using my free hand to protect my face, we emerged into a clearing. Cara stopped at its edge and I did too, wanting to assess what I'd found. It was deadly quiet. There was a sweet resinous smell hanging around.

Woodcutters: felled branches heaped to one side of a low hut and a pile of logs they'd split on the other, almost higher than the hut. Woodchips and sawdust, a wet mulch, carpeted the ground. Just like a carpet, it muffled my steps.

Bruno was growling, a low rumble right in my ear, while Cara, hackles up, was pressed so close to my side I could feel her body quivering. There was an axe, left hefted into an upstanding log near the flat slice of tree trunk that was obviously a chopping block.

I told Bruno in a whisper that I'd have to put him down and he flopped there on the sawdust, just raising his head enough to watch what I'd do next. I was restraining Cara with the rope collar, wondering indeed, what to do. I believe I'd have sensed danger even without the dogs' warning signs; there was something grim and threatening about the place. I took the axe: it had a long handle, shiny with use and its edge was unevenly serrated but very sharp. Shapely in my hand, the thing was satisfyingly heavy. I gripped it and held it against my chest as I crossed the clearing to the hut door, my steps stealthy.

I heard no noise at all from inside and so pushed at the door cautiously. It gave a little and I was debating whether to put my shoulder to it when I heard a moan. As I shoved my way in I heard another, and a loud groan. The stink in that dark smoky place, it was appalling: damp clothes and sweat. And something more foul: vomit – and something more unmentionable, worse than vomit. The intake of fresh air sparked the fire's pink ash bed into a guttering flame and I staggered over something as I took my first steps inside. It was a body under my feet. In fact, the bodies of three men were on the floor, one sprawled on his back, knees raised, the others face down, arms and legs akimbo. Vomit and excrement were pooled between them and after I shoved again at the door, opening it as wide as I could, for air, for more light, I saw bright streaks of blood in the mess.

Kneeling to peer at the man at my feet, I saw a face livid, pale yellow like a freshly-peeled parsnip, smelt the sickly and disgusting breath coming from his mouth, had to jerk back when a dribble of vomit oozed from his lips and down his chin. The man next to him then rolled on to his back and he and this fellow each let out a dreadful, deep dull groan. At that moment the third man belched and flung out an arm as he tried to pull himself up. There was a clink as something fell from his hand before he gave up, fell back. A faint gleam from what had fallen showed me it was a flask. A flask I recognised and as I looked down again I saw the stopper that must have come from it. This I recognised too.

I am sure I spoke out loud, knowing those fellows were surely deaf to anything I had to say.

'Nonna, you were right about that draught of yours … it's strong. These villains were so partial to the sweet taste of your "cordial", they've drunk the lot and got themselves into this state. Unlucky them. Assuming its effect would be a nice state of intoxication, they know nothing yet of its bitter aftertaste, the one they're going to be living with for the rest of their days.'

I stood looking down at the figures and I absolutely did not care if they died. Pathetic, destroyed creatures now but men who had been ugly vicious bullies, callously inflicting terrible damage on hapless Zantani. And who'd harmed my dogs – I was still thinking of them like that, as mine – in monstrous ways.

Nonna's 'cordial', the sleeping draught she'd made expressly for Zantani to counteract the insomnia he'd complained of while at Maser, would not be *fatal*, more's the pity. But its effects, well, the villains might think death would be no worse than what they'll be subjected to.

My grandmother was fiercely proud of her recipes for soothing liniments and cures. On her mixing days she'd close the shutters so no passers-by could see her at work. Later, on the table in the kitchen there would be an array of bottles, packets and jars. During my brief stay at Maser with Zantani I had found her there, offered to help. She was picking stalks from a limp green bundle, stripping off the leaves.

'I gathered these this morning before dawn,' she said, dividing the bundle to push some towards me across the worn surface. 'The sooner we get them in to steep the better.'

The finished sleeping draught for the Magnifico readied, Nonna told him, 'Take only one drop in a beaker of spring water. One drop.' She alerted me, 'In its neat state this draught is extremely powerful. It can drastically affect the body's functions.'

Nonna hadn't the polite words to tell Zantani the details of the draught's potency – but she made sure she got her message over to me. And it wasn't potency she was talking about, rather the opposite. 'After the hair falls out all over the body, the natural urge a man has, the one he takes for granted, that stops working. The hair may come back in time, but not that other thing,' she told me. I was thinking these men's wives will have something to say when they discover that their cosy times in the marital bed are a thing of the past.

Page the fifth

The bag and the collars are saved by Cara and I see what the villains did to the dogs

I was taking pleasure at this rough justice as I kicked out at the body nearest me, my boot making satisfyingly heavy contact with the man's rump. He was too far gone to cry out. The draught surely *was* potent. Did I think of trying to help them in any way? Was it my business whether they survived to stumble back to whatever cesspit of evil they'd emerged from? No, I was far more interested in discovering why Cara was looking expectantly up at me, while she thumped and thumped her tail on the ground.

'What's up?' I asked her, just as I saw that she was lying with her chest and front paws on Zantani's travelling bag. It was an elegant thing, made from smooth orange-red pigskin with neat saddle stitching and handsome brass studs, jaunty fringed tassels on its shoulder strap. Whenever I caught sight of his initials 'AZ' which he'd had tooled on its flap I remembered my lessons in Greek and thought of alpha and omega, God on high as the beginning and end of all things, who was and who is and who is to come, as the Bible would have us understand. In this horrible stinking hovel the bag and any thoughts of a new heaven and a new earth were so out of place somehow I needed to laugh, not real mirth, but a harsh shout of a laugh nevertheless.

I knew from the weight of it and the *clink clink* I heard as I lifted the bag that the precious contents were still intact inside. The dogs' collars, retrieved. Thank God and all his saints for their munificence. I lifted the strap over my chest. Cara was still looking expectantly at me. I patted her head and said, 'Brava!' Her tail thumped again, once, twice, she still looked up. Then I remembered as we'd left the Villa I'd seen Nonna hand Zantani a neat parcel of meat scraps. Nonna knew my dogs, knew a new owner would have to endear himself to them somehow. I fumbled to find the parcel and, selecting a morsel or two, dropped them into her mouth. Gobbled down in an instant. *Now* we could get out of there.

Bruno was still lying on his side, panting so his flanks heaved like a pair of bellows working to revive a fire made from green wood. He looked up at me, dark eyes clouded. I kneeled and patted him. Before heaving him up again across my shoulders I needed to know what had happened to him here in this ghastly place. Cara, too. I looked for clues and I found them.

I tripped on a rope, almost fell flat on to the wood chips. It was more a rough twine, of the sort that was still round the dogs' necks. It lay there, trailing from where it had been tied round a slender tree trunk. I picked up the rope's frayed end and saw it was chewed. They'd been tied and they'd chewed through to escape, one helping to release the other first, then waiting in turn to be freed.

Courage and persistence and ingenuity – I would not have expected less of them.

But stepping towards the tree my heart almost stopped when I saw what was all around it. Missiles: rocks and short lengths of log, all around on the ground. The bastards, they'd pelted these things at them. To silence them I suppose, because they'd have been barking a fury and snarling, which would have surely given away the villains' hiding place.

The men were not themselves woodcutters, they'd only been taking temporary shelter from the storm, I realised, but had obviously seen what was in the bag and fallen to drinking. Then they'd settled to finish the flask by a nice little fire. Their assault on the dogs must have been motivated by desperation because Bruno and Cara, tied outside, would not keep quiet. The tree trunk was scarred and torn where, missing their aim at the dogs, the villains had hit it. What would such things have done to tender flesh? I could answer that when I picked up a rock that was wet to my hand, wet with blood. My dogs had been ripped into, bloodied by these cruel bastards, probably laughing and jeering in their drunken state as they did it. Disgusted, sickened, I thought of that penalty for grievous sin in the Old Testament, stoning to death. My dogs, sinners? Innocents rather, incapable of hurting anyone who treated them decently.

Page the sixth

Getting back to the tavern

I picked up Bruno and settled him on my shoulders and called out 'Let's go, Cara.' She ran ahead down the path. I had lost my bearings again but headed for where the trees thinned and a patch of lighter sky indicated the forest edge. I was walking head down, Bruno's weight on my neck bending it forward and that was when I saw the gobbets of blood spattering the leaves on the path where Cara had passed. I called her back but she didn't seem to hear me. I shouted her name loudly – no luck, only when I whistled did she finally stop and wheel round to come to my side. Her right ear was bleeding copiously again now, big drops of blood, with a sticky sheet of red gore across her chest and spots of it flecking her shoulders. She can't hear properly, I thought. That was the first time I felt my head swim. I know I was staggering as we went tortuously on down that path.

Once we reached the road the trudge along it to the tavern was slow and painful. The rain never stopped catching at my back, blown by a viciously chill wind. Reaching the place at last, I laid Bruno down outside. I knew I had to get help and I banged on the door until the landlord came. He gaped at what he saw and then pointed me without a word round the side to an outhouse. A maid came quickly with a bowl of warm water and I washed Cara's wound, which started the blood flowing again. The cuts were deep, the ear itself slit in two places and the side of her head pulpy, raw and bloody. I was aghast. 'Did they *kick* you?' I asked her.

For Bruno, I searched round on the outhouse floor for a stick and contrived a splint for the damaged paw and leg, binding it as best I could with a strip of linen torn from my shirt hem. The missiles had done dastardly work, so many cuts and abrasions, red gashes in both dogs' wet fur. My hands became bloodied up to the wrists as I treated them. Both dogs groaned softly and lay limp after I'd finished. Sweat was dropping into my eyes by this time, the anxiety of discovering the damage inflicted on the dogs making my breathing tight.

'We must leave, I'll need a cart,' I told the landlord. I remember the man scratched at his ear as he stood there. The smile on his face was more like a jeer and I thought he'd say something mocking about my concern for the dogs' condition. I stopped him dead by handing him a couple of coins from the purse in Zantani's bag. Hearing the *chink* of those helped change his mind fast enough. While I waited for the transport, I had to go again into Zantani's bag to find paper and a quill pen. If he lives and if he receives this letter, I hope the Signor will excuse me these liberties with his things, I was thinking, as I called the landlord again and asked for ink.

I write a message for Signor Zantani

The note was short, not even attempting to explain to Zantani why I'd decided to head straight back to Bassano. Everything Jacopo had told me about his healing potions and poultices made me sure it was there the dogs would be best tended to. All through the long struggle back from the forest I'd been debating with myself just how much information I could pass on to Zantani. I *could* tell him we'd discovered it must have been his attackers who loosened the carriage wheel bolts, those ruffians I'd noticed at the tavern earlier. I could not have identified them as the same men lying half-dead in the hut back up the track there – but it must have been them. Zantani had so proudly brought out the collars and modelled them with his hands, how they'd look on the dogs, while we'd supped a glass of ale. The bastards saw us. I knew they had done – and they'd laid their plan to rob him there and then, done their damage to the coach and then gone ahead, knowing there would be a crash. They were waiting to waylay the carriage whenever it broke down.

I *couldn't* tell him the dogs were harmed, that wouldn't do. I could say the collars were safe, I was thinking as I wrote. More than that would have to wait. As for the thieves, those evil bastards, they'll get their just deserts in the days to come if Nonna didn't exaggerate in what she said about that potion. They'll have a price on their head if they've murdered the Magnifico, of course.

But what force of law and order would want to come looking for them up here in these wild hills? Easy enough it'd be, you'd think though, to track down four hairless men. Get them to drop their britches and their shrivelled balls will be enough to convict them. I snorted another mirthless laugh at this.

I found three more coins in Zantani's bag and passed them to the landlord with the folded note with the Ca' Zantani address written on the front. I asked him to pass it to the driver of the next coach through for Venice.

Back in the outhouse I slumped down on the straw and Cara came close to me. She let her head droop on my thigh, her honey eyes mournful as she looked at me before she closed them. Bruno did not move from where he lay. I let out a groan; it felt so good, just to close my eyes for a moment, only just for a moment.

Page the seventh

Our journey to Bassano

The wait in that outhouse seemed to go on forever, but probably it wasn't more than an hour before a boy arrived, jolting up to the hostelry door through another storm of pelting rain, sitting on a rough cart drawn by a small, thin donkey. We hurried out to him. Cara could jump on to the cart but Bruno remained lying on his side, eyes closed. Together the boy and I lifted him up and he collapsed on a couple of sacks, limp and all sprawled out.

'You know the back lanes route over the hills to Bassano?' I asked the boy. I'd decided we'd not put ourselves at any more risk going back on that road. It was the most awful journey. The long storm-driven day dragged into an evening of livid sunlight low in the sky as the donkey hauled us to Bassano. It was steep and difficult in places and bracing myself against sliding forwards, I could hear the boy's encouragement to his animal tensely clucked from between his teeth. Frankly, I can remember little of the early part. I know I lay with my body curled around Bruno, one of my arms under his head and that Cara had, in turn, curved herself against my back, her warmth welcome through my damp clothes.

Sometime in the afternoon we stopped at a poor farm, really no more than a shack by the roadside. Here I gave another coin in exchange for a dozen eggs and a flagon of milk. I mixed them with a stick in a shallow dish and made sure Bruno raised his head and took two or three gulps. Then Cara licked the dish clean. I had first swallowed a few mouthfuls of the mixture, the donkey boy gaping at the sight of this. I passed him a small coin which he exchanged with the farmer's wife for some green apples. He gobbled the lot down, just remembering to save a couple for the donkey.

I was feeling very weak as I lay there, too weak. This was more than could be accounted for by fatigue from the sleepless night or exertion dealing with the calamities. My head was swimming and I was very hot even though the evening was chill. So when I saw a shape emerging from a wraith of mist I thought I was seeing a ghost. There was an eerily insistent *clonk clonk* sound coming from behind it. Then I saw it was a donkey, the bell round its neck the source of the sound, and a herd of goats massing around it, at least a hundred of them, all of them coming steadily towards us, their footfalls muffled by the mist. A stately and almost silent procession that streamed past the cart. And then a man.

'Greetings.' The two big white dogs at the shepherd's side growled as I leaned out a hand to clasp his. He quieted them with a gesture. The dog's thick necks were stretched out as they looked up at their master and I saw how fearsome their collars were, sharply spiked all round, stark in their fur, providing protection to their throats no matter how savage the biting attacker.

We exchanged a few words the way travellers do about the safety of the routes we were taking. The shepherd pointed to the foothills he was heading to and told me he felt more fear about the wolves up there coming in the night and bringing down his dogs, mauling his helpless flock, than from any rascal trying to thieve his meagre means.

It flashed into my mind then, an image of *my* dogs' be-jewelled silver collars nestled in their soft red velvet cocoon in the bag beside me. I had to rub at my eyes with my palms. They are things of beauty, but they serve no real purpose, do they? I had to admit it to myself. Not by comparison at least, with the protection that armour I'd just seen offers to working dogs.

Page the eighth

Arriving at the house by the bridge

A murky night had drawn down under a moonless sky by the time we at last reached the town. Bassano's citizens had long since closed their shutters and only the donkey's hoofbeats on the cobbles and the cart's creaking wheels broke the silence. I was jolted awake when they went *thump thump thump* as they met the wooden planks of the bridge over the Brenta. My arm was numb under the sleeping dog's head. 'Turn left into the first street and go up to the right and stop by the second door on the left,' I croaked, my mouth dry and voice hoarse after the hours of fitful dozing. I was not feeling at all well, my head throbbing so painfully I had to brace my hand across my forehead to try and ease it.

The little donkey's long ears twitched back and she faltered to a halt as we reached the house. There was only a fractured light from a first floor window dimly streaking the street, the glow through the shutters from a dying fire in the first floor studio, I imagined. Clambering awkwardly down from the cart, I bent to pick a handful of river pebbles from the ground. I threw them up against the house and they clattered against it and fell back to the road, startlingly loud.

After a moment there was a shadow behind the shutters and I heard a voice rumbling, 'What's this foolery in the middle of the night?' Jacopo, thank the heavens.

I was so weak I had to lean on the cart as I called out my name and implored him to come to our aid. 'I have the dogs and they are sick. Come down and let us in.' What relief as the big doors were heaved open and I saw Jacopo come out and the next thing I felt was a heavy arm embracing my shoulders. I could only watch as Jacopo and the donkey boy unloaded poor Bruno, carrying him between them on one of the sacks. Cara landed heavily, stiffly, by my feet and lay down, a low groan the only noise she made.

Paolo came down the stairs then too, hair all on end and grasping at the belt of his robe as he pulled it around him. It was he and Jacopo who climbed the studio stairs with Bruno, me staggering groggily behind them. Gingerly, they lowered him to the floor in front of the fire and Cara nudged past them to flop down and huddle close by. As Paolo stoked the embers into flames and Elisabetta brought a cooking pot and hooked it to hang on the heavy chain over the flames, I gasped out some of what had befallen us. Kneeling by Bruno, Jacopo was stroking the dog's muzzle. He lifted one eyelid to reveal a glassy, clouded eye. 'Poison,' he said.

I cried out then. 'They *poisoned* him?' Jacopo put up a hand to touch my arm. 'The dogs were scavenging in the night, lad. After making their escape, they'd have been ravenous. They found something bad, carrion perhaps, or it could be mushrooms. If it's mushrooms it takes time to work, the poison.' He explained Cara was not affected so badly probably because she was a stronger dog, properly nourished since a puppy. 'You told me you don't know how Bruno fared as a puppy. That's perhaps why he's weakened so much more.' He passed a hand over Bruno's flank and said, 'Besides, you're not a young dog any more, are you, old chap?'

'Drink some soup,' Elisabetta said, handing me a bowl. My hand felt as though it belonged to someone else as I took the broth from her but the taste and the warmth of it were wonderfully good. I must have slurped and slurped.

'Yes, drink it all down and then get some sleep. By the morning we'll know whether all will be well for the dogs. I'm giving them both an antidote now, that's all there is to be done. It's grave, grave – but we must hope fervently. And pray.'

I said, 'Amen' to that and tried to cross myself but my arm was no longer acting as it should. 'Lad, are you quite well?' Jacopo asked me. 'You look completely done in, so no more talk now.' And for me, there was no more talk for some time after that.

Page the ninth

THREE WEEKS LATER

I recover and learn what has happened

Or thereabouts. I came back to myself only very slowly after the fever went down and no one here can tell me exactly which day it was that I could really be called 'well' again. When I could sit up and look about me and thought to ask what day it was I learned it was a Monday and we were in the midst of the month of July. 'July? But we've not had midsummer.' 'Midsummer? Not any more, my lad,' Elisabetta told me. It was she, Jacopo's wife, who had tended me through all the numberless days of fever, sweating and the icy chills, she who brought the tisane Jacopo concocted which was the only thing that eased the aching I felt all over my body. And it was she who explained what had happened, all I hadn't known about as I lay there in a room kept quiet with the shades down.

'It's ten days ago now the great storm came,' she said, 'and it has not stopped raining since.' I could tell the light was quite different than before, when the house was always filled with sparkling light reflected off the river. Now the light was louring and greenish and when I looked out, the sky and the river roaring dully below the house were matched in their ugly dull grey colour. Slashes of rain were blowing about in all that grey, gusted here and there by the wind. 'We're trapped here because of this,' said Elisabetta, 'Nothing's coming in or out of the town, what with the roads blocked still with fallen trees and the valley completely flooded. We lost our fine bridge too, to that cursed storm.' I'd gasped when I realised the bridge had gone, the supports in mid-river snapped off and the rest of it swept away, I supposed. The swirling water was full of debris, carrying whole tree trunks as it rushed on by and there were great rocks it had brought down from the mountain pass lying in a morass of mud where there had once been a pleasant meadow starred with daisies.

I asked Elisabetta did she know when the roads would be open again. She laughed at me and said, 'Well, who can know? But you're not the only one who's asking that. Our fine lady from Venice and her young companion are also very keen to be on their way. Until you're penned in you don't know how much your freedom matters, do you?'

I had just remembered the dogs and their plight – how did I not think of them first? – and so I gave little attention to what she'd told me. As though to match my thought, I heard a scratching sound and a squeal. The dogs? I knew it was them but still had to call out, 'Cara, Bruno, is it you? Are you there?' I heard how pathetically weak my voice was. It made me feel faint when Elisabetta opened the door and they came to me. I'd had to flop back on the bed and they made little noises of excitement when they reached me and both of them wanted to lick my hand at the same time. They were much changed. I saw that first in their eyes as I stroked their faces. And then in how they moved: no bounding and leaping, just a slow and hesitant gait, Bruno's leg still bandaged so he limped badly.

'Jacopo saved them,' I blurted out and had to look away from her because I was close to tears.

'Touch and go it was, at first,' said Elisabetta. 'Fortunately, he'd picked all the herbs to make the concoctions for them – and for you – before the storm destroyed our garden. How he knows what mix to make, I'll never understand but he had great success with his healing. You'll see that when you examine the cuts they had all over them, even that terrible wound on Cara's ear is getting better.'

Page the tenth

Jacopo explains how things are

I must have still been very weak because I wasn't allowed to talk any more that day. The following morning I was relieved when Jacopo came into the room. Now I would get a clear picture about the calamities that had befallen Zantani – and me – since we'd last been in Jacopo's company.

I wanted to hear news immediately but Jacopo put his role as my physician above being a bearer of tidings ill or good. He said, 'The fever's behind you at last,' putting his palm flat on my brow before sitting in the chair by my bed. 'Now you must take it quietly before any exertion.' I must have sighed because he looked at me sympathetically before saying, 'If it would interest you to sit in the studio during the day, then Paolo and I will be happy to see you there.'

So I am truly an invalid, I thought to myself, invited to sit and watch while others work. 'Before you come down and join us at the table for meals let me explain the circumstances in the house at present,' Jacopo continued. He went on to tell me things that were the *last* things I'd have imagined. Signora Helena was in Bassano, was in this house as a guest, trapped here with her maid since the storm destroyed any chance of leaving the town.

'She's here – *why*?' I asked. 'And what about Zantani. Is he alright?'

'He has survived,' Jacopo told me, 'the doctors patching him up as best they could. But although he heals slowly in his body, his mind is not at rest. He frets constantly and is low. Signora Helena, in despair, decided to come here for my help in finding two dogs for him.'

'Two dogs? *Another* couple?' I could make no sense of this.

'She felt only through the companionship of similar dogs would her husband ever recover. Because you see, in Venice they'd had no word you'd found Cara and Bruno and come to me with them. Your message to Zantani was never delivered.'

'It never reached him? So he'd have thought them lost forever. The poor man *would* be low. Ah, though, now at least he knows they are safe and also that I'm here and have got their collars back.'

'No, Tomaso, he doesn't – because we've not been able to get any message at all out since the storm. It has meant the Signora's been fearing Zantani will have been even more badly affected in his spirits, worrying about her whereabouts and her safety.' Jacopo sighed and then he asked me, 'Tomaso, but what's this I heard you say about the dogs' collars?'

'You didn't know I had them safe in Zantani's bag?'

'His travelling bag? Why no – we passed that to the Signora and I don't know whether Marina unpacked it for her. She has not said anything to me about collars.'

'Marina? Is this Marina perhaps come from Venice?'

'Accompanying the Signora, why yes, a lettered girl, the Signora's assistant for her writing.'

Fortune, it seemed, had something good in store for me after my pain and misery. It was the same Marina I'd first encountered while working at the Bomberg press in Venice. Come from the ghetto, she had been waiting for her father to finish delivery of his Hebrew texts for printing. We'd exchanged only a greeting then but afterwards I'd wished for a way to see her again. Now together in Bassano, that has been granted me. We meet daily.

Good fortune indeed, I quickly realising Marina's is company I'd like to have as often as I can, for as long as I can. If not forever.

'What the eye doesn't see the heart will not yearn for,' is a saying Nonna would often repeat. Seeing Marina, I still yearn. I yearn to hear her lilting voice, for example, if she is upstairs and I down, with its trace of an accent from her years in the Ottoman lands. I have grown fond.

The end and perhaps a beginning

Ending these notes, which began by recounting such terrible events, I have at least then some small optimism to report, like the first green shoot of spring to push up through the dark earth. Magnifico Zantani is alive and there is hope he will heal, the dogs are frail but getting stronger and are always spirited, as is their way, and I am leaving my sickness behind at last.

Now that the waters have gone down in the valley, the roads are being cleared and the Signora and Marina will soon travel to Venice.

Between us we have agreed a plan that I will follow them there, accompanying Jacopo. He will carry the finished portrait and I will be in charge of the dogs. We shall reunite all of these elements with Magnifico Zantani. Signora Helena has accepted this proposal at Jacopo's prompting, he having persuaded her it is the only way her husband's heart can be set to rest, his poor broken body be allowed to heal.

As to the future, it is not for me to predict whether I meet with good or bad. I can hope to be lucky in love, to somehow make Marina a part of my life. I can pray. But as always, what choice is there really – other than to allow Fortune's fickle finger to determine how our dice will fall?

CHAPTER FOUR

16 June

We group at the foot of the Villa's steps as usual to greet the Master arriving from Padua. But this time there is not the usual clatter and flurry in the stable yard, since he has brought no entourage to speak of: his valet, four scribes and two grooms only, the outriders to be lodged in the village.

'Peace at last! This is what I've been waiting for,' he calls out as he comes along the path towards us, cap off and cloak swinging behind him, throwing out an arm to take in the view down across the gardens, and beyond, the wide sky above the pastures. 'Ah *yes*, quiet days, no university business, no petitions to sign, no despatches to read, no convocations and *no* meetings,' he says, slapping my shoulder and shaking my hand at the same time. As usual he has news and he reels it off rapidly and loudly right there, the family's welfare and whereabouts, his movements.

Close to my ear he says, 'Keep it to yourself for the time being, but I am appointed ambassador again, to the Sublime Porte at Constantinople this time.' He's stroking that long dark beard of his and gives me a great grin before he says, louder, 'So, Tomaso, I intend to indulge my leisure while I'm here, since this will be my last visit to the Villa for a while to come.' He smiles at Marina, chucks the baby under the chin and pats little Carlo's head.

'Ah Paolo, you're here? Had a look at my Nymphaeum, have you? And you have been at work, some new delight to show me? Let's see it, man.' He sweeps up the steps, pulling off his cloak. Mercifully, just in time we'd got the sacks of pigment, the pots of paint, the buckets of lime and all the other paraphernalia cleared from the salon, the flagstones scrubbed spotless and polished. The Master first turns right into the Hall of Olympus but once he has spun on his heel and walked towards the long windows, he is quick to spot the new addition.

'I like it,' he pronounces promptly. This is my first proper view too, and I'm curious to know how alike what the Master observes is to the sketch Francesco showed me. Well, it is superlatively achieved as always, as far as I'm concerned. Not that I claim expertise in these matters but it would be difficult, no, I think *impossible*, to better convey that scene: the shimmering greens Paolo has used and the translucent quality of that wispily-streaked pale blue sky – so very like the one we sat under last evening. Above, a view of ruins painted so faithfully it is as though I'm glancing at them from our terrace here – the balustrade framing it is of identical white-golden stone. A morning scene, the shadows telling us the sun is on the rise. If that's Francesco's work, then the boy shows a lot of promise, I'd say.

In the foreground, a large brown dog with a white blaze on his grizzled muzzle stands, brown ears flopping forward. He left paw is lifted, he busy with it. A good likeness to my mind. But the Master, does he recognise Bruno? He does. 'Bruno,' he says. Looking at Paolo he jokes, 'I'm glad you gave him a good bone to chew on.'

I am thinking, surely the Master realises Bruno is not licking his paw after devouring a bone? No, that's the paw wounded in the attack. Rightly, Paolo has depicted the damage done, just as Jacopo, when painting the dogs' portrait all those years ago, clearly depicted the slash on Cara's ear, the one that would always remain a prominent scar.

Paolo does not react though, otherwise pre-occupied, bringing Francesco forward, to explain his part in completing the fresco and inform the Master of the mission that has brought the young man to Maser.

17 June

He is tireless the Master, a devil for detail. He said he'd come to Maser to rest but as we walk round the Villa and into the grounds to inspect the tree planting, the rose beds, the vegetable garden, the orders he throws back at me over his shoulder easily fill three pages of my notebook, close-written too. This evening he hosts a dinner for neighbouring gentry. Checking the settings on the long table in the Hall of Olympus, I'm satisfied with our work, Marina's baskets of peach-coloured roses placed at either end, and the tall sticks resplendent with twenty-four white candles. The guests will dine in their warm light, the gods up above gleaming and glowing as they look down. It gives me pleasure to see the room put to good use. We may be grumbling away below stairs but I believe we think it worth it, all the work we have to put in.

Paolo, accustomed to mixing with such fine folk, joins the table. Marina and I are between stairs, ensuring the silver tureen of cook's porcini broth (guinea fowl stock its base) gets carried up safely, then the change of plates for the course following: sheep's kidneys in red wine sauce. To be followed by fish fried with capers and preserved lemons. One year ago the Master stocked the new pool created when the Nymphaeum was built. The fingerlings thrived in the crystal spring water. Had he looked from his window at first light today, he would have enjoyed the ease with which three of the yard lads were using their rods and a mayfly bait to catch his supper.

All through the day yesterday since the Master's arrival and today too, I have had the feeling Francesco has been stalking me. I have had *no* time to stop and talk to him. Each time I catch sight of him I feel his glances are designed to inform me I owe him something. So, despite reading the notes and having the benefit of all I wrote, he has *more* questions – that's what it must be. I suppose I can't stall him forever.

We are at the top of the stairs, Marina and I, and I'm almost tempted to turn back when I see him down there, trying to look as though he's not waiting for me. *Lying in wait*, more like. Marina senses my hesitation and tugs at my sleeve to pull me back into the corridor. She keeps her voice low to say, 'He's exasperating you, isn't he? But don't give in to it. Let me finish up with the kitchen staff and you give our young guest a bit more time now.'

I nod and call down to ask Francesco if he fancies a turn in the gardens. The moon is waning and clouds scud across a night sky with a luminous purple tone to it. A jay squawks, flying past us fast and low as we take the path to the formal garden. Other than that, there is only the crunch of our footsteps on the gravel.

I'm taken aback when Francesco bursts out with, 'It's so *unfair*, what happened to you, Tomaso. I read it all, what you wrote. It made me so furious, I just have to tell you.' Taken with a bout of coughing, it's a good thing he has his back to me as I am finding it almost comical, his indignation. Unfair that Cara and Bruno were taken from me because the Master's friend had taken a fancy to them, I suppose that's what he refers to. But what good would it have done me, showing I minded? I shrug and say something noncommittal. He comes straight back to me. 'But you should mind at least mind *now*. About the injustice of it, I mean – that Zantani could come and take the dogs from you like that. Why did no one stop him, tell him it wasn't right?'

'Francesco, steady up lad,' I say. After a deep breath I go on, 'We are all the Master's here. Chattels, owned. Do you not see? No different from the table he eats at or the bed he sleeps on. For us, there is simply no say in decisions – even about things we may hold most dear. On this territory,' I bang my foot down on the gravel, 'the very earth beneath our feet belongs to the Master.'

He surprises me again by copying me – but his is a stamp of rage. The moonlight makes a flat plate of his face, two dark holes of his eyes, as he puts his head back and groans, as though through gritted teeth, 'How can you bear it?'

How burning is the sense of injustice felt by the young. Was I ever so irate? I suppose I must have been. But *unfair* – is that how I think about the hand fate's dealt out to me? '*How can you bear it?*' My life, something to be *endured*? I don't like this. I can't answer him calmly and walk rapidly away. The moon goes behind a cloud. *Ouch*, a pebble in my evening shoe. I pull the slipper off to shake out the stone and despite my irritation, I have to smile. It often takes a stone in your shoe to make you change your gait, does it not? Taking deep breaths, I'm trying to put myself in Francesco's position, see things as he does. See myself through his eyes: a man twice his age, old to a lad of seventeen.

I compliment myself how well settled we are here, Marina and I. Comfortable with my lot, without cause for discontent. I got what I wanted. I got Marina as a bride and a life once again back at Maser. But I am aware there is another meaning to 'settled': compromise, acceptance of a lesser choice because of weakness, fatigue. Perhaps that is what my life amounts to, perhaps I let myself down, giving up the chance of a skill and an independent existence? Given in, you could say, in just the way Grandfather warned me against.

If Francesco knew how the conversation had gone back then when I was the age he is now, at the time Grandfather told me the Master had decided to send me off to Venice to get a trade, if he had heard me talk *then*, he'd know what I found unfair. That conversation, the one that changed everything, had been a short one, Grandfather as gruff as usual as he told me the plan which he had just been informed about. I was to leave Maser, be apprenticed, join a printing house in Venice and learn the trade of making books.

'In Venice? I am to go from here? You and Nonna want that?' I had asked, as though Venice were the very furthest end of the earth. All Grandfather would say was that the Master had decided. In his impetuosity, Francesco might think I should have resisted, refused – since it was the last thing I wanted. But Grandfather and I, we both knew the Master gave no quarter, and that there was zero chance of questioning a decision.

I asked if it was to be forever. I remember Grandfather cleared his throat before he said, 'Look Tom, a craft is good. You have a great chance, getting to go out there in the world.' I must have tried to argue because he was gripping my upper arm, his face black and fierce as he said, 'Goddammit boy, don't you talk back to me. Just get off there and make your way.' He seemed to be shoving me off but then he pulled me back, 'Tom, my lad, there can be no buts in this. The Master's making sense, however we may feel about seeing you go.'

Then he did push me away, to look me in the face and ask, 'Besides, you don't want to end up like me, do you lad? Nonna and me, we're planted here on the farm, just like vegetables rooted in the Master's soil. There's nothing for us but to stay here and rot away quietly till death comes.' There was resignation but no bitterness in his voice.

Holding his gaze, seeing his wrinkles and his whiskers, that flat expression, I remember what I replied, 'Don't tell me that. It is a fine life here, Grandfather. For myself, I want no other.' But in *that* life, the one I loved, I had the dogs with me. Bruno and Cara were mine.

Everything changed for them too during that conversation. And, despite the fact they honoured me with their trust, it was *I* who coaxed them into that damn travelling box to go off with Zantani. I think of how enthusiastic they normally were, bounding about, all excited yelps and snuffles before we would go anywhere and then I remember how they were on that occasion, so *reluctant* to get into the box. I wonder, did they *know*? I had to push them in one at a time. Cara first, attempting to restrain her so she would not wriggle out the side as I tried to get Bruno in, pushing at his rump, my fingers in his fur. I heard him growl at me, a dog that had *never* been disobedient. Was he accusing me of betraying them? At the least, he must have sensed how much I did not want this journey to be taking place.

I have heard tell there's a religion in the East which believes dogs foretell death. I wonder about that too. No one died from what happened on that journey – although the few times I managed to talk with Zantani afterwards, I thought perhaps he might even have preferred death to his life of long-drawn-out suffering. Afterwards, during the years of his dead-while-still-living existence, did he think I let him down? Would he have said he blamed me if I had dared ask him outright? He was always what I think you'd describe as 'philosophical', resigned, despite how much he suffered. *'At last there comes the hunting hound that deals death and pain'*: I heard him say that more than once, a line from Dante's *Inferno* poem, he told me. He didn't blame the dogs, either – didn't have it in him to do that. Ultimately though, I believe he accepted that it had been as good as fatal, the love he had for them.

I don't see Francesco again as I go in to the Villa but bending to push across the bolt and close up the long doors, I realise Paolo is in the hall, close by the newly-completed fresco, holding up a candle to look at it.

'My final check on the work,' he explains. 'I always do it when I can because this light makes the definition of the forms more extreme, lets me see if I've done the shadows full justice.' He adds almost as though to himself, 'Shadows are important.' The candle flame is doing its work throwing shadows on to his face, making his long nose and high forehead almost devilish to look at. He has turned back to the fresco and I'm left in the dark as he says, 'You'll be glad to have Bruno here now, joining Cara. Puts things right somehow, don't you think?'

That triggers something in me and I hear myself blurting out, '*Right?* I can never make reparation to them.' I walk away fast after that, before Paolo can turn and see what's going on in my face. Anguish, that's what. What else would I be thinking about except blame, blame, blame? The dogs never hunted again, Cara deaf, her hearing destroyed with that knife slash and blow to her ear, and Bruno not able to run with any ease afterwards. And as to pointing for bird hunting, out of the question: his misshapen paw always giving him pain.

Should I be comforted by the thought we did the best we could for them, once they were with us? Spoiled them, titbits from cook's hand, soft beds and liberal praise, so they lived out comfortable lives. Perhaps. Not that my heart didn't wrench on the days they sensed the departure for the hunt, Bruno stirring at the jingling harness, the pack hounds' yelping and the first toot of the horn coming from the stable yard. Cara eyes brightened too, clearly knowing what was happening, although she couldn't hear a thing.

I should take Francesco to see their graves under the laurels, their headstones furred with moss now. I'll take him tomorrow. I always like to visit the place, remembering those quiet little ceremonies we made for them – no prayers, of course – when they had lived out their measure of days. Bruno went first. And then Cara, only months later. Marina scattered rose petals on her before they shovelled over the earth. She'd grown very fond of them both and as for Carlo, only a tot back then, he wouldn't be consoled for days.

18 June

I have not slept well. That dream I've not dreamed for so long came back. Years ago

I would have it often, Marina telling me of being woken by my shouts. My dream of being out in the forest: at first it is just an ordinary day and I'm walking with Cara and Bruno ahead of me. But then I look up and realise they are quite far distant, running fast. Dread seizes me as I see the direction they've taken. They must have the scent of wild boar. They are running straight into danger because I know the boar are there, deep in the undergrowth. The great heavy beasts will be foraging away placidly, snouts down, but a noisy dog appearing, they will spin on those dainty hooves of theirs to thrust with their deadly tusks.

In my dream I am whistling the dogs back, calling them to heel. I want to stroke their heads, put them on the leash, pat their heaving flanks. But this is a *bad* dream and call as I might, my voice comes out as little more than a squeak and they race away ahead, unheeding, crashing into the thickets, yelping with joy. I'm straining to hear them, follow where they've gone, pushing into dark places against thorny branches that spring back across my face, dreading the squeal that will announce one has been gored, those cruel tusks ripping into a belly or a chest.

The dream never allows me the full story. I never reach them, never get them safely on the leash. I wake from it sweating and distressed, cheated somehow. The anxiety of not knowing what happened nags at me all day.

Last night I stayed awake once the confounded dream had shaken me and I'd heaved up from my pillows with a shuddering start. What relief when at last light crept into our room and I could begin my day. My morning routine: getting the house opened up, unlocking doors, raising blinds, greeting the staff, listing their tasks, soothes me. My mood is better by the time I come into the kitchen where Francesco and Marina are at breakfast.

'Goodness, Tomaso,' Marina says, all rosy and smiling, 'Francesco has been asking me how you and I met. It has made me remember our days in Venice and I have been telling him of my father's association with Magnifico Zantani. It's a long time since I've thought of all that. Such an age ago. When we were young.'

Ah, that *was* an age ago. Young, were we ever as young as Francesco is now?

Remembering last night and my reaction to his opinion of me, I ask myself, have I reached the time when I'm to be thought of as *old*? Surely it's more that your youth stays inside you? Today's delivery of vegetables is piled up by the door. I bend and pick up a brown-skinned onion, turn it round in my hands and I think, we are like onions. I'm not trying to be clever or mystical – but we *are*. Like onions, we have many layers, grown over time, layers formed around a core that stays green and fleshy. How different the inner from the outer appearance, how juicy and fresh and vital that core, how papery and insubstantial the brown skin, so fragile it can be rubbed off with the fingers. *But*, however strong the contrast, you can't deny it is still all onion, can you? Onion all the way through.

Francesco is off again, shooting out his questions. This time he has Marina in his sights, so I can move to the table and sit quietly spreading a slice of bread with the fresh cream just in from the dairy. I am daydreaming a little, reaching for the dish of honey that's been turned into a golden disc by a shaft of sunlight just tipping the table, when I realise where their conversation is going.

'No,' I hear Marina say, 'If Magnifico Zantani ever showed my father the portrait of Bruno and Cara once Tomaso had brought it to Venice, he never mentioned it to me.'

It was from me, in fact, that Marina first heard of the painting, during our first days getting to know each other in Bassano. After the rainstorms finally ceased I was allowed to sit out on a bench in Jacopo's garden. One day while I took the sun, she came by and I invited her to join me. In one of our first conversations I described how I was spending my days with Jacopo, he devoting much time to the portrait, first sketching his canine models in all their different positions, studying them as they sat quietly or paced about the studio. Sometimes he would pat gently at their heads or bending down, stroke their bellies. Often Paolo would come over where Jacopo was and open his sketchbook, I told her. He'd dip his quill in the inkpot and begin to work.

One morning Paolo arrived at the studio before Jacopo. I watched him prowling around to find the best place to position the two objects he was carrying. Models of dogs. Yes, it was Cara and Bruno he carried, versions not much bigger than my hand but unmistakably the two dogs, modelled in warm red clay. I remember him explaining, 'I have made these as aids to help Jacopo with his portrait. He complains he can't capture the light and shadow on the dogs' coats satisfactorily because they move and shift about. Not so obligingly static as human models, are they?'

I come out of my reverie of those past days to hear Marina saying to Francesco, 'My father *did* tell me Zantani held dogs in very high regard, saying, in fact, that often he had more time for dogs than for people. Due to their nobility and selflessness.' She looks over at me then and says, 'Oh, Tomaso, you'll remember, how did he put it, Zantani, that business about the generous man and the giving of alms?'

Before I get my mouth open Francesco says, 'The man with the good eye gives the fortieth part. But dogs, they give us their everything.'

I am startled. 'Zantani told you that?'

'No.' Francesco is smiling a strange little smile.

'How do you know about it then?' Marina and I chime in unison.

Francesco's smile stays on his lips a little longer before he relents. He starts in to tell us about meeting Magnifico Zantani's niece, Maddalena. He has reached the part where they are in a gondola crossing the Venice lagoon by night when he stops and reaches a hand into his doublet, pulling out the last thing I would have expected: a fancy pair of earrings. Green and yellow stones set in gold.

Marina gasps, 'Oh, how beautiful.'

Francesco holds one up between finger and thumb and we get a good look as he lets it hang tantalisingly down in front of my wife's nose, which is practically twitching with pleasure at the sight. Only one other jewel, her betrothal ring – with which I was able to present her at our engagement thanks to Signor Zantani's generosity – only that beauteous thing had ever made her eyes go wide just so. 'Please accept a trinket from one of my collections,' Zantani had said when he handed it to me on that momentous day when I arrived in Venice and was reunited with Marina. Trinket! We were stupefied at its gold tracery, the inset gems of rose pink and sky blue.

I am wild with curiosity about these earrings and how Francesco comes to have them but the door bangs open. Paolo is there, cap on, riding whip in hand.

'Dressed like that, you are the spit of your self-portrait in the fresco upstairs, the one with the greyhound where you look in through the salon door,' Francesco remarks cheerily.

But Paolo is not here for idle chatter. 'Come. It is time. The Master's ready to ride out.' We must have looked complicit, the three of us, because he says, 'You are thick as thieves, aren't you? What *are* you up to?' but then he backs out of the door, not staying for an answer.

Thieves? Francesco wouldn't have *stolen* those earrings, would he? No, he would never be so brazen in front of us about a *theft*. He has already left the kitchen so I can't press him for the truth. Casting a quizzical look at Marina as I heave on my boots, I ask her, 'You recall that saying that it is the servants who know everything that goes on in a house, can tell you everyone's business? Well, I can't agree that has been the case here these last couple of days.'

Marina shrugs, her comical little smile showing as she voices my thoughts, 'What a relief they are all due to go soon. Left to our own devices, we'll soon have order restored.'

EIGHT

Barbaro

18 June

Today I shall ride with Tomaso around the estate, good policy to check the perimeter once in a while. Broken gates, fences down, doubtless – and a slew of poachers' snares to search out and remove. I have invited Paolo and his young friend to join our party.

A pretty day. The horses fresh, we head for a grassy ride over on the estate's eastern edge and get in a good long gallop before cutting across the forest to the northern boundary. Fanning out here, we work our way along it, two or three times having to dismount and hack the undergrowth, go on foot to lead our mounts through. We have been out a good three hours, I'd say, the sun well up over our heads when we take a slope down into a dell, a stream running along its base. Reining in, I ask Tomaso, 'This place, do you remember how Zantani loved it?'

'He always wanted to stop awhile here, Master.'

'Shall we then do likewise?' We loosen the girths and the horses step into the stream, hooves crunching on the pebbles. One whinnies and shudders and they all blow and snort as they drink. I cup my hands to drink too, the water icy fresh. I splash some on my face. Tomaso and Francesco are manoeuvring a fallen tree trunk into the shade of willows which hang their lacy branches almost into the water. We sit ourselves down, the fine river gravel pleasantly warm to the touch and the trunk good support for our backs. Sprawled, we pass an idle hour discussing country concerns, the sort of things a man's mind turns to when he gets out and breathes the air: prospects for the summer wheat crop (worrying, the rumour about black spot); the new brood mare bought at auction due to arrive at the stables soon.

After a while, midday summer somnolence silences us until the lad Francesco coughs. With half an ear I hear him ask Tomaso, 'When shall we talk about how dogs are trained for hunting?'

Training hounds? – always happy to talk about that. I don't wait on Tomaso answering. 'Hunting's of interest to you, is it? Want to know more about our sport?' I launch straight in, 'Here at Maser we have a pack of hounds trained for going after stags. Then retrievers, dogs expressly for when we fly the falcons. We'll be on horseback for that, sending the hawks out from the wrist to prey on the game birds, making their pursuit and kill in mid-flight, just as they would in the wild.'

Then a while back, we also began hunting with crossbows to bag birds, hunting on foot, that is, padding alongside the hounds through the mud. It makes me laugh when I remember how keen brother Daniele and I were to instigate those bird hunts at Maser. I explain, 'We wanted to outdo those Medici grandees who had just started a craze over in Florence. As a pastime for guests, you understand, in one of the fancy gardens with which they are embellishing the city. They would use a net, flinging it to trap the hapless birds. Then they'd give the gentlemen, some ladies too, I'm told, bows and arrows to shoot at them. Confined inside the net, I mean. Unchivalrous, don't you think? Call that sport? Here at Maser we decided we would pit ourselves against the creatures in open country, and to bring them down we would use crossbows loaded with bolts.'

Those heavy things, *oof*. In present company I will not let on how excruciating it was, learning to shoot with a crossbow, to keep steady and look accomplished while your shoulder muscles scream, to aim well while your eyes water with the effort. I go on, 'In a bird hunt we use the dogs to point and flush the quarry out, of course. And for that, the hounds require a very specialised training. Isn't that so, Tomaso?' Let him explain. It was Tomaso's ability with those two hounds of his that, after all, made bird hunting come together so well for us at Villa Barbaro.

'You are right, Master,' he says. 'They do. I was fortunate to have a couple of dogs of exceptional intelligence and obedience. In the mornings, thanks to the old Master's generosity, I was being schooled – but the rest of the day, I had time to work with the dogs on the techniques of pointing, flushing and retrieving. Grandfather gave me some tips on what to do – I never knew where he got that knowledge from.' Tomaso makes a good fist of describing how he used his grandfather's replica of a bird, one the old man had whittled out of beech wood especially for him. Tying the bird on the end of a string, he would trail it through the long grass, jerking it to simulate a pheasant's movements once it has been frightened, flushed out, that is, by a dog's presence. He stands up to demonstrate, his expression comical, and we have to laugh.

The trick, he says to Francesco, is to get control over the dog's instincts to pounce. First, so that the bird stays where it is while the archer readies his aim and secondly, so that the pointing dog focuses on cooperating with the other one, the one that's been circling the hiding place. The two of them need to act in unison when the signal is given for them to bound in and startle the bird up. 'I made mistakes in my training,' Tomaso confesses – always a modest one – 'but I tried to be consistent with the calls and signals I used, and I rewarded the dogs well for their efforts.'

'Bruno and Cara, were those the special dogs?' asks Francesco, beaming that bright smile of his at Tomaso.

'Yes. With that, as with everything, they learned quickly.'

I come in again here and say, 'They *were* fine. You did your best job ever with those dogs, Tomaso. I've never forgotten them.' Sometimes in fact, I've wondered why was it so memorable, watching that particular couple of Tomaso's at work. Never could really satisfy myself with an answer. But maybe now I will, so I ask, 'That couple of yours stood out from all the others, didn't it? Why do you think that was?'

'They were always eager, Master. Well, *all* dogs are that on the hunt. But they, they were so proud and pleased with themselves, weren't they, when they had successes for us?'

'Could it be we took to them strongly just because they were *not* noble to look at, not graceful in form, not even well-matched?' I say. 'Just a couple of farm dogs after all, no matter how fine the condition you kept them in.'

'But what I want to know....' the lad Francesco suddenly says.

I catch Tomaso raising his eyebrows and exchanging a glance with Paolo before he says, smoothly and rather loudly, 'Master, with respect, Francesco would like to hear how you identify prowess in a hunting dog.'

'Prowess sustained like Cara and Bruno's was rare, let me say for a start,' I reply, 'but those two dogs left behind a standard our kennel lads have had to work continually to try and match. And to this day you still have to be there, don't you, Tomaso? Forever at their elbows instructing and correcting.' Tomaso nods. I seem to have the lad Francesco's attention still, so I talk on, telling him what, if I were to be out with a really well trained couple of hounds, I'd reckon to be a good day in the copses.

'We would have got a bird hunkering down futilely in an attempt at invisibility', I explain. 'One hound would be standing immobile, with its paw held high, muzzle down, nose thrust deeply into the bush. The other would spring in to join it, and alerted by the commotion, the terrified pheasant would try for its escape, lumbering upwards, wings flapping, squawks of alarm shattering the still morning. There'd be a flash of silvery sunlight off its hot ginger-red and bright green-blue plumage as it gained height. It would be juddering with the effort of accelerating away. And you, Tomaso, during this getaway flight you'd be standing with your couple at your heels, yes? And all three of you would be tense, the dogs poised for your signal. You'd flick your hand or give a command in a low voice. And with that, they'd be released.'

I am in my stride now. No reason not to continue – the lad apparently still paying attention.

'At that point it'd be time for a hunter to step forward. He would have his jaw clenching, his eyes bulging with the strain of drawing the bow back to his shoulder. Then he'd release the blunt-nosed bolt. *Whang!* off it would go.' I laugh, remembering how much fortunate prey evaded those first poor efforts of ours.

'Even with a true aim,' I tell them, 'a bird struck wouldn't always immediately fall. Instead, it would fly on over the fields. When it finally did plummet to the ground the hounds would already have tracked it and be there to retrieve it. One of them would bound back with the prize drooping from its jaws. Ah yes, that would be what a good day's like. Eventually darkness would drop blue-grey over the treetops. Blurred in the dusk, the couples, panting, would still be circling the thickets, their tails waving, waving. That's the moment I'd shout, "That's it. We are for home, sound the retreat," and we'd hear the horn's mourning tone cutting through the mist drifting across the valley, signalling the end of our pleasures.'

They are silent after I finish this monologue, as though I've described something sombre. What can do I do to break the mood? I clap my hands together and say, 'Ah, yes, does my heart good, this reminiscing.'

'Signor, may I tell you what I don't understand?' Francesco's on me with his next question almost immediately. He is persistent, I'll say that, and sure enough, he carries right on when I nod my head. 'Signor Zantani was so proud of his dogs….' he starts.

Tomaso interrupts to say, 'If I may, Master? Francesco's opinion was formed when he met the Magnifico in Venice just shortly before he passed away, may his soul rest in peace. At that time Francesco was fortunate enough to be shown the portrait of Bruno and Cara that his father had painted.'

Ah yes, my dear departed friend Antonio, obsessed with those dogs and that portrait you'd had made of them, weren't you? Right up to the end.

Francesco, not put off by the interruption, starts questioning me again, 'Did he *want* the dogs shown like that, bedraggled, that is? Didn't he care they'd always be remembered in that poor state? I mean no impertinence in this, Signor Barbaro, but why wouldn't the Magnifico have preferred them portrayed in fine condition, decked out with those fancy collars he'd had made?'

'Zantani had nothing to do with the final appearance of the painting you saw,' Paolo interjects. Normally such a mild fellow, the look he's fixing Francesco with is so firm you might even describe it as forbidding. 'No', he says, 'It is time you realise it was your father who decided everything about the portrait's final composition.' Almost as an aside he adds, 'And your father who took all the risk.'

The lad looks chastened, so I ask, 'Paolo, you know this because you were there with Bassano when the portrait was made, I presume?'

'I was. And you know, when Jacopo told me what he'd decided to do, I didn't even try to caution him against it. He'd not have been persuaded anyway.' He laughs. 'I soon understood Jacopo was completely determined to fulfil the commission. He *wanted* to paint the dogs, you see. Had wanted to before they were hurt, to do this new thing, make them a portrait's sole subject. Subsequently, he became even more resolute *because* of the dogs' injuries, I think. As a finger in the face of those who had done such harm to them.'

'You are saying he had no concern that, as subjects, they could not be considered beautiful?' I ask.

Paolo answers, 'First, Jacopo was fearless about what people would think of the portrait. Then he was determined to celebrate Cara and Bruno because of their bravery. He believed they had souls and he discerned beauty in that, while Zantani ...'

I interrupt him, 'Ah, Zantani, the beauty he saw was *not* that. It was in the hounds' prowess, in their performance that he valued because it excelled over others.'

'Fearless,' Francesco is saying. 'So you're telling me that's how it came about, Paolo? Father just went ahead and did it – fearlessly.'

'Yes,' says Paolo, turning back to him. 'It wasn't for *novelty* that he wanted to paint the portrait, it was for *truth*. Your father claimed a clear justification for it: that he was only doing what Zantani had instructed. "Remember the Magnifico's words to me, Paolo?" he asked me. I did – and I gave him the reply he wanted, "Maestro, the two dogs I shall bring to you are to be painted exactly as they are."'

'My father *was* brave, *did* innovate.' I detect relief in the lad's voice.

'Yes, Francesco. Did then, still does – powered by the force of his ideas.'

There is an obvious question here. I make sure it's asked. 'But Paolo, Francesco, forgive me, aren't all you artists doing that, innovating, I mean? Isn't that what you're *for*? If not, then I must hear from you what is it that's going on in those heads of yours, all the hours you spend on a stool sitting and gazing at a blank canvas.'

They laugh, but from Paolo, obviously impatient to press on with his point, I sense it is merely politeness. 'It sounds as though that's a surprise to you, Francesco, Jacopo's innovation. How can that be, from you who work by your father's side? You've told me yourself how often he'd instruct, "*Look*, look. Only by looking will you learn to see." That was his aim, you know: to transform how we look at things. Through exactitude. That's what he wanted for us: eyes that look. And while painting the portrait of the two dogs, it is my belief it was that idea that impassioned him.'

I am lying back, eyes closed in the pleasing warmth, so I don't see the lad's expression. He says nothing and Paolo presses on again, sounding to me as though he's been waiting a while to speak like this to Francesco. Voice louder, words more rapid, he says, 'Jacopo wanted to make us see because when we see, we believe. He wanted us to believe in the nobility of dogs and their rightful place as the subject of paintings.'

'Hmm, that's original thinking,' I say.

'Original,' echoes Francesco.

'You must know what an original mind your father has?' Paolo's prompting the lad again.

'He does?'

'Why yes, *think* about it.'

To my ear, Paolo is impatient now as he says, 'Even now I'm sure Jacopo still experiments with coloured chalks, doesn't he? Others have followed him, yes, but he, all that while back, was the first. And then there are his different styles over the years, all the striking poses he tried out for his figures, how he has incorporated elements of other artists' techniques. These *pastorals* you've started on now with him, there's a perfect example of something new.'

I hear Francesco having another of his bouts of coughing. I open an eye to see the lad clutching at his chest, rocking back and forward, scrambling up and bending over the stream to scoop up a palmful of water. Turning back with a face all shiny and dripping, he seems undeterred, is ready with yet something more to ask. 'Is there then a style that sets our Bassano work apart? Tell me what it is, if there is.'

Paolo laughs before he answers the lad with a question of his own, 'What is it that

Francesco Bassano will be leaving behind as his mark on history, is that what you really want to know? You surely asked Giorgio Vasari that.'

Francesco shakes his head.

'You didn't? Well, it's a big question.'

I butt in with, 'And aren't most of you artists too busy getting by, day by day, to be answering such a thing?'

Ignoring me, Paolo persists, 'You really didn't get to speak of posterity with Vasari? That surprises me. Because one of his pet theories is that the artists before us still lend their hands to lift us higher. Although dead and gone, that is. In Vasari's view, if we succeed at all today it is because we are in debt to the great ones of the past who persist in helping us on our way.'

'As though we artists are a brotherhood?' asks Francesco.

'Very fancy,' I say, breaking in here. 'But a theory's just a theory. Pretty words don't always work out in practice. And Vasari, he who is a master of making sure his own advance matters most, Vasari himself would be the first to admit that.'

A long silence follows, each of us left to our own thoughts, broken into by Francesco's voice once again. This time he pipes up with, 'I have what Signor Vasari wants now, I believe.'

'You have enough, do you?' says Paolo.

'At last,' says Tomaso.

'At last, I think I almost do,' says Francesco.

'So, what happens next?'

'He said I should write to him at Florence.'

I have to interject, 'Write to Vasari? I wouldn't do that, Francesco. You would be foolish to hope for Vasari's attention if that's how you try to get it. Believe me, Vasari's a man with as many projects as a juggler has balls in the air.' Quite possibly *too* many for his own or anyone else's good, I sometimes think. I lean towards the lad, 'You can't rely on him reading any letter you send. It's more than likely to be opened by a secretary and added to a pile which Giorgio will never see.'

It's a hollow little thing, the lad's voice, when he says, 'Then I don't know however I shall reach him.'

'Oh, you must go there and buttonhole him,' I say breezily, lying back again. In the new silence that follows that remark I am thinking, Florence, go to Florence – well, why not? I could usefully bring forward my visit there, could I not?

Thinking more of it on the ride back, I remind myself of the matters I have in Florence on which Vasari must be persuaded to advise me, however busy the fellow claims to be. The purchase of paintings and sculpture for the ambassadorial residence in Constantinople, for example, and then the gifts of state to commission. For my presentation to the Sultan, Suleiman the Magnificent, that potentate famed for being most discerning in his taste.

As a side matter, it could be amusing too to witness this Bassano boy trying to sway Giorgio's editorial hand to favour his father. Yes, it could be an entertainment, being party to his attempts – the idea quite tickles my fancy.

Anyway, he makes for uncomplicated enough company, if one contrives to fend off his sometimes overweening curiosity. Grinning away, there he is now, repeating a little ditty:

> The hunt is up! the hunt is up.
> The horses snort to be at the sport,
> The dogs are running free.
> The woods rejoice at the merry noise
> Of hey tantara tee ree!

Charming enough and a good rhythm – but beginning to become monotonous, since seemingly he has only the one verse off by heart.

Not until we are almost back at the Villa do we speak again. Breaking off from his chorus, Francesco asks in that abrupt way of his, 'Do you believe there's bad luck in the forest?'

Paolo responds, asking in a mild tone, 'Why do you want to know that?'

'That demon I saw, that carved panel at the door to the church in Verona, where I went with Signora Elena ….'

'San Zenobio, you must mean.'

'Yes. Well, there's this demon grinning madly while watching a king hunting in the forest, pursuing a stag, his dogs' jaws almost on it.'

Curious, I ask, 'A demon and a king, Francesco, what's this?'

'Signora Elena knew the old story and she told me. She said the king had sold his soul to the demon in exchange for the pleasure of the chase. The panel shows him happy since he's on the brink of success with the kill. Of course, anyone can see disaster waits for him and he'll end up in Hell. That's why the demon's grin is so wide.' What the lad says next comes out in a spurt, 'Now I have understood about all the bad luck Signor Zantani had, I've been wondering whether you think the Magnifico made some such bargain.'

'*No.*' It is Tomaso who has spoken, shifting in his saddle suddenly and startling his mount. He *commands* the lad to silence, using the tone with which I've heard him discipline a puppy getting out of hand. It is effective, Francesco blushing and looking down. Hmm, having told us that he '*almost*' has his story, what he has so far will have to do – because I have no inclination to be pressed further on what I know. Tomaso's interjection has saved me from that risk for the moment – but how long will that last? I have an uneasy feeling the lad's instincts tell him some essential element is being held back from this story he seeks.

Antonio, my friend, the story of you and your dogs – it is really quite disturbing having those events of so long ago raked over again. You, at least, rest tranquilly in your grave now, I hope. Alas that I could not attend your funeral, be at your grave to give your eulogy – but had I been there, my words would have celebrated our times as young men together, praised your exuberance and zest. But, given that true friendship allows for acknowledging weaknesses as well as strengths, silently I would also have thought of your wilfulness and self-indulgence. Yes, I would. And I must say, of your acquisitiveness too, how when you wanted a thing you would not be nay-sayed. You felt entitled – and my, how you did insist on always getting your own way.

'May I, Signor?'

A groom leads off my mount. The hounds kennelled in the next yard signal they have heard our arrival, barking drowning out anything I might say. Hounds: with you, Zantani, there again the same thing, wasn't it? That particular couple, Cara and Bruno, of whom we've been speaking today, for example, it was from me you got the notion you could have them as your own. Why ever did I come up with that fool idea to propose we barter? Because, once it had been suggested they could be yours, you *wanted* them. Wanted them badly, didn't you, my friend? I should *never* have suggested exchanging the hounds for one of your objects.

Your objects: all of them covetable in their own way, the product of a refined taste honed by that 'eye' of yours, the eye from which you always wanted your friends to benefit. Why indeed, this very Villa is only as it is through your timely introduction of Andrea Palladio. Daniele and I are forever indebted to you for finding us our architect.

Going through the Hall of Olympus now, to my right and left are many fabulous things you led me into purchasing. The magnificent glass from Ballarin of Murano in this cabinet, for example. It was you, Antonio, who insisted I order it. First, a slender jug with a delicate lip and an elegant curved handle. Enamelled with flowers and leaves, a twisted, raised band of gold encircling its base and turquoise, dark blue, green, red and yellow singing out from a clear ground. Then, if I liked that, you said, I must look at two goblets decorated with strawberries and daisies.

'Order ten more – and why not add serving platters, a dozen plates and some delicate little side dishes too?' you asked. When you really approved of something your voice took on a honeyed tone, 'They will be exquisitely flamboyant in the candlelight, dazzling your guests around that long table you plan to have in the dining hall.' And so I did. And so they do, the beautiful, precious things.

Back then it must have been something else, something you had recently acquired for yourself, that took my fancy. For the life of me I cannot remember now what it was. One of your famous medals perhaps. Or was it entirely frivolous, a pair of gloves maybe, gloves like these I am throwing down now on the chest? I loved your gloves, you always went for subtle shades of leather and had them squirrel fur-lined in winter. Did I perhaps admire the neat buttons, beading and delicate embroidery of a pair you were carrying? Whatever the item was, you must have refused my offer to purchase it.

'A barter then? Let me have them, Antonio. In exchange, take whichever couple of my dogs you care to choose.' That I do remember saying. Extravagantly. I would *eat* those words now, if I could have them back. Then, I never gave a thought to the effect it might have on Tomaso, Bruno and Cara being handed over summarily like that. Now I see it must have been inexplicable to him, to be suddenly deprived of the dogs he'd lavished care on since he was a child as well as trained them up over all those hours.

The barter part of it all, that at least he never got to hear about, thank the Lord Jesus and Mary. Yes, thank the heavens Tomaso has never known that what the dogs went through with Antonio in the forest was the outcome of a mere whim on my part.

One rich man's idle whim to another, I can see that now. Out of it, nothing good coming to anyone. Least of all to you, Antonio. And I? Left with a lot to answer for – that is, if I am ready to admit guilt. Damnation? Well, that I know I am headed for, anyway, for all my many other sins. The only absolution I'd seek would be from you, my friend, as I told you at the time you confided the horrible truth in me. That I cannot have as things stand now, so I'll dwell no further on the past.

And if I'm frank, uppermost in my mind right now after this last exchange with Francesco is getting him to Florence and off my hands. Because, having unthinkingly offered him the chance to accompany me there, I now realise that only when Vasari's been confronted and the lad's investigation is concluded, only then can I rid myself of him and regain my peace of mind.

20 June, Midsummer's Eve

Our ways part where the roads cross. My small party, seven in number including Francesco, goes south and west to Florence. Paolo and a groom, heading north and east, will travel into the hills to Bassano. 'I shall take a day or two more and go on to visit your family,' Paolo informed Francesco as we prepared to leave. This seemed to greatly relieve the lad's concern about how his father would react on hearing for a second time about a delay to his return home. A lengthy delay too, since it will take all of four weeks, likely more, this expedition we embark on.

'I shall be inviting Jacopo to meet me soon in Venice. As soon as he can, if he's willing,' Paolo had added. 'There is more work there than we can rightly handle just at present. With his capabilities, your father will be heartily welcomed. Any of your brothers old enough to assist him, by the way? *You*, I can certainly suggest he brings along, since your worth has been proved,' he says. This brings a sudden brightness to Francesco's face.

The rest of my party trots off, one rider raising the Barbaro banner, the breeze furling it out, snapping it back against the standard, white ground rippling, red circle emblem on view. Red on white, what splendour against the blue sky. Whip raised in goodbye and about to wheel my mount round, I see Paolo leaning out of his saddle. An afterthought? Yes, introduced with a shy grin, speaking not to me but to Francesco, he's enquiring, 'Can you find out what Vasari has in mind to write about me in his new book? Do that for me, will you, lad?' His expression distinctly sheepish, he adds, 'Because I'd really like to know.'

NINE

Francesco

CHAPTER ONE

4 July, on the road to Florence

I got it wrong, thinking it a fine adventure to ride the road to Florence in Signor Barbaro's entourage. As soon as we start out across the plain the rain begins. Unseasonal summer rain flooding the fields, wrecking the wheat and barley, barely stopping for a single minute. Ten days now, slipping and sliding on the waterlogged tracks. My hands are useless, swollen red and rubbed raw by the leather of the reins. I brought no coat, and for protection I've had to beg a sack from a farmer, cutting neck and armholes in it.

I squint into the downpour and there's *nothing* ahead except flat land and a huge open sky, everything the colour of mud, fading into a washed-out horizon. I am sick of this low country, its dykes and ditches and slow-turning water mills, sick of the poor little farmsteads with their dripping thatch, their hollow-eyed people who watch us from the doorways, sick even of the geese waddling through the puddles, the way they hiss at our horses' hooves.

'Keep up, keep up,' at least once an hour Barbaro's steward shouts at our strung-out, silent, plodding party. There are grim sights on our route. One settlement we pass is deserted, nothing but a burned-out shell, a street where roof timbers' black spars lie in a mess of ash. I avert my face. No one wants to be witness to tragedy, nor take those images of destruction onward on their journey.

My mood dips lower with every passing hour. Neither looking forward nor back provides any comfort. I sense how inadequate my preparation is for meeting with Vasari. Slumped in my saddle through all these miserable dawn-to-day's-end rides, still I haven't resolved how I'll tell the story of the dogs and the painting. Tossing words about in my mind, I can't decide which ones will get and keep his interest. How *do* you grip your listener? What do you start a story with? You could say with the beginning, of course, but what if the beginning seems too dull and slow? Do you break to the finale and give away what happens, then go back and fill in the rest once your listener is enthralled? A good tale binds you with a spell. I'm racking my brain, wondering what is the most memorable one I ever heard, what captured me. How much is it the tale that does the captivating, how much the teller?

And if I choose to look forward, think about what happens next, well, what of it? I have no ready answer. *Clip clop clip clop*, the rhythm of my horses' hooves as we squelch along is the rhythm of verses learned by heart in school. I while away a stretch of track reciting what I can remember. Learning Latin, I wriggled on the bench at first but then got to enjoy texts like Caesar's *Commentaries*. And his *Gallic Wars*, sonorous even when stumblingly recited in class. Fancifully, I'm likening this journey of mine to one of the bitter campaigns fought by the Emperor Julius. The time when the Helvetii people *'resolve to go forth from their territories'*, how they light faggots, burn their houses, *'destroying the hope of a return home, so they might be the more prepared for undergoing all dangers,'* isn't that like me? I don't know if I can go back, do I? I've never crossed Father before, never turned my back and ridden off.

During a brief respite from the rain I pull out Mother's letter, but reading it again, find nothing to reassure me he is readying to excuse my pig-headedness. Then I recall Caesar's line, *'There is danger both to those who retreat and to those who pursue.'* Either way I am in trouble. *That* thought produces some sort of resolve in me: to go on, on to Florence. I must. Too shaming to turn back now. I have no choice but to take this thing to its conclusion.

But *about* this thing, the story for Vasari, I'm unsure whether I really have it all. From Paolo, from Tomaso's journal, from Magnifico Barbaro, yes, I have accounts: their memories, the ones they've been willing to let me hear, that is. But does that mean I have the truth? Is there such a thing as 'perfect' truth? How much truth can anyone bear to recount, anyway? Maybe they misremembered, it was all such an age ago. Maybe they have chosen to deceive? When I take a pen and scratch out an outline, organise the facts I've accumulated, the accounts add up. But do they add up to *enough*? Perhaps it is wrong of me to harbour doubt – but I can't help feeling something's missing.

I must have another try at getting more out of Barbaro, I decide, and it's Maddalena's earrings that provide the opportunity. I have made something of a habit of taking them out to jiggle in my fist when we sit around in the evening after eating. Tonight, the tavern owner having provided dry wood, a good fire is going, the room misted with the steam from our wet clothes but the flames flaring bright enough to catch on the gleaming green gems and dance there. *That* catches Barbaro's eye and curious, he asks me what I have, takes the earrings, examines them, and sure enough, questions what I'm doing with such beauties. I give him the bare outline.

'I see, Zantani playing the generous uncle to his pretty niece. Ah, fine things, how my friend did love them. He would seek them everywhere, select them and then make others lust after them. It was always only the best for Zantani,' he says. And then adds, 'But Francesco, since while you're with me you shall have no need to exchange those jewels for ducats, you will arrange to get the earrings back to the young lady, won't you?'

I tell him yes, I mean to. Although I don't know how that will happen, me getting again to Venice soon, that is.

'We'll have to think of some way to get you there,' he says.

Is this a hint he's thinking I might get work in Venice? I snatch at the idea with hope: something to aim for when this is over perhaps, something other than slinking home, whipped dog with tail between legs, if I get nothing from Vasari. For now, having got Barbaro's attention, it is my chance to press him on what, despite all my questioning, I still can't get clear. How did the bond between Zantani and the dogs – he obviously felt it deeply – come about? I try prompting by asking again why Zantani, who, as I'd just heard, possessed so much, and always only the finest examples, chose dogs who were not special to look at, and what is more, decided to have them *painted*.

'They were special though, how they performed, as you heard from Tomaso,' says Barbaro.

'For me, that was what counted.' He pauses, 'For Zantani? Well, I never knew why he got so obsessed with them. And so quickly. Like a love affair, a strike of summer lightning.' He laughs but he looks away. 'No, you'll just have to settle for the fact that the hounds endeared themselves to him. And as for that, can anyone really explain where true attraction springs from?' Standing to lean a hand on the mantle, head down, he kicks a smoking log deeper into the fireplace and adds, 'Mind you, afterwards Zantani could never forgive himself for....'

At that he stops. He realises he has said more than he should? Aah! I wait, *willing* him to say more. At that moment the door swings open, our food brought in. I'll not be able to keep Barbaro's attention now. He crosses to the table, knife in hand to hack at what's on the platter. Roast fowl! My mouth waters. The others start milling around. I'll not hold back. I'm ravenous.

5 July

So, I know there's more to know. I *haven't* got to the bottom of it. But now, almost at the end of the journey, what likelihood is there I'll discover what's missing? On the road, while riding, un-saddling, while sitting around at the tavern after supper, I listen to Barbaro's conversation. I learn a lot. As well as an envoy, he is a leader of academic thinking, he and his brother involved with the University at Padua. He has been helping them make practical advances there, setting up a Botanical Garden, where medicinal plants will be studied, for example. And he has changed attitudes by extending a welcome to Jewish scholars, for training as surgeons and in law. From his valet, I learned that it was Barbaro who encouraged Tomaso to betroth himself to Marina all those years ago, despite the opposition they faced because of her religion, she being from the Ghetto. Offering them employment at

Maser, Barbaro gave them the means to be together there and build a life.

I feel admiration. Barbaro knows so much, has travelled so far and talks so well of all he has seen and how it helped him form his interesting liberal views. But I can never quite square up my admiration with another, deeper feeling: my scorn about the way he used Cara and Bruno. I knew he acted impulsively in handing the dogs over to Zantani but now I learned something different: he explained that it came about through an act of barter between them. On the evening he chose to speak of this – his lips perhaps loosened with one draught too many of grappa? – it shocked me hearing him quite casually mention this barter as being his reason for taking Bruno and Cara away from Tomaso. How could he feel no shame openly admitting to a stupid, unthinking act like exchanging the dogs for some frippery belonging to his friend, the fancy most probably of merely a moment on his part? But then I realised it was just as Tomaso told me: Barbaro, as the one who had ownership of them all, the animals and the man, could do exactly what he liked, when he liked, answerable only to himself.

Of course, there can be no expressing any of this to the Signor, ever, least of all now while under his protection. 'Button your lip, boy,' I tell myself, but behind my silence I am disturbed, disgusted actually, that he, *anyone*, could behave so heartlessly and apparently feel no remorse. My questions obliging him to go back over the story, I wonder whether they might be forcing him to acknowledge some responsibility? It's fanciful, I know – but were it to be so, it would at least mean that when you take the long view, nothing ends up being for nothing.

CHAPTER TWO

8 July, Florence

We come to an escarpment's edge and there it is, Florence, spread out beneath us. Sunlight is breaking through heavy grey cloud, lighting up the Arno as it bisects the city, flowing full and wide, strangely yellow in colour. Our little party is silenced by the grandeur of the panorama of glinting red roofs and over it, the Duomo presiding so magnificently, the tall Baptistery tower beside it. The enormous scale of the great curved red-tiled dome astonishes me, that great golden ball adorning it. '*Stupendous*', a word I heard Giorgio use: now I'm making it mine.

From afar, I thought the city welcoming but now here, I dislike how it closes in around me. The solemn grey blocks of the buildings, their high windowless walls and heavily studded doors seem to discourage entrance. It's a building site – although what else did I expect, after hearing so much of the marvels of its architecture? The noise! deafening, the sound of shovels breaking earth, the *chink chink* of chisel on stone, the screech of pulleys hauling up buckets. After the silent, wet journeying through countryside virtually empty of people, it's a shock to be inside the city's walls, crammed up against its confined spaces. Everywhere you turn there is disruption. We have to watch ourselves as sweating work gangs push past, their carts piled precariously high with stone blocks, slipping along the mud-slimed surfaces, cursing when the oxen stumble and tangle in their traces.

As soon as we have left the horses at the tavern – a better-looking accommodation than many we lodged in these past two weeks – Barbaro's ready to seek out Giorgio Vasari. 'Giorgio's been granted a place by the city authorities where he can live and work. We'll go there.' We make our way through the packed narrow streets leading to the market, careful to dodge the Florentine shoppers' elbows and bulky baskets, the horses with their loaded carts, bulging sacks of vegetables, live chickens, bleating lambs. I'm assaulted by aromas: frying onions, well-peppered. And baking, something sweet, cinnamony to my nostrils. It feels like weeks since I've eaten good food. I keep my eye on Barbaro, his blue-feathered red cap bobbing above the crowd, hoping he knows where we are going because I'm utterly muddled as to whether we head north, south, east or west.

Eventually we reach Vasari's place through some poor little criss-crossing streets that fan out from the main piazza, going that way because the wider road fronting the river and all the space around it have been torn up. We are warned there's a vast hole where foundations are going in, the thoroughfare entirely blocked with a mountain of sand. 'Another of Giorgio's projects, I understand,' Barbaro tells me. 'To be public offices on a very grand scale for the Medici overlord. He and his clerks will have a fine view over the Arno and the old bridge. And as for Casa Vasari, Giorgio has elaborate plans for decorating his abode, he informed me last time we met. If I know him, he'll cover the place with frescos top to bottom. He did just that at the house he built in Arezzo, ceilings as well as walls.'

Taking yet another dark street of tall buildings where only a mere streak of daylight penetrates, we arrive at an imposing studded door. Barbaro lifts the great ring of the knocker and raps. Over his shoulder he says, 'Not a man for half measures, our Giorgio.' Well, good, I'm thinking. If I am finally to reach Vasari, finally to unburden myself of the story he asked me for, well, let the fates induce the man to deal full measure with me.

A servant opens the door, announces his master is not at home – but most likely the Signori can find him in the Duomo. 'In these days Signor Vasari is very taken up with the work begun on his frescos for the dome,' he tells us.

'Let me show you this other thing of Vasari's before we go and cajole him down from his scaffolding,' says Barbaro as we step away. He steers me to the end of the street where we cross another great piazza and then go up the wide steps of a vast church. How many such edifices are there in this city? Already I've seen the Virgin has six dedicated to her: Santa Maria Novella, Santa Maria Maddalena, Santa Maria Maggiore, Santa Marie dei Candeli, Santa Maria degli Angeli, and of course the Duomo, Santa Maria del Fiori. This is Santa Croce. 'Santa Croce,' I am told by Barbaro, 'is a church of the Franciscan order, a suitably grand final resting place for our most eminent men, those who have led us, those who have elevated our minds.'

Once inside, he waits while I, head craning back, adjust to its scale. I feel awed and dwarfed. The nave is huge, very long and very high, wood-beamed, with chapels leading off. Jewelled rose windows illuminate the church's sacred space from a great height and the bare stone walls are studded with plaques. There are many funerary monuments too. Barbaro has me by the elbow and this time steers me down the right aisle until we reach a huge, ornate and impressive one. A large plaque, its capital letters in Latin, a bust of a fine-looking man high up above a casket ornately sculpted from black marble, all surrounded by painted drapes where cherubim disport, chubby fingers playing with the fringed tassels. From the inscription I decipher this is the tomb of Michelangelo Buonarotti.

'The city was determined to have him back here, to make Florence his final resting place, although he had lived in Rome for years. And died there, of course,' says Barbaro. 'Vasari abetted the city fathers so his *"divine genius"* would be close by him here. So that he, Vasari, would be the one to create the most fitting monument for his beloved Michelangelo.'

Vasari designed *this*? How many more skills does this man possess? If it's scale that makes a monument 'fitting', this one is massive. My eyes go up, up high and then down, down to eye level where I marvel at the lifelike, almost life-sized, sculpted women, three of them, sitting so casually on a ledge, leaning forward almost conversationally. Vivid, natural, they are not like cold stone at all and make we want to touch them, want them to reach out those delicate fingers and touch me.

From behind me Barbaro says, 'You realise they are personifications of the arts: Painting, Sculpture, Architecture? This is how Vasari portrays the *paragone*, that eternal argument as to which of the three should take precedence.' Yes, I see. The middle one, a veil over her hair, her face the most despondent of the three, holds a pencil – she must be for drawing, that prerequisite to painting, the skill Vasari told me he considers 'the father of the arts'.

Barbaro has me by the sleeve yet again. 'This site, here at this end of the church is where Michelangelo himself expressly selected as his burial site. Now why?' I have no answer. 'Because, you see, at the last trump, when the gates of Hell gape wide, Santa Croce's doors burst open, its roof comes off and Michelangelo sits up in his tomb, he claims he'll be rewarded with the finest possible view of the Duomo's dome. And if Michelangelo is to have one final sight in his afterlife, he wants it to be of that golden ball atop it. For which, of course, he provided the design. Now there's an *anecdote* for you, Francesco – how do you like it?'

As usual, Barbaro allows me no time to answer. I have to trot to keep up with his pace as we head back towards the Duomo through the swarming streets. The closer you approach, the more awe-inspiring it is.

Once inside, beneath our feet there is a floor of wondrously pleasing mosaic shapes, squares, circles, a harmony of black, grey and white. Walking down the long central aisle through a miasma of dust, I'm struck by the bizarre sight of ropes dangling down from the impossibly high dome. They hang from its centre right down to the floor, swinging idly between the ladders that lead up to two scaffolding platforms either side. Other ladders go up even higher from there, hundreds of feet it must be. 'I'll not have to go up?' I ask Barbaro, my voice a mouse's squeak. The mere idea of taking the rungs, placing foot after foot to that height makes my head swim. Voices sing out up there, echoing strangely, so that if they are commands or even a greeting, I can't make out the words. In the flickering lantern light it is impossible to see the state of the frescos.

'*The Last Judgement.* Terrifically ambitious. And typical of Vasari to take on the entire Apocalypse. Thinking to outdo Magister Giotto, eh? His Medici Grand Duke patron's idea, no doubt,' Barbaro informs me. But how the scenes are conceived, or indeed if Vasari is even up there sketching out the design or slapping paint on to damp plaster is a mystery to us.

'Watch out below,' comes a shout from directly above us and we've just time to step back and avoid being knocked by a basket plummeting towards the floor. Halted just before crashing into the mosaic, we can see the jug set within it. Smell it too, *phew* … so that's how they manage bodily needs once up there for the day's work. Next, another 'Halloo!' and now a man is sliding very fast down the rope nearest to us. Springing off, bending his knees on impact, he almost bounces before standing up while the rope, released, jerks and flails wildly.

'Magnifico Barbaro?' he asks. 'I'm an assistant to Signor Vasari. My master received your message. He has finished drawing for today and gave me this for you.'

Barbaro reads the note and tells me he's invited by Vasari to dine this evening, 'You, Francesco, he'll see tomorrow.' I am to be back at the house in Santa Croce by nine in the morning. I am not to be late. 'You are on your own for that, mind,' I am informed. 'I've appointments elsewhere I must keep.'

I spend the rest of the day walking. For a hundred and more years this city has been building, building, wanting to outdo all others in prestige. How do the architectural ideas I've only heard talked about look in practice? Away from the centre the crowds thin out and the city begins to show itself to me. I cross the Arno and climb to a viewpoint and from there, looking over terraced gardens giving on to the river, I get some sense of its symmetry. I try sketching a fine façade, some details of statuary, but I drip with sweat and my hand fails me. I end up tearing my smudged efforts in two. I buy a glass of ale but it doesn't refresh me. Restless and irresolute, anticipation crouches on my head like a fat toad, emptying me of energy, of appetite.

At night it's hot, humid, airless and I can't sleep. What I went through in Venice at Titian's Casa Grande keeps flashing into my mind. There I was all anticipation too, and how did that play out for me? I toss one way, asking how could I have been so naïve to think Vasari was really extending friendship? To *me*? 'Call me Giorgio', huh? How could I have supposed he would help someone like me? He is as 'big' a man here in Florence as Titian is in Venice. And I? I'm a little person, only of interest to Vasari if I can be used to his advantage.

I was warned. Barbaro warned me on that hot day in the meadow at Maser. Zantani too, he warned me – didn't he say, 'Vasari is a man who'll make best use of anything that comes to his hand'? I twitch off the sheet and toss the other way. A glimmer of hope favours me briefly and for a few moments I let myself believe my story *will* please him. Well, why *shouldn't* it? It has its twists and upturns, it has villains and victims, it describes courageous action, ends with pathos. But then, what do I know? *Ach*! to be going powerless into the presence of someone to whom you matter nothing is a situation no person in their right mind would seek out. Yet once again I am about to do it.

There are two ways only it can go: either Vasari grants me what I want or he turns me away. Imagining that, I rear up, groan and have to thump at my pillow. Vasari, he'll be full, replete with what, trustingly, I lay at his feet. This thing I've sweated over to bring him will no longer be in my keeping. What kind of fool will I look, empty-handed, open-mouthed, when he rejects it as worthless?

9 July, Casa Vasari

The morning has come. Nine o'clock not yet struck, on Vasari's doorstep again, I'm feeling rough, sore-eyed, as though I got no rest at all. Led up a flight of stairs to an anteroom, the servant leaves without showing me where I can sit to wait. I stand over to one side, awkward. On time but to be kept waiting – no doubt intended to make me even more aware of what little significance I am to Giorgio. Minutes pass and then I think, 'To hell with this.' I give a push to a half-open door and enter the salon I've glimpsed beyond it, a square room with a large fireplace and high-beamed ceiling, empty except for a table under the tall window.

But ah, it is here, in this inner sanctum, that Vasari will fresco – because, in fact, the work has begun. There are the initial *synopia* designs, sketched on the plaster either side of the fireplace. I step closer: standing and seated figures are demarcated, male and female, and a series of arches, trees forming part of a sweeping vista. On the table, a spread of designs. Of course, I can't stop myself from crossing the room, avid to discover what grand vision Vasari has in mind for the room.

I never do get to know though, because suddenly he is there behind me, catching me out in my attempt to sneak a look, But then didn't he himself sneak in, silent-footed in his velvet slippers? He is all in velvet actually, black quilted dressing gown enveloping him to his feet, a black cap perched on his head, its huge scarlet tassel dangling by his chin. He puts up a hand to pat at this distractedly, then passes his hand over the tight mass of curls springing out on either side. He is somewhat bleary-looking. Has he been tumbled from his bed?

'Good morning, young man,' he greets me before making a yawn so wide I can see his back teeth. If he minds my presumption in wanting to see his work, he does not say. He is looking past me, anyway, his eyes on the drawings. Suddenly I'm chagrined by the thought he may not remember who I am, let alone know why I'm here. He *is* glad though, it seems, to have me as an audience because he starts expounding the ideas behind his design scheme. Out it all spills, the fables and myths and moral tales his panels will recount, the individuals he will honour with painted busts replicating sculpted marble high up near the ceiling, how with his choice of palette he'll bring the soft greens and yellows and terracottas of the countryside into the salon, to sit alongside the rich reds, deep greens and bright whites of his characters' garb.

I am not invited to respond. Each time he has made a quip he particularly likes he looks up in anticipation of a nod or grunt of appreciation from me. I feel I must oblige. Eventually it dawns that if I don't interrupt him, he will carry on this wordplay until it is time for his next appointment. He doesn't like it at all when at last I seize on a small pause in his flow. He frowns and what I want to say comes out clumsily, my throat dry as a brook in the drought months. I cough and then I croak out, 'I have it, that story you asked for.' Silence. I add, 'The one you asked me to get, you remember?'

Still he does not speak. Anxiously I burst out again with, 'It is good, my anecdote, you'll like it, I'm sure. About a portrait. A portrait of dogs.' *Still* he says nothing, just holds my gaze, his expression hard to read: withdrawn – or is it calculating? My face is burning. What else can I try to arouse his interest? In desperation I add, 'You'll see how what I've got is interesting, intriguing, like you asked me for. For the Bassano entry, I mean – the one you are putting in your book.' He's still frowning but finally, his voice flat, he says something. What he says is, 'For the Bassano entry? In my book?'

It is then I have that feeling, the one you get when you're out and the wind suddenly comes up and you go cold. Everything around you starts to flutter and flap. The light changes, becomes hard and bright and you know a storm is brewing. At that moment you are still dry – but the rain is coming, almost on you now. You're going to be hit. Even before the first drops fall, you are chilled and dread how dire it will be, the inevitable drenching.

'My book, ah yes, yes, *my book*.' He strokes at his beard, infuriatingly slowly, his fingers not so ink-stained now, two or three of them sporting heavy rings. He smiles – not at me though, an *inward* smile – and then he says, 'But my dear young man, my book is finished. Already done, off to the typographer – the excellent Signor Giunti you know – it must be oh, three weeks ago at least by now.'

I have to turn away from that supercilious smile, not wanting him to see my face. But I can still hear him, the way he sounds almost merry as he says, 'Ah, *Bassano*. You're young Bassano. We met in Venice, no? *Now* I'm remembering. And you managed to get some information for me, did you? My, my, my.' He steps to the window, pushes it open. 'Let's have some air in here, shall we?' He turns, saying, 'Last night, talking with Barbaro, I did take a minute to wonder why he had asked me to see you. Of course, had he turfed himself out of bed to speak with you this morning, he could have saved you the trouble of coming here, couldn't he? Informed you my *Lives* are finished and done with, I mean.' He gives me a look as though he is confiding something important. 'A fine dedication for the Grand Duke Cosimo were the last words I wrote before finally throwing down my quill.'

He laughs again. He must see how aghast I am. But no. 'At least you're not one more hopeful come here begging for a job,' he says, rubbing his palms together, the smile a grin now as he adds, 'I assure you I'm utterly overwhelmed with applicants.' It is like a spurt of bile in my mouth, the sudden loathing I get for him, his vanity, his smug meanness of spirit. Grinning there in triumph and self-congratulation. Always outdoing others in everything, that is how he has to be. *Tick tack, tick tack, my jack wins over your jack.* That's him, Vasari, every time.

I am stock-still, feeling my head has gone black inside and is tingling in a peculiar way. My eyes are fogged. Not so fogged that I can't still see Vasari, though. At the table he pushes idly at the pile of designs. I think he starts to draw. Although I don't want to speak to him ever again, I force myself. I have to know what he has written about Father in the book. If anything. He must have written *something*? I ask my question of that turned back, pained at how pleading I sound.

Facing me now, yes, Vasari has a blue chalk in one hand. He pats again in that pathetic way at his hair and I see his fingers smudge one curly lock with the colour. On his face is that smile, the one I now recognise is just for show. He says, 'Oh, a small mention for Jacopo, certainly. Forgive me, Francesco – it is Francesco, isn't it? – if the details of just what I wrote escape me right now. A small mention, something about his skill with animal representations, I think I recall.'

I croak out the other question burning me. 'Oh Titian?' he replies, 'Well, oh yes, plenty. I have written a properly detailed chapter for *Maestro* Titian, of course. Praising his colours of course, but with nevertheless some small note of caution that that his design skills could be better – but otherwise, no less than he deserves.'

I have no memory of how I leave that room. Are there courtesies and farewells between Vasari and me? More likely, I just spin on my heel and stumble away. It is a first for me, discovering disappointment can knock you senseless, turn you momentarily into a madman, wild words in your head, no different from the ragged creatures I'd been avoiding as they gibbered their nonsense on Florence's street corners. Does the servant pull back the bolt on the door or is it I who pushes at the heavy thing? As I get myself out of the horrible place do I as good as fall into the street? Because that's where I find myself, crouched over, gasping and blinking, fuming and muttering as I fumble for my kerchief.

CHAPTER THREE

23 July, on the road home

Going back, back through the same places, basking in sun that is at last warm and fitting for the time of year. Yet I'm finding I'm no less depressed than I was in the drenching rain. Anxious was how I was then. Now I am sore, angry, resentful. My feelings skew my vision, I know it, but honestly, I've had it, done with my fool venture, done with this drear journey. I long for home. I want to be up off the plain and in hill country, riding under old trees, hearing the Brenta rushing past, being in sight of our great mountain, counting the clouds pushed by the wind to graze its top.

So, you fool, I am thinking, all you turned your back on, rode away from, that is what you yearn for now? To be in Bassano at the house by the bridge, to be sitting and eating a meal cooked by Mother, to be jostling elbows with the little ones while we joke and laugh, yes, that is all suddenly very appealing. As is the thought of getting back to work in the studio, even that.

Barbaro is barely speaking to me. As we ride, he keeps ahead and each time we stop for the night he calls his scribes around him. They huddle together over their papers, making plans for projects they don't choose to share with me. I suppose I'm nothing but a footnote in the account he will make of his time in Florence. An embarrassment too. In that, we are agreed, it *is* embarrassing how abject a failure my mission has been. One there's nothing to be done about, according to Barbaro.

'Too bad, my young fellow,' was his idea of consolation – or all he had to say when he heard what happened.

The nights have warmed. Twice already, when we've stopped and made our camp, fed the horses and lit a fire, we have slept out instead of offering our tender skins to the bugs in a hostelry's straw pallets. We have the same plan tonight. The site we choose is sheltered, down in a dip, at its edge a copse of trees. We found pork meat for sale in the last village and after gorging on it, sprawl around two or three glowing logs. A sultry evening, a high sky tinted a warm orange by the departing sun.

The night has not yet quite closed in when they come silently from the wood, the women. First one, then two more, and then another two. The first I know of their presence is the faintest tinkling of bells, the swish of feet stepping lightly through the grass and a strange, sweet scent I can't place. I look over my shoulder and realise, gypsy women. Not an attack, an overture – which is why they have been permitted to come this far by the guards at the horse lines.

They stop just at the edge of the glow cast by our fire. Then the first one steps into the circle so that we see can see her. Quite silent, not looking at us – but wanting us to look. Not asking permission, but with something urgent to announce, she raises her arms above her head, splays her fingers, tenses them to a shape like the beak of a bird. The rhythm starts as she lifts her head high and back, throat exposed, her spine a sinuous curve. *Clack clack clack*, from the castanets she's holding with those fingers. At first their beat is slow – but it is insistent.

We have ceased any idle talk, eyes only for this. The woman moves to a faster beat now, her hips swaying. She is circling herself and also circling wider, back and forth, close to one of us, then another, then tantalisingly retreating, whirling her tasselled shawl off and on her shoulders. Her skirt is spangled, her hair in a long plait, ribbon-tied in many colours, swinging out behind her, wafting a musky scent each time she nears.

The *clatter clash rattle* of a tambourine comes in from behind me as the second woman steps on high-arched feet into the circle. The *rat-a-tat* rhythm quickens both dancers' movements. Weaving and dipping around each other, their feet are bare but they stamp their heels down hard on to the bare earth just like impatient young colts. And they *twirl twirl twirl* before me. My head spins as I try to keep the face of the second woman in focus as she flashes past. A girl only she seems, hair loose and flying, glowing red like the blaze of autumn leaves.

Their dance ended, a third woman enters our circle. Carefully she puts down two flasks at Barbaro's feet, placing a small copper bowl beside them.

'We're to get some gypsy fire coursing in our veins,' the scribe sitting next to me says under his breath. We wait while Barbaro tips his head to gulp some, swiping the back of his hand over his lips, passing the flask on. I, of course, think of Nonna's potion, of poison and punishment. Banish that thought! I will not miss this. Besides, these rhythms are about life, not death. There is joy in the dancing which is why the copper bowl is for coins to pay – but for the liquor, not for the dancing.

The beat is in my blood now, my feet tapping. The tune is taken up by two fiddles. I glance to the side and there are the musicians, two slight men, with rings in their ears which glint against long dark curls. Their heads bob, their bows saw back and forth furiously. The music moves up tempo. The women respond, faster, faster, using every part of their bodies. They are like flames, crackling red and gold and green. They hold their hands down by their waists and clap them together furiously. Their knees are lifting a little higher each time as they swirl their skirts side to side, revealing flashes of their thighs. Their fire roars now, their flames leap up. I'm leaning forward, rapt. We all are. I want to get close, I want to feel this, I want to dance.

And then we do, following Barbaro into the firelit circle after he is invited by the first dancer. All it takes is a flick of her hand for him to be up and stepping towards her. We dance, we pause to drink the liquor. We dance again. At one point, we rest, the fiddles gone quiet. The women sink down, limbs akimbo, their bright skirts collapsing around them, as languorous at rest as they are energetic in movement.

After that I whirl and whirl. I am partnering the girl with the red-gold hair. She's with me and yet not. I try reaching for her. Stamping and clapping, her face stern, she side-steps me, swirls past, turns, brushes my shoulder, turns again. By the time the beat slows and she is making again the sinuous movements with which the dances started I'm not noticing – nor caring – where Barbaro or the others are. I want to pull her to me, move with her. My feet are clumsy but I won't stop. I go in close where I'm warmed by the heat coming off her body. She comes near, smiles up into my face and I'm clumsy no more, feel myself light and free, floating, her hair brushing across my cheeks as now we're touching and touching, turning and turning.

She takes my hand – at last – says with her eyes, 'Follow me.' And I would follow her anywhere: even into the darkness where she leads me. Where she wants me. And I her. And then we're together and I'm willing this night to go on and on, this joy, this blaze of red and gold stars behind my eyes, these soaring 'fireworks' of my mind. May they never end. I'm willing that forever I shall stay here, between her breasts, enveloped in her musky scent, my blood thrumming to the music our bodies are making.

24 July

As dawn breaks it does end though, she stretching, getting to her feet, waiting for me to stand, leading me back towards camp. We reach a clearing fringed with bushes dotted with small round orange-red flowers. I don't recognise this wild bush, its blossoms the colour of her hair. It perfumes the morning, bitter-pungent, disturbing. I get a sudden conviction: this scent I'll never forget.

The path diverges here. She points one way, looks at me insistently. I don't move and her smile has a touch of the taunt in it as she pushes me to the right. She puts a finger into her mouth, still smiling, swaying where she stands, holding my gaze. Is she picking at the pretty gap in those white teeth? No, she is licking that finger, then she's putting it moist to my lips. A fleeting pressure. Her farewell.

We are about to part and *still* she will not tell me her name. However many times I ask she only smiles and shakes her head. Mine, she knows. 'Francesco', she repeated when I first told her, my palm flat on my chest. Her voice is throaty, my name in her mouth sounding strangely guttural. Now she pulls away from the arm I've slipped round her waist and says something rapidly, words in her language that I don't understand. She says the same thing again, I think, more slowly this time. I shrug and open my hands.

I pull her close again. At least my actions can speak. She twists to catch at my right hand, using both of hers to flatten out my palm, pressing something into it, folding my fingers closed. Something cool, its surface smooth. My palm open, on it there's a river stone, creamy white, dappled with warm brown spots, three-sided, irregular, perforated almost at its centre by a small, round hole. She is smiling when I look up. She breathes in sharply and touches the stone with one finger, saying clearly, 'Francesco luck.'

A charm! All gypsy women tell fortunes, don't they? There's one who comes to Bassano, she has travelled there with the summer fair every year since I was a child. She drapes shawls for a makeshift booth and once night-time comes, plenty of folk want to consult her. That old gypsy's face flashes into my mind: leather, the skin wrinkled like a prune, coloured almost as dark, a black headscarf edged with jingling silver coins. And teeth, such teeth that remain to her, gleams of jagged gold in the cavern of her mouth. Nothing could be more contrasted to this soft-skinned beauty in front to me. A beauty giving me a charm to remember her by (as if I could ever forget).

My beauty is pointing at her eyes. 'Eyes?' I say.

'*Your eyes are for looking. Look, boy, look. And keep on looking.*' Father's voice, uninvited inside my head.

Bright brown, liquid, the eyes of my beauty are darting side to side, her head is bobbing and she is saying, 'Yes. Eyes. Animal eyes.' This time her finger is pointing at me, jabbing once, twice for emphasis.

'Animal eyes watching me?'

She nods, 'Francesco luck.'

One last beam of a smile from her before she is gone, with a bunch of her skirts grasped up into her hand, running down the track, bare feet raising little clouds of dust. Gone as though never there. Before I turn towards camp I clutch my fist to my face. I keep it there as I walk, so I can breathe in, for just that short while, the scent of the blossom and leaves crushed in it.

CHAPTER FOUR

25 July

Barbaro, alone, the fire reduced to pink ember and white ash. Crouched over, chin on fists, he seems far away. Perhaps I'm not to be reprimanded. Perhaps he didn't notice that I … perhaps he himself…?

'Sit here, Francesco,' he indicates the space beside him on the log. 'Wild night, eh? I don't suppose you've experienced many as gaudy as that?' He sounds stiff and doesn't smile. So, he did notice – although seemingly he has no interest whether I reply or not. Something on his mind?

'It's a complicated business, this life, Francesco,' he starts.

Oh, a discourse on his philosophy. I bite back a yawn.

He clears his throat, 'You are just at the beginning of yours, with many more experiences to come.'

And? This is painfully stilted.

'And if you were to ask me for advice, I'd say learn from them all, these experiences.' A pause while he straightens his back. 'And fear none.' His voice rises, 'To be fearless, that's the gift your youth gives you, you see, lad? Gives you the freedom to experience deeply – and then move on.'

'Thank you, Signore,' I make myself sound dutiful. Lecture over?

He sighs. 'I have not told you everything about what happened to Zantani.'

Aha, *now* it starts. He is about to spit it out. *Finally.* How galling it is *now* he comes up with it. Now, when whatever it is can make no difference, neither to me nor to anyone else.

'Let me explain.' He twists himself, looks at me. 'Before, I could not tell you

because a promise made to a friend is sacred. You'd agree with me there, Francesco?'
I nod. Another sigh and then, 'It came about like this. Some time after it was all over,
my poor friend Antonio decided one person only should be told about what took
place in the forest. It was in me he confided. I know what even his wife does not.' He
sighs. 'I believe you said you saw his manuscript?'

'I did Signore, but could get very little from it.'

'I am sure Zantani would have told you that the whole story was in the manuscript.
Not true – it skated over many details, things too painful for him to record. Much
later, it preyed on him that he had dissembled and he reached the decision to reveal
the truth. He asked me to listen. After I'd heard what he wanted to tell me, I swore it
would never go further. That has been my situation: faced with your questions, alone
in knowing the facts. You understand my withholding them as I could never have
allowed the story to be published?'

I can't think what to say.

Barbaro also is silent until he bangs one fist against the other and bursts out with,
'However much Vasari wanted lively anecdotes to titillate his readers, he wasn't to
get hold of what I knew. It is not for consumption by a curious public, that sorry
demeaning tale.' The public? It's me that's curious now, of course, ravenously so,
about what Barbaro knows. But 'sorry, demeaning', what depths is he going to reveal
to me? It is alarming me, his tone. The master of the light touch and always so much
in control, never before has Barbaro spoken in this fierce, clenched way.

Thrusting himself up to standing and looking down, he says, 'But you Francesco,
you I believe, should be privy to that knowledge. Now that Vasari's book is safely out of
the way, it is right you are told. I have reflected a lot and have come to believe you are
owed that, at the least.'

'Oh Signore….' *This* is something, now. He's agitated, scratching at his beard. I
had questioned my trust in this man. With reason, as it seems to be turning out – but
now he wants to put it right. Best I keep quiet and let him do so.

'Yes,' he says. 'I know that by telling you I'll be forswearing myself. But otherwise

I will not rest. It is time to close the circle. I must. Closing the circle, that's something I hold dear.' He taps my shoulder and points a finger across the horse lines. At the banner, the Barbaro standard that has been displayed by our party all our long journey down country and back. 'Perhaps I am influenced in that by my family insignia.'

The white flag emblazoned with a red circle hangs limp. I shudder, remembering Paolo telling me about the insignia, how the red circle is intended to remind all who see it of blood, serving as a gruesome connection to a Barbaro ancestor, a sailor commanding a Mediterranean fleet. This commander's ship was overrun by Moorish pirates who hauled the ship's pennant down and torched it to demonstrate their victory. Barbaro and his crew fought back; somehow they vanquished the marauders and tied them up. Grabbing one of the Moors by the arm and pulling a scimitar from the man's sash, in a trice Barbaro had brought down the blade to slice off his captive's hand. Then, ordering the man's white turban to be snatched off and laid on the deck, grasping the severed hand he used the blood flowing liberally from it to mark out the Barbaro circle on the cloth. The crew hoisted the trailing fabric up the rigging where it was caught in a stiff breeze. The rest of the fleet, reassured by seeing their commander's pennant once more aloft, took courage. Fighting on, they sent the remaining Moors packing.

What I now hear is gruesome too. Also it is shaming, ugly and bitter. Had we been by the firelight with a flagon, the shadows masking our faces, afterwards I'd have thought it was the wine that had embroidered the detail, that my memory of the story's horrors was a fuddled one. But no, Barbaro and me, we sit in the pale light of a summer morning, the sort of light that would normally fill me with optimism for the new day. Today, neither of us show any sign of that mood. Thanks to the gypsies' brew, I have the sorest head and have to hold a hand pressed to my left temple to quell the pain. Usefully, as it happens – what I learn making me thankful I can keep my expression hidden.

At first though, it starts gently enough: I hear that Zantani, there in the forest while he sat out the storm, was quite probably singing.

'Singing a song?'

Barbaro replies, 'Yes, I'd not be surprised if that's what he was doing when the attack took place. He had music composed, you know? By San Marco's cappella master, Willaert, for example. So he might easily have been far away in his mind, his inner eye lifted to the Basilica's twin choir lofts. Perhaps he was recalling how the harmonies poured out from either side of those golden heights, melding as they washed over him.'

I allow myself a fleeting memory of the beauty of the Basilica's interior as Barbaro continues, 'Having pulled his cape right over his ears, Zantani told me he couldn't hear much, had not realised the rain had eased.'

I ask, 'Where were the dogs?'

'Why, there under his knees, huddled with him in the cape's folds. I suppose they had got quite a fug up in there. So Zantani was sitting like that when one of the robbers crept up from behind and threw a noose of rope over his head, the way you'd rein in a horse you're going to break. The attacker tightened the rope until Zantani, almost throttled, was pulled over backwards, gasping, too shocked to shout.

'The dogs then? Well, they had already launched themselves straight into the attack. But *forward*, attacking two other men, ones who were approaching from the front. Even as Zantani was thrashing on the ground he could see Bruno going full on at one of the bastards, the big dog straightaway getting the man flat on his back, pinioned.

'"Bruno had his four paws braced on the fellow's chest," Zantani told me. "I could hear how he was growling, more like a roar. The villain was wild-eyed, blubbering with terror at the bared teeth gnashing next to his neck." He told me he could see Cara too and that she had her teeth locked on to the upper arm of the other man. He was screaming, a high-pitched squealing note, and swinging round in a circle, trying to get her off. The dog was being lifted right up in the air as he flailed about – but she was not letting go. Off balance, staggering, the man was batting at her futilely with his other arm, unable to reach her. He too, he was down on the ground in no time.'

'Heroic,' I say. What other word describes such brave acts, such loyalty?

'Yes,' says Barbaro. He is back sitting beside me again on the log. He groans and scratches at his beard, his head. 'The rest of this, it's not pretty, Francesco. And not heroic. Because this is the point when a *fourth* villain appeared. A brute of a man, if Zantani's description's to be believed. He was brandishing a long knife as he came into the clearing and Zantani heard him yelling, "Call them off, call your dogs off." Still approaching, he yelled again, "Call them off or I'll kill you." What would you have done, Francesco, helpless there?'

Barbaro is not really expecting an answer from me and he barely pauses now in his account. 'Zantani told me he hesitated. The man lashed out with the knife and there was a shriek of pain from Cara as he slashed down once strongly at her head. She was still worrying the arm of the man she had brought to the ground, but even with a knife wound she wouldn't let up. The man came close and bent over to yell again, this time right down into Zantani's face, "Call them off right now. Do it – or I'll cut both of them into pieces. We'll roast them and eat them. You too, I'll stuff your mouth full – you'll be gagging on roasted dog meat while we're hanging you." He pushed the blade under Zantani's chin, kept it there while he said, "We'll hang you right there from that tree."'

Thank you Magnifico Barbaro, *now* I'm getting the truth. *This* is what Tomaso didn't know – couldn't have. Couldn't even have dreamed of. *Dream?* This is worse than the worst nightmare. I don't want to hear more but I have to. 'So Zantani called the dogs to him. What else was there for it? Cowardice, was it? You might want to call it that, Francesco. Zantani asked me once if I thought it so. I don't know that he was reassured when I told him no, trussed just as though he were a beast readied for the butchery, he'd had no choice.

'The dogs hesitated a moment, one heartbeat, another, he told me. "The noose around my neck was yanked, once, twice," he said. "I was all but choking as I called 'Cara,' 'Bruno' again, my voice sharper this time. They released their prey and they came."

'"Tie them. Tie them so they can't bite," he was ordered by the man behind him, who yanked on the noose again to prove his point. The big brute, the fourth one, made sure Zantani could see him touching the pad of his thumb to the blade of his evil knife.

'"One of the bastards had his knee braced in my back while the one with the knife slashed four lengths of rope from the hank he'd picked off the ground," he said. "He threw them down beside me. The dogs had answered my command to sit. I was ordered, 'You tie them with these. You knot round their necks with one first and then use the other to tie their jaws tight. And no funny business while you're at it.'"

I am incredulous. 'So first they must have had to untie him and then he was forced to tie up the dogs?'

'Yes, he said the villains loosened the ties on his arms just enough for him to do it, his fingers clumsy on the rope, some sort of greasy twine that slipped in his fingers as he tried to make the knots. And he was doing this while forced to be down on his knees.' Suddenly Barbaro sounds as though he's choking, 'Francesco, they got him, my friend, so noble and refined and a Magnifico of Venice, *they got him on his knees in front of them.* They reduced him to that. They made him lower than them. The blinding cheek of the bastards, abusing my noble friend as though he were a criminal to be put in the stocks. Or like one of those desperate penitents scourging themselves before struggling up the Scala Sancta's cruel marble steps. The *humiliation, the suffering* of it. Even now it's unbearable for me to think about him being degraded like that.'

Barbaro's voice has gone high now. He's distressed. I am too, at this scene he's conjured. But there's a question I have to ask, 'Did the dogs just stand there and let him strap them up? I can barely believe that.'

'You heard Tomaso tell how he had trained them. That was how they were. Cara and Bruno would never disobey. So, while they were tying him up again the man with the knife gave more orders, shouting again at Zantani. "Hand the dogs over. Give me their ropes. I'm taking them now." So Zantani did it. And they went....'

'Zantani *gave* Bruno and Cara away?'

'He had to,' the words said like a box snapping shut.

'So those vile men went off with them. They must have been dragging the dogs by force, they'd never have gone willingly. And Zantani was left there, thinking they were going to be killed and *eaten*. It's *horrible*.' I am squeezing my eyes shut but the image is there in my mind, the dogs spread-eagled, their limbs like that man-root, their flesh about to be skewered through, put to roast over the flames of a cooking fire.

'Yes, and even though Zantani had done what they wanted, that didn't stop the bastards from nearly beating the life out of him. Before they took off they did him huge harm, irreparable damage. He was lying there and they kicked at him, a man helpless, trussed up and down on the ground.'

Not a single word have I forgotten of Tomaso's account. Barbaro does not need to say more about the injuries inflicted on Zantani. Mother's letter had described the grief those very injuries had brought to Signora Helena. *Now* I understand what it was the Signora was crying about in her room at the house by the bridge, why she raged out loud every night about what had happened to her husband. 'Irreparable damage', words with the most bleak and hopeless sound.

'I'm glad I've got this over.' Barbaro is slumped down as though exhausted. He groans out, 'Is there anything more you want to ask?' In the silence he adds quickly, 'I shan't want to return to this subject.' Nor me, nor me. I do not speak. Right now, I don't even want to think. I shake my head.

CHAPTER FIVE

27 July, on the road to Bassano

Since then we haven't spoken, Barbaro and I. We have ridden for two days and arrived at the crossroads from which we set off more than four weeks ago. Dismounting, stretching, I have to groan, remembering the person I was then, the me that felt so carefree, my head full of hunting songs and *hey tantara tee rees*. Adventuring off to Florence, convinced of my own importance, foolishly optimistic Vasari would commend my efforts, would want to make use of what I brought him, hopeful that what he would do for me then would change my future.

What became of that optimism? Recalling how I tried to explain to Vasari what I'd got for him, it's ashes I feel in my mouth now. And the hands that trustingly held out my offering, what do they hold now? Nothing but gritty sand. Knowing the full horror of the story I sought so ardently, the story that all this has been about, I'm asking myself, why did I *ever* start out after it? Maddalena, I've thought of her too. This story I have, this is not something you'll want to write about, Maddalena, of that I'm sure.

I have confided none of this in Barbaro. Why should he care, anyway? I think bitterly. He'll be feeling any duty he had to me was despatched after we sat together by that burned-out camp fire, any business we had together now past and over.

In this, I'm proved wrong. He comes across to where I'm sorting my saddlebag and it turns out there *is* something he wants to say. He indicates that while his riders water our horses we should get out of earshot. The sun blazes down on us and he's having to screw his eyes up against it as he starts to speak. Clearing his throat, he says rapidly, 'Go away with this from me, lad. Think of it as my parting shot. Remember it.'

He clears his throat again and I am dreading what further homily he'll make. 'What I say to you about fear, it's important. Francesco, know this: fear will break your will and spoil your life – if you let it take hold. Fear will stop you advancing. Are you with me?' I nod and he continues, 'Best to forget, to move on. Me, I always say a short memory is a gift from the gods. But you can work at it, you know. You can *choose* to have a selective memory.' He's scratching at his beard as he tells me Zantani wouldn't ever do that, would never let himself forget what he had done, how he'd been made weak, betrayed his honour.

'You know, there was just that one incident where he failed his own code. But that was it for my friend, his life broken, in ruins. He was hurt of course, but his body would have healed if he could have got over the pain he held in his mind.' He sighs. 'Others suffered because of it. Helena: the marriage was empty for her after that. They had no children. By the end, even his objects brought him no pleasure.' He sighs and that seems to be it, Barbaro has no more to say to me. Turning away and going ahead back up the track, the last words I hear from him are, 'Zantani was never able to rebuild his life. Learn from that lad, embrace your disappointments, banish fear.'

═══∞═══

I ride off, alone for almost the first time in this whole long journey. Riding beside wheat fields that begin to be tinged with gold, this fact only dawns on me after I've gone a mile or so. I realise that except for when I waited on the step outside Vasari's front door, there has barely been a waking moment in the last weeks when I haven't had someone by my side. Someone from whom I have needed to beg attention, to wait on an answer, to be helped along on my way. I have been so *needy*! What a weight of requests I've carried with me, thinking to offload them on to my hapless informants in exchange for what they could tell me. Today it's a different weight I carry: heavy like a millstone slung round my neck. The story as I now know it, how happy I would be if I weren't burdened with it. Nothing comes without a price – but I didn't think I'd be paying like *this*.

How much advice I've had on my search. I've listened each time. People telling me what to think, what to learn, what to *feel*, how to succeed. People proposing what it is I should do next. And, lastly, people telling me how to forget. Is the wisdom Barbaro wanted to impress on me the best of the lot? Let go, move forward fearlessly, do not look back – are these the mottos I should be striving to live by?

It's too hot. I can't go on. Every leaf and blade of grass in this landscape is burnished by the sun. I'm wincing, parched and muddle-headed. I stop by a stone bridge and slide weak and weary-boned from the saddle. My horse and I step into the water to the knees, cooling ourselves and drinking deep. Then I tie my mount to a tree and stumble down the bank to the shade of the bridge's arch. All I want is to sleep where it's cool and I sink down, my face to the damp velvet of lichen.

I sleep but dreaming, I do not forget. Faces parade in front of my eyes, faces with frowning expressions indicating how urgent it is, what they have to say: Father, Uncle G, Paolo, Tomaso. Are they warning me? Or scolding? I can't hear their voices. They're drowned out by the music, gipsy rhythms but played crazily fast and harsh in tone. The old crone from the Bassano fair, grinning, one scrawny arm holding a tambourine up high, leads away a procession of dancing women. It's disappearing fast. I'll have to cross over the river in front of me to catch it. My girl is the last in the line. On her beautiful face is that always-taunting smile and she is reaching back, stretching out her hand, urging me, 'Come, come.' But then it's Maddalena who is there. She's standing on the far bank, throwing back a dark hood from her face, calling, 'Francesco, your story, the story of the dogs, I will write it.' Then louder, '*I will write it for you.*'

I've dreamed of this river before. Red, it splashes over rocks, it's viscous, it smells like paint. It's Titian's river again. And there across it are the dogs, Cara and Bruno, barking at me from where Maddalena stood. One great leap and they launch themselves into the current. *Whoosh*, a flaring noise behind me, a searing light and all at once the length of the river is on fire. Aghast, I watch as the dogs swim across, points of flame licking at their coats. I hear a yelp and there's a smell of singeing. But then they're by me, wet-muzzled, gape-mouthed, bracing their legs, shaking their coats. Thick red drops fly all around and on to me, hot. I feel the prickle on my skin as though I've broken out in a rash. I try to brush them from my arms and yes, they are warm to my touch. I hold up my fingers to my face: these drops, they *are* paint? But oh, no, no, they are blood.

Awake with a start, I pull off my boots and peel my clothes and stumble to plunge as deep as I can in the river, desperate to get the substance off me. A great fish, startled by my arrival in its pool leaps up and twists away in a flash of silvery scales. The water feels good. I dip my face and head three, four times under the surface, let my hair float out. If only I could scrub my mind clean.

As I ride on into the evening I feel the benefit of my ablutions. My head clear again, I'm thinking perhaps I can ride away from the anger and frustration, I *can* forget and leave them behind me down here on the plain. In the end, I ride all through the night. Why stop? The light softens but it stays very clear, limpid and beautiful, throwing the trees along the horizon into etched relief. A white-gold ball of a full moon comes into view, glowing, rising steadily in a silent sky. My ears prick as the bark of foxes at play reaches me from the ridge. My horse makes one long, high-pitched whinny. The air freshens as we climb into the hills and I hold my face up to get the breeze on my cheeks.

At last, there on the skyline is the mountain. Monte Grappa, I'm coming back. Like a migrant bird responding to the pull of the high country, some signal is telling me to be done with the softness down south. Back in this landscape, I step once again inside the frame of my Father's paintings. *'Look towards the north and the rising sun,'* another line from Caesar's Gallic Wars in my head. Is that where I should look for hope? The sun *will* rise and as dawn breaks, looking forward, I feel new energy. Soon I'll be home. Then to find out what welcome awaits me.

28 July, at the house by the bridge, Bassano

The warmest welcome, it turns out, is the puppies'. Stretched out on their backs in a patch of sun by the front doorstep, all their eight paws are up, their eyes closed, their round bellies gleaming. Cesare's coat is like a shiny piece of coal and Fiammetta's as firelit as her name. I call their names. They stir, blink and totter to my hand, snuffling and mewing at my fingers, little tongues licking at my wrist. The door of the house and all the shutters are open. A trickle of water from a window box above my head is dripping down to the paving, someone giving the red geraniums a drink.

'Mother?' I call out. 'I'm home,' I call louder as I go into the hall, cool and dim after the sunlight. As I dump my saddlebag by the stairs I hear quick steps across the upstairs landing. 'Mother?' A faint whiff of lavender lingers, yes, it's her, she's up there. She must have heard me. Of course she recognises my voice. 'It's me, Mother.' But the only sound is the door to her room closing, the *clack* as the latch falls. Calling out again, waiting for the door to open, for her greeting, silence is my only answer.

Trying the studio next, I fare only a little better. On the stairs up I cross with my brothers coming down. They burst through the door, jostling to be first, hungry for their lunch, of course, as the midday bell has just struck. I stop and look up at them. 'Francesco,' they say in unison, a high surprised whisper with no warmth in it.

'Boys, are you well? How's it been?' They look away from me, anywhere but *at* me, and their answers are no more than mutters. Giovanni has one foot pointing down and is studying it carefully. 'Busy are you, Giovanni? Looking forward to having me back?' He juts out his chin, providing me my answer. I try to ruffle Leandro's hair as he pushes down past me but the jerk he gives his head makes my hand graze over it, fall to my side.

At first I think there is no one in the studio. I am surprised at how my heart sinks: Father's not here? I have been resigning myself to a chilly reception, wondering what I'll say, what *he'll* say, whether it'll be worse than chilly, that he will reject me because I've crossed the Rubicon once and for all, as far as he's concerned. Now I have come to face him and he's not here? But then going round behind the easel I see him, sitting in his usual corner, the window casting a pool of clear midday light on him. A leather-bound volume is open on his knees, a heavy great book I recognise as the Bible in Italian he was so proud recently to bring back from the bookseller. He's oblivious to my arrival. For a quiet moment I watch him. *Look, boy, look. And keep on looking.*

Have I ever done this before, really studied you, Father? His lips move silently as he reads, one hand lightly stroking his beard. My breathing slows. I watch the motes of dust in the sunlight's shaft, how they circle around his head. That old head of his, the hair – greyer, surely? – but as tousled as ever. I turn and tiptoe away, take the stairs with care to muffle my steps.

Up to now I've never given much thought to the strength of Father's faith. And I? Well frankly, I've taken the Bible's teachings for granted and if I have thought about them, it's been merely as a source of good narratives. Even during our row, I didn't pay much mind to what Father said: that all future work is to be inspired by Our Lord's teachings. I see that attitude of mine will have to be different from now on. From somewhere a faint hope stirs in me: that painting I'd planned, that *Return of the Prodigal Son* I wanted to do, can I not start on it now? Might that be the way to placate Father?

CHAPTER SIX

I am in need of a friendly greeting even if I must pass over a coin to get it. Few drink in the *Three Quails* at this time of day, so I am glad to discover Stefano mooching there. We sit at the table by the window, below us the Brenta frothing and churning its way under the bridge. Stefano eyes me over his beaker, 'Back, are you?'

I'd like to talk – well, boast – about what I've been up to: invited into a Venetian palace, a grand *terra firma* villa, to dine al fresco in Verona, to eat delicacies and drink deep from crystal glasses. And to impress him with the women I've met. I touch my doublet, feeling through the fabric to the inside pocket where the gypsy girl's stone is. I'd like to show him that, talk about her. The stone clinks against Maddalena's earrings. Wouldn't Stefano like to know how Maddalena and I took that cosy night gondola ride together, crossing the lagoon as dawn rose?

Stefano's only interest though, is the reception I will get here in Bassano. 'Got yourself into a tub of trouble, I bet, haven't you? Going off like that, a fine fight with your father, by all accounts.' That sneery laugh of his, it grates. 'You haven't tackled him yet but you're hoping you can come creeping back into his favour, is that it? Like a right little prodigal son.'

'I was pig-headed.' I'd already decided now is not the time for pride.

'Pigs, is it? That's good – because yeah, in the Bible story doesn't that prodigal son end up tending the pigs, right there in the sty with them, up to his elbows in muck and swill? Has to eat their food, isn't that right, because he's penniless? Bit of a come-down, eh, after all that loose living he'd been doing, running through his father's money? That what you been up to, eh?' He sniggers.

I don't answer. But Stefano can well snigger. He's got a point. I was *with* pigs, the human kind. I've learned how bestial it's possible for men to be. No, in fact, Zantani's attackers were brutal torturers, degenerate men who apparently got pleasure from doing far worse things than any beast could be capable of.

I'm nudged by Stefano's elbow. He's grinning. 'Back to work with your father again now, are you? If it's like in the Bible, you'll be on your knees, begging him to take you. And you'll be paid like a hired labourer. You'll not find that fun, will you?' No, I will not. On my knees for an act of contrition? I shudder, that's too raw. Zantani on his knees in the forest and I, on my knees under the brambles for the act of love – but here at home and in front of Father? That does not fit at all with my idea of being treated as an equal, now the day is so near when I should be acknowledged as adult and independent.

But what Stefano's said presses on the sore point of my unease: what if Father won't take me back? What *will* I do? *'Father, I am no more worthy to be called your son'* those are the words I remember from Luke's gospel. Are those the words I'll have to say when Father and I meet at last? 'You're loving this, Stef. Aren't you? Creep.' I give his shoulder a good shove. He cackles and grabs at me. I feint, give him a good cuff back – but then I have to get away from him.

═◊═

I take off fast out of the town on the path to the foothills. When I find a shady place I sit there a while. But no matter how much I strain, it's not with thinking that I can resolve how to approach Father. My mind veers away each time I try, keeps returning to the painting I suddenly know I want to make, *must* make. My *Return of the Prodigal Son*. With its themes of repentance and forgiveness, what else could I possibly consider starting to work on? He is an empty-headed idiot, Stefano, but in this, he has got it. Spot on.

The painting: I haven't forgotten one detail of the ideas I had for it when in my fury I was riding away from here, south to Venice on my oh-so foolhardy quest. Now those ideas are back in my mind, those shapes and colours to interpret them too, forcefully and with clarity. I I want to use them immediately to make a great painting. That anger I was feeling, I must harness and tame it and put it to work. Father will see. Painting something splendid is the best way to get him to appreciate the seriousness of my intent. My hands make an involuntary twitch. I've got it again, that itch to get started.

How shall I compose the scene? For the setting, the mountain will be there. Of course. As for the frame of the action, I shall demonstrate what I've learned from observing Paolo: arches, architraves, a flight of steps, a temple with columns. Mastery of tricky perspectives to show off the skills I've acquired – but also because architecture of grandeur is needed, to signify how important it is, this scene of reconciliation. I shall make the figure of the father richly robed and girdled with gold, in stark contrast to the son, who will be barefoot, bare-chested, his breeches in tatters. I shall show how the light gleams from the lustrous silk robe the servant proffers, the garment with which the son will exchange his soiled rags.

To capture the mood, there will be servants sounding trumpets of triumph. In the centre, I shall place the fatted calf, strung up, butchered for the feasting. I shall put in that monkey I had sourced for the pastoral paintings. I like that monkey, it will add interest to the foreground. And then a dog, there must be a dog. A spaniel at the merciful father's feet. That will please *my* father. It shall resemble Cara. Yes, yes, this is good. Father, if you'll just let me *talk* to you, I think I can get you interested in what I shall do with this subject.

═══◇═══

I hear the evening angelus as I take the steps back up to the house. Suppertime, Friday and ah, the smell of frying fish. Mother's food soon to be in my mouth, at last – I hope. I slip in by the back to leave my boots. As I enter the kitchen I'm hoping against hope I can just go through to the table and find a place has been laid for me.

'Mother! You are here.' A frying pan sizzles on the stove, next to it a large pot which she is stirring. She eyes me, no smile, keeps stirring.

'Pass me the salt, Francesco.' A generous pinch, she drops it in, stirs again. 'Will you taste the soup? Artichoke. Needs pepper?' I reach across to take the spoon and there is a thud and a crunching sound as something falls to the floor. I look down. Eggs. I've knocked a basket of eggs off the table; fragments of shell are everywhere and all the golden goodness is pooling on the tiles. I'm flustered, looking round frantically. Where's the cloth?

'Oh dear, oh dear.' I really did *not* want this – especially not just now.

Mother, by contrast, is as calm as ever. 'Leave it, leave it, son. They're for the workshop, not our supper. Not to worry. The hens are laying well so we'll have plenty more eggs tomorrow for your father's tempera.'

'But the mess ....'

'Go in for your supper. I am coming with this tureen. The maid will clear the mess.' She has come around the table, come close, is looking up at me. A hand to my shoulder, the briefest touch.

'I'm so sorry, Mother.' She must know I mean it for more than smashing a dozen eggs to the floor. Do I see the faintest hint of a smile?

She looks up at me, very straight in the eye. 'Son, it's what we women are good at.' And then the relief of it, that little chuckle of hers that I love. So she is smiling when she says, 'That's it, isn't it? We women clean up the messes, we put right the clumsy things men do.' There is silence between us. A strand of hair, strayed from her bun, is stuck across her cheek just where it dimples. I want to reach out but her hand is there, pulling it back into its place.

'So go in. Go and speak to him, son.'

He stands by the table but I don't get a chance to say the poor words I've rehearsed. There's no time. Before I can speak I'm grasped and pulled and folded into a great hug and held there for a long moment. My face is crushed to the rough stuff of his jerkin and I can't hear what he's saying. Maybe it's just noises – maybe the noises are coming from me. We pull away.

And that is how it is left, nothing said on either side. As I brush back the hair that has fallen in my eyes, there's the scraping sound of stools being pulled out. There is one for me, my usual place set. The soup bowls are passed, the steam coming off mine warms my face so that I need to reach for a napkin and wipe my cheeks. It comes away wet. I take up my spoon, plunge it in and taste the soup. Mmm, good – but in need of pepper. Mariana, solemn, sits across the table from me. I watch her lift the big spoon to her mouth. To one side of it an unblinking eye peeps at me. I wink. There is one still moment and then the eye winks back.

CHAPTER SEVEN

29 July, in the studio

I am in early, ensuring I'm ahead of Father. I'm expecting there will be mess, brushes muddled and neglected, bristles stuck together. But the materials are in good order, a respectable stack of canvases and a plentiful supply of pigments, freshly ground. That is something: Giovanni and Leandro must be pulling their weight.

I look around, recalling Paolo's studio organised for efficiency, the way he worked with all his *garzoni*. And Vasari, his team of assistants. And Titian, how processes in that great workshop of his were streamlined for speed of production. Then I glance again at the table of our materials: oh no, that heap of vermilion over to the side, it has lumps in it!

Father has come in behind me. All business, I point at the cone of red powder and without even turning to greet him say, 'I'll work on this and get it perfect for you.'

'I don't want perfection.'

'You don't want…?'

'I want to have you, son, here with me.'

'But, but Father….' Better to bluster than to cry more tears. Enough of those fell last night to float a boat beached as high on the Brenta's bank as it's possible to pull it.

'And to have your understanding.'

He is holding me, one hand on the top of my arm. He raises his other one, palm straight up and then, when he knows I have seen it, lets it fall to his side. He *entreats* me. Father entreats *me*. For once I am glad of the need for my kerchief to cover my face, to turn aside, to cough and splutter. Then I don't know what else to do but to get back to business, so I point at the pigment and say, 'They can do better than this, the boys. I'll show them how again. If they are to work with us, they need to be properly trained.' I take a deep breath, 'Because Bassano and sons, that is what I'm thinking, you see, Father.'

Yes, that's what I'm thinking and I realise something as I say it out loud. I hear the strength – and somehow the symmetry of it – and at the same time I think of Titian. I realise you haven't got that, Titian, have you? For you there is no family coming after you with sufficient talent to go forward into the future and bring pride to your name. Yes, you may have perfection in what you achieve. Yes, genius you are, but alone, unsupported in your old age. All that public acclaim, and yet all along, that isolation is what Fate has had in store for you. But we, we have a dynasty, that is what has been spawned by my family here in Bassano. Together, unified, we can do work, lots of work, work that will go far and wide, ensuring we are known now as well as remembered in the future.

Father turns from the table, his arms folded low across his chest. It looks as though he's cradling a baby. He is smiling as he looks down, swinging those folded arms side to side. He says, 'Even our babe-in-arms, even he can one day join us, do you say, son?'

'Even Gerolamo, Father.'

Later in the morning we discuss and agree a working method for my *Prodigal Son*: initially I shall execute the overall shape and then focus on large areas such as the figures in the foreground. Father will retain some key elements of the narrative for his attention, such as, in this instance, the interaction of the father and son figures as they reunite. I accept Father will want to correct my work, pull my broad strokes of colour into disciplined order, define the figures with his sharp charcoal strokes, and that he will take responsibility for its general finish. But perhaps it will not always be that way. Now he has dominion over me – but not forever.

'Before beginning to draw, you might want to refresh your recollection of the text,' he says once we have finalised all that. 'My bookmark is in the page.'

The Gospel of St Luke, Chapter 15, the parable taking up twenty-one verses. I heft the big book from the shelf and sit, conscious this is where Father sat yesterday, *this* is what he was engrossed in. As I read, I decide I will take time to think about the meaning of redemption and to give devout thanks for the love and graciousness of the Lord that I see reflected in my Father.

But not just now. Just now, what I must do is get back to the easel. I'm keen to flex the muscles of my painting arm, get them back in shape. I want to grasp a brush and get going, apply brilliant colour thickly on to canvas.

Father is holding up a sheet of rough paper. On it, he has inscribed some letters with charcoal. 'See, this is how I propose we designate the work we shall do together. Expressed crisply but unmistakably. Our names. I, the father and you, my first son: "JAC.s ET FRANC.s FILIUS P."' I am at the shelf, choosing my paper. Sheets of our best blue is what I pull out, the only choice for this. Red chalk gripped between finger and thumb, I begin. May my hand remain steady, may my line be smooth and true.

EPILOGUE

Francesco

14 September 1591, Casa Grande, San Canciano, Venice

An urgent rap on the door wakes me: a message from Mother, summoning me to Bassano for my Uncle's funeral. Dear Uncle Gianluca, gone to his rest, I shall greatly miss his warmth. And his wisdom, accumulated over a generous span, close to ninety years, it must be. Long-lived, as the Bassano men are.

Like my father, even at over eighty vigorous enough to be still in the studio every day, every morning rising obsessed by one painting, his great altarpiece, **The Baptism of Christ**. The question is, will he live to finish it? Perhaps he doesn't want to. I for one can't imagine the studio without the compelling presence of that canvas. Father's nocturne of nocturnes: the black night, the white dove, dawn rays that glimmer behind a snow-clad Monte Grappa, that show of astonishingly red cloth, the gleam on the boy angel's golden dress and his parted lips.

But then nor can I imagine the studio without **him**, Father, hunched on his stool, eyes heavy-lidded but still piercing, right hand aloft, poised to ply the extraordinary loose strokes he favours these days. It occurs to me that this is where and how Father would like to die, brush loaded with his beloved vermilion, leaning forward, straining to the last to reveal to us the light that is there in the darkness.

Anyway, it's high time for a visit, to check on him and the pace of studio production. I shall find Father fine, I know, still barking instructions at Giovanni and Gerolamo as though they're know-nothing little boys, not grown men. Men with their own ideas about how things should be run, as they tell Father all the time, clashing with him about methods and management. With me, they clash about money. When an enterprise takes off, as our family business has in these last years, that's when the rifts open. Money is the soft way to explain our difficulties; the hard truth is that the root of it is jealousy. It has always been the bitterest competition amongst us boys, to be the one most praised by Father. Nothing much has changed: brothers, artists, yes – but no unity in brotherhood, no, not us.

They, of course, think I, as the firstborn, had it the easiest. Not true. Even if you take no account of my illness, **hard** is how I've had it. From the beginning, it was me sticking my neck out, me going head to head with Father. The things I struggled for, the others have simply sat back and benefitted from.

Brother Leandro is the prime example. The third of us four, certainly endowed with some talent (although probably less than he cares to take credit for), he would not be in Venice at all, let alone outdoing me, if I hadn't convinced Father to establish a Bassano family studio here. Finally. Years and years it took me to get that agreed, despite the sound business sense of it.

For me, independence was granted only long after I'd gone futilely off to Venice, to Maser and on to Florence, chasing recognition from Giorgio Vasari. After that episode Father made me wait. I learned to submit to him, to experience both the soreness and the sweetness of that. Once in tandem though, Father and I, we did make brave work together for a good long while. Sought-after too – so many of the grand new houses here, in France, in Germany, acquiring a set of our pastoral cycles or our allegories. (Royal houses too, it should be said – fifteen going to the King of Spain's palace.) Father ensuring of course, that however bucolic the setting, the paintings' narrative always included a religious teaching.

This sickness of mine: afflicted with it since my childhood, an unbidden fellow traveller, one I've never managed to shrug off. 'Afflicted' ugh, that has a pathetic sound to me. I don't like how it brings poor unfortunate Zantani's long decline back to my mind. Although pathetic **is** what I've become. I've even caught myself groaning out my pain while at the easel. Nowadays I destroy my kerchiefs. I could not ask any laundrywoman to deal with linen so blood-drenched.

'Rest,' they tell me. I was in bed trying to do so a few days ago when I was shaken from *uneasy slumber by another messenger at my door. This one handed me a lidded basket, something very alive inside, scratching at the wicker. From Maser, Tomaso had sent me a gift. A puppy. I tipped it out: mewling, comical-looking, piebald, a splodge of black around his right eye. Only 'Arlecchino' will do as the name for a dog like that, a dog sporting a costume like a clown's.*

Travelling to Bassano, I'll tie Arlecchino's basket behind me on the saddle for the two-day ride. Afterwards, coming back on the barge, the journey will be easier. The puppy can have the run of the deck and me, my leisure for a week. A dog on board: it will be like the accounts I heard of the journey Father made those years ago. The time he travelled downriver after he'd finished the portrait of Bruno and Cara, on his way to deliver it to Zantani in Venice.

On board then, along with Father and the canvas, were Tomaso, Cara and Bruno – none of whom Zantani was expecting to ever see alive again. (Signora Helena had conspired with Father to keep her husband in ignorance of all of this. She and Father, they shared a sense of the dramatic, you have to agree, since it was not until the moment the Bassano party reached the palazzo's water gate, that the Magnifico had any inkling the three of them had survived, let alone of the portrait's production.)

I've tried to imagine that moment. What must Zantani have been going through, I've wondered, as the two dogs got themselves out of the gondola and padded haltingly towards him? When he saw their injuries, no more truly healed at that time than his own? And what about when he saw the painting of them, what then? Tomaso too, what must Tomaso have been feeling, to be back again in Venice, faced with handing Cara and Bruno over to Zantani, with losing possession of his hounds for a second time?

I have tried to picture the little band of travellers being received at Ca' Zantani, the surprise at first and then how they would have been invited to sit by the wellhead in its elegant courtyard. How the explanations must have taken much time, more than a few tears falling, no doubt, and how confused, complicated and conflicting must have been the emotions resounding off that courtyard's walls.

Poor broken Zantani, there half-prostrate, white-faced under his red fox fur rug, despite the noon heat. But not failing, even for an instant, to show himself deserving of the title 'Magnifico'. Even though in still a very wretched state after the attack, remaining a man of magnificence in his vision and principles. After greeting the dogs fondly, holding their heads to look in their eyes, stroking their muzzles and ears, he breathed a sigh and stated that Cara and Bruno would not stay in Venice; that they were to go with Tomaso.

Then, the dogs' jewelled silver collars having been unwrapped by Tomaso and placed in Zantani's hands, the Magnifico provided his listeners with another surprise. Immediately he declared the things would be auctioned and the proceeds go to the Foundation for the construction of an Incurables' Hospital, a charitable concern which he and the Signora had set up. Because, far from allowing his misfortune to affect his charitable plans, even in convalescence Zantani had been determined to do more, deciding to also dedicate a church for the Hospital, the architect Sansovino already commissioned.

Father, always reticent about praise for his work, never did describe Zantani's reactions to the painting. But one time I got him to relate what he had learned of this project of the Magnifico's. Zantani and the Signora Helena been moved to do it after observing the plight of the hapless sick in the city, it seems. Such unfortunates were often abandoned on the Rialto to die, their festering sores distressing to see, the stench of them insupportable. (Even myself, those years later, I was made witness in Venice to piteous sights which, wholesome country boy that I was, I found hard to take.)

And so then, what of that other country boy, Tomaso? Well, life delivered to Tomaso exactly the desserts that the dear steady man deserved. What Father described made the pieces of Tomaso's story finally fall into place as far as I was concerned. I learned that after that Venice meeting the Barbaro brothers brought him back to Maser to manage the transformation of their old manor into the new-fangled Villa Barbaro, via the inspired designs of Andrea Palladio. Revoking Tomaso's apprenticeship to the Bomberg printing house, the Barbaros freed him to leave Venice, to woo and win Marina and to take her as his bride to Maser. And so there it was that Cara and Bruno went too, to live out their days easefully.

Before I leave Venice today I must send thanks to Maser for the companionship

Tomaso and Marina have provided me with in Arlecchino, Turkish-rug-chewing, favourite-slipper-destroying, crazily cock-eyed pup though he be. Tomaso, I know, will be saddened by the news of dear Uncle's demise. I'll not be surprised if he rides up to Bassano to attend the funeral.

By contrast, I can't imagine Leandro will deign to accompany me. He will say one or other of his Venetian social engagements can't be sacrificed. He likes it a lot, his hobnobbing with the city's high-born. And how fast he has moved up, in just the one year since he arrived. When you slice your knife into butter you never know where it'll slip and slide, do you? For Leandro, his pole has been well-greased, society proffering him invitations and commissions of a sort I never had. But it was **I** here first, smoothing his way. I who smiled so nicely. (Did they not like it perhaps that, behind my smile, they saw my eyes had a fevered glitter?)

I tried, yes, I tried so hard. And got so little. But Leandro? Leandro is left thinking that what he's achieved in Venice is a direct result of his charm. He'll continue to paint serenely, successfully away at those portraits of his, austere as they are in their greys and browns and blacks.

For me, although I had chafed against Father's restraints, it was merciful, that delay in my finally getting to live in this city. Because of it, I was spared from the plague of 1575 and 76, those years when the disease scourged Venice in the worst way ever, a death toll of tens of thousands. In the heat of one putrid August it took Titian off, a man well over eighty by then, but – it has to be said – up until then, still impressively active, still our Maestro.

Titian **never** got my forgiveness for belittling me. Although I did mature enough to blush recalling the youth I had been, the one who felt imposed upon when passed the Maestro's palette to hold. Especially after hearing that the Maestro, when painting at the court of Charles V and his brush happening to drop to the floor, was embarrassed when the Emperor, the world's most powerful ruler (in mid-pose for his portrait) was the one who bent to retrieve it. The Emperor knelt, Titian protested. Then, demurring with words designed to once and for all humble my shameful pride, the Emperor said, 'Titian deserves to be served by Caesar.'

Vasari died too. Not of the plague, but in Florence, the Duomo frescos unfinished. Lying snug in his bed, I bet he was, when he went, most probably looking up, chin jutting proudly while he congratulated himself on the excellent artistry of his own ceiling. His passing would have been neat and quick, just like him. And however many and grandiose his endeavours, the spark of them all snuffed out like that: poof! gone! One breath only needed for the job.

His death came not long after his Lives' Part II was published. When his name comes up – it often does when art's discussed – I tend to keep silent. Let others question the account Vasari renders of this artist, that artist. Some of what he wrote, you can't blame people, can you, for asking, 'How much of this did he make up?' My private thoughts are, 'Giorgio, your "inventory", your "toil in an honourable cause among men of talent", all your fine, fine words, what do they add up to?' Fickle-funny, taunting tease that you were, you've left such things for us to puzzle out, no? Your work: is it fact, is it fiction – and are we ever to distinguish between the two?

Father's mention in The Lives was nothing more than a few words (mine non-existent, of course.) True to himself, Father appeared not to be bothered in the slightest. Vasari did describe Father's paintings as 'beautiful' – but frankly, the adjective 'beautiful' is so over-used in the book, I would say it hardly counts as praise. The worst irony for me was that Father's meagre appearance was put **within** Titian's chapter. The ignominy of that....

Paolo fared somewhat better in terms of length but still had no chapter of his own. Much of what Vasari said regarding Veronese is found within other practitioners' entries, for example in Tintoretto's and in the architect San Michele's (Paolo's mentor). Paolo, who I'd always found the most genial of men, grumbled mightily about this. Often his plaints about being overlooked would come while on the scaffold, most likely when lying next to me, flat on our backs, faces up against a Ducal Palace ceiling. Because yes, it came to pass that I worked comfortably beside Paolo on many collaborations in Venice.

It was in the year 1578 that I came to live and work in this city at last. I had been determined to secure Casa Grande, to take as my own what had been Titian's studio – a kind of perverted yet triumphant vengeance being my motive, I would say. Not so grand, the place, any more in actual fact. Ransacked after the Maestro went, left a ruin for years. But despite the weeds pushing through the cracked masonry, it was where I wanted to be.

I had become a family man by then too, recently making Giustina, a Bassano girl, my bride. Paolo's boys were growing up. I remember he confided he wanted them to one day spend time in Bassano, just as he had. Loyal fellow, he would always declare our family's facility for portraying animals excelled all others. Paolo would like it greatly, I believe, to know Carletto, his youngest, went to work in Father's studio when Leandro left last year for Venice, and that he still stays there now.

Ah, Paolo, you were taken too early. A flu – no one should die from catching a cold while out on the Easter parade. I was forced to finish our commissions alone while mourning the loss of a cherished friendship.

In friendships, family, fortune in general, my luck hasn't been so good. Gambling, well, maybe yes – but I was young then. In my really low, low times I've wondered whether the evil eye is on me. Did I forget to touch iron one time? Or is it because I no longer have her charm, that stone with the hole in it that she pressed into my hand, the gypsy no-name girl? My ingot, always kept safe in my jerkin pocket. Safe until it was gone, that is.

Leandro, did he steal the stone from me? Does that account for why he, pleasure-loving and seemingly leisured, succeeds in Venice? While I, working so hard, reel with exhaustion yet receive rewards I deem inadequate. Less acclaim and more pain. Much more pain, every day getting harder to ignore.

From what the gypsy told me at the time of our tryst, I thought her prediction of animal eyes watching over me referred to the eyes of dogs. I was **happy**, picturing a life ahead with devoted hounds by my side. Since then though, I've feared that the watching eyes are sinister: that they're the yellowed, slitty, pus-filled ones of an evil goat, perhaps. Titian, **you**, are you still here with me, a malevolent presence persisting even beyond the grave? Am I never to be rid of you marring my prospects?

That old crone fortune-telling at Bassano fair is long gone. But I'll not be consulting her successor, nor any other soothsayer because, frankly, it is past the time any spell can fix what's gone wrong for me. There are only so many tries you can make to put a thing right, *that's my view, anyway. For example, my debt of thanks to Maddalena. I wanted to meet her again, look in her grey eyes and deliver the true record I'd promised. The fortieth part, or more, just as I had declared.*

I wrote three times to Ca' Zantani. Don't ask me why, but somehow I thought Signora Helena might relent and at least answer me. I got no reply. When I could, I found my way to the palazzo again. By chance, the boatman was sunning himself on rio San Toma's steps and I got out of him the name of the convent where the Signorita was ensconced. A nun! That prettiness locked away to waste behind high walls. Shame.

Carefully I parcelled her earrings and a small canvas, a devotional scene (remembering she'd once wanted to see my work), sent them, asked her to let me come during visiting hours. Her reply was kindly – but adamant she'd not receive me. With her letter she enclosed the blue scarab ring. As if I'm bothered about having that thing back.

I took time to write out the dogs' story for her, aware I must be clever and omit the harshest aspects of what befell Zantani. I waited on a reply but felt no real surprise not to hear from her again. As a novitiate, her concerns had become of a very spiritual kind by then, and I supposed the brief episode of our joint endeavour irrelevant now to her devotions. Maybe not, though. From time to time maybe she does finger her rosary to murmur a quiet prayer for the boy who walked away at dawn along the lagoon shore path.

So now the way to the north and the mountains awaits me again. 'North to the rising sun,' those were the words on my mind that time I rode back to Bassano not knowing if Father would forgive me. I needed that forgiveness – but I still planned to surpass him. There was a possibility I could, I thought. Possibility is what provokes us to action, isn't it? With luck, I thought I could do it. But the Lady Fortune had other ideas.

In the Preface to **The Lives** *(and damn it, in the end I read both of Vasari's books cover to cover) what Giorgio wrote about the Lady is that she will take you to the top of the wheel and then, for amusement or* **out of regret**, *return you to the bottom.* **Her** *regrets? What about mine, I ask?*

Father, he is my true north and my furthest horizon. I know I shall not travel beyond him. The truths I can't shy away from are that my sun is no longer rising and that my best work is behind me: ideas no artist wants to accept – but sometimes acceptance relieves the mind of struggle. Like everything else, ambition has it limits – and can outlive its usefulness.

I'll always remember how marvellous it was, seeing for the first time Paolo's frescos at Villa Barbaro. And there, up in the Room of the Dog's ceiling is an image of his that always stays with me. Against muddied grey-brown clouds, a dog (well, of course) witnesses an altercation between two women. The finely dressed figure is Ambition and she's expostulating as she tries to wrest away the riches which Fortune, the nude on the right, holds in her hands. A third woman, Envy, seated to the left, observes. She has a dagger, is concealing it from view, hand clenched on its hilt.

Recalling that ceiling now I say, **no**, don't hide it. Rather I say, 'Envy, bring it out, yes, your dagger. Let me see your knife. Hold it high, show it me. Lower it now, let me touch it, test the keenness of its edge.' Yes, I say, let this knife blade embrace its destiny, serve its purpose: let it slash the umbilical cord, slash the ties that bind, slash the hanging rope.

I am done pretending Ambition will succeed on my behalf, that my brow will ever be garlanded with laurels, that I'll take the winner's spoils. No, I accept that for me Ambition will not prevail – no matter how many times I turn to a fresh page, pull down a blank sheet, reach for the sharpened crayon, begin again.

The sky will darken. Let it. The world changes when the sun has set. So, let the clouds roll in, let the bells clang out. The rooks will fly up, caw caw caw. Noisy black-flapping rooks. Not for me the silent flight of golden eagles. I won't care. I will be able to close my eyes, no need to look anymore, freed to sit and wait while the rays of a sun low in the sky warm me one last time.

But before that, I've duties to fulfil, a final journey to make. I take down my cloak and hat, latch the shutters, grasp the key to lock the door. 'Arlecchino, come boy. Time to go.'

Acknowledgements

Thanks are due to all in the team at the Unicorn Publishing Group's Universe imprint for bringing this book to its final form, with special appreciation to Lucie Skilton, my skilled editor.

The Eyes that Look was begun during my year of study at Bath Spa University for the Masters in Creative Writing. Grateful thanks go to the tutorial staff there, in particular Celia Brayfield for her rigour, Maggie Gee for her enthusiasm and Fay Weldon for her unfailingly sparky and inspiring insights, and also to my fellow students for their encouragement.

Also to Jim Crace for his judicious instruction at a mid-draft Arvon Foundation course.

Early readers and friends to whom I owe a debt of gratitude for their energetic engagement with the story include Annie and Tony Hastings, Anne and Paul Swain, Storm Stanley, Brian Parkins and Sarah Jones. At a later stage, the contribution made to narrative development by the Nairobi Writers' Group was inestimably helpful. To Lisa Forrell and Marcel Berlins thank you for time - beginning, middle and end – spent in Paris.

In online study I was fortunate to have the enlightening teaching of Dr Emma Rose Barber through Oxford University Continuing Education and of Dr Michael Douglas-Scott of Birkbeck College for a Courtauld Institute short course. At Corsham Court, James Methuen-Campbell graciously shared his knowledge of the Methuen Collection Bassanos with me, while at Bristol Museum Dr Jenny Gashke, Curator of Classical Paintings, provided me with the thrilling opportunity of close hand observation of the Leandro Bassano *Return of the Prodigal Son*.

I'm grateful to Pip Falkner-Lee, contemporary dog portraitist, for helping my understanding of what's involved in working with live subjects, and to supreme colourist Mary Collis for our discussion about red. Thanks are due too for the generous hospitality extended me at Montecastello in Tuscany by the book's cover artist, Barbara Becarelli, and her husband, Jens Schmidt, from whom I gained new perspectives on the evolution of hunting with dogs in Italy.

Of overarching importance has been guidance from Dr Giuliana Ericani, art historian and former Director of the Museo Civico, Bassano, who gave unstintingly detailed attention to the manuscript. As well as providing the novel's pre-eminent resource through her work *Jacopo Bassano and the Amazing Trick of the Eye* (with Alessandro Ballarin), Dr Ericani steered my research towards the Veneto's key Bassano fresco locations.

Other key sources include *Art in Renaissance Italy 1350–1500* by Evelyn Welch, *Venetian Colour: Marble, Mosaic, Painting and Glass 1250–1550* by Paul Hills, *At Home in Renaissance Italy: the Italian House 1400–1600* by Marta Ajma-Wollheim, *The Cardinal's Hat: Money, Ambition, Housekeeping in a Renaissance Court* by Mary Hollingsworth, *The Hunting Book of Gaston Phebus*, preface by Claud Christian and *The Hound and the Hawk* by John Cummins.

Finally, love and devotion are due eternally to my husband, Viri, without whose staunch support the tree might well have flowered – but almost certainly would not have borne fruit.

Author's Note

Although in this book Jacopo Bassano and his family, Antonio Zantani, Titian, Veronese, Marcantonio Barbaro and others – people who actually lived – mix freely with a cast of fictional characters, it's been important for me to follow the documented record where it exists. Staying faithful to the facts and rendering the particulars of my historical characters' lives as accurately as possible, I've nevertheless wanted to allow for the imaginative leaps and assertions that these same facts' possibilities seemed, to me, to be inviting.

Regarding this dilemma Hilary Mantel says, 'Guesses should be made only where there are no facts to be had. Where gaps occur, the way you fill them must offer a plausible version.'

It was while I was tussling pleasurably with plausibility and motivation in relation to the conundrums presented by Bassano's dogs' portrait that the larger aim I was harbouring for my novel revealed itself: perhaps, in highlighting the Bassano family story by digging deeper into my characters' emotional lives, I might succeed in calling attention to the particularity of Jacopo. I might cause him to be more celebrated, not only as an artist and innovator but also as an individual whose attitude to animals demonstrated extraordinary prescience.

As Francesco predicts, the products of his family's workshop went far and wide, in his lifetime and after, with the happy result for enthusiasts today that Bassanos are on view in galleries and museums worldwide.

Italy offers rich pickings. The Museo Civico in Bassano del Grappa houses many Bassano paintings gathered from local churches and buildings, along with Jacopo's frescos from the *Casa dal Corno*. His fresco of Marcus Curtius, badly faded, is still *in situ* on the gatehouse of Porta Dieda. Other frescos are to be found in the churches of Citadella, Cartigliano, Lusiana and Enego. In Venice there are paintings in the Galleria Accademia, the Palazzo Ducale, and the churches of San Giorgio Maggiore and San Giacomo dell'Orio, while in the Veneto region there are examples of altarpieces and devotional paintings in the churches of Holy Trinity in Angarono, St Anthony in Marostica, the parish churches of Cassola, Mussolente, Pove, Borso and Asolo and the Cathedral in Belluno.

These are the locations of the paintings in the novel:

> *Two Hunting Dogs:* Musée du Louvre, Paris
>
> *The Good Samaritan:* The National Gallery, London
>
> *The Last Supper:* Galleria Borghese, Rome
>
> *The Return of the Prodigal Son*
>
>   – by Jacopo and Francesco: Galleria Doria Pamphilj , Rome
>
>   – by Leandro: Bristol Museum and Art Gallery
>
> *The Baptism of Christ*: The Metropolitan Museum, New York

The *Assumption of the Virgin* by Titian remains in the Frari's Basilica di Santa Maria Gloriosa in Venice; his 1566 *Annunciation* is in the church of San Salvador, Venice.

Paolo Veronese's *Conversion of Mary Magdalene* is in the church of San Giorgio in Braida, Verona and his *Martyrdom of St George, Happy Union and Conversion of Mary Magdalene* in The National Gallery, London. His *Sacrificial Death of Marcus Curtius* is in the Kunsthistorisches Museum, Vienna and *Supper at Emmaus* in the Musée du Louvre, Paris. The six rooms of Veronese frescos at Villa Barbaro, also known as Villa di Maser, are open to visitors www.villadimaser.it.